LOW LOVE, LOW FIDELITY

LOVE BELVIN

MKT Publishing, LLC

ISBN: 978-1-950014-62-0 (Paperback)
ISBN: 978-1-950014-61-3 (eBook)

MKT Publishing, LLC
First print edition 2023 in U.S.A

Cover design by **Visual Luxe**

low Love, low fidelity

by Love Belvin

Chapter One

Lennox

Staring at the two suitcases splayed out over my bed, almost filled, I sighed. With my fists burrowed into my hips, I turned to my closet. Something was missing, and I didn't have the time to forget or to have lingering thoughts on anything. I needed to be headed to the airport soon. The big coat, a needed accessory for possible low Jersey temperatures in late October, took up much of the space in the larger suitcase. But something was missing. Then it dawned on me. I paid myself an inspective gander from my ankles all the way up to my shorts. My pajamas. I needed to pack the ones I wore.

Oh!

I turned for the bathroom and pulled out the pre-packed bag from a drawer. Then I carried it to the larger suitcase. Immediately, a sense of still calmed me.

I think that's it…

Soft raps at the door startled me. Peering over my shoulder, I saw Scott craning his neck inside my master bedroom. His golden skin was blemished with mild acne, distracting from gorgeous, orangey freckles, and I could tell he hadn't washed his hair recently. But the teenager was handsome, resembling his uncle in his heyday.

"Yes, honey?"

"I fixed MeMaw's breakfast," his southern, nasal intonation never failed to tickle me. "She said you want me to wait in the car?"

Rubbing my lips together, I nodded, glancing down at the suitcases on the bed, then my pajamas. "I'll be right out."

Scott's eyes fell for a few seconds before he nodded with palpable melancholy. Then he backed out of the doorjamb.

"Hey," I called out to him. When those hazel-green irises appeared again, I saw the looming sadness. "This is just for a few days. Remember?" I smiled his way for comfort.

Scott nodded then sniffled, followed by a gauche swiping of his nose. "Yeah. You go every year."

"And every year, I return."

His gaze lobbed around the room. "Yeah, but this year…" His eyes swiped over my face for just a millisecond before continuing to whip around the room as he thought hard, long, and cautiously. "Since…" Scott shook his head, causing his long, greased, blond tresses to sway. "Fine. I'll be in the car."

As he dashed out of my line of sight, my heart thundered in my chest.

Fully dressed and carefully strutting in heels, I pulled my luggage behind me as I entered the living room of my home. The sounds of flesh violently hitting flesh, along with spirited shouts, had my attention flying over to the mounted plasma television. Two Black, effeminate men were going to blows; arms swinging, and heads down as they windmilled each other.

Zeus Network…

I turned in the opposite direction. There, on my sofa was Kelly-Ann. Her strawberry-blonde hair was wet from a recent shower. The ringlets close to her scalp fell just at her shoulders as she held the plate of boiled eggs and waffles, narrow jaw collapsed as her eyes oscillated from the television to me.

Internally, I shook my head. A white woman fixated on Black reality television was a dangerous thing. She watched them all: "Real Housewives of Atlanta," "Love & HipHop," "Growing Up HipHop"—the whole gamut. She'd even watch reruns of the reality shows no longer in production. But this *Zeus Network* was a new charge to my account. I paid for it all, even the couch she sat on, and the roof over her head.

"You comin' back?" her southern drawl was less eloquent than her grandson's.

Supplying a smile, I advised, "I live here. Why wouldn't I be?"

Kelly-Ann's eyes faltered like her grandson's earlier. "I'm just sayin'."

Pulling in a quick, tempered breath, I reminded myself of the flight I had to make. "Kelly-Ann, I want to remind you I will not be accessible the rest of this week, into the weekend. For the next four days, starting when I pull off in my car, any emergencies will have to be addressed by the adults they involve. Do you understand?"

"Yeap." She was motionless when she followed with, "You told us that." She tossed her chin toward the front door. "I don't know what that meant for him."

I took off, pulling my suitcases toward the door. "Well, for the next few days, he'll be with his other grandmother. If she reaches out to you with an issue, you both have enough living experiences between the two of you to come up with a solution."

I couldn't get to my car fast enough, but halted at the sight of the mangled *BMW* taking up half of my driveway. Its mere appearance propelled my motivation for a needed break.

We pulled up to Scott's grandmother's home in Knightdale. After paying the two-story home a full gander, I observed Scott.

"We're good?"

He nodded. "Yeah." The kid wouldn't even look me in the face.

"Scott, you'll be fine. Sunday will be here before you know it; and on Monday, I'll be fussing behind you to get out of the house for school on time."

One side of his mouth lifted, telling of his relenting worry. "I'll be on time." He rolled his eyes in the most adorable way.

"And so will I," I assured him. "Now, you have the number to the hotel where I'll be staying. And remember our secret—"

"I know. Don't tell anyone you'll answer for me."

"Yup!" I enunciated the *P.* "You and only you." Then I elbowed him gently. "You're going to have a great time. Your grandmother will get you to school on time and pick you up. Then you'll make that special visit on Friday. So, she's picking you up early."

Scott's nod still consisted of dejection, making my tummy toil. I offered him my fist.

He returned it with a gentle pound. "Can you, at least, let me know when you land up there? It'n it cold up North?"

With my chin resting on my mounted fist, I nodded. "Just got cold, which is strange. October's the best flex for those last days of summer temps, although it isn't summer."

"You miss it?"

"Miss what?"

"New Jersey," Scott clarified. "I mean, I know we're in North Carolina and all, but Raleigh ain't the country."

I smiled even broader. "No, it's not. Raleigh is mildly metropolitan. But my hometown, East Orange, is a lot different in pace...and culture."

"You didn't answer my question."

"Which was?"

"Do you miss it?"

Taking in a deep breath, my eyes drifted, and I considered that for a moment. Honesty. It was my new approach to the people in my life. Swallowing, I admitted, "Lately, I have been."

"See! Shit, man!" Scott curled over his lap, yanking his blonde hair at the skull.

"Scott..." I warned him.

"I'm sorry. I really am, but something just feels off." He lifted and shook his head.

"Look at me," I demanded, voice controlled. The torment in his eyes jumpstarted my anxiety about this trip. "Like last year, the one before, the one before that, and so on, I'll be back. I promise, Scott."

I saw it. Scott, a thirteen-year-old who'd lived through more trauma than I could imagine, braved himself for the worst. Scott needed endless reassurance after the week we'd had. I knew nothing about this role, had no manual for it.

Reaching into the backseat, I heaved my purse into my lap. I pulled out the cash I'd set aside for Scott and handed it over to him. "This isn't for you to ball out with. It's for you to not go hungry or thirsty. It's for your independence. If they offer, let them pay. If you're in need and they don't offer, you pay for yourself. You hear me?" He nodded. "And you know how to use my *Uber* account for emergencies. You have your key to the house, and I am accessible to you—"

"Yeah, yeah." Scott took the folded cash from my hand. "And only me. Let's just keep it that way. Be safe, and for chrissakes, get back home."

When the door was closed, and he pulled his suitcase from the backseat then slammed that one, my heart lightened a little. Scott was displaying normal hormonal acts of a teenager I could identify and appreciate. I watched him approach the house. His grandmother answered the door, allowing Scott inside. Her little, wrinkled, porcelain arm with the "lunch-lady loose wing" jiggled as she waved. I returned her greeting before drawing in yet another deep breath and pulling off.

I'd made it to the airport on schedule. Checking the time, I had twenty minutes before boarding, and my agitation had been spiking since I parked my car in the lot. With my larger suitcase checked, and only so much time before takeoff, I felt restless. Glancing around like a lost child, I saw a bar. Given the amount of people inside the restaurant, I knew it was open. Rolling my carryon inside, I got the attention of a waitress right away.

"*Mauve*. Premium—vintage," I corrected myself.

"Sorry." She tapped her device. "We only have silver and gold here. V.S. and V.S.O.P."

I nodded, understanding. "Gold it is."

"Got it."

"Double on the rocks."

"Is that all?" I nodded, biting my lip. "Okay. Give me just a second, and I'll have that right out for you."

Distracted, I pulled out my chirping phone.

Mya: *Which hotel are you staying at again?* 😳

My pulse rocketed.

Nisha: *It's freezing. I hope you packed a coat and tights.* 😕 💀

I kept tabbing and scrolling down my text thread.

Lisa: *Hey. You mind if I meet you at your hotel? I need to chat with you about something. I'll drive us to the pub.*

A zip of panic coursed through my belly. Lisa was driving in from Easton, Pennsylvania. Would she need a place to crash? This was a half-a-weeklong event. She wouldn't finesse me by springing on the need for a place to stay out of the blue. Right?

I tapped my index nail on the table, anxiety encroaching again. The waitress appeared in my peripheral suddenly, placing my drink on the table.

"Thanks," I murmured, trying for a smile.

Lisa's text still lingered in my head. The woman was married with kids. Responsible. Asking to crash with me at the last minute would have been a "broke college student" move. I glanced at my phone, considering my reply.

Then my spine tingled.

Tobias: *125 Nirvana Ln. Samsara*

Samsara. It was a small, river-town between Englewood Cliffs and Closter. *Bergen County wealth.* I'd never been and, honestly, had never heard of it until recently.

Shit...

Don't! I chided myself.

To distract my nerves gone atwitter, I began responding to the texts in the order in which they were received.

Me: Red Carpet Inn. Budgeting. 😔

Me: Remembered to pack it at the last min. 🫠 🙏

Me: Sure. I'm staying at the Red Carpet Inn though in case you wanna meet some other place. I'll text you when I get there.

I hoped that was a successful deterrent. Lisa was from a suburban town in the state of Delaware. She hated Newark, New Jersey. Thought of it as dangerous. Something it could be depending on where you traveled and what you were up to. But I was familiar with it, being from East Orange. It was like home.

Before my next response, I decided to allow the alcohol to medicate me for courage. The *Mauve* was delicious, aged in oak to a smooth texture. Present were notes of thyme, grapes, and nuts. The Very Superior Old Pale liquid relaxed my limbs almost immediately. My toes inside my pointy-toe, knit *Balmain* booties curled as they warmed. I closed my eyes, rolling them contently behind my lids as I felt suddenly blanketed.

Opening my eyes, I took a meditating breath. This week would be mine. I wouldn't cower to my fears or the expectations of others. I'd be uncharacteristically selfish. Put me first. No plans outside of anticipating fun and good times without guilt, shame, or...fear.

Me: Affirmative.

Dropping the phone, I went for my drink again, peering out of the window to the tarmac. A thousand thoughts sprinted through my mind.

Tobias: *Had to look around to see if I was at the hospital. Affirmative, my G?*

I rolled my eyes, fighting my amusement. My phone chirped again.

Tobias: *What size shoe are you?*

Me: Why?

Tobias: *Because I know you ain't pack ya sneaks. We running this week.* 😴

A violent beam burst on my face, splitting it in two as I shook my head, staring into the phone.

Tossing the decorative pillows onto the mildly stained sofa, I turned back to the queen-sized bed. Then I pulled the comforter and sheets down on the side closest to the window. The first thing I searched for were bedbugs. Waiting, I brushed my eyes all over the all-white, open beddings. I was sure to push the remaining pillows apart, still observing closely.

Standing back, I pulled my phone from the desk to check the time. Learning I hadn't missed any calls or texts relieved me. That's when I remembered to send one myself.

Me: Hey Scott! Landed and arrived safely at my hotel.

My dutiful attention returned to the bed. No black dots or movements.

Okay…

I punched the pillows, comforter, and mattress. Moving down the bed, I did the same until the bed was no longer "perfectly made," but ruffled and used apparently. Then I went to the large, opened suitcase and pulled out the pajamas I woke up in this morning, tossing them aimlessly onto the bed. Next, I retrieved my toiletry bag from the suitcase and carried it into the bathroom. I unpacked the essentials: toothbrush, toothpaste, a bar of soap I sat inside of the sink under running water, deodorant, mouthwash, lotion, and basic makeup.

I shut off the faucet, placed the *Grayson's Skincare* soap inside the shower, then ran the water. Next was placing the floor towel in front of the tub. The second I turned off the water, I caught the chirping of my phone, out near the television. Giving the bathroom a last inspection, I ambled back out into the room.

Scott: *Glad ur safe Hve fun*

A smile opened on the inside and outside of me. I was grateful for his concern, and hoped he'd have a wonderful rest of the week, into the weekend. Changing a thirteen-year-old's schedule on a Wednesday to the point of him being away from his home could be a challenge, especially after the past few days we'd had.

I spent the next few minutes unpacking my things, setting my old shoes in a corner near the dorm room-sized fridge, strewing random shirts and pants over the sofa and office chair. The goal was to create a realistic, pell-mell appearance. *Why? This isn't necessary.* Yet and still, I worked my planned agenda. The moment I felt satisfied, I exhaled, stomach turning over again. The *Mauve* from the Raleigh-Durham airport was long gone from my brain at this point. Now, unmedicated, my nerves ran wild.

I almost leaped in place when a rap at my door sounded.

With shaky hands, I pulled the door open. "Hey girl!"

"Lennox!" she playfully shouted. I backed away to allow Lisa inside, hugging her as she passed by me. "This place ain't as bad as I thought."

"You think I'd stay at a rinky-dink hole in the wall?" I followed behind her to quickly grab my things.

"*Nuh*—yeah." Lisa laughed at herself. "That's why I was tripping when you said *Red Carpet* in Newark. I didn't think this place fit your style."

I snickered. "It's convenient…close to the airport. Besides, I only plan to sleep here this week, into the weekend. I have so many people to see and hug. You're the first." I grabbed my coat. "Let's go. It's still early. Let me treat you to happy hour. *Checkerboard* is open. We can chat there then head over to the pub."

"That club Ragee, the singer, owns?"

I nodded, noticing my friend hadn't lost the weight put on by her last child, who was almost three-years-old. "Yeah. It's really nice. Decent food and excellent drinks." I winked.

"You've been there before?"

"*Yea*—oh!" I suddenly recalled. "You came late last homecoming. I forgot. Yeah. I got us a booth there. It was really nice. How lucky were we that Ragee just so happened to be there that night!"

"Oh! I remember." Lisa grabbed her forehead, keys in her hand. "He didn't perform."

"Right."

"But he had dinner at a table not too far from y'all."

I nodded, remembering the night with fondness.

"Okay, girl! I'll be courted any day. It ain't like Aaron's on his job in that department no more." She rolled her eyes.

Laughing at her joke, I observed out loud, "You look good, Lisa. You really do."

Her hands automatically went to her hair. "Me? Really?" Eyes wild and uncertain. "I don't know anymore. With this baby fat and the bags under my eyes. My knees cracking like a granny. Gurrrrl!" She rolled her eyes as I laughed.

"Join the club. When they told us beauty is fleeting, so run alongside it like a damn shadow for as long as you can…" We snickered. "Girl, we should've listened."

"You know!" She lifted a hand for a hi-five. "But you look amazing as always. I see you with that tiny waist. And those natural curls and blonde streaks still popping!" Her torso swayed side-to-side rhythmically.

Subconsciously, my hand went to finger my curls. "I was considering cutting it all off. Sculpting into my Halle Berry."

She gasped. "Don't cut that pretty hair off, girl. You crazy?"

I rolled my eyes then winked. "Come on, woman. I'm starved."

With my coat and purse in hand, I grabbed the Do Not Disturb tag on my way to the door.

"You leaving the television on?" Lisa asked from behind me.

Opening the door, I fastened the laminated hook onto the doorknob. "Yup."

I tried to manage my expression. "Really?"

Lisa nodded. "Cheated on me, girl. We've been married for almost six years, and he was sneaking around with her for over a year."

"And his job was how you found out?" The story sounded crazy.

"Yup. HR was made aware of it from them being 'inappropriate' a few months ago in a storage room," she repeated the detail. "And I really think they were caught on tape having sex."

"I'm not sure about that." My brows met as I considered several scenarios of similar incidences in my line of work. "Depending on their policy, Aaron could have been terminated if they were caught in an actual sexual act. They were likely in too close of proximity or petting in an unauthorized zone of the building."

"Maybe you're right, but that's the reason he told me." She sighed, rolling her eyes. "I couldn't sleep for a week."

"This was back in the summer. Right?" She nodded. "So, you guys are working through it?" She hadn't said they were splitting when she began this story as we finished our salads and fries.

When Lisa said she wanted to talk, this topic was the furthest thing from my mind. I was still confused as to why she'd only share it with me privately. We had been good friends since our college days, but not more than any other girl in our crew.

"I forgave him when he told me. He cried, saying he didn't want to lose me and the kids. He even put in for a volunteer transfer." Lisa shrugged. "That made me believe him. When it got approved, I thought maybe it could work. Maybe he's sincere. Now, he has to drive an hour and ten minutes to a remote office." Her attention drifted to the piano where a woman sat and fondled the keys melodically. "I just…" Then her eyes landed on me. "I hope I'm not a fool for staying."

Aaron was an older man in mid-level management at a tech firm in Pennsylvania. Lisa met him sometime after we'd graduated. They dated for years, and had their first child, AJ, a namesake for his father. Seven years his junior, Lisa was in love with a man who'd been married before. The previous marriage lasted all of two years, and no children were produced from the union. By all accounts,

Aaron had lived a full life before Lisa, something her parents warned her about.

Needless to say, once he proposed when AJ turned a year old, Lisa quickly obliged. She'd been living with him practically since they met, refusing a long-distance relationship, considering Delaware was nearly three hours south of Easton. She earned a degree in English when we graduated, but never had a plan for it exactly. She eventually got her teacher's certification, and began to teach in Pennsylvania. However, when AJ was born, Aaron insisted she stay at home with him. That was where Lisa had been ever since.

With my fingers splayed over the base of the wine glass, I noted, "You're not feeling secure about your decision to stay."

Lisa's eyes roved away. I didn't push. This was a touchy subject. I was the queen of domestic, touchy subjects.

That led me to ask, "Is that why you're pulling me aside to share this? You want my opinion?"

Lisa snorted, confidence visibly low. "Mya would have a printout of all the local shelters and divorce attorneys ready for me by the end of the weekend. It would be her way of calling me stupid for still being there all these months later."

I shook my head. "Mya's life isn't perfect either."

Lisa's tone was low, but brows arched when she challenged, "Can you prove it?"

I could but didn't participate in talking shit about anyone's marriage. I'd grown beyond that. I also understood how intimidating Mya could be to surface readers.

Skipping over that topic, I placed a hand over hers. "I cannot stand in judgement of your decision to stay with your husband. Mistakes happen. I think marriage can be a series of joy, pain, and recovery."

"Damn." She chortled wryly. "That sounds depressing."

I shrugged. "I think it's human nature. We're talking two human beings, trying to walk one path. Both will get it wrong several times over."

"Yeah, but to the point of pain?"

I nodded. "I think a successful marriage has less amounts of reckless pain and more joy. But please believe, they have both."

"And the recovery?"

I twisted my lips. "It's like…grace. That period of vulnerability, which requires understanding. It's needed after the pain."

"What if it's too much pain?"

I couldn't look at her when I answered, "Then you'll be ready to receive Mya's printout."

From the table, we watched Nisha and Lisa finish the *Cuff it Challenge* everyone had been attempting on social media. I was sure to cheer them on. My table wasn't alone; several people in the pub joined in. I couldn't believe this place held the same feels it had nearly ten years ago when I was a freshman.

Neil's Pub was nestled in Montclair. It was close enough to catch the college crowd, yet just off campus, making it assessable to the public as well. We'd been here for over two hours, drinking, nibbling on appetizers, and catching up with each other and a few other familiar faces. It was cool to see a few folks returning for homecoming weekend. The event was typically held in early October but had been postponed a few weeks due to delays in putting the final touches on major upgrades to the campus. To encourage endowment, the school wanted to be sure the property was in pristine condition.

"Look at y'all!" Mya gassed the girls up as they approached the table, out of breath and giddy.

"Girl," Nisha panted, plopping down into her seat. "Those four movements are fucking work. Okay!"

"You know who killed it on *TikTok?*" Mya's eyes were wild with wonder.

"The Nigerian kids?" Lisa asked. "They be fucking shit up!"

Nisha snapped her fingers. "Toya…Lil' Wayne's baby's momma, on that little yacht after her wedding?"

Mya shook her head, fingering her long, curly weave. "Shi-Shi," she finally revealed. "The dancer. She's been in the *Asè Garb* ads."

"The Black girl, twirling in their trench coat in the commercial?" Lisa seemed confused.

"She did more than twirl in a trench coat in that commercial," I corrected. "I've seen her in like two of their commercials, and in *Vogue*. She looks amazing."

"Oh!" Nisha lowered her drink. "She was on the *Times Square* billboard wearing *Asè Garb*. Right? The one who used to date Austin Seers?"

Mya nodded. "She's so dope."

"They're cute together. Her long legs and toned thighs! Whew!" Lisa fawned. "I wish I had that body." She grabbed her protruding belly through the turtleneck sweater, making us all laugh. "I hope they get married finally."

Mya's neck snapped back. "Try again. She has a whole baby!"

"Who?" Again, Lisa appeared genuinely confused.

"Shi-Shi," Mya laughed. "You keeping up?"

"I didn't know. When?"

"Earlier this year. Cute little girl." Mya's mouth twisted as she nodded affirmatively. Then her eyes fixed onto Lisa. "Too busy vacuuming floors, I see," she murmured before taking a sip of her drink.

Nisha fell into my arm, snickering hard.

We'd had a few drinks, but I didn't find it all that funny.

Lisa rolled her eyes, brushing it off. "When did she have the baby? I feel like I just saw them together on *E!* or something."

"Nope." Mya explained. "Shi-Shi put out a press release saying they broke up last spring'ish. Then last summer, she posted pictures of some brown-skinned guy with muscles." She used her hands to demonstrate. "They were at some beach and on a boat, partying with a bunch of people."

"Then how could you say she posted pix of her and the guy like they were together?" Nisha challenged.

Mya licked her lips, eyes squinted toward the ceiling wistfully. "Because of the way she held him in some of the pictures. She took usies with lots of people, but she didn't cup any of the guys the way she did this particular one. It was like a…lover's grip."

"Was he better looking than Austin? That mofo fine!" Lisa met palms with me.

The actor, Austin Seers, was handsome. I wouldn't deny that. However, he was a little too *"Disney"* for me swag-wise. I preferred a dash of cayenne pepper in my ideal man.

Mya nodded with a confident grin. "This guy was *pretty* special. And I think that's who gave her a baby." She winked, voice reduced to a conspirator's volume.

"Shit," Nisha breathed.

Mya nodded. "That's why Derrick and I played no games when dating back here on campus. I was not for him being the football jock all the girls fucked around with. If he wanted to be with me, it had to be only me. And when we graduated, I was not about to wait years for a proposal after we'd dated for most of our undergrad days." She rolled her eyes.

Lisa's attention brushed against me before I looked away.

"Shi-Shi's dope," Nisha followed up with, fingering through her long, jet-black box braids. "It's funny how you can be with one person for so many years, you break up with them, and *boom*! She's pregnant. Male or female." She shrugged. "Or maybe she just didn't want to live in his shadow, you know? As we can see, a bitch pulling in her own bag!" She slapped her hands together and twerked in her seat.

"Okay!" Lisa agreed, peering into her phone. "And from what I see on her *TikTok*, that baby ain't do no damage to her body."

"She's a little thicker in the butt." Mya disagreed.

"She could afford to be," Nisha injected. "She's tall, but not too thick. A little extra booty never hurts a girl like her. But now I wanna know what happened between her and Austin." She shrugged. "Body's right; bag's secured. I don't see what's to talk about."

"That reminds me of a certain someone at this table," Mya's eyes swung around.

That caused everyone else to do the same. Everyone but me. I knew where she was going with that.

Apparently, Nisha did, too. She rolled her eyes softly. "Lennox is fine. Like I said: body's right and bag's secured. And, might I add, the bitch got it out of the mud."

Mya cleared her throat.

My brows plucked and head angled as I peered her way. This wasn't unusual for Mya. It was only a matter of time before she'd turn the spotlight of her criticism my way. After going off on her two years ago at this same event, Mya now pushed me further down the line in her passive-aggressive verbal shots of judgement.

"Are we doing this again?" my tone was calm, clear.

Right away, Lisa appeared uncomfortable.

Mya laughed, waving her hand dismissively. "You know me. I'm pushing to get into your head. But for real, she does remind me of you, in a sense."

"How?"

"I don't know. Just how she makes life look easy, although, clearly, there's been trouble." Her words spilled slowly, cautiously. Mya wasn't confident in her pursuit of knowledge.

"Okay." I lowered my chin, looking her dead in the eyes. "So, I'm going to choose, once again, to not get offended by your inquiries into my personal life."

"Personal life." Mya scoffed. "We're practically best friends."

"We're old friends with history," I qualified. "It wouldn't matter if we were sisters. When I set a boundary, you either respect and adhere to it, or you can choose to walk away from me. I'm not demanding anything I don't give, Mya."

She giggled again, possibly off her game. "Don't be so extreme. Of course, I respect your boundaries. We all have and do—"

"Then what's the problem?" my volume reasonable as I smiled warmly.

"The *Red Carpet Inn?*" She used her hands to express incredulity. "I mean, who stays there? Not local people."

"I live in North Carolina, Mya. I'm no longer local."

"But you have money," she argued.

"Here we go!" Lisa laughed nervously at Nisha.

"No," Mya tried. "I swear, it's not like that. I'm saying. Y'all know Lennox is a class act. Staying there sounds crazy. You could have stayed with me, Derrick, and the kids."

My brows met. "When do I ever stay with you and your family? Is that what this is about?" I scoffed. "You wanna play sleepover?" When she rolled her eyes away, I knew I'd struck a cord. "Mya, I plan on doing a lot while I'm here. I have my grandmother and her home to check in on. We"—I motioned around the table—"have a packed itinerary. There was no need to stay at the *Ritz Luxuriate Hotel* when I only plan on sleeping in my room this week. No, I'm not broke, but I can be practical, too."

"I know that's right," Lisa rolled her eyes.

"Ladies," Nisha interjected. "We only see each other once a year now. Let's enjoy the time we have together. These have come to be some of the best times for me over the years."

I cupped her hand with my own. "You're right. I'm sorry if my energy has detracted from that."

"It's all good," Lisa assured. "I'm still tripping off this Shi-Shi thing."

Mya leaned into the table, her conspiratorial mien back in play. "So, you know Derrick's brother works for *The Garden*. Right? Well, he told Derrick how he saw Shi-Shi backstage, kissing a brown-skinned, tall dude holding a baby girl before she prayed with the dancers and took to the stage."

"What concert was it?"

"Alana's," Mya answered.

"Whoa…" Lisa breathed with wild eyes.

Mya nodded with an even wider smile. "Shi-Shi moved on to another man."

Chapter Two

Lennox

I pulled up to the opening of the driveway, expired leaves relieving themselves of their posts on branches all around, even in the dark. Squinting behind the steering wheel, I tried making out the house number. My GPS led me to Nirvana Lane, then began re-routing. I had to be sure the two-story, wooden ranch sitting yards off the road was the 125 property. *Samsara* was such a closed off, almost rural town. Most of Raleigh was better populated than this place, with less trees and closer-spaced homes. *Samsara* gave off a secluded, rural-suburban vibe.

"Arrived," the system announced, and I sighed audibly.

"Really?" I muttered back.

Good. This neighborhood didn't seem like the type to be friendly to lost travelers. My stomach growled again, reminding me I hadn't eaten a full meal since lunch at *Checkerboard* with Lisa. Lifting off the brake, I pulled into the long driveway until a well-lit, two-car garage came into view. Both doors were open. A large, black, tinted *Suburban* was parked just outside on one side. My stomach knotted as I cut the engine. Slowly, I climbed out of my rental, closing the door behind me as I observed the SUV. The windows were as black as the night at this hour. I swallowed on a dry throat when the passenger's window rolled down.

"What it do, Lennox?"

With pinched brows, I craned my neck to peer into the truck in search of those gravelly chords.

The man chuckled then leaned his husky frame over toward the passenger's side. "It's Danny, girl!"

My forehead lifted and I pulled in a hefty breath. "Danny G! Oh, my god!" My hand flew to my chest, and I laughed at myself. How could I not see a six-foot-plus, nearly three-hundred-pound man? *Well, at least, I know I'm in the right place.* "What are you doing here?"

"Working, my girl."

Panic struck. "Raj's in there?"

He snickered again. "Nah. The boss and his family been away for about a month now. They started in *Saint Justin* for their anniversary. I pulled that shift. Then they flew the fam out to Haiti to visit their son's family."

"Oh."

Danny G's boss, R&B superstar, Ragee, and his wife, Wynter, didn't have biological children. The couple adopted three boys of different racial and ethnic backgrounds a few years ago. Not many were privy to this information. One of the most popular blogs "reported" on it a while ago, but they were the same outlet to tell the world a few years back how Raj and Wynter's marriage was fake. Considering my talks with Tobias about the couple, I'd never gotten "fake" vibes from him, so how credible could that "reporting" be?

"Yeah. One of the boys' pops got people out there. Boss lady wanted him to meet his fam, so they put it together."

"How sweet!" That was really touching. "So, you're off?"

"Not really." He tossed his chin toward the house. "I still got side hustles."

I laughed at that. "I'm sure he gets the family discount."

Blinking adorably, Danny G shook his head. "Oh, that nigga

pay. Sometimes I charge him extra because his ass don't listen, thinking because he ain't a celebrity, he ain't at risk."

Smiling goofily, I nodded, understanding his point.

"I kicked it with ya pops last weekend." The switch in topic had the muscles in my face collapsing. "The nigga doing good. Real good."

I swallowed, fighting for congeniality. "No surprises here."

He tossed his chin toward the house again. "No worries. I ain't seent you this week. Ol' boy in there expecting you, though. The door inside the garage is open."

Hearing music pouring from the house, I nodded with a twisted smile. "It's always great seeing you, Danny G. I hope you're taking care of yourself."

"You always say that, Lennox, man." His big hand met his chest. "Thanks."

I tapped the inside of the truck through the open window, smiling as I turned away. Trying to shake off that mention of my father, I strolled through the empty garage with just a motorcycle inside, and into the house. Immediately, I was doused with a deluge of garlic and herbal aromas, causing my hunger pangs to recur. The delicious traces were louder than the Afro-beats streaming from hidden speakers. Following the long, lit hall, I learned it opened to a huge kitchen. Long, black-painted wooden cabinets with brass hardware, a colossal gold-vein marble island centering the room, and a brass-trimmed range hood over the stove where he stood filled the space.

He was comfortably shirtless, with a kitchen towel tucked inside the waist of his low-hanging army fatigue, cargo pants. The man wore fresh *Timberland* boots at the stove. *The butters*! Parts of his back flexed infinitesimally with each subtle move he made when shaking a medium-sized, stainless-steel pan with a loaded cream sauce in the air, over an open flame. This was effortless masculinity in a way I couldn't be sure I'd seen in a while, if at all. The intricate grooves in his broad back resembled an African warrior. His dark, low-cut hair formed miniature waves, fading toward the nape of his neck. The tattoos etched on his back and arms were artful. Some I'd seen;

many I hadn't. Right away, I knew this was all a bad idea. This week, into the weekend would be no good for me. Those anxious feelings leading up to today had been a warning.

His phone rang under the music. I watched as he reached for it on the counter next to the small bowl of what I assumed was fresh parsley.

"Yeah," he grumbled, and my heart was near exploding at this close adjacency to him.

What was wrong with me? I'd played this scenario over and over in my mind for more than a month. I'd had countless conversations with myself about this very week and the proximity we'd share. This was *not* looking good for me.

"What?" he somewhat barked, snapping me back into the here and now. "When?" Within seconds, he followed up with a grumbling, "Fuck…"

His powerful frame steeled for seconds long, and my pulse beat thickly in my neck. I watched him turn the eye of the stove off, reach for a remote on the counter and press a button, lowering the volume of the music. Next, he pulled a shirt from a nearby, displaced barstool belonging to the enormous island. I bit my lips together, watching him manage the thin, black t-shirt over his head. The striae in his back and arms flexed again, making a work of it until the cotton fell over the waist of his low-hanging pants.

His head dropped forward, a clear showing of frustration. Then, slowly, his broad shoulders turned a one hundred-eighty-degree angle. The first vivid mark of his frontal beauty coming into view was his deep brown beard, manicured with precision around his mouth. My lids fluttered and belly followed. He faced me, chin low, thick lidded eyes inaudibly admonishing me.

"Curry," he throatily greeted.

My brows plucked, creating deceptive confidence. "Mr. Elliott."

Quickly, his eyes melted into a soft squint. "Oh…Mr. Elliott? So, I'm middle-aged with bad knees already?"

"If I am." I shrugged, switching the weight in my heels. "You started it."

He scoffed, neck collapsing again. A cheap smile softened his face as his chin nearly reached his chest. Then Tobias sauntered over to me, shoulders stiffly aiding in his stride as he rounded the island. His woodsy-floral scent pouring over me was downright lewd.

When he arrived to me, I watched as his eyes roved up my body. They didn't linger for long before he raised his palms above my head for a playful greeting. "I ain't know you were on your way."

I slapped hands with him in the air. "And I didn't know you were having company over."

His brows shot up. "Pardon?"

I tossed my lips behind him. "Cooking for a dinner party?"

Tobias reached for my purse, pulling it from my shoulder with his eyes low. "You're my party. I cooked for your big head ass. Don't insult me now."

My head swung back as I grinned hard. "*Excuuuse* me. What's the occasion?" I stupidly giggled.

"Your trust." He walked my purse over to a barstool parked at the island. "Can you eat?"

Eat? Suddenly, my stomach couldn't decide if it felt pangs of hunger or butterflies of...excitement?

"Was starving until I walked in and saw all your wing meat exposed."

Tobias, back at the stove, turned to peer at me over his shoulder. "Knock it off, Lennox."

That's more like it...

Being less formal relaxed me, I guessed. God, I was so tense. Those long pep talks to myself were totally ineffective at this point.

I watched Tobias pour pasta with seafood, tomatoes, spinach, and a white sauce onto a plate. He scooped up freshly shredded parmesan cheese in his hand and held it over the mound of food. His auburn irises raised to meet mine. "Parm?"

"For me?" I swallowed. "This is for me?"

His head angled. "You gotta wash your hands first."

Grinning, I nodded. "Yes. Please."

"Tell me when."

After his second sprinkle, I expressed, "When."

"The sink's over there." He used his forehead to point across the kitchen.

After pulling out of my coat and placing it on the back of the barstool holding my purse, I ambled over to the sink and washed my hands.

"Where's your suitcase?" Tobias gestured with his eyes toward the hall I'd traveled from to get to the kitchen.

I dried my hands with paper towels near the sink. "In the car."

"Pass me the keys." He placed the plate on the table. "In the trunk? I'll get Danny G to bring it in."

I rolled my eyes. "I can get it, Tobias. Aren't we about to eat?" I couldn't express how thoughtful of him making dinner was. All the phrases I conjured while washing my hands felt corny now.

"Nah. *You're* about to eat then take a nice, hot, bubble bath." He brought a cloth napkin over, along with utensils. His striking body distracted me. Seeing it live in the flesh gave his countenance new energy. My senses were on overload with appreciation.

Stupid.

Stupid.

Stupid.

Stupid body. My stupid brain.

"And what are you going to do?" I couldn't help my antagonistic deflections. "Watch me?"

Shit…

Bad choice of words.

Tobias didn't answer right away. Instead, he strode with unhurried confidence, just outside of the open kitchen area to what was clearly a glass wine cellar. I watched as he decided over at least a dozen bottles, neatly stacked symmetrically. His hand brushed over one before reversing in direction and selecting another.

"I think you'll like this red blend." Bringing it to the table, he showed the label, holding the bottle at the capsule and heel.

"*Château Blevin.*" My brows lifted. "Whoa. Who did you rent this place from?"

Adorably, his gingerbread-hued face wrinkled. "Why?"

"Because they have good Jersey wine in their collection."

Tobias turned to glance at the glass cellar. "That's *my* wine from my even bigger collection at home."

"My bad. I didn't know." Self-conscious, I pulled at the ends of my hair.

"Because you ain't been to my crib yet, Lennox."

"Stop."

"Okay." He took a deep breath and raised the bottle again. "Wanna try?"

"Sure, I do. But you haven't answered my question."

Tobias sauntered over to the island, pulling out a drawer for a bottle opener. "Which was?"

I stood for my purse. "Why is the table set just for me?"

"Oh. That one."

Placing the keys to the rental on the island, I snorted. "Yeah. That one."

"Well," He pulled the cork from the bottle. "—that's because I got a call from Dale an hour ago when I started cooking. He asked me in to an 'emergency' meeting tonight."

I resumed my seat at the table. "Tonight?" My eyes roved around the kitchen.

"Yup. Said it's important. He's in Jersey, staying at the *Ritz Luxuriate Hotel*. I told him the timing was perfect. I'd meet him there by eight, the latest."

"You forgot about me?" Splaying my palm over my chest, I feigned offended.

"Not at all." He plucked a wine glass from a hanging rack and poured a small amount of the red liquid. "Actually, you were my motivation."

"I just got here, and you're leaving me in a rented home in *Samsara*. How did I motivate anything?"

"Because I know your fuckin' anxiety is through the roof about this week. I figured I'd give you time to get settled in from a long day of traveling and kicking it with your girls. Like I said, when you're done eating, go soak in the tub and unwind. I'll be back before you know it, and we can kick it then."

Once again, I glanced around. "You're leaving me in a place

I've only known for all of five minutes, Tobias? That doesn't sound like you."

He scoffed, looking too good doing it as he backed away from the table, grabbing the keys to my rental. "Charles is in New York tonight. That's why Danny G's here. Somebody you know. He'll be posted up outside 'til I get back."

"Hmmm…" I braved a long gaze into his auburn eyes. Tobias held me there while slipping the keys into his pocket. I could feel a force emanating from him, one I couldn't articulate. It made me want to comfort my friend as much as I wanted to antagonize him. This week was a big deal for him, too. "You're paying one of the senior, armed security guards of music superstar, Ragee, to guard little ol' me in this suburban neighborhood while you skip off to a meeting with another luminary icon, Dale? This can't be real life."

Tobias chuckled silently. "It could be, but you're down in North Carolina, stuck in a hospital."

My attention rolled over my plate, mouth secreting, telling of my appetite returning. "A hospital paying my bills, sir. And others'."

His big, hot hand clasped my shoulder lightly. My lids turned heavy at the new juxtaposition of his scent. "I know it does. Let's not go there. Anyway. This place has five bedrooms. As promised, you have your privacy on that side," He pointed past the wine cellar.

"That's it? It's just down there?" I asked. "I don't get a tour? Just a homecooked meal?"

"I've got every faith your resourceful ass will find your room. Mine is on this side, near the garage."

"Who's got the master?"

Tobias smacked his teeth, eyes shrinking with a smile. "C'mon, Lennox. We both do. Yours is just a little bigger because I know you overpacked." When I gaped his way, expressing my unease, he reminded me, "I'll be back."

"So, all this food is for me?" I gestured to the stove.

He turned, following my line of vision. "Nah. I packed a plate for Danny G, and I'm eating when I get back. Don't crash on me." Tobias grabbed my coat and headed down the hall I entered through. "I'll hang this in the coat room!" he shouted behind.

Taking a deep breath, I turned back to the table. *Seafood pasta.* Scallops, shrimp, and lumped crab meat were easily identifiable against the spinach and cherry tomatoes. If he were a different man, I'd assume he ordered in from fancy *DiFillippo's*. But nope. The man could throw down in the kitchen. It just hadn't been a practice of mine to sample his skills. Any of them.

My eyes scanned the table. The stemware was tall, large, and clearly high-end. I rolled my eyes closed while shaking my head. Jersey, *Samsara, Château Blevin,* and Tobias.

This definitely couldn't have been my wisest decision.

Couldn't...

love belvin

Tobias

I carried her suitcase to the door of the house, inside the garage. Lennox packed light, and that shocked the hell out of me. She'd turned into a diva over the years. Slipping her car keys inside my pocket, I didn't know how to read that. The one thing I did know was she wouldn't dip out on me while I took this meeting.

"Yo." I stopped at the driver's side of the *Suburban.*

"Yo." Danny G lowered the sports talk radio.

"Your plate's in the warmer. Take her suitcase in when you go." I rubbed the back of my head. "I got her keys on me."

Danny G laughed. "Yo, dawg, you wildin'! You got Chino's daughter up here? You's a wild one." He shook his head. "That puppy love on some shit."

There wasn't shit puppy about O.G. Chino's daughter, Lennox. The tiny glitter in her soft pink lip-gloss had my head spinning. Lennox had put on a few good pounds. I saw it in her thighs and curved ass through her tight jeans. Her commitment to lifting weights had been paying off. And those damn dirty blonde waves that were dark brown at the roots looked so fucking good on her. They framed her dimples so well. The girl wasn't just beautiful. She was cute...something precious.

So, I took it. I'd let Danny G talk his shit. The shit was crazy. That was my very thought all month long, leading up to turning around seeing her standing in the kitchen, looking as impeccable as I'd ever seen her. And she'd never been anything less than perfect in my eyes. I had to play it right, though. These were her rules, but there was no game on my part.

"Thanks for this," I told him instead of responding.

I hated to leave her, and so soon. When Dale hit me, I almost told him no. Then I thought about Lennox and how not to over-whelm her this week. This was a huge step for her.

Danny G sighed, wiping his face with his hand. "You got it."

"I'm out. I'll be back soon."

"Yeah. I know yo ass will!" He laughed behind me. "Tell D-A-L-Ezee I said whaddup."

"Yo!" I greeted, making my way to Dale and Luke, his best friend and one of his managers.

Dale, wearing sunglasses, sported his usual friendly smile as he approached me, giving dap. "My man!"

"That's on playa," I returned playfully, when greeting Luke next.

"One love, my G." We dapped it up, too.

"So glad you're here, man," Dale expressed. "Looking good,

too, G! What's this? The new *Asè Garb* avi leather?" He referred to my jacket, whistling his approval.

The shit set me back almost four bands a few months ago. It was good to have someone else identify and appreciate it.

In response, I harmonized the chorus to one of his old hits, "*Licker*," speeding up the melodies.

"Ah! See!" Dale yelped, holding his crotch while turning to Luke. He pointed at me. "These producer cats, who swear they're so hard, never like for people to know they can blow, man!"

With a hard scoff, I warned, "Pause."

We busted out laughing as Luke backed up to the white, linen-top table I figured they were seated at when I came in. *The Ritz Luxuriate Hotel* was not only holding strong in opulence for guests needing overnight accommodations, it also had a Michelin star restaurant, which featured a piano bar. As we took our seats in the bar section, my ear tickled with awareness, hearing keys being stroked from the other side of the room.

"You hear that, huhn?" Dale asked, face still lit brightly from that signature smile.

I listened for a minute, holding my phone in my hand. There were no vocals accompanying the harmony. "Oh, yeah. Duke Elling —*oh, nah*! That's…" I snapped my fingers. "Monk. Thelonious Monk. "*Straight, No Chaser*." Yeah. That shit. People say he's second only to Duke."

"See what I mean?" Dale shouted, happy as hell, to Luke.

Luke laughed, nodding.

"What?" I chuckled.

"You know your shit, man," Dale explained, head swinging back, giving Stevie Wonder vibes. "This is what I've been talking about. I just turned forty-four, and I knew that was Monk, but I'm feeling lost on transporting that same level of timeless music to a generation with microwave-level attention in terms of consumption. They don't let shit marinate. Just chew, swallow, and on to the next 'hit.' The shit that's up now is the noisiest, most boring, and quickly-thrown together cultureless shit of all time."

I was scissoring the hairs on my chin when he removed his

sunglasses. Dale's face was tight as he expressed his feelings about the current state of music. This was a redundant conversation in the music industry. Had been forever.

My argument remained the same. "That ain't true for everybody."

"I said *this* generation," Dale clarified. "I ain't a part of it. I ain't got the ear."

"Okay…" I pushed him to make his point.

Dale's eyes squinted as they moved from behind me to my face. That charming smirk returned. "I'm ready to get my thang-thang wet again."

Luke took a sip of his drink, face not giving away anything at all.

Slowly, I regained my damn wits. "Well, shit." I snorted. "Good for you, man. You're a fuckin' legend…too seasoned to be keeping the porch light on."

Dale, a platinum selling artist since his teenage years, hadn't had a studio album in about five years. His last hit album, *"Telling it All,"* was a cultural phenomenon and went five times platinum. That shit was almost fifteen years ago.

He nodded, likely accurately sensing my calculations of what all of this meant. His smile widened. "Yeah, my nigga." Dale nodded hard as hell. "You feel me?"

Luke scoffed, rubbing his mustache.

It was my turn to smile. "Who you in bed with?" My brain quickly spun the rolodex memory. "*RCA*, or you goin' indie?"

"Nah, man." Dale beamed. "No indie over here. I need the marketing help. *Arista.*"

My eyes went wild. "Okay! Going back home, in a sense."

"Yeah. And they givin' ya boy a nice bag for it."

I nodded, not expecting this when he reached out wanting to kick it. "You and D.J. getting the band back together?"

"Can I get you a drink, sir?" An Asian waitress with dark red lipstick appeared at my side.

"Oh, nah. I'm good."

"You sure, man?" Dale looked concerned.

I didn't mean to be rude. "Yeah. I got something happening at

29

the crib. I flew over here on my *Multistrada V4*. Can't stunt on her while loose in the head."

"Okay. Water?" the waitress offered.

"Sparkling with lemon," I requested. "Thanks."

"You got it." She turned to leave.

"So, D.A.L.Ezee's gonna be recording again with Mr. Daryl Joubert?" I repeated my question.

Dale and Luke caught eyes. "Nah," Dale murmured, looking my way again.

"Oh, word? Then who?"

"Somebody that ain't seasoned like D.J. and me, but somebody with an ear older than ours."

"T. Trouble?" He was a new cat out of Philly, shooting out hits for Pixie, Mario's comeback album, and Alana. *Shit.* Dale had a feature on one of Mario's new joints that was dope as hell.

Smiling, Dale shook his head. "You, man."

I felt my forehead stretch. I'd had keyboard credits on one of his failing albums about seven years ago as his sales took a trending dive. I remembered being hyped as hell about being in the studio with Dale for the first time. Every producer coming up at that time would sell their accumulated points to trade places. But Dale was hard-pressed about working with mediocre writers and producers. I sold his team a track—the best-selling one from that particular LP. However, they left me out of true production of his vocal arrangements. The shit infuriated me back then as a budding producer.

"Me," was all I returned.

"C'mon, Tobias, man. We know—the *world* knows—you've been the brainchild behind Raj's wild success over the past three-four years. The nigga went from like…Elton John to Prince doing Michael Jackson's numbers!" He fell out laughing.

Nah, bruh. Actually, Wynter did that…

I could have never copped to that. It wasn't my place to. Besides, it would have played into the very reason Dale had seemed to be asking me for my help.

D.J. was not just the producer of most of Dale's tracks on his "*Telling it All*" album, his best to date, but he was also the curator of the vibe the album conjured. People believed the stories Dale sang about regarding his recusant love life. D.J., through Dale, wasn't just selling music; he sold a storyline about wicked romance, and the world bought and ate it the hell up. *This* was why dude was coming to me. It's what I'd been doing for the past few years with artists.

"Everybody's been watching your work with Raj. Just like with D.J. and me with *"Telling it All*," you know how to create cultural nuances for the listeners. Look how long and widespread that one line from Raj's joint, *"No Bed Needed*," went. All the *TikTok*'ers, the challenges on *Instagram*. They posted fuckin' Tori McNabb singing it at their annual fundraiser. Hell, even Brielle and her dancers included it in their choreography for her world tour that year! The shit was up and stuck!"

Luke nodded, sipping on his drink. The waitress arrived with my water, giving me a moment to think.

Dale was right. We'd poured a lot of creative juices into Raj's last two studio albums. Ragee was at a point in his life where he was ready to reveal more, and it was about damn time. The nigga had been closed off to the point of weirdo-ism.

"What's it gonna take?" Luke finally spoke.

"For what?" I asked.

"For you to do the album."

I asked for clarity, "The whole album?"

"The whole shit," Dale qualified. "Executive producer. Full LP. You determine the number of tracks and the producers you wanna call in to co-create with. I'll even give you a credit."

"One credit?" That was an okay start, depending on the other details. I just needed to fine-tune the specifics. "How much bread?"

Dale looked Luke's way.

Luke placed his tumbler down. "Two seventy-five and another fifty for the EP role."

"Fifty to executive produce the joint?" I laughed dryly.

"C'mon, man. Think about the whole pie," Dale implored.

"Dawg, I just sold a track to Young Lord a month ago for one and a quarter. *One* track. You're asking for a full LP, which would be mostly my tracks. No disrespect to you, O.G., but that shit ain't math'ing."

Luke asked, "What's Raj been giving you?"

"Something that would reveal just how low your ball is."

Dale's expression dropped. "Ah, c'mon. Now, I'm lowballing you? Don't do that, Tobias, man."

"Nah. I ain't even gonna sit here and stunt on a whole legend. I'm flattered. I really am." I placed my palm over my heart. "Truly grateful. I just have to make sure the details work well for me. Quarterback'ing a *"Thriller"* attempt or even a *"Telling it All,"* requires a lot of work on my part. It's basically like spending a bunch of time with you, playing therapist and shit. I'll need to see what's going on in your heart and head to create a thematic album and provide authenticity. I won't just be throwing a bunch of empty tracks from my vault at you and telling you to have at it. My preference is to start from scratch."

"I know, man." Dale exhaled, attention sweeping the area around us as his mouth twisted. "I ain't gon' front. I heard you had a process with Raj. I know you're a beast in the studio…period, diggin' into peoples' heads. I'm willing to do what it takes."

I checked the time on my wrist. "Then start with valuing me."

"What do you want?" Luke asked again.

"Shit." I sighed, scratching my brow while shaking my head. "For starters, to EP a Dale album with this expectation, I'm taking no less than two points. And two hundred seventy-five thousand dollars for six to eight tracks—depending on where this shit goes—ain't gonna get it done. Fuck a EP fee. You can't put a price tag on the passion I bring." I sat up in my seat. "Speaking of passion," I took a sip of the sparkling water. "I've gotta put some in action tonight. I'll let y'all politic on the numbers, and get back to me. In the meantime, I'll start drawing up a plan for the direction of the project."

Once again, Dale and Luke looked at one another. Dale's smile was faint this time. Luke's expression ain't give away shit.

As Troop's "*Spread My Wings*" pumped through the speakers of the sunken-style family room, I dropped down the two-step entry-way, twirling creamy pasta around my fork. Feeling her jovial mood, I rocked from side-to-side as I chewed. Lennox had changed into her pajamas: ivory silk pants and a purple terrycloth robe exposing her tiny waist. *Damn.* At five feet and three inches, and about a buck-thirty, the girl was fucking stellar. Her natural, wavy curls were blonde at the ends and a light brown from the root. The color combo worked well for the season.

While she danced as though no one was watching, I ate with butterflies shooting around my damn belly. I couldn't believe she was here. Back in Jersey with me. And Lennox was dancing. After the hellish week she'd had—the shit she was currently going through—my girl was still able to find joy in a fucking singular moment.

When Lennox moved, swinging her arms in the air around the room, I smoothly moved behind her, around the furniture. She sang some of the parts, using the remote as a microphone. It wasn't until she turned the corner of the sectional sofa that she sensed me. I froze, and Lennox turned around with wide eyes as she shrieked hard as fuck, covering her mouth.

I tossed my head back, laughing before catching myself. "I'm being an asshole. My bad." Covering my mouth with the hand holding the fork, I tried hiding my humor.

"Tobias Lenart Elliott, you scared my lungs from my chest!" she panted, tapping down the volume on the remote. "Is this how you want to start this week? Do you not want to be roomies in this dope ass house you rented?"

Sobered by that fucking question, I straightened, swallowing my food. "Is a pig's pussy pork, girl?"

Slowly, her eyes grew even wider, and her mouth fell open. Lennox looked to be ready to cry before she let out a hard ass laugh. "What did you say?" She grabbed her belly as she howled.

Grinning, I twirled more pasta onto the fork, being sure to catch a shrimp. "You heard me."

"Boy! A pig's pussy? Really?"

I shrugged. "What you know about Troop, youngin'?"

Slowing her laughter, but still exposing those sexy ass dimples, Lennox explained, "My neighbor, Trina's mom. *Duh!* And you ain't but a year older than me, son-son."

"Oh, word? She used to rock out to Troop? That's what's up."

"I only know like two or three of their songs—*oh!* Like this one!" She pointed the remote, pressing into a button until the volume was high again.

"*All I Do is Think of You*," played next. That one brought back memories of being in talent shows. This time, I found myself singing with her in between eating. Lennox lip-synched as though she'd written the lyrics straight from her heart. I understood. The track was that catchy. At one point, coming out of my playful state, it hit me again.

I'm here with Lennox. She's here with me. For a little while.

You could have pinched me. Nah. *Fuck that!* Never pinch me when I'm dreaming of Lennox. Even when not in her presence, the thought of the girl, alone, was a fantasying-escape. But she was now here with me in the flesh, singing one of the most adorned, adolescent love songs in Black culture until its end. That was until she stopped to watch me, and her smile faded.

"What?" I was confused.

With a faint smile and low eyes, she answered, "You can really sing," as the music faded.

Shit…

I straightened, going for the last bit of food on my plate. "I play around."

"You can't help your gifts, Tobias." Lennox lowered the volume of the music as Guy's "*Groove Me*" intro'd. "It just dawned on me that you don't use that gift. I mean…" She feathered her hair, sitting on a sofa. "At least, not that I'm aware of. It's not like I'm with you often at all."

I nodded, hating that fact. "I work my gifts all the time. It's given me a great life." I spoke with food in my mouth.

Her dimples deepened as I placed the plate down on the coffee table. "You ate. Good."

"I told you I would when I got back."

"And now you're back." *Fuck*. Her smile did funny shit to my insides.

But I played it cool, gesturing to my empty plate. "What did you think of it?"

"Well!" She inhaled deeply, popping her lips dramatically, making the both of us laugh. "It was pasta and seafood. All of my favorites."

"So, that's it? It was a'ight because they're your favorites?"

"Well!" Lennox repeated again, popping her lips. "The chef put his foot in it, though." She gave a dramatic wink, making me crack the hell up. "How was the meeting? I don't even know how long you've been back. You fixed a plate and all."

"I pulled up about twenty minutes ago. Had to kick it with Danny G before he left. Then I washed up, and fixed something to eat. I was fuckin' starving." I rubbed my stomach.

"Awwwww! The Tobester was hungwee," she teased, sounding like a toddler.

I snickered. "Fuck you, Lenny."

"Get in line." She motioned with her arm, rolling her eyes.

"Pause."

She bit her bottom lip, dimples intensifying. Lennox clicked her teeth as she snapped her fingers. "Right. Bad response. Anyway…"

"Yeah. Anyway. What's on the agenda for you and your girls this week?"

Lennox rolled her eyes, smirking. I didn't mind. She was here. The girl could slap me and I wouldn't be offended. "Well, tomorrow is grooming and relaxation. We're meeting up at *Crystal K. Spa* around noon."

"Where's that?"

"In Central Jersey." I nodded, acknowledging her answer. She continued, "That'll pretty much be an all-day affair. There are restaurants on the property with so many amenities. We have facials, massages, and meditation booked. Then Friday, we're having breakfast at Mya's before—"

"Mya." I scoffed.

She shook her head. "That part. She was on her 'Mya-tribe' earlier today. Anyway…" Another deep breath. "We haven't decided where we'll land on Friday night. There are a few Greek parties happening. We said we'll decide tomorrow at the spa."

I lifted a brow. "You partying?"

"Yup." She swung her arms in the air above her head.

"Make sure you learn how to dance while at it."

Lennox laughed, covering her mouth. "I'm getting better. That bomb ass twerk is loading." She winked dramatically again, making me shake my head.

Then things went quiet again. Soul For Real's "*Candy Rain*" played low. Thanks to my dumb ass excitement of being in the same room as her, I skipped a beat in the conversation flow.

"You look good, Tobias," her voice was so small…insecure. She was vulnerable, and so fucking femininely divine, my brain froze a bit.

I raked my hands down my face, inhaling deeply. "Yeah. If it's one thing the kid gon' do, it's stay fly."

As I held a straight face, she spit out air. "Kid? You're about to be thirty years old. Far from a kid, old man."

"You're saying what I'm about to be like it's *my* birthday that's coming up soon."

"Yeah. But I'll only be turning twenty-nine. Your next birthday is the big three-oh, buddy!"

Nodding, I conceded. "You got that."

"How does it feel?"

"You asked me the same thing a couple of months ago."

"I know. Aging is a real freaking thing. Whether we're prepared for it or not, it happens. If we're not ready, it'll leave us on our asses."

I nodded in agreement, digesting that. "This is true. To answer your question, I've been giving more thought to my future. Investing has been a big push for me mentally."

"What about it?" Lennox curled her legs, placing her feet beneath her on the sofa.

Was this her facial expression when we'd talk on the phone for hours when we could?

"It's something I need to do."

"You dabble in real estate."

"Not for real, for real; I'm learning. Back in June, I was lucky enough to have lunch with a few millionaires—even a billionaire was in the house."

Lennox's eyes burst wide. "Jay Z? Diddy?"

I shook my head. "Azmir Jacobs."

Her face fell. "Never heard of him."

"Yet, he hit the billionaire mark *before* Jay and Puff." It was her turn to nod. I continued. "Funny, though, because it went down at *DiFillippo's*. You ever been there?"

"No. I heard the food is superb, though."

"It is. I hope to take you one day." I needed to move smoothly past my offer and dive back into the story. I wouldn't make this shit weird. "Well, Jacobs owns the place—"

"Is he Italian? Jacobs doesn't sound Italian."

"Nah." I shook my head, grinning. "The man's darker than me. He Black, Black. But that's what I learned about him. He's a master investor. Stenton Rogers was at the table—"

She sucked in a breath. "StentRo?"

Nodding my head, I explained, "Young Lord was there and a few other cats. Jackson Hunter invited me." My eyes lifted to her. "Another funny thing?"

Her dimples deepened as she smiled, anticipating my next words. "What?"

"As I'm walking into the private room, I hear loud, boisterous talking. Security let me inside, and a bunch of dudes were standing around the dinner table. Azmir Jacobs is up giving Jay Z dap."

Lennox dropped her chin. "*The* Jay Z? Beyoncé's husband?"

I lifted my right hand. "I shit you not. Those two went to high school together!" She gasped. "I know. Right? Small fuckin' world. Anyway, Hov must've gotten word Jacobs was in the building and popped into his private room on the way out. It was the craziest shit."

"Who is this Jacobs guy that he knows Mrs. Carter's Mr. Carter."

I laughed. Chicks swore Beyoncé contributed to Jay's success. They put her on this high ass pedestal; they did the same with Brielle.

"Anyway. The point of the story is Jackson invited me without telling me exactly what the vibe was. These cats sat there and talked money for like two hours straight. And not bragging on what they got; they talked about how to get it. Raj's business partner, Zebedee Baker, was there giving so much real estate game. It made me realize how small my wallet is."

"You're far from broke, Tobias. Come on."

"But I'm not wealthy."

"I'm saying." She flashed her palms in the air. "I've never seen your bank accounts, but you own several properties, travel the world, and you're one of the most sought-after music producers of contemporary times. Cher's been to your studio—played alongside you—at her request."

"And with all of that, I haven't secured generational wealth. My current portfolio would help Elia if I died today, but that ain't enough. I still don't have a *wife*—shit. I want more kids. That's more mouths to feed, more kids to groom to carry on the Elliot legacy." I shook my head. "I've been getting money for about eight years now. Millions have come and gone. My current move is to harvest them. To have my money make more money for me while I sleep. You know?"

Lennox's nod convinced me she did understand. "How do you plan to do that?"

"For starters, by not just accepting any deals thrown my way. Dale just gave me a good offer, but it wasn't great."

"What's great?"

"Raj gives me great. He trusts and values my gifts. It's taught me to do the same."

A sad smile lifted on her face. "I'm glad you trust you. You're a good guy, Tobias. Honorable, protective, giving, and trustworthy. *And* you're self-made. Not many can say that. You know?"

My fucking chest tightened, and eyes went lazy as I stared at her.

Shit.

Was this week a good idea?

Lennox gave me the same feels I had when I first met her at nineteen. The days when I sold myself—and my talent—short just to get her attention. Now, the woman, Lennox, was giving me her approval. That simple deed did shit to me I should have been embarrassed to feel. Instead, I chose to be more intentional with my time with her.

My throat was dry when I asked, "How was Scott?"

Lennox's wide eyes blinked as she processed, "Scott?"

Chapter Three

Tobias

Lennox blinked, fucking jarred. "Scott's...to be expected, considering the circumstances of his little world."

Shit...

I didn't mean *to*—

"*Ummmm...*" She rubbed her lips together, eyes toward the floor. "I'm feeling a little...parched from the drinking earlier. Mind if I go grab some water?"

"Sure. There are cold bottles in the fridge, and room temperature ones in the pantry." Lennox, domesticated, grabbed my empty plate before leaving the room.

My head collapsed backward in frustration the moment she disappeared.

Don't do that!

I chided myself until she returned. Lennox carried a bottle of water and a glass of wine.

She handed it to me, her baby-soft flesh accidentally brushing against my hand caused sparks to discharge in my chest. I watched her spin then drop onto the sofa across from me, those blonde ringlets cascading in the air. Her legs curled beneath her as she opened the bottle of water.

"So," she exhaled after taking a gulp from the bottle. "I've seen the type of deep-dives you've done with Raj—well... You've told me about some of them. The long conversations, the push for honesty, the heavy disagreements. All of that to get him to be more transparent in his art. If you're going to work with Dale, what will you do?"

"The same."

"The same?"

I nodded, thinking about it. "Yeah. That's all true R&B music is made of: vulnerability, love, hope, expression. It's hard for Black men to embrace those elements, but it's what resonates. It's what sells."

"Seems like what's been selling to me is getting high and cheating on your significant other." Her brows peaked.

"Because your Ragees, Dales, Joes, and John Legends haven't put out work consistently or concurrently—" I shook my head, quickly having decided I wasn't articulating myself well. "They weren't on their posts hard enough. Tank's been in the fight by himself for that generation. The Luthers, Stevies, and Teddys are not around or interested in new work. A lot of male R&B artists play in pop music equally or to a larger degree. And let's not mention the extinction of groups. There are none filling that space. All of these components and others answer the question of why the genre has been compromised. It's the foundation of music, yet no one wants to carry the banner."

"Except for Tank."

My head seesawed. "Raj has been doing his part these last two albums. Lucky Daye's been making some soulful noise. Honestly, there are lots. But when you have legends like Dale, making a resounding resurgence on the charts, the culture is inspired."

Her intentional attention could send me on a blissful orbit if I didn't remain grounded. "But first, you have to infuse that inspiration into the artist."

Slowly, I affirmed, "Bingo."

"How?"

Getting my shit together, I took a deep breath while sitting up, and reached for the glass of wine. "Like I said. Same shit." I took a sip, enjoying robust, fermented grapes exploding on my tongue right away. "Convincing him to get open. Maybe trying to pry because, while nobody's as closed off as Raj's ass, I still feel like Dale is like Brielle. They're from that pre-social media, popstar era, heavily reliant on public relations professionals."

"There was '*Telling it All*,'" she lowkey argued.

"A body of work based on the experience of another man. Who *is* Dale? Thanks to "*Licker*," we know he likes head. But does he enjoy reciprocating? A moody bitch? Does he like to fuck in public or is he rather reserved in his destinations? Does he still have a penchant for older women or, now that he's arguably a middle-aged man, do women his age catch his eye?"

Lennox nodded. "You think you can get all of that?"

"It's up to Dale. Will he pay me what I'm worth? Will he do the emotional work necessary?"

"The work," she echoed in a whisper.

After taking another nip, I emphasized, "I'd be interested in hearing what his needs are."

"What are your needs?" Her eyes ascended from the water bottle she rolled between her palms.

Was Lennox flirting with me?

"What's sitting across from me unassured."

Countless time was stolen over the stretch of two shallow breaths.

Her lips slowly parted as she regarded me, locking eyes. Lennox shook her head, murmuring, "Is that what you think?" I didn't answer because I had no damn clue. She was here. That had to mean something. "I found my way to my bedroom." She snorted, dimples forming. "Printed words of affirmation leading me straight to the door. Precious, worthy, desired, enduring, brilliant...I can't remember them all, but felt each one of them. Protectable. That was one of my favorites. Then black, long stem flowers on the bed, forming a heart around a purple *Andretta*'s box."

Licking my lips, I nodded, fighting for bravado. The last thing I was feeling was confidence. Subconsciously, I busied myself by pulling the wine glass to my mouth. It was tasteless this time.

"I've got something in common with Ragee now?" I hardly heard her.

"What's that?"

"I've been stuck in a house with you, and enjoyed your culinary skills." Her smile caressed my groin. "It was amazing. I had two plates." Lennox fell into the sofa, laughing at herself.

"Did you really have that much to drink today?"

She shook her head, still in a fit of laughter. "No. It was really good. It's just that I was a little piggish is all."

"I don't mind that even a little bit."

That comment seemed to sober Lennox up. I didn't know if that was a good thing or bad.

"Guess what I bought last night?"

"I have no idea."

"A book. Care to take a guess at whose?"

"No clue."

"Nyles Adams'."

My brows flew into the air. "Word?"

Smiling animatedly, Lennox nodded. "Yup."

Nyles was a Black, contemporary spoken word poet. He verbally sparred with our culture, specifically our generation, using compelling, colorful words, creating imagery for enlightenment. It was funny how Lennox and I both dug his work.

I grinned her way.

"You're tired." She observed, tapping the face of her phone.

I rubbed my face, fighting back a yawn. "I'm good."

With a conspirator's grin, Lennox pushed off the sofa, toed around the coffee table, and planted herself at the far end of my side. She handed me her phone. "I'm bushed. Read me a few bedtime stanzas."

On the face of her phone were words to a familiar piece. I snorted, "I don't need that." I gently pushed at her soft arm, rejecting the aid of the book. "That's my shit—*Remember*."

Lennox curled her legs beneath her, settling into the sofa. "Oh, really? What you know about *Remember*?"

I lay my head back on the soft, suede cushion and exhaled. Then my mind settled on what my heart felt at the moment with having her so close to me. *"I miss what I never had. I want what was never mine. I wanna be a kid again. Maybe then I'll understand this world I'm living in. Maybe then I can settle down, not be lost but found."*

"Mmmm!" she quietly hummed her encouragement of my selection with closed eyes.

"But right now, I'm stumbling in a haze of mumble rap and Instagram fame, foreign hair and body shame. But as long as I remember..."

I peered over to Lennox, catching her lids cracked as she looked to me. She finished along with me, *"I damn sure won't forget."*

Lennox

"Today?" I asked, fingers suspended over the keyboard of my laptop while I gaped at the phone propped on a pillow next to my hip.

"Yeah." Mya giggled. "We can grab breakfast from the *Brown Baristas* near your hotel. I know you're crazy about their coffee and pastries."

My stomach growled at the same time a lance of panic struck my chest. Unhurriedly, I gazed around the plush suite, mutedly admiring the sage-hued walls, stark white sofa across from me, and the thick, quilted bedding I was nestled inside of. It was all calming, a relieving harbor from my truth and the chaos accompanying it.

"I can come pick you up," she amended, rivaling my refuge.

Before I could conjure an answer, a soft, yet announcing rap sounded at my door. Quickly, I tapped to mute the call. "Come in. I'm on a call," spilled as a whisper.

The door cracked, then slowly swung open to a rolling cart topped with food. The churning of my belly intensified as did the fright. Tobias' eyes were sagaciously on me as he wheeled the food to the side of the bed. His presence had me questioning my consciousness, and his scent made me feel loopy.

And shame. Sudden recollection of his essence here in the bed last night, long after I left him for the night had me feeling embarrassed. Thigh-clenching and heavy breathing preventing me from falling out as quickly as I should have, considering the length of my day. Seeing him yesterday caused a cavalcade of emotional and physical responses I hadn't planned for. Maybe it was because I was way out of practice with making myself available to men, or Tobias was just that damn tempting, but I was undeniably attracted to him.

Sporadic *FaceTiming* and regular scrolls down his *Instagram* page painfully reminded me of how handsome he was over recent years. However, being with him—alone—in the flesh did things to my mind and body I hadn't accounted for when agreeing to staying with him this week. Last night, I wanted to touch myself. The pounding of my sensitive flesh between my thighs was downright painful. The secretions smeared on toilet tissue when I forced my way to the en suite bathroom was evidentiary of my attraction to him.

Thinking slowly, but moving swiftly, I unmuted the call. "That's not going to work. You coming north to Newark, just for us to drive down to Central Jersey—"

"Girl," Mya scoffed. "I'll drive. Ain't no biggie!"

Tobias' auburn irises were locked on me as my jaw collapsed. I was hyper-stimulated between his unbelievable, virile countenance and Mya's unrelenting attempt to get into my head. Too much was going on at the sight of his thick frame in slim fit joggers and a black, dri-fit shirt with black ankle socks. The man oozed generous masculinity from each pore. That and delicious cologne, which I now confused for his natural body odor; I was so unused to this physical proximity to him.

"Oh, you *would* drive if I'm the out-of-town guest," I was sure to inform Mya. "But it wouldn't work. I have a few stops to make before hitting the road. Anyway, girl, I need to go. Breakfast just made it to my door."

"*Eh?*" Mya squawked. "*Red Carpet Inn*'s got room service?"

Rolling my eyes, I hissed, "Bye, Mya. I'll see you at *Crystal K*'s." Without leaving room for another word, I disconnected the call.

"You trying to fatten me up with all this cooking?" My eyes roved over the tray.

French toast, bacon, sausages, eggs, grits, coffee, and condiments all packed neatly.

Tobias stood, holding a napkin, fork, and knife. "I told you if you trusted me this week, I'd make sure you didn't regret it." Speechless and caught off guard by his transparency, all I could do was stare at him. "You damn sure got that fat-fat all by yourself."

That caused me to blink. "I told you I'd get my weight up three years ago."

"And you damn sure did," the growl in his voice couldn't be missed.

I blinked hard, attention going back to my laptop. "Lonnie was a good, albeit an unsolicited, suggestion."

Three years ago was the first time we'd seen each other in the flesh since I'd moved down to North Carolina. I was depressed, underweight, and in crisis. Crisis had been my normal arrhythmia since my college days. Even now, I'd developed a way to coast in it. We irresponsibly exchanged numbers, and when we finally spoke over the phone, the man's veracity was brutal and needed. Tobias told me if I didn't gain a hold of myself, I'd have the body of a prepubescent child within a year or two. Even further, he insisted I get a personal trainer instead of going at the pursuit of fitness alone. Incongruently, I obeyed. Two months later, Lonnie began training me in the hospital's fitness center four days a week and provided a meal plan. Within eighteen months, he'd eased on tracking my food, but we'd still been training.

Ignoring me, Tobias tossed his chin toward my computer. "We didn't agree to this. Working on ya days off."

I exhaled, closing my laptop, and placing it to the side. "Yeah. The old, pasty, demanding board members who hate me." I rolled my eyes. "I got an email at exactly eight this morning, requesting the most recent quarterly reports. The hospital knows I'm off. The board…"

"Don't give a fuck." He pulled a tray from the lower level and arranged it over my lap, covered in the white, fluffy comforter.

"Not a single one," I agreed, watching him bring the plate of food over. Next came my coffee, cream, sugar, and syrup. Gently, and with thoughtful care, Tobias prepared a hearty meal before me. "This is nice—a lot, but nice."

"But your ass is going to eat it up, though."

Pretending to cry, I nodded. "I am!"

He chuckled, pouring my coffee. "Greedy ass," he muttered. "And the sad thing about it is, I'm about to go for a run—a run I was supposed to have company for, but I have to share you with your girls this week, I see."

"Not my fault you have hidden agendas. I did not agree to running with you this week." I pointed to the adjacent wall. "Those kicks are dope, though. I've got a workout fit that goes well with them—two, actually!"

Tobias cocked his head to the side. His natural, hooded eyes narrowed, but twinkled the way they always did for me, making me squirm over the mattress. I forced myself to laugh instead of revealing how mesmerizing he was.

"Tobias, can I ask you a serious question—a personal one?"

He folded his arms, breastplate bulging unfairly as he leaned away from the bed. "Ain't nothing too personal between us. You know that."

"Why are you single?"

His eyes burst wild. "Damn." He scoffed, "I wasn't expecting that." I rubbed my lips together nervously. "Well…"

47

"I'm sorry. I don't mean to go deep." I shrank. "You don't have to—"

"Nah. Nah." He sat at the foot of the bed, turning his strapping, upper-torso to face me. I didn't need the respectful distance, but appreciated his attempt at integrity. "*Ummm…*" Tobias shrugged. "I ain't single, exactly." My eyes widened, and I swallowed hard involuntarily. "It's like this." His tongue rapidly swiped his lips. "I remember back in the day when I was running hard, trying to catch my first hit. I used this popular studio in the City the record companies had contracts with. Pretty much the same taxis worked the area, picking people up from the building, knowing many of them coming out of the studio had dough. Even though I didn't for a while, I would get this particular cabbie often. His name—well, we called him Herk because we couldn't pronounce his name displayed on the dashboard with all his credentials. Dude was like…Middle Eastern, maybe?"

He used his hands as he continued with his story. Tobias had the most captivating stories. It was one of several distinguished talents he had when I met him as a kid over ten years ago.

"Well, anyway, we'd talk from time to time when I'd catch him. Kicking it about…life." He shrugged. "The cat was cool. Herk kicked it with everybody. We all knew him. So, fast-forward to when I got my first break with "*Children of Fate*," I was hyped as hell. It was so big, my management team planned a party. So, boom. One day, I was catching a cab to *Bar Pitti* over in South Village for this meeting with a record exec, and Herk pulled up. He'd heard about the "*Children of Fate*'s" lick and congratulated me right away. I invited him to the party, and he said he couldn't come."

"Why?" I asked, already enrapt.

"Because he was about to head back home to get married that week. Now, mind you, the nigga looked to be every bit of in his fifties. So, I asked why he waited so long to get married. He explained how in his culture, they'd just moved away from mandatory, arranged marriages. He said his parents had just missed the old tradition when they'd gotten together as kids. Some families still did it, but the younger generation coming up pushed hard against it.

This included his generation. So, the shortie he was going home to marry was the one he'd been wanting since they were like preteens, but her family knew she had some…gynecological issues."

"What?" I chirped. "As a preteen?"

"He'd been feeling her since his preteens. I don't know when they assumed she had these issues. Well, anyway, for a female in their culture, it makes you undesirable as a wife. The shit is so deep, her father ain't want her married either."

"That's horrible! Why?"

Tobias shrugged again. "Reproduction is essential to preserving culture. A barren woman holds no value in some of those tradition-led ethos. Herk said he ain't care about having kids, but somehow because of that, he wasn't able to secure her hand before he got an opportunity to come to the U.S. He never forgot about her, though. Always kept in touch, and never laid a hand on another woman. He said they call it teetotalism. No sex, no companionship, no nothing."

"Wow…"

"Right." Tobias stood from the bed. "But he got his lady. They got married, and he brought her here. Saw him a month after that. Dude had a glow to him." He headed to the door. "So, call me Herk. I'm on my teetotaling shit."

My belly flipped, burning like acid with jealousy.

Wha— "Who are you waiting on?"

"You," he answered with his back to me.

"You totally made that story up!" I called out to him, deathly curious.

"Everything except for your last question," his nonchalant voice carried.

I was effectively confused at this point. "Wait!" I shouted at the opened door. "Then how true could the last be if the first was totally made up?"

The trail of his scent left behind had me closing my eyes in shame.

And did I say thanks for the food?

"I'm not ready to leave," Mya wined, stretched out with her arms over her head in the oversized, leather reclining sofa. Her contented grin was soft as she gazed into the crackling flame of the fireplace.

We were all clothed in robes and plush, sheepskin slippers with rubber soles. *Crystal K.* was top tier in resort spa services. We'd been here for just over six hours, receiving facials, massages, manicures, pedicures, mineral spring baths, adult beverages, a full meal, and snacks.

"Me either," Lisa's groan wasn't much different from Mya's before she yawned. "I'm dreading tomorrow. It's gonna be such a long day for me."

"You're still coming back out tomorrow. Right?" I asked, curled into my recliner, debating on texting Tobias.

I missed him.

Shit…

Here I was, staying with him in a rented house this week and missing him at the same time. Who was this Lennox?

Lisa answered, "Of course, I am. I hate that I have to leave y'all tonight."

And I hated the indisputable desolation in her voice.

Nisha nodded. "Same, chile."

"I don't know why you didn't just stay with Lennox," Mya inquired. "Split the room."

Lisa rolled her eyes closed. "Girl, I'm lucky to be here. Aaron's never happy when homecoming rolls around and he has to be daddy daycare." She yawned, head reclined. "I swear. The shit I know now; if I knew back when…"

"Tell me about it," Nisha agreed.

Mya sat up, back leaving the cushioned sofa. "What would you have done differently, Nish?"

Nisha didn't reply right away, gazing at the wine glass between her palms. "*Hmmmmm…*"

Her eyes narrowed. "Judge-free zone?"

Mya gasped. "Of course. Don't insult us."

Nisha eyed Mya warily. Lisa and I exchanged a knowing glance. We knew who Nisha was referring to.

It was confirmed when she twisted her neck, looking Mya dead in the face. "You remember that when I'm done. Anyway… If I could go back in time—especially since undergrad—I would have given this young professor a chance."

This time Mya gulped in a heap of air. "A professor? Who?" Her head swung my way, long weave flying in the air. "Did you know?"

Ignoring her, my attention went to Nisha, who rolled her eyes. "Dre. He was a sociology professor."

"And you fucked him?" Mya asked.

Nisha's eyes rose from the glass to the flames against the wall. "No, but…" Then she shook her head. "Doesn't matter. My point is he wanted to explore dating."

"How?" Lisa asked. "Isn't that against school policy?"

"He was leaving for a position at *William Paterson*. It started back in our junior year. I took his class. He knew he was leaving at the end of the school year. He was starting a doctoral program the same fall he was starting at *Willy P.*"

"His doctorate?" Mya repeated, clearly shocked. "How old was he?"

Nisha shrugged. Again, glancing down at her glass. This was really emotional for her. "Not even ten years older than me. He was young. Did an accelerated program for his master's degree when he was getting his bachelor's."

"Was he a perv?" Mya's eyes lobbed, telling of her racing mind. "Do I remember a young professor trying to holler at students when we were there?"

"No," I answered. "I don't recall that."

Professor Dre wasn't a perv. That was the first thing we assumed when he would stare at Nisha all the time before approaching her mid-fall semester. He was chill. We *Google*'d him for like a week.

Mya, finally reading the room, shrank. Then she shrugged, falling back into the sofa. "I'm just saying…"

"So, you're saying you missed out on your one opportunity at happily-ever-after?" Lisa asked, concluding.

"No." Nisha answered. "I don't know. I'm almost thirty, and still single. All I do know is it's scary out here for people like me who want something real, equitable, and monogamous."

"I thought love would be easier for you at this age, versus marrying right out of college," Mya noted. "You don't have that buildup of resentment collected from shared experiences over the years. Love is easy when you're not fighting against bad memories created from the marriage. Love is the best when unalloyed." Her words spilled dreamily.

"But marriage is defined by those spoiled moments when you remain resilient." The girls' heads snapped my way. *Yeah.* I shocked myself, but I believed that. So, I nodded. "Love is fun. Marriage is work."

For a spell, all you could hear were the relaxation-inducing musical notes playing from hidden speakers and occasional crackles from the fireplace. I took the time to type the *Samsara* address into my phone in the *Maps* app, wanting to see how long the ride would be and if there was traffic. I was ready to go, but didn't want to be the first to announce it.

"Do you have any regrets since graduating college?" Mya asked Lisa. "Would you have made different choices?"

I glanced up to find Lisa's attention take to the ceiling. She nodded after a beat. "I would have traveled before falling in love. I was too quick to look for that happily ever after." Lisa inhaled deeply, expression turning felicitous. "I was so young and had no damn clue of who the hell I was."

"Right," Nisha nodded. "Same. That's what scared me about the young professor. I ain't even 'know' Quenisha at the time. How could I take on a 'for real' grown ass man? Dude was in the real world already."

52

"And about that," Lisa interjected. "The world is so much bigger than New Jersey, Delaware, and even Pennsylvania. I found this collection of children's books by a Black author. She writes about different countries and their cultures. Just basic stuff about it, but they have these cute illustrations. *Some*—" Her budding excitement hit an extreme halt. "Sometimes, I fantasize I'm there based on the images." Her eyes closed. "I wish I'd traveled before settling down."

"Then you wouldn't have Aaron," Mya reminded her of the obvious.

Lisa didn't respond.

"Awww. C'mon now! We were in a great sharing space," Nisha playfully chided Mya. "You mean to tell me if you could go back to those days and retract some of your decisions, you wouldn't? You think all the calls you've made were correct?" Her tone was kind, inviting.

Mya's mouth twisted as she appeared to think. She shook her head. "Not really. My kids are great. Collectively, their gene pool is amazing. I wouldn't change that." Her head swung to her lap.

"But there'd be no D.J., Miley, and Andrea if there was no Derrick," Lisa threw the obvious right back to Mya.

"Yeah. I know," Mya muttered with less confidence than she was known to exude.

"Think about your needs now," Nisha aided her softly. "What attributes does twenty-nine-year-old Mya need she maybe muscled through life without coming out of college?"

She didn't answer right away. Nisha, Lisa, and I crossed each other's lines of vision.

Mya's tone was the softest I'd ever heard when she murmured, "It would be nice for Mya to be given more patience when she's frustrated with the kids. She could use a soft hand sometimes, and not always have to be the regulator. It would be nice to share some of the responsibilities of the house like recurring bill payments and things like that. We both pay the bills, but I don't like being the lone secretary. And when this advanced-aged Mya expresses her opinion, it would be nice to be heard by her partner and not blown off all the time." She nodded, glancing around the room at us. "It would be nice to remind Mya she's a human being with feelings that get bruised from time to time. Words hurt, and ill-actions wound. I'm not always as tough as I seem. Mya could use wooing and pampering." Abruptly, Mya giggled, maybe at the fact of speaking in third person. But I thought it was cool, so long as she could be real. "I bet you feel the same," she posed to me.

She was right and wrong. I knew what it felt like to be coddled from time to time, though very limitedly. In recent years, I'd also been reminded that I was human, capable and deserving of being pampered.

"But seriously," Mya continued with a dramatic pause. "I wouldn't go back and decide against Derrick one bit. He can be all of those things—is all of those things. You know?"

I couldn't answer. Was too busy typing my text.

Me: Leaving in twenty minutes. Should I pick up dinner?

Back at the house in *Samsara*, I peered down at my kicks, feeling giddy as I walked toward the live, circumfluous musical flow. On the ride up from Central Jersey, my excitement multiplied by the mile at seeing him again. It was stupid. Childish and reckless compulsion is what it was, but I'd defer self-judgment until next week when I returned to my real life.

I stopped at the doorway of the formal living room where Tobias sat at the grand piano, stroking its keys with his eyes closed and head cocked to the side. His posture on the bench was different than I'd seen him back in the day, playing at my grandmother's church when the regular organ player quit for a paying gig at a mega church in Upper Montclair. My grandmother said Tobias' hands were anointed by God. She was smitten with him until she found out he wanted me.

Tobias' eyes squeezed and chin twirled in the air; he was so caught up in the melody. I understood because, in no time, I was captivated myself. The notes were complimentary; some soft, others dominating, but all worked together to cast a spell of decadent peace. Finding myself leaning into the arched entryway, I got lost in the beautiful, sweet arrangement.

Second by second, it was wondrous to not feel a slapdash of anxiety—a flash of terror entering your orbit, caused by reckless decisions made by others. The suspension of worrying about the phone ringing with bad news, or the access demonic havoc had on your life. It could walk through the door of your home at any minute and cripple you into irrevocable circumstances. The perpetual, gut-churning state, from being calm and unsuspecting, to receiving disturbing news. Having a moment of simple peace was priceless and undervalued.

In these moments, I recognized the gift of heartsease. I told myself I would find that very thing this week and bask in it. I wouldn't run from happiness or watch it parade by me. This week, I'd chase it with courage and ride the wave with hopeless intent. No crying myself to sleep or twisting and turning before I could find rest. I'd latch onto it until it dissolved in my arms.

"You look…" the sound of his husky tenor thundered in my chest. My eyes burst wide. "…interesting. Good, but interesting." Tobias observed me from head to toe, taking in my attire.

An emerald green, off-the-shoulder tulip dress. It fit perfectly. However, incongruent to its elegance were the *Nike* running shoes he purchased for me this week. My attention trailed up to him across the room.

"They all fit."

His syllable spilled monotonically. "I know."

"How?"

"Because I pay attention, Lennox."

"Maybe I shouldn't be shopping while on the phone with you." I fought a heated grin. "I was going to buy it."

His brows plucked as he shifted his legs around the piano bench to face me. "Maybe I should have let you. Marked down or not, that shit is expensive. I thought *JAGMisha Boutique* had killer deals."

"It's *Valentino*." I shrugged, taking in his stunning beauty. Tobias' features were soft, eyes imposing as they ran across my body. Again, I wasn't used to this proximity to him. Did he always exude this passion when sharing a space with women? I swallowed while hooking my finger into the twenty-four-inch necklace running into my cleavage. At the base, in white gold, was my first initial. Captured at the top of the letter and bottom were several small, glistening, disbursed diamonds. It was soft, dainty, and with an intentional message. "Couldn't have been as much as this *Andretta*'s."

For a spell, neither of us shared a word. A crackle of pending tension sparked the air. Suddenly words weren't necessary, and quite frankly, I'd given enough out today at the spa with the girls. At this hour—in this space—my needs were different. I didn't want to lead. I wanted to be understood and tended to for once. Even if it meant just standing here, being seen in clothing, jewelry, and shoes he thoughtfully purchased for me. I wanted to be seen as something more than an invariably in-control heroine.

I didn't want to be a silent survivor like pigeons in the inner city. I needed to be a dove once in a while. Doves weren't seen in my neighborhood coming up. At least not the all-white ones. They were beautiful, rare sightings. Doves had better reputations and were believed to be precious. That's what I wanted to allow myself to be, and the man across the room from me had been the only to, not only express interest, but capability as well.

Flustered, I cleared my throat. "What are you thinking?"

Tobias licked his lips, peering me dead in the eyes. "How I wanna spank your ass."

"You say that a lot. This time, I'm afraid I believe you."

His spine straightened over the bench. "You should."

"Why do you want to beat my ass?"

"I said spank. And I want to do it for a few reasons. One is because you took so damn long to give me this time with you. So fuckin' long that I don't know if I'm in a dream or if this is my real life. Do you need another reason?"

My groin churned. "Please." I hated the unintentional whisper.

"Another one is you spent too much time away from me today," he delivered throatily. I switched weight on my hips, feeling that unwelcomed moisture between my thighs again. "I know you're up here for homecoming, but you being here with me is sort of my homecoming. You know?"

"Do it."

His forehead expanded. "Do what?"

"What you want to do."

"There's a lot of things I want to do to you. You have to be more specific."

My heart trembled as I crossed the room to him. It was truly an outer-body experience if I'd ever had one before. I didn't feel anything, hardly saw anything but him. All I could feel was my pulse beating in my head and my heart pounding inside my chest. Who was this intrepid, vixen person hidden dormant inside me?

I stopped inches away from his feet.

"You're scared."

"Of you?" My mouth was as dry as the desert. "It's not like you're going to hurt me."

"Actually, I am. C'mere." He turned on the bench so his back was now facing the grand piano. When Tobias patted his thigh, my lungs seized in my chest. His dense brows, hooded lids, curly, lashed auburn irises, and classically sculpted nose, all made for a temptingly handsome man I decided against years ago. Tobias' mouth was ajar, too, eyes expressively bright on me. "You want me to ask you again?"

He didn't. I moved toward him in this new position. Tobias reached for me when I leaned over. Together, we adjusted me onto his lap. My head near the wooden floor, breasts crushed against his one thigh, and pelvis covering his other. The pulsing thickness of his dick pushed into my belly as I panted.

Tobias hiked the skirt of the dress, rendering my rear cheeks to him. Instantly, I felt debased, exposed…bare. All the things I'd fought against each day in my micro, yet unstable world, I allowed him to bring me to.

"This wasn't the plan," he muttered over me.

With a chest heaving against his thigh, I croaked in a whispered, "I know."

"*I*—I…"

"I know," escaped even lower.

This man had been nothing but a gentleman, even while in illegal pursuit of me. I'd allowed it…even grew to want it. Tobias and I expressed our physical attraction to one another when we'd met as baby adults. The emotional department was what we had to grow into these past three years, even if it was under forbidden circumstances. I trusted this man with my life. A small glimpse into his intimate world would be worth an awkward, undignified act between us.

Even from this position, I could feel his unrelenting force. His thighs and hands were hard and hot. His hold inescapable.

Damn.

Last night and this morning, Tobias was my personal chef. Tonight, he was my aggressive captor. I blinked deeply as I anticipated the first sensation on my exposed ass. Curled over his lap, I focused on not clenching my cheeks. They'd look awkward that way. The tension was so powerful, the temptation imminent. But the first thing I felt was exploratory, slightly callous fingers at the waist-strip of my thong. He ran a finger underneath, the examining graze burning a trail on my skin.

Then Tobias yanked at the strip between my cheeks, creating a pull from the lips of my sex. It squeezed my swollen clit, churning my groin. He tugged again, and my clit thickened more from arousal. The state felt foreign on his lap. My bare skin pressed against his hard body. By the third yank, I forced my throat closed, fearing a mewl shooting from my lungs.

TAP!

That lash was not only unexpected, but eye-crossing. I winced over his hard flesh, my spine curling into him. And my mind subconsciously viewed my antagonist as an ally. His big, hot, and misted palm wiggled my cheeks. That provoked my libido, causing me to lubricate even more.

SPACK!

Another blow. This time to both cheeks. I gritted my teeth at the smarting from it. Did Tobias enjoy this? Did I? Even more burning than that question and the sting from the blow—what other women did he do this to? The question numbed me momentarily. Tobias wasn't mine—*well*... He was my friend; a dear one. A trusted and intimate one, albeit platonic at my insistence.

Until now—

POP!

My lids closed in forfeiture and my body tensed, lungs seized against the bite from that one. Although it was only the third, I understood the pain would ease momentarily. I released a contented sigh after the initial sting subsided.

"That's enough," Tobias grunted as though angry. My frame tensed all over for a different reason this time. I'd been anticipating more. He straightened my dress over my butt and helped me to my feet. "You good?" His big hands gripped my waist when I stumbled. Nodding, I didn't want to reveal how disoriented I was, how my mind was bustling more than Grand Central Station. Tobias removed the sneakers, exposing my red toes. "Here..." He guided me to the other side of the bench and grunted as he lifted me to sit on top of the piano. There wasn't much space, but I was stable. "Good?"

Blinking hard and still reeling from an adult "spanking," I muttered, "I'm afraid to move. I don't want to break..."

"Nah. You're on the music rack," he explained with curled lips. "That can hold you."

"And what about my feet?" *How long can I sit on this hard surface before my ass begins to burn?*

Gently, he swung my legs toward the left, placing my feet at the corner of the opened top. "They'll be good here," Tobias murmured, before returning to his seat on the bench.

While trying to find a place to relax my hands, I heard the first of the melody. Tobias began playing a tune I soon recognized as the one he'd been playing when I interrupted him. Fighting my way to comfort, I struggled to get out of my head about the awkward act we'd just committed. Tobias just spanked me. A man struck me. *On my ass, though…* Was it punitive? If it was, was I okay with it? This is Tobias. Tobias Elliott. He'd never hurt me.

But he *spanked* me.

And I liked it…

I was, once again, affected by the vibe of the tune. It was as though each note compelled me to a new orbit. It was seductive and provocative and rich. Time disappeared. Spa time with the girls was but a foreign memory. Despair, my real-world attendant, was at a comfortable distance. No calls from my home in North Carolina. No calls regarding my life in North Carolina. I wondered if the world was on fire outside of this *Samsara* home, would peace be this dominant while lost in this space with Tobias? That's what this music did. It ensconced me. Us. And it was also bewitching, allowing me to transport to wherever I wanted.

Except I didn't want to leave. Didn't want to escape this space. I wanted closeness with my friend. Finding anchoring stability on the piano, I managed to lean into him. Tobias' eyes were closed as he played. His head swayed, but I could capture him if given a few inches. I didn't have too much work to do. His eyes opened, almost sensing me. They were alert, yet thick and smoldering.

My heart galloped against the wall of my chest as I inclined just a bit more to make clear my intention. As predicted, Tobias met my emotional need and pushed his lips against mine. My body trembled with anxiousness. It had been months since I'd been kissed. The last donor of the affection was the man himself. So soon into the embrace, I told my brain to calm itself. Tonight, I wanted to push the bounds of his willpower. Except, the moment I parted my lips, ready to taste his mouth, he pulled away. Hands still tapping the keys fluidly.

Tobias' attention was keenly fixed on me when he evenly warned, "I've been here playing for five hours, fantasizing about your name and mine being on the deed of this house." His words poured like sweet honey from a jar, slow and voluminous. "I've been telling myself this was an ordinary day, and I'd wait for you to get home from work." The key transitioned higher. "This is what a creative, desperate mind can conjure. That's how bad I want you.

I've spanked you." His jaw clenched with tension. "Your tongue in my mouth again'll push me over the fuckin' edge, Lennox."

My heart twisted, stung from the rejection. I lifted my torso, trying to reign in my emotions. Maybe he wasn't ready. Clearly, he'd put some thought into it. But we'd kissed several times over the past eighteen months. Embarrassed, I turned my head away as Tobias continued to play. Self-doubt had been a familiar foe, Tobias being a prime example of defeat to it.

Within seconds, I felt his big hand at my ankle, pulling it from the wooden corner. My head whipped down, and I watched as he played with one hand, using the other to arrange my right foot over his left shoulder. My left foot followed as I gripped the shiny wood for anchorage. He hiked it onto his right shoulder. Instantly, I was bare to him but for my thong panties. The scent and heat of my arousal was now aired out directly to this man. The position mortified and further roused me.

Tobias' penetrating gaze seared me as he played beneath my open thighs. I could feel each flex of his shoulder when he reached for a distant key. He wanted me to watch him while I was opened... to him. Not once did he look between my legs, not that it took much effort to see down there. I could feel my nipples swell and push against the fabric of the off-the-shoulder dress. My breathing hiked; breasts lifted toward the ceiling as I balanced myself on the tiny board inside the opened piano.

When he leaned in and pressed his soft lips against my knee, I shivered. His electrical touch so reverent, Tobias didn't stop there. As his hands finessed the keyboard, his mouth busied up my quivering thigh. The strain to keep still now elevated the ache in my butt. I endured the torturing pleasure until he arrived inches from the seat of my panties then stopped and began on my other thigh at the knee.

Tobias paid the same sensual patience, traveling up my inner thigh. I clenched my misted palms around the raw wood of the instrument, eyelids fluttered at the teasing pleasure. Each decadent second of carnal sensation made me feel like a novice. Like a prisoner denied sunlight for twenty-three hours of the day, like an incubated child without maternal touch, I felt deprived of intimacy. But tonight, I'd received every ounce made available to me.

I was so swollen, so wound up. Between the tenderness of my cheeks, the music enchanting my mind, and Tobias' gifted touch of intimate places on my body, I was teetering on the edge of insanity. When he pushed his mouth into the bed of my panties against my engorged sex, my neck gave out and head collapsed backward. A forceful gush of air broke through my throat.

Perceptively, I could feel the muscle of his tongue push into the wet, silk material. It swiped weightily against my clit. And then again. And again. Each time he lashed against it, pleasure mounted until my feet pushed against his shoulders, hips lifting to meet his strokes. This wasn't good. This wasn't me. But this man was me. He'd been the closest thing I'd had to a friend and emotional refuge virtually since I'd known him.

Cognizing a man this close to me—between my legs—while playing beautifully at a piano, sent my mind adrift. My body floated, lifting in venery. Nyles Davis' descriptive expression whispered over the sirens blowing in my mind. *"For hours, I tongue-kissed your essence, pleased you, squeezed the juices from your damn soul as you screamed and moaned."*

"Tooobeeee!" I cried out as an onslaught of delicious tremors impaled first my core, then blossomed out to my chest, legs, and arms.

Every doubt, insecurity, and regret haunting me daily silenced as I cried his name over and over while my stomach contracted, and feet curled over his hard shoulders. *And he played on.* The music never ceased; the cadence never dropped as I lived through a blissful bodily explosion.

As I came down, trying to wait out the fog from a powerful orgasm, Tobias soothed my discomfit with a line of suckling kisses down my right thigh. My heaving was just under control when he made it to my left one. Only, I wasn't soothed; the oral care revved my hunger all over again. I think Tobias knew. His pining gaze was on me again between my propped legs.

Having never heard this song, I believed I was Tobias' number one fan, knowing all of his published music. I'd researched them all when he re-entered my world three years ago. That being said, this nameless, unfamiliar track vibrating beneath my tender ass was indisputably my favorite of them all.

Tobias reached up, and with two forceful yanks, ripped my panties. Leaving the bed of them hanging low near the keys, his right hand resumed playing the piano. The chords changed. Tobias began a new song. My mind was too preoccupied to truly appreciate the switch, with his blazing eyes observing and busy mouth working up my thigh again.

I watched as his tongue snaked out in slow motion and swiped inside my swollen lips. My belly contracted again, understanding what was taking place. I wondered who was this woman controlling my bold behavior here in Jersey; now, I questioned who was the man. There was a fire in Tobias' eyes—an unapologetic hunger and confidence I wasn't accustomed to—even having known him previously as a lover. My, how things had changed.

Evident in his touch, Tobias was skilled beyond music. But this shocking reveal blew my mind. He was eating me with slow mastery, being sure to explore each unseen inch. He flapped, twisted, and curled his tongue, never missing a nerve ending. This time, he didn't just focus on my clit; Tobias explored me, teaching me where pleasure could be hidden.

When he was ready, he found my nub, and pounded it with the firm tip of his tongue. As pleasure mounted, I did recognize the new song. "*Spread My Wings*." His version was slower, more dramatic. And so was my orgasm as I lifted until I reached my crescendo in his face, flying high.

"*Tobeeeee!*"

Chapter Four

Tobias

"*Tobeeeee!*"

The pitch in her cry was about more than inescapable pleasure. Lennox hit a plateau she was unaccustomed to, a place possibly never visited. And my manipulative ass knew it. This week wasn't supposed to be about this.

I swear...

Our bedrooms being on opposite ends of the house was strategic. I didn't want to seduce her, just spend time with the girl. But instead, my ass got jealous about her spending time with her girls. I'd suspended lots of shit on my itinerary when she finally agreed to spending half the week in the same house as me. I sacrificed a lot, but I knew what I was getting myself into.

So, why the fuck you spank her? Lennox! This is Lennox!

And my low-key, possessive ass couldn't even make it two full days and nights without crossing the line. You have to understand, shortie didn't live in the same state as me. The times I'd seen her over the past three years had been stealthy and timed to be brief. She'd give me longer *FaceTime* calls than face-to-face visits when they were possible. Still. I should have been patient.

As my tongue glided away from her clit, down to her thigh, I wanted one more. Lennox could come again on my face, I knew it. But I also knew I should stop while I was ahead. That first orgasm came quicker than I thought her self-consciousness and good sense would allow her. The second was more fun because I got to explore. Swallow her essence. Ingest her pleasure.

My girl's pussy was pretty, too. Lips plump, soft, and well portioned. Her hair was low and waxed in the shape of a martini glass. And it tasted like…her. A natural oil enhanced by a delicious artificial fragrance.

Just fucking perfect.

Sucking on her thigh as she panted, chest toward the ceiling, pussy spread before me like a feast, I decided to end the song. She'd had enough. Her harsh breaths hit my face, saturated in her satisfied concession as I licked the evidence of her state of negligence on my lips. I pressed harshly into the final keys, paying her an inspective glance. Lennox was spent. Affected. Disturbed. And something inside me was happy with that. It was long overdue. She needed to become undone, even if for a night.

Once the ending note was complete, I pulled her legs together and hooked them over my right arm. Then I scooped Lennox from her heaving back, lifting her from the piano. As I walked out of the living room, I studied the hardness in her expression. Lennox kept her eyes closed as she struggled to steady her breathing. I understood. That was a lot. There was no way I could go in for another orgasm. That would have really done damage.

Traveling the hall, I held her in my arms and chest, physically, the way I did emotionally. Lennox Curry was one of those feminine gems born into the earth, who men fucked up with mishandling. It started with her father, Chino, and went on from there. Sometimes, I considered myself in that mix. Shit, I could have prevented it if I'd just bossed up back in the day. I could have shielded her from a lot of bullshit. The shit that had her crying the moment we passed the doorway of her bedroom.

A tortured cry ripped from her belly. Lennox tried to catch it, covering her mouth, but the sharp mewls reverberated in my chest as her body convulsed in my arms. This was why the third—or fourth—orgasm wasn't appropriate. I kept her in my arms as I made my way to the bathroom. Managing the light switch, I carried her to the tub, sitting on the lip to turn on the water.

Both of Lennox's hands were now covering her pretty face. She didn't need to hide shit from me. She couldn't. I hurt for her and with her. To the world, she may have been a fierce, self-controlled woman, filled with confidence—and, for the most part, she absolutely was. However, Lennox was weighed down, being burned out from the baggage she'd been carrying for too many years.

I leaned down and kissed her forehead. "*Shhhhhh…*"

Her muffled wails didn't lessen as I rocked her in my arms. I waited on her and the water, even found her bodywash and squirted a bit in the tub to give it fragrance. If this was a different scenario—if this had been planned—I would have had all the tools necessary to care for her.

When the tub was filled and Lennox's wails had stopped, though her tears had not, I moved my mouth, tight from her dried essence, down to her ear. "I can take your clothes off for you. I can bathe you, too, but…" I hesitated, always did with her. "I know you wanna be alone right now." Taking a deep breath, I waited for her to speak. "Am I right?"

Lennox nodded. That tiny movement from her neck reminded me that I needed to trust my know-how of Lennox Curry to assist me in dealing with her. I managed to turn off the faucet. Then I arranged my arms beneath hers, lifting her from my lap. Lennox staggered right away, but I anchored her at the waist then stood.

"You good?"

Her face was to the floor when she nodded.

"Should I…" I hesitated again, struggling with the call to leave her alone again. "…wait out in your room?"

The blonde curls of her head swayed left and right. "No," she croaked before a hollow, wet sniffle. "I'm good."

And there it was. She'd made the call.

I left Lennox to do her self-care.

Lennox

She placed the office phone down on the receiver and smiled. "Give us a few seconds. We have someone coming now to escort you to Pastor Williams' suite."

Will today be a good day?

I nodded at the woman of Asian descent. "Thanks."

Then I pivoted away from the reception counter, and mindlessly found myself observing the images on the wall. Formal portraits of elderly people, all ranging in ages, hung in a symmetrical arrangement. Their names engraved on brass squares along with their occupations appeared official and warm at the same time. I imagined they were mostly wealthy residents of the private convalescent home. I'd also bet most of them were dead. I mean…that was the final step before leaving here. As pristine and home-like as the facility was, it was a final resting place.

On second thought, that was not totally true, I eventually remembered. This particular campus may have been for hospice and assisted living; however, the sister property was for nursing and rehabilitation. According to Tobias, one-third of flash-famed, quick fizzled rap group, *Korrupt Hearts'*, Lil' Guap, was on the other campus. He had been in a practically vegetative state for years now. There had been rumors of his slow, yet present progressions, but they were just that. I'd always suspected that to be the motivation behind my father selecting this company. Chino Curry was a true O.G., a hip-hop head, too.

Based on the thick and glistening, sealed hardwood flooring, beautifully detailed drapery, and thick floral carpeting, whatever my father had been paying for this place was worth something. Over the five years I'd been visiting here, there wasn't a speck of dust in sight, neither was there a note of staleness in the Wayne, New Jersey facility. Each corner was tended to, and apparently, the air, too.

"Mrs. Richardson?"

I leapt in place, spinning around, startled. Taking a moment, I swallowed. "*Ye*—yes."

"Sorry to alarm you," the short, stubby brunette with thick glasses spoke softly. "Pastor Williams will be happy you're visiting today."

But will she know me?

That was something they said each visit. I knew it had to be a part of their communications protocol, particularly for a segment of their population. I appreciated it. It demonstrated them putting their best foot forward in terms of customer service.

We traveled the facility, which greatly resembled a modern village. There were residential suites planted all over in between miniature shops like an ice cream parlor, nail salon, popcorn shop, and hair salon. They were decorated vividly, going beyond just imagination. Even being warped in utopia, I had gut-churning fears.

Will she be lucid today?

Will she remember?

Along the way, we passed residents and staff, each person smiling with their greeting. It made me wish I'd be running into her on the way to her room. I really needed to visit more often. As the head of her estate, I should lay eyes on her in-person weekly. It was impossible with my distance and demanding job. Sadly, I almost missed her this trip, thanks to being overwhelmed from including Tobias in the itinerary. But my gut told me I shouldn't. As I ran and had breakfast with Tobias earlier today, the inclination to visit today, before the evening circuit with the girls, grew stronger.

The stout woman knocked on the door, though I could see my grandmother's legs from the front window, above it a floral awning. They were covered in thick, nude hosiery, a hue too light for her. My stomach roiled even tighter. I followed the brunette inside, being immediately overtaken by a miscellany of scents; one dominating was vinegar.

"Pastor Williams, you have a guest today," the attendant announced. "Look who's here."

My grandmother's head slowly rotated over to me. Her tapered, gray wig appeared dry. Her caramel skin, bare of makeup, but for the coral-hued lipstick, glowed, blemish-free. The modest-sized pearls gracing her ears were a touchstone of her impeccable style and grace. But her cognac eyes were empty. That's when I knew.

My grandmother was far away, trapped in her brain, unable to participate in reality in this moment. This wasn't the case each visit. I'd seen and spoken to her when she had been present and lucid. We'd have lively conversations, making me forget her dementia. But dementia was still our adversary. It had been for at least seven years. According to her doctors, the onset occurred earlier than we recalled her bizarre behaviors. I'd been in North Carolina for about two-and-a-half-years when I'd gotten the call that she'd had a break-down, crying, shouting, and being distrusting of her pastoral staff.

Once, she had a problem getting inside her home in East Orange. She couldn't locate her keys. The neighbor watched grand-mother shuffle back and forth from her car on the street to the front door of her home, appearing irritated. It went on for so long, they called for help. Neighbors had been noticing grandmother's odd behavior for a while. Her closest friend, Evangelist Sherri Monroe, the woman she had standing manicure and pedicure appointments with since I could remember, arrived and tried getting her to calm down. However, grandmother didn't even recall her diva-compadre. She thought Evangelist Monroe was trying to rob her home.

It didn't take many incidences like that for us to concur, dementia was looming. After tests, fights, and loads of tears—hers and mine—my father moved in with her. Well, he had his own place, but would coordinate nights there along with Evangelist Monroe and another woman from her church. That lasted for a few months before my father realized just how futile their attempts of babysitting her for most of the day had been.

Because grandmother didn't have the strongest or largest congregation, it did not take long for her church and ministry to wither. They were down to about thirty members, on paper, anyways. I came up from North Carolina to "close her books" one year. While now, at twenty-eight years old, I had no desire for church communities, and no longer found religious organizations appealing, closing down my grandmother's life's work was still unbearably painful for me. It had been her blood, sweat, and tears since I could remember.

And now…gazing down at her spiritless shell, it was painful to recall the once spritely diva, who didn't resemble a pastor at all. Grandmother loved her two-piece suits or embroidered dresses, high heels, costume jewelry, colorful nails, and carefully laid makeup. She was known for her impeccable taste.

Pastors and deacons from larger churches all around loved to see her and her crew of three when she was a guest speaker, and would engage in subliminal coquetry. I understood it before gaining a full vocabulary. The women in those neighboring churches hated her. That could be felt before I understood that jealousy and catty behavior was a thing for some women. But I had zero recollection of my grandmother's conduct being anything but graceful. She never had a husband or boyfriend I knew of, and she didn't pine after men.

Today, she was in a floral dress. It was one I didn't recognize, but better than the sweatpants they had her in during one of my first visits. Grandmother wouldn't be caught dead in sweatpants. In fact, she only wore pants on occasion when vacationing, which was rarely. I had to be sure my father wasn't approving any and everything just for a smooth ride. Grandmother's dignity had to be preserved.

"You look pretty," I finally found the words.

Grandmother didn't respond. Her attention stayed below at the stereo playing one of her favorite gospel artists, Albertina Walker. I was sure it was in rotation with other musical favorites I made sure she had here. I just wanted her safe and healthy. At seventy-two, grandmother was still young. However, those were the only two desires I could come up with for her. Her brain returning to the function it once had would take a miracle, and I was low on the expectation of wonders meter these days.

"Would you like to take this in the kitchen with your snack?" the brunette asked grandmother.

That's when my attention was drawn to the plate of sliced cucumbers drenched in vinegar and sprinkled with salt and pepper. The dominating scent of the place now made sense. The fork, laying next to the plate, appeared dry and unused. It was a sign of despondence. I turned away, subconsciously checking out her place, which was tidy and resembled her home in East Orange.

Just when I thought I'd have to participate in a one-way conversation, I heard a spritely soprano pitch, "Oh, my! What do we have here?" Grandmother smiled and my heart jumped to my throat. She peered over to the brunette. "Do we have someone in need of prayer again?" Those fiery irises appeared on me. "You're the young lady from laundry. Am I right?" Her smile, though less vibrant than once revered, had arrived. "I never forget a face as pretty as yours."

Grandmother's wrinkled, veiny, caramel hand went to the center of her chest. "Awwwww! Baby, I can see it. I see all around you. Looking like log weights all over your head...on ya shoulders. The Lord said to cast your cares upon Him, for He cares for you. And here you are, carrying them around." She smacked her lips together, something she was known to do. Then grandmother pointed toward the adjacent sofa. "Dear," she referred to the brunette. "You mind handing me the altar blanket right over there."

"Oh, sure!" the brunette chirped, leaping on her toes. She turned to me with an apologetic smile.

I nodded my consent to adjust to my grandmother's reality of the hour. It was clear to me the staff allowed her to pray for people. I couldn't be more grateful, understanding how much people's spiritual beliefs varied. And nowadays, the topic could be offensive to many. So, yes, I'd go along with this role grandmother conjured for me today.

The woman retrieved the blanket and opened it on grandmother's lap with practice. Then grandmother clapped her hands together. "Come, my child. You thought I didn't recognize you, but I did." She winked beautifully. "Now, come on. Kneel before me so we can petition The Great I Am. *Haaaaallelujah!*" she began her chant. I recognized that, too, as I lowered to my knees. "*Hallelu-jaaaaah!*" her preacher connotation, merged with her impeccable singing voice, kicked in. "Oh, *gloray!* Thank you, oh, God!"

She clasped me at the back of my head, inviting me to lay my head on her lap. That didn't feel unnatural at all. An imminent emotion stirred in my belly as I took to an intimate, beseeching posture at my grandmother's feet. Instantly, it felt like a forfeiture of sorts. As though I was actively seeking refuge or transferring powers. I hadn't felt this tease of lightheartedness in more years than I could count. As she spoke in tongues over my head, I began to cry, another thing I didn't allow myself to do much of lately. I figured Tobias' spanking broke a dam. It was a prelude to this moment where I could embrace my grandmother in her "other" mind. She hadn't prayed over me in years. But today, even if she thought I was some random laundry staff member here, I'd let her do what was innate to her existence. Pastor Clara Williams was a prayer warrior and, therefore, a woman of faith.

My life was a mess. It was something I didn't count on. Something I would have never chosen had I been given better counsel, and had simply taken the time to think. Rushing towards something that isn't ready for you is like choosing to run a marathon wearing shoes two sizes too small. You burn out fast and will endure inevitable pain. I'd been running the marathon with the wrong equipment.

"You've been willfully carrying these logs for too long," grandmother spoke with confidence. "It's your decision to drop them right where they belong." Seamlessly, she continued with her praying.

If only it were that simple, Grandmother...

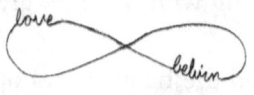

72

"C'mon, Lia! C'mon, Lia!" I barked on the roaring field while lunging down the sideline pitch alongside the ball and players.

"Go, Lee-Lee!" her mother shouted behind me.

She stopped, chucked her little leg back for a promising kick, and…missed. The whistle sounded just after the buzzer, and the ref called the game.

Shit!

Half the crowd cheered as the other half—my side—either grunted loudly or sucked their teeth. Her shoulders fell in defeat. Seeing that felt like a kick in the gut.

"Lia!" I called out to her. Soccer could be brutal. So could basketball, volleyball, tennis, and cross-country. "Lia!" I called again. When she looked up, I waved her over.

With slumped shoulders, she made it to me. I took her by her little shoulder, and before I could speak, my cousin, Charlie did.

"Lil' Lee, you good girl. They ain't ready for you out here." His eyes scanning the busy pitch filled with kids, parents, and officials. "Fuck them."

I tossed him a look, ready to check his ass. The nigga smelled like weed, something he knew I fucking hated. It was one thing to smoke to your heart's desire, but an entirely different thing to reek of it in public. He felt my heat, mumbled a few words, and walked off. Shaking my head, I turned back to Lia.

"Yo, what's up with that pouting?"

"I missed the goal, Daddy." Tears welled in her eyes.

"Is it the end of the world?"

She twisted her lips, looking away while balancing with one leg crossed over the other. Then Elia shook her head.

"Okay. So, what now? What should be the course of your brain now?"

Her attention was on me again, eyes blinking heavily. "How I can do better next time—but—"

I shook my head this time. "Nothing can be done about what's done until your next opportunity to do it. Getting in your feelings is what?"

"A waste of brain power."

"My girl." I heard the whistle being blown again. "That's where I need your head to be now. Not in your chest with your heart."

"Coach wants them," her mother, Krista, announced over us.

Elia reached towards me for a quick hug and kiss. "Call me," was all she gave before running off to where her team had gathered for their coaches to take them to the locker room.

I stood up, feeling my phone vibrate in my pocket. I pulled it out as Krista stepped closer, chewing on a damn grin. Red hair topped her head while she wore her scrubs, likely not having time to change before getting Elia here.

"I ain't think you could make it today?"

I paid her a glance before tapping into the alert.

Missus: *Dinner around six?*

It was Saturday. The official homecoming game for her school was likely happening at this very moment. Why would she be asking about dinner?

Me: I thought you and the girls were outside tonight.

"I had time," I answered Krista. "I knew she'd be in her head about this team."

"Awwww! She was good, though. I had a talk with her on the way." Krista chuckled. "I actually told her to think about what you'd say if you were here."

"Thanks for that," I mumbled, reading Lennox's text.

Missus: *Told the girls I'm tired. No partying tonight. We'll be on campus for a few more hours but I'm bailing after. Dinner? Maybe somewhere local?*

Another text came through as I was reading.

Missus: *Unless you're working*

Me: I got you

I looked over to Krista again. "Good looking out."

"Have you thought more about my proposal?"

I pulled in a breath. "You're asking me for more money. That's not a proposal."

"It's for a home for your daughter."

"My daughter has a home already. Two, actually. It's not for her."

"She lives in a three-family house, Tobias. That's basically an apartment."

"She lives in a unit of the three-family house her mother owns. A house I helped her cop when she requested it. Had you asked for a townhouse, I would have made that happen. If you wanted a standalone, one-family unit, I would've helped with that, too. You see where this is going?"

Krista was pretty level-headed. She did right by Elia, which was all I could ask for. So, we've had little trouble co-parenting over the years. It took a few years for us to regulate our relationship, transitioning to a platonic one, but even that went over well. Krista dated a few cats over the years, always playing it safe when it came to Elia, something I respected about her. She'd been dating her current guy for about two years. I didn't know him, but Elia didn't have any problems with him, and that's all I asked for.

"I can't grow, Tobias? What's wrong with me wanting better for myself and my daughter?"

I turned to fully face her, voice even. "The fact that you're going into this with a grown ass man."

"And whose business is that?"

"Mine when he wanna go fifty-fifty on everything."

"I'm bringing a daughter into this. Your daughter," she argued.

"My daughter has more homes than she needs. You want her to come live with me? Will that help ease you into a fifty-fifty situation?"

She stepped back, neck readjusting. I'd hit a nerve. "Don't go there."

Krista was getting upset, and I ain't want the smoke. "Look,

Kris. I've never held you back from reaching your endeavors." I tried to support her with whatever needs she may have had to always remain independent. Every few years, I paid for a new vehicle. I'd even sponsored her career. Back when Elia was first born, when she jumped up wanting to be a nurse, I paid for her nurse's aide certificate and then practical nursing license. When she wanted to earn more money, I took care of the tuition for her bachelor's degree—a piece of paper I was still paying for because she was taking her sweet time finishing the damn program. "You know I've got your back. But when a man enters the picture with staple dreams like housing, I gotta fall back. I don't want to feel like an ATM."

"That's *not*—"

"I'm just being honest, Kris," I remained calm, not wanting to trip in public. Krista's eyes swung over to Charlie, who tried to make do in his phone. We didn't beef, and I didn't want to start over this issue. I would stand my damn ground, though. "Something about contributing to another man's life goals feels off to me. Anything I can do to support you and Elia, I'm down. When your life plans start merging with your man's, I'm expecting him to be your partner and step up."

Krista pinched her nose, looking frustrated. She shook her head. "I don't want to do this. He is stepping up. We're expanding our housing situation. I don't understand why you can't see how that involves Elia."

My brows jumped and head angled. "And I don't understand how you can't see this is about me contributing to my daughter leaving a home her mother owns to live with a man who's carving out his turf in said home already."

She rolled her eyes then muttered, "Allah will provide." Taking a deep breath, she straightened in stance. "Anyway. How was Africa?"

Across the tiny table from me, Lennox's head tossed back, and she covered her mouth as she laughed quietly in the restaurant. "How was Ghana? Is that how she got out of the fight. That shit was smooth!"

I nodded, smirking at that truth. "That's Krista for you."

"But she's pretty level-headed. Nothing like the unreasonable baby's mothers I've heard of."

Shaking my head, I argued, "But this is unreasonable." Lennox didn't react, just looked at me. "It's wild for her to think I'mma shell out cash...pouring shit into another man's home."

"Makes you feel some kind of way, huhn?"

"Yeah. Krista got me fucked up. She thinks I'm her brother and not just Lia's father. I've got my own shit going on."

"Do you think she takes advantage of you?"

"I think her asking me to do this is taking advantage. I've told you the shit I've done for her financially. The way I see it is if Krista can be her best, having goals and reaching them, then Lia will see it coming up and subconsciously understand what feminine development is. She doesn't have examples of that on her mother's side of the family. *Shit.* It shocked the hell out of me when Krista jumped up saying she wanted to be a nurse just before giving birth to Lia. But I supported it."

Lennox nodded soberly, mouth twisting before pulling her glass of water to her dulled, pink lips. "How was Ghana? I don't think I asked. When you called after coming back to the States, you blind-sided me with the proposal for this week."

She was right. I checked in with Lennox as soon as I returned home from a three-week trip to West Africa. I'd been out there for work. When I called to check in with her, Lennox mentioned her annual homecoming weekend. I didn't have time to think before blurting out a half-baked proposal.

Now, this is what you call a proposal, Krista...

"Ghana was chill. I didn't do much tourism because work was the priority. But the love the people showed in hospitality and food!" I groaned, head falling back at the memory. Lennox's giggle encouraged my dramatics. "I'm serious, man. I did a lot of running out there, but not a full gym workout, because I had to. I ate shit I can't pronounce, even discovered a few favorites."

"Sounds good." She brought her elbow to the table.

"It was. You should go." My eyes rolled up to her. "With me."

Lennox's lashes clapped a few times, effectively taken by my flirting. "And how were the women? Did they treat you right?"

That shit doused me like fucking ice-cold water in the dead of my sleep. Swinging my attention behind her, I shook my head. "We got along."

"How well?"

Then my chin dropped to my chest. "We really doing this?"

"I'm joking. Kinda." She sat up. "Anyway. You were able to visit Nigeria, too, right?"

"Yeah. Another artist making waves was there. I was able to get in like…two studio sessions with him before flying back out to Ghana to finish Ogya Boy's album."

"Is that what you were listening to when I showed up on Wednesday?"

I didn't recall. Actually seeing Lennox in the flesh stole my breath.

"Probably. The engineer sent the polished tracks back over. There were a few tweaks I knew had to be made. But it's done. I finished it two nights ago when you went to bed."

"In *Samsara*?"

"Nah. I ran over to my studio at home. I needed my equipment for that. It took a couple of hours…three, maybe. Then I sent it back."

"And you went for a run yesterday? When do you sleep guy?"

"I'll sleep when I awake from this dream."

We locked eyes for a bit. Lennox's expression was deadpan, studying me. I had no shit to hide. In fact, I welcomed her inspection of my innerworkings. Every inch of me was made just for her. Whatever she needed, I'd flip the fucking earth to bring it to her feet.

When she broke her gaze and fingered her loose golden curls, I knew she'd found what she needed when seeing into me. I understood her situation and would continue to practice patience until she was ready.

"How was your time with your girls?"

"Well…" She sat back in her seat, pulling in a breath. "Very interesting for sure."

"What does that mean?"

"I've gotten lots of revelations."

"What?" I pretended being shocked. "No empowerment?"

"Not exactly. This year Nisha, Lisa, and I played it smart with Mya, understanding her 'busy' ways. But the glimpses I got into their personal lives let me know we all have problems. All with imperfect lives. All with the same genesis of that campus. We were making big girl decisions when it was time to leave."

"And?"

"And none of us are completely happy—well, of course, Mya professes to be."

"Of course," I mumbled.

I knew Mya for a brief time back in the day. When I was trying to get with Lennox, she did silly shit to get my attention. She had a man, but would engage in risqué conversations, asking personal questions. She stared at me a lot. Mya even gave me her number when shit turned cold between Lennox and me, saying she had a cousin she wanted to hook me up with. I tossed the paper with her number as soon as I got home that night.

She was competitive, and obviously unsure of herself, which was evident in the way she'd often compare her body shape and size to Lennox's. Both girls were petite in stature, but Lennox was slim. Mya was more voluptuous, with sizeable tits and hips, and a mild fatty in the back. She was nice, but so was Lennox. It took Lennox a few years, but her ass and thighs were now spread, firm, and shapely. Simple perfection. Her boobs were a modest size, but never failed to make me skip a breath when we greeted each other with an innocent hug, or two nights ago when they pushed into my thigh as I spanked her. Whether or not Lennox picked up on Mya's insecure ways back then I didn't know. But I had.

"She did it again," Lennox shared. "Mya watches me a lot. She doesn't actually talk so much as she…takes everything everyone says and goes in. Then, she blurts something harsh, definitive, absolute, or subliminally braggadocious. Earlier today, when we hugged good-bye, her wedding ring got stuck in my hair, and she made a comment about how I should have straightened it for this week. But she gets to rock the same curly weave she's been wearing for more years than I can count."

Lennox had natural wavy hair. Some confused her for a mixed girl. I loved her hair, even wrote her a poem or two about it. One day, I was fingering through it without really being cognizant of my evident adoration of the girl. Mya called me out. She said it was weird to play in a girl's hair, and how Lennox needed to change her style. She told her the curly look was bland and played out, and she should cut it to get an edgier look. The next few times I'd seen Mya since that day were the last times I'd seen her until recently. Each time, she rocked a massive wig or weave with similar curly ringlets to her girl, Lennox. Insane.

"Yup. But I could see right through her. I just wish she could admit her life isn't perfect when she's inquiring or judging the imperfections of others." I watched closely as Lennox rubbed her lips together. It was something she did often when in deep thought. I wondered how well that translated at her job. "It's okay to have bumps in the road. It's okay to say you've made a few bad calls, or you need to recalibrate or reroute."

"Is that another revelation from this week?"

Lennox didn't answer right away. "Yeah. But…" Those sweet lips rubbed together, and her brow-line tightened. "Maybe not the biggest."

"And what would that be?"

Her head shook and curls bounced softly when she revealed, "I don't want to come to another homecoming with my life in sham-bles. I'm sick of the anxiety I feel, waiting on someone to ask the wrong question under the guise of catching up with me. I'm tired of carrying this load."

"Does that mean no more homecomings?" Why did my chest tighten in panic at the idea of that?

As Lennox fingered her long, blonde curls there was another pause before she murmured, eyes on the table, "It just means I need out of the jungle."

Time was of the essence, and I wanted to switch gears. So, I stood and walked over to her chair. Lennox squealed when I lifted her into the air. She squirmed against my chest as I carried her to the empty chair next to mine and planted her there. When I sat down, I dragged her chair next to me, and pulled her into my side, holding her little body close to mine.

"Well, today's Saturday." I nuzzled in her ear as she giggled.

Within seconds, a soft beam grew on her face, recognizing right away my swift change in direction. "It is, Mr. Elliott."

"How was your short week back at home?"

Lennox took in a deep breath, chewing on the question. "A blur, *really*—"

"Really?"

"Well...yeah. Things got fuzzy after Thursday night." With her mouth ajar, Lennox's eyes remained below, where I'd threaded my fingers with her soft ones.

Thursday night. The night I spanked her soft ass. I thought that would have made Lennox stumble yesterday. She was so damn emotional afterward, and I got it. But in true Lennox fashion, she woke up yesterday, and took up my offer for a run in the sneakers I'd copped for her. We got our cardio in mostly in silence. After, she let me make her breakfast before I had to leave out for a meeting with my accountant then run errands with my grandmother. By the time I got back to *Samsara* that night, Lennox was still out with her girls.

"What about Thursday night, Lennox?" I made a point to roll her head up by gently pulling her hair so I could look into her pretty, cognac eyes. They were outlined with chestnut rings. "Did something...*any*thing happen that made you feel uncomfortable or violated?"

The smiling waitress arrived with the bill. "Have you changed your mind about dessert?"

Lennox's gaze lifted to me.

"Nah. I think we're good. Thanks."

"Okay. I'll take care of this when you're ready." She placed it on the table and left us again.

"So?"

Lennox snickered, rolling her eyes away. "So?"

"About Thursday?" I leaned down and nuzzled into her neck, feeling dizzy in excitement from her flowery scent. "I need to know," I whispered. "In less than twenty-four hours, you'll be back to your regular life. I don't want to check in with you in a few days just to find out you blocked my ass."

Snickering, she shook her head. Why was my heart pounding? Mouth dry out of no damn where? I needed something from her. When I heard her come in last night, I let go of a fucking sigh I didn't know I was holding. I thought for sure at one point she'd been turned off and decided to stay at her hotel. My thoughts went to how I'd get her things left in the house to her. Lennox still had my ass strung up like a love-struck kid. She had to know I'd never hurt—

"At first, I wondered if I should have run to East Orange for a gun, then drove back to *Samsara* with a deadly vendetta." My body steeled next to hers, hand clasped over hers. *Damn!* Was I so eager, I went too hard? *Shit!* I knew it. I knew I made the wrong call. Knew I should have been satisfied with her agreeing to the week and gone at her pace. "It humanized me…humbled me," she murmured, facing her lap. But then, Lennox went quiet for a while, and my lungs disappeared until her next words. "Gave me a rare feeling of not being above reproach. It was a human touch, a familiar, primal interaction still settling in my mind. But the irrational part of me feels I…need more of it."

I couldn't breathe when I asked, "More spankings?"

A gust of amusement shot from her nose. "Not in *a*—I… I'm not saying 'please, daddy, spank me. I've been a bad girl.' I'm saying, I feel like I had human contact from it. I didn't know you had that type of kink in you either. It scares me, but…" She slowed again. "It reminds me of how sheltered in place I've been physically and emotionally."

I understood but pushed. "What does that mean?"

"I mean hanging with the girls was cool as usual. We laughed, reminisced, and caught up. Good times. Still, they treat me like a fenced animal; something I've caused. But it's the only way I can be around them. I don't want to come home year in and year out, and cry about my shit. Coming back to Jersey is my escape from the madness." Her eyes crawled up to my face. "Being with you..." She busted out laughing. "Spanked by you." That made me laugh, too. "In some 'I've finally lost my mind' way, it made me feel alive. I want to be free. Alive. You know?"

I cupped her chin and leaned down to kiss her soft lips. Centimeters from meeting them, Lennox sucked in a breath and shivered at the same time. Her fingers curled around mine in a tight squeeze as our mouths caressed each other slowly. Her other little hand cupped my jaw, making my dick stiffen.

I pulled back. "I don't want you to go. Feels like you just got here. We didn't spend any time together."

"I know, which is why I wanted to have dinner with you tonight."

It wasn't enough. With Lennox, it was never enough. We'd gotten back in contact about three years ago. Because she lived in North Carolina, it was impossible to see her. Throughout the years, I manufactured ways to be in the same room as Lennox; sometimes, even from a distance. It was hard going at her pace. Nonetheless, I knew if my endgame was forever, it was at her comfort that I'd get there.

But when I have her so close like this...

All the goodwill of passively listening and understanding was hard to practice. I wanted to bury Lennox in my chest and hold her there until my last breath. I wanted her in my arms to be adored and coddled. I wanted to eat her pussy until she cried from joy. I craved for her to one day feel loved and appreciated by all who knew her, especially me. I wanted to become one with her, fuse souls until the day arrived for us to meet our Maker.

"C'mon. I'm not trying to spend my last few hours with you in the back of a small Indian restaurant."

Nodding, Lennox looked stuck. I shelled out a few bills for the check then helped her into her coat. On our way to the door, her stroll stopped abruptly.

"Oh, no," she murmured.

Then I saw it. From the door and front windows of the restaurant, gallons of water spilled from the sky.

I went for my phone. "I can order you an *Uber*."

"And what about your bike? We came together."

"I'll drive behind you?"

"I'm not leaving you to drive in the rain alone."

My forehead went tight. "I can't leave the *Multistrada* here. The neighborhood's mild and all, but baby girl needs supervision." Rubbing those lips I couldn't stop staring at together, Lennox's eyes went to the rain beyond the restaurant. "I'll call an *Uber* for you," I repeated.

Her head swung to me, curls flying in the air. "No. I'm coming with you."

"You sure?"

She nodded. "I'll put my purse in the storage space. That way my phone won't be damaged."

"You sure?"

"Are you a broken record?" She grabbed my hand, walking toward the door. "Let's go." Lennox waved to the smiling waitress behind the counter. "Thanks for everything. The food was delicious!"

Then we dashed outside, hand-in-hand, to quickly stash her bag, throw on our helmets, and mount up on my bike.

Chapter Five

Lennox

At night, in the pouring rain, the ride was joint-tensing. I kept my eyes closed as I lay against his broad back while he guided us through the quiet, suburban town. Riding on his motorcycle in the rain was a different experience than it was going to the restaurant. Going felt like a classic, romance movie. Returning to the house in *Samsara* resembled apocalypticism. But I knew I was safe. It concerned me how much I trusted Tobias.

For years, I fought against the instinctive draw to his calm, yet in-charge, persona. Since the first day I met him, I sensed his strong determination and independence. Well before I learned his story of coming up without his parents, I could see the guy exuded fearlessness and an old charm that could only come from long-term survival. Tobias chased me from the mall, all the way to my grandmother's small, storefront church in East Orange where he played the organ for almost the whole summer. Little did I know, those short months were the most pivotal ones in my life.

That summer would color my lenses for what I saw down the line for my life. I wouldn't know for years to come how I should have, perhaps, slowed down for a moment, and given myself more time to develop and allow Tobias to as well. I could never forget the day he came to my grandmother's house, broken and regretful. We'd just met a few months before, practically falling into a deep connection, when he learned he was going to be a father soon. Hurt, I broke things off with him. It was easy to: my grandmother and others from the church family voted against me being with him. I chose against him.

I was wrong.

Sauntering out of the en suite bathroom to my suitcase on the sofa, I rubbed the towel over my wet hair. Tobias was kind enough to go back out, using my rental car, of course, to drive to the local *CVS*. I needed shampoo and a good conditioner to wrestle with my tangled hair after what couldn't be tucked beneath the helmet got soaked from the rain. I was able to find my brush inside a toiletry bag when I realized I didn't have a blow dryer.

"Shit!" Dramatically, I closed my eyes to a squeeze. "Shit. Shit. Shit."

I was used to air-drying it, especially when in a rush or uninspired to style it. But it was nighttime in New Jersey. There would be no fresh-air drying. I had to leave early in the morning to get to the airport on time. Certainly, my hair wouldn't be completely dry by then. But I wouldn't ask Tobias to go back out in that wet mess. I had other plans for him as my eyes brushed against the box of condoms I purchased after dropping off Scott on Wednesday. My fingers grazed the box as a wave of anxiousness lanced my belly. I'd been considering this.

For a while—years, actually—I'd wondered what Tobias was like as a mature lover, and if it resembled who he was, now, as a friend. As my friend, he was sensitive, patient, caring, anticipating, and enduring. Too many days in my wondering head, and nights in my cold bed, I fantasized about being beneath *this* Tobias. I'd be leaving tomorrow and had no idea when I'd see him again. It could be months. I wanted this. I wanted Tobias. With shaky fingers, I put the large box of condoms into the pocket of my housecoat.

On foot, back into the bathroom, I told myself there was still time to talk myself out of it. In the meantime, I needed to get this wild mane of mine under control. I went right into sectioning it off, beginning at the back, to detangle. It took a little more than twenty minutes, but I'd successfully, smoothly brushed it to the nape of my neck. The leave-in conditioner was another great call. As I gathered and secured it into a bun, my phone pinged of an alert. A specific alert. The sound was distinct, causing my stomach to churn. I clasped my bun with a hair claw then slowly reached for my phone.

The notification was from one of my credit card companies. Apparently, the authorized user had met its limit, and a purchase attempt was unsuccessful due to insufficient funds. Saliva thickened and soured in my mouth, both familiar responses to this recklessness. I fell into the vanity, feeling my pulse race.

"You couldn't finish the program for once, Kelvin?" I whispered, scrubbing my face with my palm.

When I realized my breathing had turned deep and slow, I fell to my haunches. No. I wouldn't allow this to happen. This was my escape, my refuge, my timeout.

One foot in front of the other...

Hang on till the next moment...

Soon, this will be a faded memory...

You won't break...

You're built to survive even this...

I was okay. Really, I was. Why I allowed something so small and common to affect me had to be because I'd done a good job of "leaving my cares behind." Emotionally, I'd moved closer to my goal of putting myself first. But this uninvited reminder threatened the well-crafted bubble I'd put myself into this week.

Then my brain jumpstarted, and I brought my phone up to power it off. Otherwise, a barrage of calls would commence, and the ringing or vibrating wouldn't end. As I pressed the button into the side of the phone, I heard hard steps. Within seconds, a hefty, bearded frame filled the bathroom doorjamb.

His thick brows were knitted, eyes ablaze with concern. "What's going on?"

Without thinking, I vocally fumbled, "Had to detangle my hair. Burnout."

With his head cocked to the side as Tobias closely examined me, he spat, "Bullshit. The fuck, Lennox?"

I jumped to my feet too fast. My bun shook, and housecoat lurched. Thanks to the weighted pocket, it opened at the front, exposing my naked cleavage and pubic bed. My eyes rolled from my body up to Tobias' angry expression. Quietly, he sauntered into the bathroom. My pulse raced again, loud this time. He reached for my pocket and pulled out the box. After studying it, his eyes roved over to me.

"You trippin' over this?"

No!

I mean...

Confused, and now, embarrassed, I tore my gaze away.

He croaked, voice thick, and somewhat standoffish, "I lit the fire in the den. Figured we could talk out there." Tobias turned to leave. On his way out of the door, he mumbled, "I see now, I gotta keep you off of me."

Curled into a ball, I struggled to breathe, laughing so hard.

"Word, yo! And she used to go in!" Tobias continued his recollection. "*Oh, oh, oh, precious God! And may he have a good life by a good woman. Cover his body so he can fill Your earth with healthy, beautiful, babies, oh, God!*" His head swayed left to right as he sing-songed under the glow created by the crackling flames. "Because remember, Pastor Williams could sing her fine ass off!" He snapped his fingers. "And what was the other fox's name?"

"Deaconess Wright with the gray wig."

We lay on a mountain of plush blankets Tobias had compiled.

There were fluffy pillows around as we allowed our chatter to fill the air. Two mugs, once filled with steamy green, mint tea, were within arm's reach of us both. The captured space was nice, intimate. It was like a cove carved for just the two of us.

"No. The one who used to wear high heels all the time like Pastor Williams," he recalled.

"Oh. Evangelist Monroe."

"Yeah. Her, too!" Tobias pushed up from his elbow next to me, straightening his spine. I missed his heat immediately. "Yo, she was a baddie, too." I rolled my eyes. If I had a dollar for every time I'd heard that coming up. Crazy thing was, both my grandmother and the evangelist were well aware of their favorable aesthetics. "They used to check a lil' nigga out." He stroked his beard. "They ain't press me, but they knew the kid was ready, whenever and wherever."

Lying flat on my back now, I hollered toward the ceiling, holding my belly. Tobias' tone and demeanor were rather calm, but his "fantasy" tickled me.

"You would have cheated on me with my grandmother and her bestie?"

"Nah. This was before I laid a finger on you. This was when I first started playing there. They wanted the kid."

"Oh, stop. You were a cute kid and all, Tobias, but I think it was your talent that got them. Grandmother used to say your hands were anointed."

"Damn." He shook his head. "If that's the case, I got lucky. It ain't easy playing for preachers. You gotta learn their cadence and pace. Then when you get one like your grandmother with a voice..." His eyes closed and head shook. "Damn. That voice, man. She was powerful."

"Still is." I nodded. When I could feel his questioning gaze on me, I added, "I went to see her."

"When?"

"Yesterday, after you left for your day."

"How is she?"

"Healthy—*well*... You know her condition. But she's physically healthy and safe. That's all I can ask for."

"Word," he breathed.

"I cried," fell from my lips.

Tobias' eyes flashed wild. "Cried."

I nodded. "Apparently, this trip back home has not only gone by in a flash, but it's been unusually emotional for me. Your spanking evoked something…opened the floodgates of my tears." That was a partial joke.

Quickly, yet smoothly, Tobias leaned down next to me, kissing my cheek. "That was not my intent."

"I know. But damn were you good at it!" I teased him. Tobias' smile was wry. "How many women have you done that to?"

"Lennox," he groaned.

"I'm busting your chops, Tobias."

"Don't."

"Why?"

"Because I don't wanna represent anything negative to you. I'm trying to appeal to your heart."

"Okay, Mr. R&B lyrics!" I joked. "You wanna appeal to my heart, huhn?"

Tobias went motionless next to me. The masculinity he exuded had me feeling more self-conscious than I appeared. I was still unaccustomed to this proximity. And Tobias liked to touch me. Gentle, innocuous grazes or kisses on the cheek were doled out heavily tonight, since laying out in front of the fireplace. I wondered if this was his norm with women. All night, I'd been considering if I liked it.

Even now, Tobias' eyes traced my face. "I love you," sounded to have crawled out from the depth of his soul. My throat closed and belly turned over. Tobias' expression was blank when he added, "I've been in love with you since you were nineteen, and ain't nothing changed."

"That was so long ago, Tobias." My limbs were shaking. "We were kids."

"I was a man. Shit," he scoffed. "I created a whole baby. I wasn't a kid. I was just young and reckless. Misguided. I should have never let you go."

I felt a sensation lance through my chest. "My grandmother should have never flipped on you. I'm sorry for that."

Tobias chuckled. "You always say that shit, Lennox. We were adults. I should have pushed harder."

"I didn't let you."

He shook his head. "You didn't. And that's why my punk ass gave up. And look at us now."

I held my breath to tamper down another cry. "Back where we started." My lips trembled. "Sneaking."

Tobias leaned down and kissed my lips, his beard caressing my chin and upper-chest. "Can you imagine feeling like someone was created just for you?" His hand snaked beneath the lapel of my robe where I was bare.

I shivered when this thumb plucked my nipple on its descent to my flinching belly. Tobias' hand stopped there, his palm on the flat of my belly as he kissed me slow, his tongue beseeching, tasting like the young Tobias I met. It felt like our first time—definitely, my first time. However, those two things could not be less true. Tobias and I had been together sexually years ago. Back then, he didn't lead with the confident energy he'd been emitting since Thursday night at the grand piano.

"I know you don't feel the same. I get it," he explained throatily. "But I don't mind earning your love. I've been working on your trust. You can trust me."

"I do." My whisper was defensive. "I'm here." I tossed my attention down to my naked body beneath the robe.

Tobias leaned down to kiss the delicate space between my breasts. "But you're not mine yet." I watched as his tongue trailed down my belly, causing it to contract. My heart beat out of my chest when he naturally positioned his big body down next to me and grabbed my thighs to arrange them around his head.

The first stroke of his tongue evoked a strange cry from the back of my throat with my thighs coming together around his head. "Let me in, Lennox." The switch to authority in his voice compelled me into action. My hips felt tight as I widened my thighs. "That's it.

Thank you, baby," he whispered against the hot puddle he'd created at my apex.

Then Tobias pushed my knees by the back of my thighs. He scooted closer on his stomach, and pushed his tongue directly into my sex. My eyes rolled to the back of my head, lashes fluttering as he rubbed against my sensitive labia. The sounds created from his need to please me further diluted my mind. This was Tobias Elliott with his mouth on me. A talented one, too. I lay there enduring his mastery, struggling to think of the last time I'd had this type of pleasure before Thursday. When did head feel so good?

Why am I not freaking out?

This is Tobias...

That's why there was no awkwardness to the act. This mutually-made companionship felt so natural. He didn't judge, he didn't condemn, he never lost patience. The man had been my only ray of sunlight during my incredibly cloudy life, even on those days where it rained in torrential amounts, similar to what he was creating right now between my quivering legs.

My groin churned and churned until my hips began to buck of their own volition. Heat filled my body from my shoulders, down to the pads of my feet. My spine loosened at each stroke of his tongue against my clit. Opening this way to Tobias was foreign before Thursday. But tonight, he left no room for unfamiliarity. He reached up and plucked both of my peaked nipples, causing ripples of pain to shoot through my chest and reverberate in my thighs. Why would he ruin the trajectory of the moment? Within seconds, I understood why. As the ache subsided, a coat of tingling pleasure began to heat my body anew. Pleasure obliterated every bit of pain and heightened to a degree my body couldn't contain. My hips rolled, chest caved, and shoulders lifted and rotated—all rhythmically.

With each stroke of his tongue, I knew one thing for certain: Tobias was falling to a level within me he could never recover from. I knew this was no random, erogenous episode he was known to engage in. This thing, born out of our erotica, was soul-binding and timeless. Incongruent to my circumstance making our union impossible, my endurance to pleasure broke, and I came hard in Tobias' mouth.

My ass lifted from the blanket as I thrust into his face, understanding his vulnerable position. It was one Tobias never minded taking for me. He sucked and sucked until my hips gave out and I dropped down to the blankets. That's when his mouth softened to reverential kisses as his big, hot hands caressed my hips and thighs.

Imminent was the powerful draw to him. I wanted more. "Tobe," I cried, eyes closed.

"Yeah, babe."

Breathless and recklessly, I demanded, "Make love to me."

I needed it, and I wasn't sure I'd ever experienced it. Nonetheless, I knew the one man who could make this happen.

Trying to control my lungs, I watched as he reached over my head and onto the sofa. He pulled back the box of condoms. I grew fidgety beneath his big body, desperate for him. This depth of connection with Tobias was the only thing missing between us now, and I didn't want to lose a second of it. Feeling myself swell all over again, I watched raptly as he pulled his t-shirt over his head, revealing the swollenness of his chest.

The man worked out nearly every day of the week. People thought his keen discipline was fanatical, but I knew it to be methodical. Tobias ate mostly clean and worked out in fear of facing the same fate as many of his peers. His late hours, coupled with sitting at a piano and studio keyboard from the evening into the midmorning hours, allowed for unwanted weight and cardiovascular diseases.

He'd put on fifty pounds at the beginning of his career, not wanting to see much outside of the studio. Tobias ate whenever he wanted, even indulging in simple cravings. I recalled the pictures he sent me when we began communicating three years ago. It was an insecurity of his that Tobias had to acknowledge and rectify. Oddly, it was why he could express with such confidence back then that I needed a lifestyle change, and aggressively recommended a fitness trainer.

Thankfully, I lay here, witnessing the results of his discipline as his pecs bulged and biceps curled while he pulled down his lounge pants, revealing his full-on commando status beneath. Tobias' dick sprang out thick and spritely. In recent nights—and days—I found myself performing brain exercises, trying to recall the exact measure of his girth.

Here it was, thick and pulsing as it hung hook-style mid-air. The wide crest head of Tobias' dick curved downward as though pointing toward its destination. There was a bead of precum sprouting from the opening of his fat head. When my eyes roved up his sculpted abs and hilly chest, I noticed his heavy-lidded gaze. Those thick brows were knitted in a way that could have intimidated me, but I knew better. Tobias would finally have me again after almost ten years.

Willingly…

I reached for him. My trembling fingertips meeting his tight abs. Tobias' beard was toward his chest as he observed me, exploring him. When I raked downward to lay back, my middle and ring fingers brushed against his erection, and his abdomen contracted.

Tobias groaned, eyes closed as though he was in pain. The passion he wasn't afraid to share excited and intimidated me at the same time. Could I be just as transparent? He reached for the box, ripping it open with animalistic savagery. My mouth watered as he deftly peeled the lubricated rubber from its packet and glided it onto his thick rod. Then Tobias' eyes were on me again as he stroked himself.

"Can I kiss you?"

I licked my dry lips. "Please."

Slowly, he dropped to all fours, dipping his mouth toward my belly, and licked his way up the middle until his talented mouth met my own. His big frame casted a shadow over me against the glowing flames. Uncharacteristic desire ripped through me, and I took Tobias at the back of his head and kissed him wildly. Our tongues lapped against each other's with eager abandon. His heat. His heaviness. His attentiveness. His desire to please me. There was a liberty in this space with him, one that transcended time. So, lost in the moment, I didn't realize he'd positioned himself over me properly until I felt the first attempt at breeching my sex.

My head swung upward, detaching from his mouth, shoulders off the floor. The pain was sharp.

"I'm sorry," he graveled in my ear before planting a gentle kiss on my neck.

I shivered, instantly relaxing. "I'm okay."

"You sure?"

"Yeah. Come on." I lifted toward his thickness, the head of him hitting my sensitive clit, causing me to shudder again.

"You sure?" he whispered with concern.

I nodded profusely, reaching for his bearded jaw to pull into a kiss. My body tingled all over with impatient need. Even the taste of me from his mouth turned me on. I wanted him so badly. I whispered in between tongue strokes, "Try again." Then lifted my pelvis toward him for emphasis.

Tobias reached down and swiped himself against me, lubing himself, and driving me wild. Then he reared his hips just a little, attempting to enter me again.

He kissed my nose. "You're straining around me. Relax, Lennox."

"I'm trying. Maybe…" I exhaled.

Tobias froze. "You changed your mind?"

My head swung left to right with adamance. "No. Not at all. I was going to say, maybe I want it too bad."

"It?"

"You. *Maybe*—" I grunted from blunt intrusion.

Tobias was inside of me, at least halfway.

"You want me?" He circled his hips.

I nodded, mouth agape as I concentrated on his girth. Back when we first met, I didn't have loads of experience with penises, so I never fully evaluated his package. I only recalled the discomfort from his sex.

"I do."

"You're so fuckin' wet," he whispered with a lazy jaw, stroking gently.

I breathed in deeply, taking in his masculine, woodsy scent. His thick arms were around me protectively. I liked it. The strain in his thrusts, the heavy beating of his excited heart. The dew sprouting from our shaking frames, the combustible energy ready to explode. Within minutes of feeling him drive deeper inside of me, I began to ease into his crushing weight. At one hundred thirty-five pounds, Tobias rested, what felt like, half of his two hundred-twenty pounds on me. I was eager to accept it all, wanting to get lost inside his generous passion. *This.* All of it had been why your favorite artists flocked to Tobias Elliott. Moving my hips against his plunges, I considered how he exuded love and acceptance and wisdom and patience. As he made love to me, I felt it all. It was privileged, sacred, and rewarding.

It was also powerful when I felt his dick swell even more inside of me. Sweat lifted from my pores again as his plunges grew wild and his face turned hard as stone. Tobias' hips were poetry in motion. His strokes weren't random or rigid until now. His breathing grew choppy.

"Let it go," I encouraged him before taking to his lips again.

I stroked my tongue as deep as I could into his mouth. Initially, Tobias tried joining me. But once he understood how wild my attempt was, a deep, subterranean groan rocketed from his belly, and he bucked deeper, nearly breaking me in two. As his orgasm assaulted him, I clung to his robust frame, ignoring the ache from my core. He was delicious.

Undone.

He was mine.

The sun had just fully awakened, and my heart swelled in my chest, gazing at his puffy, heavy eyelids. His soft, pouty lips peeked through the full beard. The raised scar beneath his lower lip sparked a curiosity I was never afforded. A young, rumbustious Tobias brought a sudden, unexpected smile to my face. His broad chest, dotted with tightly coiled hairs, lifted and dropped at a peaceful pace.

We'd done it. I'd finally opened myself totally to Tobias Elliott. And with the proverbial "morning after," there was still palpable dissatisfaction. A barrier could still be felt like a wedge between us. Yet, I still felt an indescribable joy. Four years ago, I would have never imagined this connection. Before Tobias came back into my life, I wasn't kind enough to myself to allow this sizeable victory. I leaned over and kissed his forehead.

"Why are you awake," he mumbled, eyes still closed.

"I didn't mean to wake you."

"Girl," His big body shifted. "I been up."

Stumped, I didn't know if I should believe him. "Were you up, really?"

"I was up when you went to pee and brush your teeth around four-thirty—I was able to go take a leak myself—and I was up when you turned on your phone just to have it ping back-to-back, frustrating you to the point of powering it off again. And I saw when you were looking for the box of condoms to pull one out and stash it somewhere underneath you." *Wow.* Tobias had been awake. Apparently, only his eyes rested. He licked his lips before uttering, "Today's Sunday."

"It is."

Then his tight eyes opened, imploring. "Stay longer."

I whispered, "I can't."

"You'll kill my fantasy."

Kissing his soft lips, I explained, "This will be our new reality, Tobias."

His dark eyes ran between mine, brows knitted. "I'll buy the house. We can leave all the bullshit behind, and finally—"

I kissed him again. This time, I boldly ran my tongue against his lips then dipped inside his warm mouth. I didn't think about morning breath until I was inside, but didn't smell or taste anything other than the ruthless concoction of despair and hope, the contradiction our bond had been built on. Tobias sat up, pushing his fingers into my hair and gripping my scalp.

Needing to be close to him, I lifted to straddle his big frame. As though the act was natural, Tobias pulled me into his lap. His supplicatory gaze stayed on me, shredding my heart into pieces. I handed him the condom he accurately described as me hiding. Then I scooted back onto his thighs and yanked at his boxers. With Herculean strength, he lifted us both, and I managed them down until his thickness plopped out of its cotton hold, greeting me with eagerness. My mouth watered and I swallowed then rubbed my lips together.

With my head, I motioned for Tobias to apply the condom. His face was hard with preoccupation, but he obeyed, adroitly ripping open the package and smoothly rolling the rubber down his hard, curled erection. His head pulled up and before he could speak or gesture, I stood to my knees, crawled up his muscular thighs, and angled my throbbing sex over him.

"Help me," I whispered over him.

My hand cupped the back of his head, my chin resting on the top as I waited. Tobias' big hand was at my waist as he pulled me down onto him, directing the entry point. Once there, I recklessly pushed down on him, stretching my already tender walls. I pulsed around him, immediately feeling a line of sweat above my top lip and throughout my scalp. Tobias could easily break me, but instead of fear or being turned off, my mind and body yielded to his masculinity. I wanted the pain, the trembling, and fullness of him inside of me.

I plunged down onto him until satisfied with his depth. Tobias' stony expression hadn't melted, though his mocha nipples were pebbled, and dick was hard as steel inside of me. Leaning into him, the tension lessened, and I was able to stroke him without much force. Tobias' finger and palm grip on me didn't loosen although my sex had. He was tense, and still preoccupied with what was to come.

This all made me feel like shit, but I couldn't stop rocking over him. I wouldn't allow anything to disrupt the final minutes we'd share. I thrusted onto him until I enjoyed the stretch, until I wanted

the most intimate indentation of him inside of me. This felt different, though. I'd never known Tobias to be stubborn, but we'd also
pushed the bounds this week. I had to be as patient with him as he'd
been with me practically since I'd known him.

So, I stayed at it, taking mental snapshots of how he felt this
close to me. The adult Tobias. His hands eventually worked their
way to my ass, gripping me with need. I even leaned over to kiss the
man, appreciating the strokes of his tongue. But then I pulled back,
wanting to see the muscles in his abs tighten with each squeeze of
my pussy over him. I could do this forever. Could live with this man
inside of me. It felt so natural to be invaded by him this way.

And then when all the carefully crafted muscles of his gorgeous
face collapsed and Tobias' chest caved inward, lungs empty in a
tortured cry, my heart sheared even more. Frantic, my arms shot
around him, hips bucked faster, and I kissed him.

With urgency, I whispered forcefully, "I love you. I want us."

I didn't know if Tobias could process my admittance, because
his head fell back as he groaned while thrusting into me from below.
His big body shook just as it did when he was on top and then
behind me. Tobias had reached his pinnacle. He was shooting into
me a passion I quickly decided I never wanted to live without again.
So desperate for him, I stroked and stroked, until Tobias' bear paws
clenched me in place. He was done, and within seconds of his
orgasmic bliss ending, I'd be a terrible person. So, I held him tightly
in my arms until his spine trembles stopped, and heart rate slowed.

"Stay," he pleaded throatily, letting off a rumble in his thick
chest. "I got something to show you. Something I wanna teach you,
Lennox—"

"*Shhhhhh…*" I quieted him. "I have to check out of the hotel
before getting to the airport." I struggled to steady my voice.
"You're going to stay right here while I shower, get dressed, and—"

"*Lennox*—"

"*Shhhh*! Stay right here. Stay here and think about how you've
proven your point this week, and how you're releasing me to go
clean up my mess, so you'll have no need to prove anything to me
ever again. You'll soon be able to simply show *me*—"

"When?" he demanded.

I kissed his open mouth. "Soon. Now, promise me."

Tobias' eyes darkened as he stared at me deadpan. I knew he'd obey but wouldn't be happy about it. Not wanting to delay the inevitable, I lifted from his pelvis, feeling relief from his pulsing fullness, and an ache of longing as we separated. My knees wobbled as I stood from the floor. Quickly locating my phone, I paced to the back of the house for my bedroom.

It was an out of body experience to relieve myself, shower, get dressed, and pack up the last of my things. A self-protective wall I had been far too acquainted with over the years buffered me as I wheeled my suitcase to the front door. I could have gone to the garage, but my heart negotiated a balance. I ambled past the living room, and without changing pace, caught a glance of Tobias' big frame still in the place I left him. His robust frame leaned back into the sofa, the bulbous muscles of his upper arms wrapped around his head and face. He'd obeyed. My gentle, patient beast remained in place.

"April third."

His deep tenor stopped my stride. My voice was stolen.

He faced ahead, toward the fireplace as he declared, "You have until April third of next year to be mine."

I swallowed involuntarily, my lungs strained and irritated. "And if I…"

With unwavering confidence, Tobias returned, "I'll leave it to you to get used to the idea."

After a spell, I let myself out, not stopping until I made it to my rental. I managed my things inside then slipped behind the wheel and charged the engine. That's when I felt lightheaded and let out a breath I had no idea I'd been holding. I collapsed over the steering wheel, not expecting the upending bellow shooting from my belly. My body quivered violently, juddering the car. The pain I felt I imagined was equivalent to having your heart ripped from your chest.

I reached back into the car for my purse and coffee. After locking the doors, I started toward the hotel's entrance. My head was toward the cemented ground as I dragged my heavy heart behind me. So many thoughts coursed my brain, countless scenarios. However, there was one over-riding declaration: I would not put myself in this situation again.

"Lennox?"

My head shot up. I couldn't believe I'd made it to the entrance already, and that Mya was standing just outside the lobby's door, holding two coffee cups.

"Girl," she sighed, head tossed back. Then she chuckled. "I thought I'd missed you."

"Why?" was all I could ask in my stupor.

Her expression dropped. "Are you okay?" Mya stepped closer. The traffic from the street played the soundtrack, reminding me of just how metropolitan the city was. "Your face is swollen."

"I'm fine." I managed a smile. It would have been nice to vomit all the shit I was carrying—had been carrying—right then and there, but over the years, I managed to deal with it all internally. "Just a little nostalgia episode before heading home."

"Oh." Mya seemed stuck.

My brain kicked into gear. "What are you doing here?"

"Oh!" this one delivered as a chirp. "I knew your flight out was this morning. I tried calling you all night and this morning."

Shit...

My phone had been powered off virtually since getting out of the shower last night. I powered it on twice to check a few things, but then I went off the grid again.

Then my senses kicked in again. "For what?" I'd said my goodbyes to the girls when I left them yesterday.

Mya's eyes circled before her words leaked. "I *uhh*—I was going to make sure you were good before leaving."

"You were calling for that?"

"*Yea*—no." She sighed, rolling her eyes. "I just... You know, you're so closed off. I just wanted to check in with you alone. Without the girls. Then I freaked out when you didn't pick up or text me back last night or this morning. So..." Her eyes settled on one of her hands. She brought one of the coffee cups toward me. "I knew you'd start your day with your favorite java."

I lifted the coffee mercifully in my hand. "I just came from picking up my *Brown Barista*."

"Oh! I must've just missed you. The place was packed. That's why I try avoiding the one over here." I nodded, trying to figure out why Mya was here. "So, are you packed? I see you're up and at 'em already."

"Almost. Do you want to come up while I finish?"

Please say no...

I wasn't in the mood for company, much less one of Mya's probing nature.

"Ummmm..." She poked her lips out. "Sure."

I managed a giggle as I rounded her for the door of the building. "Come on. I've gotta get to the airport."

Chapter Six

Lennox

"I can't wait to get into my bed," Scott mumbled as we drove into our neighborhood.

"Mmhmm." I rubbed my dry lips together. "Same."

He shifted, spinning in the passenger's seat to face me. "You sure you're okay?"

I looked his way, smiling. "I'm with you. Why wouldn't I be okay?"

"Because you seem sad. Did anybody up there mess with you?" Then he sighed, apparently suddenly hit with a revelation. "Did they mention Uncle Kelvin? Did somebody ask about him while you were up there?"

That made me snort. "One or two, but it was no biggie." I shrugged. "I couldn't go back home without someone asking about him."

"And now, you're back home—here—and you're sad," he mumbled, chewing on the meat of his fingers, moping.

I reached over and pushed his hand from his mouth. "I'm fine, Scott. Would you cut it out? I'm actually happy about your great news. Don't ruin the moment."

"Yeah," his tone dry. "I told her she better not do anything stupid in there to get more time."

"She'll be ready." I assured him.

"And what about you?" Scott asked as we turned a corner.

"What about me?"

"When she out, how're you gonna feel?"

I caught the storm in those gorgeous, hazel-green irises. "I'm going to be okay." Whipping his neck to swing a few blond strands from his face, he looked away. "Scott, listen. I need you to hear me. I look after you. I enjoy doing it. You're no burden to me. Never have been. But I'm not your burden either. You reuniting with your mother is the best gift in the world. I want that for you."

"But—"

"But nothing. Terry will be released in January, and you will return to her, and spend the rest of your childhood being nurtured by your mother."

His head whipped my way. "And what if that never happens?"

"What if you believed good things can happen for good people?"

"She killed my father. Does she qualify as a good person? Can she be one after all this time? Has it been long enough?"

I slowed the car to a stop in the middle of the suburban road.

Voluntary manslaughter. Scott's mother, Terry, had been incarcerated for murdering his father nearly ten years ago. They were young and high and passionate. Like his father, Kyle hit women. Terry, a relatively young, impressionable girl, found herself in a toxic relationship with him. One night, high off meth, cheap vodka, and God only knows what else, their interaction grew violent and ended his life.

"Your mom was really young when that happened. She deserves a second chance from everyone, including you. You know she loves you."

Scott scraped his bottom teeth so hard against his top lip, his skin turned red. Ironically, so had his face. I'd never grown up with white people. At least, not until college. It was funny how now I lived with them. So, I got to see their physiological tendencies as well as many of their thought processes. The heated neck, for Scott, was a sign of anxiety. He'd been thinking about this. He had to think about too much at his young age for far too long.

"My experience is a lot different from yours."

"Not really. You have one parent who's dead, and another who was locked up once. Sounds about the same to me. Your father's home now, and you still don't fool with him."

"I do, Scott. Just not often."

He exhaled, frustrated, and turned away. "Okay."

Uninterested in continuing the conversation, I let off the brake and continued to the house.

"Do you know what you want for dinner?"

He shook his head. "Wonder what MeMaw wants."

I checked the dashboard for the time. It was already five in the evening. Five, and I hadn't heard from Tobias yet. I knew I wouldn't. He never called first when I left him since our first kiss about a year and a half ago. This was one of the few times he'd flexed his stubbornness. "She's probably already gotten her food for the night. She didn't know what time we'd be getting in."

"Yeah," Scott sighed, gazing out of the window. "You're right."

We were two houses away when I saw a familiar *Chevrolet Malibu* illegally parked in the street. Outside, on the passenger side, a tall man in jeans, a hoodie, and sunglasses leaned against the vehicle I paid the insurance on, lighting a cigarette.

"Oh, shit," Scott griped under his breath.

I pulled into my driveway, and observed the contorted *BMW* on the other side, still annoyed by the sight of it. Frustrated at life all over again, I took a deep breath. *I'm built for this...* Scott left the car first. I reached over to the glove compartment and fingered through papers until I found my rings. Once I managed to slip them on, I met Scott at the trunk. That's when I noticed Billy slipping into the *Malibu* not wanting my wrath.

"No matter what," Scott advised lowly, "just ignore him. You don't need his shit right now. You just got back into town."

"Scott, your mouth."

Without acknowledging me, he pulled my smaller suitcase from the trunk while mumbling something incoherent beneath his breath. He then went to get his own bags from the back seat. I managed my larger luggage from the trunk, and was pulling it up the driveway, when the screen door burst open, and a six-foot, seven-inch tall, crooked tree branch filled the doorway.

Kelvin's eyes were pink and tight. His normal, smooth, pecan-hued skin was marred with current scars and healed wounds, reddening at the neck and lower face. His thin, shapely lips appeared to be cut. Just the sight of him made my stomach twist with anxiety.

"You fucking turn your phone off, Lennox?"

"Lay off of her!" Scott spit, rounding his uncle to enter the house.

"Mind your punk ass business, boy!"

"Scott!" I ordered. "Straight to your room to unpack."

"Do you hear me?" Kelvin demanded, following me inside when I passed him.

He didn't bother to assist me with the large suitcase. I didn't expect him to either. Chivalry was never really his strong suit.

As expected, his mother was on the sofa—my sofa—watching mind-numbing television per usual. She was my first stop. "I don't ask you for much," I began out of breath, pulse racing. "Never have. The one thing I do ask of and expect is support for his recovery. You couldn't do that for me, Kelly-Ann?"

Her freckled faced opened in alarm. "What?"

"You picked him up from treatment is what. Is that what we're doing now?"

"What're you talking about?" she argued, exposing the missing tooth in the center of her bottom row. "You just came in, and I'm just here watching T.V."

Stating the obvious was her defense?

"That's what you should've been doing yesterday; but instead, you checked him out of the only program we could find him last week in a crisis?"

"He was sick. Miserable in there," she spat back. "He's my son!"

"Yeah. Your only living son! Is there no solidarity when it comes to his well-being?"

"Hey!" Kelvin barked from behind me. "Don't talk to my momma like that! Who in the hell do you think you are? This is my life. I ain't no damn kid."

I turned to his lengthy, stick-like frame as he glowered down over me. "But you're not well. Do you know how much your accident out there is going to cost me?"

"We have insurance, Len. That's what the shit is for!"

"You think you driving while high, and wrapping that car around a tree in a school zone, is going to cost me only what I pay in premiums? If so, you *are* a kid, Kelvin!"

More than just being in the vicinity of a school, Kelvin, and one of his tweaking buddies, were on the property of a school. *Scott's* school. It was the most unlikely, inescapable situation. The incident happened while some of the students were at recess. Although cell-phones were prohibited at the school, without a doubt, several students recorded the scene with the police, firefighters, and EMT pulling Kelvin from his totaled *BMW*, attempting to get him on a stretcher as he was high out of his goddamn mind.

Scott was justifiably humiliated and traumatized. Quite a few kids at the school knew Kelvin Richardson, the former basketball *League* player, and Raleigh's golden boy. They also knew he was Scott Richardson's uncle. The Scott whose mother murdered his father. And that mother was currently in prison. All of that was too much for a thirteen-year-old to have to deal with.

"And you're a *bitch*—"

"Kelvin, don't start your shit!" His mother warned. "She just got back in from her class reunion. Don't nobody wanna come home to your shit."

My body whipped to face her. "Thanks to you, I have, Kelly-Ann." My delivery less animated, though I was seething.

"Don't fucking talk to her like I ain't right here and I ain't a grown ass man!" Kelvin took a step closer to me.

I took a step closer to him, refusing to allow the monkey on his back to intimidate me. "Well, grown ass man, with his 'suspicious, chain-smoking, junkie friend' waiting outside for him by his mamma's car, why were you calling me?"

"Because you're my fucking wife, Len!" he barked. "You forget that? I go to use my card yesterday to get some snacks at the gas station, and it kept coming up declined."

I rolled my eyes, massaging my forehead. "That happens when you've reached the limit, Kelvin."

"Limit? How am I at my limit, but you up in Jersey, at homecoming?"

"Because I work, Kelvin. I pay my credit card bill and *yours*."

A reddish-pink hue shaded the borders of his constricted, green irises. "You have money to spend, but I don't. What type of sense does that make?"

It was the attempt at logic that snapped me out of my anger. I couldn't do this. Wouldn't. I had to claw my way out of this cycle of gloom I'd found myself in. This. This is what I'd be doing when I could no longer bare children. The fighting over money and accountability with a family that wasn't mine would be what I'd be doing when my hair began to gray. I'd be exhausted, fighting to pay for Scott's college tuition and then his portion for his wedding. By that time, Kelvin could be dead, and I'd still be here, burned out and bitter. I'd be far more uninspired and desolate than I was before...

Before Tobias re-entered my world and rekindled a passion I'd totally forgotten I possessed. Before that, I'd been functioning in a dark world, only seeing light when at work. My life was monotonous, filled with dread and emptiness.

Last week, into this morning wasn't about sex. It wasn't totally about escape either. With the advice of my therapist, this year, the point of my annual trip was to mentally and emotionally take a step away from under the umbrella and feel the rain. Yes, I threw in the possibility of sex, something I knew blindsided Tobias, and was specifically what my therapist advised against. However, it felt good to be selfish and make a decision for me.

And it started in a moment like this where all of my roommates and dependents were all around. It happened with the adjutant of my misery glaring down on me, taunting me, and waiting for my next move.

I took a deep breath, deciding on my next words.

"None. It makes none, Kelvin."

"Good." He scoffed, eyeing the new piece around my neck. "Then give me a few dollars so I can pay Billy back what he had to kick out for me when my card came up declined."

"What happened to your cash, Kelvin?" My questions were repetitive, at this point, when he asked for cash. "You get money at the top of every month. Where did it go?"

"I got robbed."

"I'm sorry to hear that, but this month you were robbed, last month, you lost it—"

"Gambling!" he shouted. "I lost the shit gambling, yeah. Damn! You like this game of reducing me to a kid like I'm Scott. I'm a grown fucking man!" he barked, stabbing his finger toward the floor.

Remain calm...

You were built to survive this...

Out of nowhere, a pale hand appeared, holding a bundle of cash. "Here," Scott grumbled. "It's all I've got."

Kelvin's wild eyes shot from the cash to me. While staring him dead in the face, I moved Scott's arm away, declining his offer.

"Absolutely not again," I made clear. "Kelvin, you need to get back into treatment."

"I'm not going back to that hellhole!" He fingered his loose coils, and I subconsciously wondered when was the last time he'd been groomed. "I don't need treatment. You know I'm just fucked up about my career."

"And what are you doing about it, Kelvin?"

He grew visibly agitated, face screwed. "I spoke to Coach Cal. He said he'd see me soon."

"Soon," I repeated, entertaining this conversation in front of his mother and nephew purposely. "Did Coach Cal tell you exactly when he'd see you and what he'd be looking for?"

Kelvin shook his head, exhaling roughly. "No!" he whined. "His assistant—" His mouth twisted tightly. "I didn't speak to him. I'll call this week. We'll talk."

"About what, Kelvin?"

"About me playing again! The fuck!" he roared.

I blinked deeply, rearing my head. The basketball *League*. The professional basketball association. They're going to let Kelvin Richardson back into the *League*?

"Kelvin, that's not going to happen."

"And how the fuck do you know?" he demanded so harsh and loudly, his thin frame twisted on one foot.

I remained calm. "Because one of your vertebrae shifted out of place because of a stress fracture in the bone."

"Don't talk to me like I'm a fucking dummy, Len!"

"I'm not."

"Then why would you say shit like I don't know my own medical history?"

"I don't know. Maybe for the same reason you brought up playing again." A car accident while he was high caused Kelvin a severe spinal injury early into his second season with the *Charlotte Hornets*. He had to have surgery, which improved his condition, but couldn't repair what was needed for Kelvin to play. He still suffered from back pain. "Your injury won't allow it."

Kelvin waived me off dismissively. "I'm not about to stand here and listen to you try to break me down." He scoffed. "Picture that. A broke bitch from East Orange, New Jersey, who I pulled out of her humble circumstances, and paid her tuition for two degrees. I go down, and now you think I ain't shit. You think you can snip my balls. You wanna know why I crashed last week? It's because I'm drowning, being married to your miserable, controlling ass. Out of all the girls dying at a chance with me, I let my agent and manage-ment team convince me you were the best choice to marry. I knew they were wrong." His long arms shot up in the air. "And look at me now, just as miserable as you."

"You don't have to be with me, Kelvin. No one's forcing you to stay," I tried to reason with him.

"Because I'm down! I'm trying to get my shit together. But you don't believe in me. My own wife never believed in me. She only believed in the money I was getting when I got drafted. Now, you got my nephew here brainwashed, so he don't believe in me either. You got my momma here, giving me the side-eye every other day. She's starting to not believe in me, too. Lennox, you're like a fucking cancer. You think you're special but you're really not."

"Oh, no?"

He snickered. "Hell no! You may have good hair and be light-skinned, but you ain't all that *pretty*—"

"Hey!" Scott shouted.

I raised my hand to silence him. These were verbal bullets used frequently when Kelvin was low in spirit. I'd turned numb to them after year three of him being let go from the *League*.

"Shut the fuck up, Scottie. She knows it's the truth. Trust, when you grow up and start getting girls like your dad and I did, you'll see. Your uncle chose the bottom of the barrel. Her pappy's a goddamn thug. And before her grandmom lost her mind, she tried to groom this motherless child into something great. Too bad I didn't leave you there in that shithole of a town, and let her finish the job. You ain't nothing special, Len. Nothing. I can still line the block with badder bitches than you with this fucked up back."

"You're full of shee-at, Kelvin," Kelly-Ann hissed. "Full of shee-at, just like your daddy." She shook her head.

"My daddy?" He smiled, reminding me of the ghost of his natural, good looks. Kelvin Richardson was presumably the total package back in his *Princeton University* days. Good looking, mulatto kid. A by-product of a Black father and white mother, he had the most alluring features. Something a young girl's heart couldn't resist. "My daddy liked white-trash girls. Irving may not have fallen far from that tree," His attention rolled over to me as he pivoted in stance. "But I had the sense to try out Black trash. You limit my money and then berate me for not having a job because of my injury. How in the hell am I supposed to win in life with this kind of fucking negativity around me? I'm out, man. I'll just figure the shit out myself. I'm used to it." In classic fashion, Kelvin turned to leave, after making a spectacular production of feeling sorry for himself.

"Kel," I called out to him. He turned back, hand on the screen door handle. I dug into my purse for my wallet. I pulled out all the cash I had. In true addict's fashion, my husband leaped around and took lunges toward me. I held the money in the air, stalling. "This will be my last time giving you money. No more having you as an authorized user on my credit card. No more allowance at the top of the month. No more sob stories of you being in pain. No more tragedies of you being assaulted or robbed. I'm no longer enabling and covering for the drama that is this household. Starting with this exchange, I'm done."

Kelvin snatched the money from my hand so fast and violently, he scratched me. My first instinct was to haul off and hook his ass, but I caught myself. I knew he meant to be rude, but not to scratch me. Along with every piece of shit this man had slung on me since I agreed to marry him, I swallowed this, too.

For the last time…

"You fucking done," he mumbled. "I been fucking done with your controlling, bitchy ass. You can suck a dick!" That's all I heard before the door was slammed closed.

"I swear to God, I love my uncle, but I hate how he treats you! I wish my dad was here. He'd beat his ass!" Scott cried. Again. The little guy cried. "This is why I thought you weren't coming back from Jersey. You're strong, Lennox. Too strong to keep taking shit he shoves your way!"

Initially, when Terry went to prison, it was arranged for Scott, who was three at the time, to live with her mother. And he did, for some time. However, Terry's mother lost the home that had been in their family for over seven decades, and the court forced them to arrange for better housing for Scott. That's when Kelvin and I stepped in. Well, I'd stepped in. Kelly-Ann had been living with us, so she couldn't exactly take on custody for anyone. Kelvin had been indifferent, but I always thought Scott was a good kid with horrific circumstances. They were ones I could relate to.

While this episode was light-weight in comparison to Kelvin's tirades when tweaking, it was sad that he'd been separated from his parents due to tragedy, and was now living through trauma with us. Just sad.

As I gathered him into my arms, I gaped Kelly-Ann's way. She couldn't even look at me.

But that was fine. As I told her son, no more.

Tobias

I stretched out on the chaise portion of her new sectional. Pulling my arms up, I folded them over my face as I grunted.

"Mmmmhmmm…" she hummed from across the room as she knitted something with a soft yellows and blue yarn. "That look like a heart issue."

"What?" I mumbled from behind my arms.

"That shit weighing you down is what?" My grandmother didn't mince her words. Ever. At seventy-eight years young, she had a fiduciary obligation not to sugar coat.

I opened my eyes, looking up at the ceiling. The color contrast from the soft gray walls to the stark white ceiling sparked a memory.

"You ready to bring your patio set in for the winter?"

"Nah. I figure I gotta few more weeks before it's too cold to sit out there. October's usually good to me. Now, you! Who done died?"

"Nobody, Grandma."

"Then it's Len-Len."

I laughed. Hard. "Grandma."

"You seen her, huhn?"

I shook my head, eyes closed. "Yup."

"Alone."

"Yup."

I could hear her distinct teeth suck, or in grandma's case, her dentures click. "You kiss her again?"

"Yup."

"And now she back down south with that crackhead, basketball player of hers?

I laughed again.

"Something like that, yeah."

"What you gone do if she let you smell it?"

Grandma, I did more than smell it. I made a few meals out of it…

And that was what fucked me up. Never in a million years did I think I'd have a chance at Lennox's body this trip. She even let me spank her, another unexpected miracle. I've been wanting her so bad and for so long. I manifested having her back in my life. When it happened three years ago, it boosted my ability to have long term faith, and to focus on specific goals. Manifestation was some real shit.

"She ain't pregnant by that crackhead, basketball playing husband, is she?" My grandmother's forceful words of inquiry shot from her weak diaphragm.

I wish that would be the announcement two months from now…

But it wouldn't. We used condoms, something that felt unnatural with Lennox. Being a single man who travels frequently for a living, and one that does well financially, I did my fair share of fucking. Flavorful, festive fucking. Protection was paramount for a man who had become a father unintentionally at twenty years old. Notwithstanding the gift that was Elia, her conception was such a traumatizing event in my life because of the circumstances surrounding it.

"Well, is she or ain't she?" My grandmother demanded.

I shook my head again then lifted it from my shoulders while still on my back. Mattie Mae was leaning forward now, in her leather recliner. She was hella curious.

"You's a nosy old lady, ain't you?"

She raised her crooked fist in the air and dramatically declared, "Before I close my eyes for the last time, and meet my maker, that child gone be my granddaughter-in-law."

"Grandma, stop!"

"I'm serious, Tobias. I am. I ain't never seen no pussy-whipped pup like you a day in my life." Her face went tight, and I dropped my head back onto the sofa, cracking the hell up. "I 'clare, you worse than your grandfather when he took me from my first husband. That man followed me around by my *secretions*—"

"Grandma!"

"You know how when the man animal can sniff when the female animal in heat?" she continued, ignoring me. "That's how your granddaddy used to follow me around town, sniffing up my ass. He did!"

I tried to stop laughing to ask, "That's messed up. Is that what you think of me? I'm a whiny simp? Woman, this simping got your house gutted and rebuilt. It's what still gets you down to the casinos in Atlantic City and up in Connecticut."

"Yup. All that romantic whining in them songs got me to feel on them football players' arms." Her wrinkled face opened in a scandalized smile as she grinned toward the ceiling, demonstrating groping a man. "They like it, too."

"Actually, they don't, woman. Tell me this: what're their names?"

Her curled body resumed its natural posture as she thought about it. "I got it. Shrimp Jordan and Johnston Bailey! That Shrimp know how to work them hips, man!" She attempted to gyrate in her chair. My grandmother may have moved half an inch.

"You're crazy, lady!"

"Yeah. I am," she murmured, going back to the task at hand. "Crazy and missing that ol' fool." Now, my grandma sounded sad, her words pouring slower as she knitted. "I know I tease you about that child, but I really hope it works out for you after all these years."

Me, too...

"I'm being patient, but trying not to go overboard with my expectations. Lennox's got a lot of shit on her plate. I hate it for her."

"Mmmmhmmm…" My grandmother hummed. "Ever tell you how I ran into that so called grandmother of hers? The pastor," she spat.

I brought my head up again. "Pastor Williams?"

"Mmmmhmmm…"

"Grandma, when?" I was shocked as hell.

She hummed she didn't know. "It was a few short years after the young lady left for down south. Deloris dragged me over to a bingo hall over there in East Orange. You know I like to stay on this side where it's classier. But listening to that fool, we went. Soon as I sit down, I see her high-yellow ass, wearing that red lipstick and sparkly jewelry, and thangs." She rolled her eyes while sucking her dentures. "I wanted to drag her by that goldilocks wig she had on. You know what I did?"

"What?" I couldn't believe she was saying this shit.

"I went right on over there to her table and told her who I was. I told that cow she was dead wrong for dismissing my grandbaby for that boy just because he was going off to play that ball. You don't do that to young peoples. You let them fuck up or find they own happiness. I told her I hope her grandbaby don't end up lonely and miserable at bingo halls at our age. And you know what, Tobias?"

"Eh," I squeaked, so fucking stunned.

"That lady looked at me with them pretty eyes, and asked me who was my grandchild. When I told her the name, she then asked what granddaughter did she have. I told her who, and that woman looked at me like I had more than three heads and said she ain't know none of the peoples I was talking about. I told that liar she was a fool. You hear me? A fool! Then she finna cry, and her friends started talking they shit about leave her alone: she ain't feel good." Another sucking of the dentures.

"Grandma, that's probably when her dementia started kicking in."

"Yeah, well…" She kept looping and hooking. "God don't like

ugly, Tobias! I can't even leave peacefully cause ya heart ain't whole. I'm old as hell, boy!"

Swinging my eyes toward the ceiling, I slammed my head back down on the sofa. "I know, Grandma, but you do have a great-grand child." Elia was her only. She had three grandchildren. I was the only by my pops, and my uncle, Smite, had two children, but none reproduced. "That's something."

"Yeah. But I could'a had like eight by now."

"Eight? Elia's eight!"

"A baby every year." She scratched her nose, looking me dead in the eyes. "My grand-momma did some shit like that. Look at you: all successful. You could'a had as many, and taken good care of them."

"Take care of who?" My uncle, Smite, dropped down the stairs.

"His chirren."

"He only got one." I stood as he made his way over to me to give him some dap. "You good?"

"I'm good. You good?"

"He ain't good."

"Grandma, knock it off," I tried to beg without begging.

I'd always been comfortable confiding in my grandmother. She'd been my rock since I could remember. My family unit was tight, but most shit I only shared with her. Grandma was the type to trivialize every problem in the world, and try to explain why nothing was worth stressing over. So, in an event like this, she'd invite my uncle into my shit. I wasn't interested today.

"Knock what off?" The O.G. flexed. His eyes bounced between the two of us. After being in and out of prison since I was a baby, and after doing a sixteen-year bid the last time, Smite assumed the role of the enforcer in our family. As a grown ass capable man, I didn't need protecting, but my grandmother did. So, when I got her house done over a few years ago, I asked him to stay with her. She was getting older, and I didn't want any surprises happening here as far as she was concerned. He agreed; and provided groceries and paid some of the utilities. I took care of everything else. I could sleep at night knowing he was here with his nose clean. "You good. Right?"

"When am I not good?"

"I 'on't know. When somebody die. Raj pops' good?" Smite asked.

"Yeah." I nodded. "He's been straight since that hospital stay."

"Then it's Lennox." The muscles in his face dropped. "You seen her?"

I nodded, annoyed by the topic, as my grandmother hummed.

He turned to me. "Today?" When I didn't answer, just stared at him, he followed up with, "Lil' Lennox was in Jersey?"

"Homecoming."

"Where she stay?"

"With me." I could have regretted that truth but didn't. Lennox didn't want people to know each time she was in town, but it was silly to deny this time because she came to every homecoming.

Smite blinked. "She been by to see Chino?"

My grandmother's gaze rose to hear the answer.

Lennox's father, Chino, and my uncle were locked up at the same time during his last bid. They were close on the streets since they were younger. Both in their fifties now, they were considered O.G.'s in Essex County and beyond. They could still pull rank if needed. Smite knew the complexities of my history with Lennox, and so did Chino.

"I don't think so. No."

Smite whistled with wild eyes. "You had Chino's daughter up here this week, fuckin' her, and Chino don't know?"

"Ant-uhn!" My grandmother grunted, shifting up in her chair. "You ain't say she let you smell it, young man!"

"I'm out." I headed toward the kitchen. "You got the plate fixed, Grandma?"

"Yeah, but wait a damn minute here!"

"You got a whole healthy-ass chef at home. Why you coming to get Mommy's Sunday dinner?" Smite inquired to my back. "Ah, damn, nephew. You really fucked up, homie!"

Chapter Seven

Tobias

"You sure, Daddy?"

I stood outside of my car, happy the *Bluetooth* transferred. Reaching back inside, I grabbed my to-go plate. I snorted, "Why do you keep asking me that?"

Elia laughed. "I don't know. Because you sound different."

I closed the door then headed inside the garage. "You sound like Granny earlier."

I could hear the breath she sucked in. "You went to see Granny today?"

"Yeah. I'm coming from Irvington now. Got a plate."

"A plate? Where's Pedro?"

"He's been off for a few days. He'll be back tomorrow. Why?"

"Because he cooks you that healthy stuff."

That was hilarious. "I grew up on Granny's fine cuisine. Turned me into a healthy boy then a strong man. Plus, you know I gets down in the kitchen. Pedro don't cook all my food."

Ignoring me, my baby asked, "Did somebody die? Is that why you're sad, Daddy?"

Abruptly, my steps halted inside my garage. I turned around as though looking for someone. "You, too, Elia? Why do you think I'm sad and that somebody died?"

"Because you're always happy." She giggled. "But Daddy, wait. I have something to tell you."

I hit a button to close the garage door, and managed tapping the keypad while wedging the phone between my ear and shoulder, holding the bagged food. "I'm listening."

"Okay. So, you know how you always say don't wait till the last minute to tell you what I want for Christmas?"

"Uhn, huhn."

"Well, I know what I want."

As I strolled inside towards the security pad, I entertain my cutie pie, fully aware of her finesse game happening in the moment. "Okay."

"*Disney!*"

"*Disney?* When I was eight years old, I ain't never been to no *Disney*, and you've been like eight times!"

"But when you were eight, you were poor, Daddy," she sounded offended.

Shit. *I* should have been offended for her pointing out half of the obvious. On the one hand, she was correct: I was relatively poor as a kid. But the other half of that coin was how poverty escaped her because I was poor *as a kid*. I worked hard to make sure she wouldn't be poor as a kid or an adult. I even named my publishing company after her.

"I was, I know. And you're not: we know. But you going to Florida for Christmas means I won't get either holiday with you."

"Yes, you will."

I stalked down the hall of my empty home, passing the laundry room and heading toward the short set of steps for the main level. "Nah. You'll be with your family in Boston for *Thanksgi*—"

"*Ohhhhh!*"

"Yup. So, that'll be both holidays without my Pear Bear."

"Daddy!" she whined. "You could come, too."

"You didn't invite me. I wasn't in mind when you came up with this." When her silence confirmed it, I asked, "Who did you plan on taking down there?"

"Mommy, JuJu, his mom, Pinky, and her auntie, maybe?" Elia didn't sound very confident, now conscious of leaving me out.

"JuJu, too?"

"Daddy!" there was more bass in her voice. "Daddy, please!"

JuJu was a little boy who had been friends with my daughter since they were old enough to make friends. The boy was cool, but was still a boy. The dad in me didn't want my baby to have boys as friends, especially not travel companions. But lucky for me, little JuJu was as feminine as they came. If the boy hadn't declared his sexuality yet, I'd be surprised. He walked and talked with more vibrant femininity than my Elia. He was a smart kid, too. Very respectful and talkative as hell. JuJu stayed asking questions about the artists I worked with. The kid knew the stylist Ragee worked with, and who made Brielle's wigs. All the shit I had no clue or care about. On the other hand, if he grew up to be heterosexual, I'd die of a heart attack: the joke would have been on me all these years. The kids spent a lot of damn time together.

"Okay, Pear Bear," I relented. "Have your mom give me the details. We'll make it happen—"

"Thank you, Daddy!" she shouted into the phone. "I love you! I love you! I love you a thousand times!"

"Just a thousand?"

"A bagillion!"

I smiled, shouldering out of my jacket. The girl knew she had me wrapped around her finger. It was similar to another finger my heart, and now my fucking dick, was melted all over.

Lennox...

I sighed, leaning into the island countertop and rubbing my face. "Thank you, Pear Bear." I managed a smile.

"You sound sad again. You wanna just come?"

I laughed. "Nah. Daddy's just tired. I'm gonna warm up this plate Granny made me and eat."

"Okay. Daddy, after that, do something to make yourself feel better."

I thought I was doing that these past few days. Now, I realized the thing about longing was the impatient anticipation before was less painful than the bereavement after.

"I'mma do that, baby girl. You all packed up for school tomorrow?"

"Yup."

"Don't forget to brush your teeth. And when you pray tonight, be sure to pray for daddy's heart and mind. Okay?"

"Why?"

"Because they never get along."

"Oh." Her eight-year-old mind sounded all confused. "Okay." There was a brief pause before she offered, "Night Daddy."

"Night, my love."

When we ended the call, I took another breath and gazed around my kitchen. It was cleaned and organized and...empty. At this rate, I should pay Krista to buy a bigger home with her man, and let Elia stay with me full-time. This lonely shit at my age wasn't for me.

After washing my hands, I had dinner at the table in the kitchen. Not really tasting the food as I downed it, my heart grew anxious for a purge. In between feeding my face, my fingers tapped away at invisible keys.

Before I knew it, I was too anxious to make it down to the basement where I had a well-functioning studio. Settling at the grand piano in my living room met my urgent need. I began to finger through a few notes. Not really measuring time, I stayed at it until a melody occurred. A while later, a harmony was born, and I began to feel intoxicated.

"*My tears...*

My tears." I sang, seeking more.

It took a few minutes before I continued with, "*Blessed are those who mourn...*

For our tears fall on fertile soil.

All my hopes and dreams will one day be released.

One day they'll swell your belly.

Soon, oh so soon, this debilitating pain will cease.

And just like my former longing,
My love for you will transcend the years.
Oh, my tears,
Will water my fears.
No longer will I be torn,
Because blessed are those who mourn."

Lennox

"You're sure?"

I peered into the screen on the small table in a private room of the *NC State* library. It was where I took my therapy calls via *Zoom*. The school was within walking distance of my job and shared a partnership, allowing me access to the campus. Here, I had the privacy needed for honest and personal conversations.

"I am."

"Have you told him?"

"Who?"

"Tobias," my therapist asked from her New Jersey office.

I shook my head, giving her a definitive 'no.' "Not in direct terms, no."

"Which terms did you use?"

"Ummm..." I rubbed my lips together, thinking back to four, cloudy mornings ago when I left his big body on the floor of a strange home. I still felt like shit, and still hadn't heard from him. "It was time for me to leave...to go to the hotel so I could make the airport on time. He said he had something to show me. I told him he'd be able to soon."

"Soon," she echoed. I nodded. "Just soon?"

Suddenly, I felt insecure. "Yeah."

"And by that you meant leaving your marriage?" I answered with a nod. "And have you told Kelvin?"

"Indirectly. When I got in on Sunday, the last thing I told Kelvin, before handing him almost three hundred dollars, was him taking it would be for the last time."

"And that was your way of announcing your divorce?"

I readjusted myself in the leather seat. "I thought you were in support of this. Why do I feel like you're alluding to me doing something wrong here?"

"I am in total support of your decision. I'm just assessing your communication on it and seeking clarity. Have you heard back from Kelvin since Sunday?"

"In a way. He came home that night. More like the early morning hours, which is typical. I heard him go down into the basement. This morning, he watched from the living room window when the tow truck finally came for his totaled *Beamer*."

My therapist nodded. Taking in a deep breath, she exhaled when mentioning, "Yeah. And there's that. You should be more direct with Kelvin. Is there a reason you can't do that?"

I considered it for a moment.

My husband was a full-blown addict. Threats and warnings had been hurled his way by all who loved and hated him like missiles, mine included. I'd done everything I could think of and was reasonably advised to help him down his dark descent into drug addiction, including neglecting my own mental health.

I met Kelvin at nineteen, in my sophomore year of college. Mya and I attended a *Princeton University* basketball game one night on her wild search for a rich man. It was her thing since I'd met her, even after she'd been dating Derrick. She always wanted bigger and better, always preparing for her real adult life. Mya felt owed the glam life, and had been in serious pursuit of it since I'd met her. She used to say she wished we attended *Blakewood State University* so she could be guaranteed good stock on her very own campus. I never understood that because what did it say that *she* wasn't enrolled there? If she wasn't "good stock," why did she feel she deserved a man who was? But hey, I was young and floating through life.

I'd been into a guy we'd met at *Garden State Plaza* mall months before, but hadn't committed to being his girlfriend at the time. So, when we managed our way into the afterparty of a game they'd won, I didn't get excited when we found ourselves encircled by the top guys of the *Princeton Tigers*. Kelvin was there, smoking weed and drinking while sitting on the back of a sofa, feet planted on the cushions of the seat. While I was returning texts to the guy I'd been liking, Mya had sparked up a conversation with the jocks. By the end of the night, she felt accomplished leaving with two telephone numbers.

The next day, she came to me with odd news. The captain of the team, Kelvin, wanted us to hang out with him and his friends that following Saturday. Initially, and against Mya's impossible attitude, I declined. I'd had enough of playing her wing-woman. But the guy I'd been "dating" was a budding musician, and had a gig in the City that Saturday night, so I relented.

When Saturday rolled around, I talked to Kelvin a bit. He couldn't stop telling me how pretty I was, complimenting my curly hair texture and the unusual color of my eyes. Similar to that, all topics were surfaced, but I did discover how attractive he was. The guy was six-feet, seven-inches, had fine hair, and hazel-green eyes. His smile was picture perfect in spite of him being a little asshole'ish. Okay. Kelvin was very handsome, but his personality yielded very little endearment. That night, after chatting for a bit, he asked me to a back room. The same "back room" invitation Mya had consented to earlier. I froze.

No.

There was no way I'd do it with this Kelvin Richardson guy. I didn't know him—*now*... Granted, I'd only been knowing the musician guy for a few months, and I, uncharacteristically, had sex with him...twice by this time. But that was different. *That* guy was really cute as well—thicker—but also extremely sweet, patient, always around, and closer to my age. His fixation on me was more than I'd ever felt from anyone, including my, recently released from prison, father and Grandmother combined. This Kelvin guy was a senior at *Princeton*. He was three years older, which wasn't old, but I was only nineteen.

And sex? Did he smell I was easy? Is that what the musician guy felt, because it definitely felt easy with him. The only other guy I'd had sex with before him was a guy I'd dated for three years in high school, Dayron. And that took a while.

That night, when Kelvin asked me to go to a back room, if he thought I was easy, the musician likely thought I was easy, too. That made me wonder if my grandmother sensed the same thing. And God help me if Pastor Williams believed the one young woman under her tutelage—in her home—was fast! I couldn't have that. Needless to say, I was repulsed and turned him down. Kelvin abandoned the conversation and me minutes after.

About a week later, Kelvin called me. I'd forgotten about giving him my number when the conversation was good before the sexual invitation. He asked if he could take me out. I'd just learned horrible news about the musician guy and told him I needed space, much to his chagrin. To distract myself from the ache of the musician's "sloppiness," I agreed to go out with Kelvin. I'd go out with Kelvin lots after that initial date. In fact, the *Princeton* jock had begun to grow on me. He intrigued me once I got over his slight arrogance. Eventually, I grew smitten enough to sit through an "interview" with his "team" where I was complimented on my "beautiful" features. It felt very "audition'ish" or, more specifically, like the models experience in "go-sees." See, Kelvin Richardson was on his way to the pros. He was a promising draftee for the *League*'s draft that summer.

Oh, yeah. Richardson was big time back then. He was rolling over into a stratosphere the average guy I grew up with could only imagine. What I didn't know was that I was being vetted for optics. They knew Kelvin had rogue tendencies, so they curated an image for him. That image included sobriety, focus, dedication, safety, and me.

When he met my grandmother, it was a wrap for me. She fell in love with the guy before meeting him. He attended her church one Sunday, and the whole congregation were instant basketball fans, declaring their loyalty to whichever team that drafted him. It all happened so fast, nauseatingly so. I didn't see Kelvin outside of what I now understood was him securing our future. Perhaps I didn't understand the play because, simultaneously, I'd been nursing a broken heart thanks to a starved musician who'd been trying his damnedest to re-earn my trust and affection.

Kelvin proposed to me a week before draft day. I was torn and jaded by the advice and hard push by Grandmother. The musician was visibly wounded when I met him at a local pizzeria and broke the news to him. He begged me to give it some time before making such a permanent decision. My hurt from his betrayal made it difficult to heed to his wisdom. Then Grandmother and her cohort of clergy girlfriends were the icing on the cake in my unwise judgement. My father, whom I'd never had a real relationship with, tried to intervene. He didn't agree with the pace of the decision. But I didn't trust him enough to take his advice either. He was a virtual stranger, one I'd seen about a dozen times before he'd been released from prison that year.

By twenty years old, I was married and had moved to North Carolina where he'd been drafted by the *Hornets*. A week later, I was due to begin my third year of undergrad. I'd returned to Jersey to take care of paperwork at the school and check in on my grandmother when my father approached me in an unusual fashion. It was at night, hours before my flight back to North Carolina. He came with a check from my grandmother's account. It was his money, and boy was it a lot from an ex-con, fresh off a fifteen-year homicide bid. Yup. My father, Chino from Amherst Street, was a proven O.G.

Uncannily aware of his distance from my orbit of influence, my father pleaded with me to not go into the marriage without a safety net. When I shared I didn't understand, he advised me to buy a house, even if it was down there. He said if things were to fail between Kelvin and I, I'd at least have a soft landing. I reminded my father I had no job or way of paying a mortgage and property taxes beyond a deposit. He suggested I buy down south, and if I needed help with anything, he'd make sure I'd get it. Oddly, naivety aside, there was a spark of hope in that moment for the man I didn't know. Something instinctual told me to hearken to his words. And I did, which proved to be a lifesaver later on for not just me, but Kelvin, too.

I finished school mostly online, flying back and forth until I'd graduated. Life was such a blur, meeting significant, rich, and even famous people. I never had a honeymoon or downtime with Kelvin to really get to know him. Kelvin didn't play much the first season. He wasn't a breakout star like his peers. The Bookers, Towns', Russells, et al eventually became the names ringing mental bells. Richardson out of *Princeton* was not. And yes, *the* Michael Jordan took joy in whooping players like Kelvin's ass on the court off camera. Unhappy with his bench-side view of the court, Kelvin would gripe about it. But he'd show up to work and practice as agreed upon in his contract. It wasn't long before there were rumors about infidelity. They were plentiful, but not loud enough due to Kelvin's lack of celebrity.

So, yeah. Unfortunately, I couldn't be a Kardashian to the Richardson brand. However, the isolation from my family and new husband had been the spark of hunger for my own endeavors. I created them just before Kelvin's career came crashing down. After graduating with my degree in nursing, I immediately enrolled into a master's in nursing administration program at *UNC Charlotte*. A month before we were married, Kelvin purchased a beautiful, eight thousand square foot home just outside of the city. The place was so huge, it was easy for him to have his space from me. And that's what he did. He also had a nice home built for his mother in Durham.

I didn't know what to expect from a husband. So, I tried to listen to his cues, cook, clean, and arrange for anything he needed to excel. Even with that, there was a distance we had never been able to mend. There was occasional sex, some outings which were business obligations, and his regular family gatherings for the holidays. I obliged them all.

In all honesty, after year four of marriage, I didn't believe Kelvin had ever loved or had been in love with me. For him, I'd become a necessary associate in his pursuit of life. I learned in the second year of our union that drugs had actually been Kelvin's preferred, primary, and priority partner. He smoked weed. A lot. Sometimes, it would simply calm him, make him more amenable to stand. Then, he'd be despondent. I'd come in from work when I didn't have class and find him staring at an unpowered television screen in the family room just off the kitchen. At first, I'd try to snap him out of it. Eventually, I'd caught on and understood, mentally, Kelvin was at an exclusive party in his head. I was not invited there with him.

I didn't take to his lifestyle easily. Because we didn't spend much time together, it took a while for me to grow agitated with his recreational escapes. His job did before me. The coaches and management complained and sanctioned him before I did, even before I caught on. Addiction didn't happen overnight, but it blossomed like a flower. It eroded from within before withering on the exterior. The car accident into that second season with the *Hornets* was when the world caught wind to the existence of his problem. Before then, the organization tried getting him therapy and narcotics anonymous assistance. Kelvin wouldn't show.

It wasn't until he overdosed in our home eight months after his back surgery did Kelvin finally show interest in therapy. I supported him, going to sessions I was asked to attend, hearing him detail traumas of his childhood. He shared about his abusive childhood at the hands of his father, who died of alcoholism when Kelvin was in high school. The man had beaten his children often to the point of child protective services getting involved. His mother, Kelly-Ann, couldn't or didn't intervene. This trauma drove Kelvin to sports, including basketball. It pushed his older brother, Kyle, to a deep dive into drugs and alcohol himself.

No one paid attention because, eventually, Kelvin's path into developing his game took precedence. He worked hard and became popular locally, eventually earning an athletic scholarship to *Princeton University*. His youth and elite athleticism outshined his nasty pastimes, and Kelvin was able to get by, just like he was able to sweep his imposing "golden boy" imposter existence onto me. No one knew the demons he hid. That was until the *League* let him go, and his three-point-eight-million-dollar contract, eventually, was no more than a United States postal worker's starting salary: it didn't match our expenses. That meant the house we lived in had no provisions of being paid off, neither its taxes. The same went for the home he had built for his mother in Durham. There was still an outstanding mortgage on it.

Her home was the first to go into foreclosure. The sheriff seized the property, putting all of Kelly-Ann's belongings on the side of the road. We managed to get her into our house, which would follow the same doom. I was so stressed out between his reckless living, school, and working a full-time job. I didn't know what to do. Under unbearable duress one morning, I called back home to a mentally-decaying grandmother who, unbeknownst to me, ran crying to my father. Crying. Grandmother never panicked or turned to her only child.

Within ten hours, my father and a van filled with twelve goons descended on my property demanding answers. I was flustered, in a state of fear mixed with embarrassment from the way Chino from Amhurst Street aggressively pulled up on my husband, demanding answers. I hardly knew the man, but he presented himself with such extreme authority. There were gang members in my foyer, flashing the most frightening mugshots, while swaying left to right. The most notable was a petite female wearing a tapered cut and a boy's two-piece pantsuit. She had a huge nozzle, perfectly arched brows, and wore no makeup. It appeared she was the number two in charge. Just when I thought twelve goons was enough, four more pulled up with local accents. My home was under siege.

Within eight hours of my father, et al.'s hostile appearance, most of the furniture and all of my belongings were relocated to the house I'd purchased in Kelvin's hometown of Raleigh a month after our wedding. From visiting there several times since I'd known him, I took a liking to the town. I managed to find a realtor, and purchase a nice piece of property. I used it for short-term rentals. Thankfully, during this time, it had been vacant for the past two months.

On the way to Raleigh, my father suggested I return to Jersey "and give Kelvin time to figure his shit out." I refused, reminding him of my job and school. I was midway through my master's program at the time and needed the clinical experience to reach my goal. I couldn't drop everything and leave. Besides, I'd been an ex-pat at that point, and didn't feel I had any "home" to return to. In his own brusque way, my father begged me. He shared how he didn't trust Kelvin and never had. My father even blurted he knew my husband was a fiend by their second meeting. That angered me. Why not tell me then? He only urged me to buy property as a backup plan. The head- and heartache that pertinent information could have saved me.

I was still young, now insecure, secretive as hell, prideful, and virtually unfeeling. I moved through my education like a machine. My life was all about the books and clinical work. There was no emotion attached. My pursuit wasn't ambition in North Carolina so much as it was survival. I was trying to make it day to day with my sanity in a foreign world with a man I didn't know.

Needless to say, I stayed behind when my father's goons mounted up to leave. Before they did, two additional cars filled with more gang members arrived at my place in Raleigh. Kelvin and Kelly-Ann eventually made it to the house, too. His face was swollen with dry blood, and a sole mark on his forehead. Kelvin looked beaten. He wouldn't give me any eye contact, and neither would his mother.

My father may have acted quickly on his mission, but the man's thuggery had been well thought out. The last of the thugs to arrive were local gang members. My father explained to Kelvin how, just because his daughter was living in Kelvin's hometown, it didn't mean she would not have protection. The man demonstrated he had eyes and "guns" everywhere, including Charlotte and Raleigh.

Not too long after that day, I realized how significant that move was. Raleigh loved Kelvin. He was their golden child, even after he'd gotten cut from the *League*. They all knew and supported him, from the police department, to the mechanics and the hospitals, which was how I got my current gig. I didn't exactly qualify for it after graduating from my master's program. It was because of

Kelvin's former coaches and trainers who knew people with pull at the hospital that I'd secured a job I should have had at least seven more years of experience to qualify for. I'd been there for three years, excelling. I ignored the naysayers and learned my craft to earn my title.

But I could never learn how to connect with my husband. My father, during the one visit, may have convinced Kelvin to not harm me physically, but all bets were off for my mental and emotional health. Kelvin never shared a bedroom with me in Raleigh. He moved into the finished basement, where he'd have the privacy he preferred to get high and disconnect from the world to his content. This meant no intimacy, no physical contact, no building, no repair —essentially no start—to the marriage we'd been in for three years at this point.

Yeah. In between his bouts of drug binges, I'd support him through recovery attempts by way of programs. If Kelvin stayed clean for a month or two, we'd occasionally go out to dinner and perhaps a movie. We'd even have sex sparingly during years four and six of our marriage. However, there was no magic, no romance, no longing. Just two adults trying to function through a union they signed up for. Even that came to an end in year six.

Kelvin and I hadn't been intimate in two years. I couldn't do it anymore. The attraction I once had for Kelvin had withered over the years of seeing him leaning over while standing, falling into a reposed state charged by heroine. The blisters and crust around his mouth from poor hygiene and a lack of grooming. The glassy, reddened eyes. The slurred speech. The stealing, the lying, the blackouts, and despondent episodes. None of it stroked my libido. And if I were honest, Kelvin hadn't been banging down my door for sex either. The chemistry simply faded.

I was very naïve fresh into my legal adult years. This was something I now realized. It was also why I'd clawed through the first five years of my marriage. I held myself accountable for my decision. It didn't matter that it was naivety. It was a decision, and I'd chosen wrong. Instead of allowing myself to be a victim, I took accountability by understanding what I'd done.

Often, I wondered if my maturity back then would have been sharper with my mother still around. I took Grandmother's guidance because that was what her guardianship had always represented to me. Not having a mother for Lennox meant no back rubs, no soft touches during loving instruction. No smiles and giggles to develop me against firm discipline. I'd been with my grandmother since I was a preschooler, and never once had I confused her maternal role in my life. She'd always been Grandmother, never mother.

Grandmother wasn't affectionate physically or emotionally. She was far from a mean woman, but tended to instruct from a femininize formality approach. In other words, her intention was to prepare me to be a woman suitable for the triple M destiny: marriage, motherhood, and ministry. This included college. She stayed on me about my grades until I got into a decent state college. Boy was I not prepared for how swiftly she'd turn over the reins of my custody once there.

It was under her advisory and resolute push that I married as soon as I could the moment I was of legal age. It was faulty advisement and had done damage no one considered. In our fighting throughout the years over his addiction, Kelvin would resort to calling me ugly and speaking ill of my family. He used words and nasty energy to attack my image and existence. Did I believe him when he called me ugly? No.

However, after being told that so many times, I'd developed a coping mechanism which was work and school, when I was still enrolled. Between those two, I didn't treat myself well. No trips to the beauty salon, nail salon, or regular grooming maintenance despite my well-endowed salary. I worked, schooled, and even slept in scrubs until I got the position at the hospital. The first six months, I rotated between four suits.

It wasn't until the musician reappeared in my world that I grew a conscience about my appearance. And when I stepped up my game by way of exercising, eating well, and getting groomed regularly, Kelvin's disdain for me tripled. Each conversation with my husband turned volatile for him. When Kelvin was irritated, I'd be every ugly, selfish, stuck-up bitch he could conjure. And I took it, having become immune to his vitriol.

So, to answer my therapist's question, 'no.' I could not tell him I was divorcing him, and expect him to believe me and act accordingly. I honestly didn't think he'd care.

Shaking my head, I murmured, "I don't think the focus should be in the details with this, so much as it's in the end goal. I'm done. I'm leaving him."

Slowly, her head began to bob as her mouth twisted. "I see. And last week?"

"Last week?"

"Your time in Jersey. Specifically, your time with Tobias. Has that inspired this decision?"

I scoffed. "I've been seeing you for almost two years. I've always shared my desire to break free from my marriage."

"You also began seeing me at the push of Mr. Tobias Elliott." She shook her head as my eyes widened. "It's my role to be sure your motives are present and clear to you. How did the week go?"

Stuck and slightly embarrassed, I dawdled.

She cleared her throat. "You said he pointed out how you rub your lips together when stuck in your head. Why is sharing about it this difficult?"

"Because I slept with him."

I watched as her face opened in surprise for a split second before she relaxed the muscles. "Okay."

"Is it really?"

"You don't think it is?"

"I think it's caused me to lose my mind, if I can be honest."

Her head swayed to the side. "Why?"

I caught myself this time and separated my lips.

"Was it a bad experience?"

"It was…" Tears welled in my eyes "…beautiful. It was absolutely perfect—almost."

"What kept it from perfection?"

"The fact that it felt rushed. My time with him was so limited. We didn't even talk much. I mean… The first night I got there, he fed me then left to take a meeting with Dale. I was starry-eyed, reminding him how well he could sing and stuff. Then I had my itinerary with the girls." I shrugged, truly bothered by this over the past four days since being back home. "I've shared with you my favorite feature of Tobias is his conversation. He's so transparent and open to whatever. There's no machismo with him. But because of my 'cloak-and-dagger' agenda up there, I didn't 'see' him."

"But you managed the time to have sex."

It felt like a bucket of ice water had been doused over me. My mouth twisted in embarrassment. I pulled at a piece of lint on the hem of my skirt. "It was organic."

"As it should be."

"Then why, again, am I feeling like you're telling me I did something wrong?"

"It's not my intention to make you feel that way, Lennox."

"Then what is it?"

She froze, appearing to be regrouping, then took a deep breath. "What's your plan?"

"You mean the divorce?"

"I mean all of it. What is the plan?"

"Well…" I caught my lip-rub. *Damn you, Tobias!* "I'm scheduled to meet with the divorce attorney next week." She was in the middle of litigation, and wanted to see me instead of having her paralegal take my information. A Black counselor-at-law, she was recommended by a friend of a colleague. "I guess I'll know what's next after that."

"Really?" she asked with hiked brows. "Once the divorce is finalized, what will happen to your mother-in-law? Scott? Will you remain in North Carolina? What would become of your relationship—*well*, affair now—with Tobias?"

"What do you mean what would become of it?"

"Will it be pursued full-force, in earnest?"

Taking a deep breath, I considered that. Of course, I thought about what my post-Kelvin Richardson world would look like. I thought about it all, but never the fine details. Scott was still so young and vulnerable. Kelly-Ann couldn't be trusted to provide him stability because she wasn't exactly independent herself. She was now a couch potato and bike-week enthusiast.

Yup.

The woman lived to go down to bike week in Myrtle Beach. She did not own a motorcycle, but would rent a mobility scooter to go look at men on their *Harley's* for the entire event. That was the extent of Kelly-Ann Richardson's life. No matter what my mother-in-law decided to do with her existence, it was hers to decide. I didn't have Scott's future worked out now that his mother would be getting released soon. But one thing was for sure.

"I'm going to be with Tobias."

My therapist blinked successively. I nodded my head in the same fashion to express my confidence.

"So, you're leaving North Carolina, and moving into his home? Didn't you mention wanting to leave your job and work in the nail industry?"

My face went tight. I had. It had been a burning desire of mine to effectively secure a chain of Black-owned nail salons along the Eastern border. The idea was broad, more or less in training and management, rather than providing manicures and pedicures myself. But it had been a dream of mine for years. I had very few of them, another being giving this thing between Tobias and me a shot. But packing up my life down here and shipping it to his address in New Jersey? That plan seemed...wrong. I didn't want to lose my security and independence. Hell, my fantasy was to walk around my empty home ass-naked after work. That could be viewed as an imposition on Tobias' property. I would never impose on another man or be dependent on him.

My belly churned as I fingered through my hair.

"*Nuh*—yeah." I cleared my throat. "Not exactly all of those things in that order."

A cool smile spread upon her face. "Then we have some work to do, don't we?"

Chapter Eight

Tobias

Coach L plucked a string on his ax while clutching a burning stogie between his teeth, then went back to polishing it.

"What's that on there?" Raj, sitting at the small table with us, asked him.

Launz's face stretched horizontally. "This would be my lil' Laundria Zo Buggy's—."

"That's drool?" Raj's face was twisted.

"Drool, food, juice…who knows," Launz muttered, polishing the wood. "I play to my baby at least once a week when I'm home."

"Respect." I saluted him. "How old is she now?"

"Baby girl just turned one last week while I was on the road."

Raj snorted. "Feels like she was just born."

"Yup. And now PaPa's Zo Buggy's one…and a messy eater." His scrub was concentrated on a particular spot now. "Her birthday party cost her grandmother a few bricks." Launz chuckled, wiping down the guitar. "I skipped parenting babies, so I'm all out of the loop with what's appropriate."

"I am, too." Raj snickered. "I'd go crazy if I had a daughter. Word up: I'm so grateful the only female precious to me was delivered as a grown ass woman. She'll kick my ass if I fuck around too much."

I found that funny as shit. His wife, Wynter, was no damsel in distress, that was for sure. She checked Raj's moody ass each time it was needed. *She* was needed. Wynter, a former social worker of sorts, managed her husband's mercurial episodes like a champ.

"*Mauve*, Coach?" the bartender on duty at Raj's club, *Checkerboard*, called from across the room.

"Coach?" I barked back.

"I know!" Raj chuckled. "Who the hell keep the lights on in this joint? Who's getting your 'Coach-happy-ass' paid every week?"

The guy behind the bar laughed. "My *Kings* winning this season is just as important as me eating, boss. You feel me?"

Launz Pierce, also known as Coach L by many, was the head football coach of the *Connecticut Kings*. He was in the thick of his season, but found a few hours out of his busy schedule to tend to one of his passions: music. He'd been playing for R&B superstar and actor, Ragee McKinnon, for years when not pursuing his career in the professional football *League*. Launz was a studio guitarist for Raj and not a touring one because of his schedule. This meant Launz created the tunes that his ax-peers would have to follow and reproduce when Raj went out on tours or did spot performances.

I laughed while Raj shook his head, going back down to his device where he was reading lyrics I'd written to a number we were going to expound on tonight, grow them.

"That'll do, my guy," Launz replied to the bartender, finding it funny, too. "You do grandiose celebrations for lil' Elia?"

"I think she's had her fair share." I scrolled through the text notifications on my phone. "When she was younger, I let Krista figure all that shit out. Now, she's eight with a damn appetite for entertainment. She called me last week, talking about *Disney* for Christmas."

"Damn!" Raj groaned, blowing out smoke from his cigar.

"Yup." I nodded. "Having girls can be tricky. I'm sure if I had a son, shit wouldn't be so sweet."

"Damn sure wouldn't." Raj chuckled.

"Yeah. With boys, you gotta prepare them to be providers, not to be tricked on," Coach L noted.

"Yup." I agreed.

"You going?" Raj asked about *Disney*.

I shook my head then placed my phone on the table to stretch back in the chair and rub my face. "Not even invited, bruh. Only my wallet." We all laughed at that. "It's crazy because she's already spending Thanksgiving with her moms' people out in Boston."

"Damn." Coach L's eyes pitied me. "No end-of-the-year holidays with the old man, huhn? Your end-of-the-year in parenting is sounding a lot like my shit all of my kid's childhood."

Launz may have delivered it lightly, but it was still fucked up that dude had a son for twenty years before he knew. Lil' Zo's mother contacted Launz out of the blue with the news. I knew it had been a hill for father, mother, and son to climb, but they were making it work. I guessed the silver lining in the whole nightmare was that Launz was there when Lil' Zo's baby, Alaundria, was born. Baby girl had been the apple of her grandfather's eye. There could be beauty buried beneath years of pain, I figured. After spending time with his family for over a year now, I could see there was authenticity in their recently-formed unit.

My sad ass wondered if the same could be true for me. But as I scrolled through my text messages, seeing the last correspondence from Lennox had been the night before she left, a week ago, I wondered if miracles of love happened only once every seventy years, or simply to coaches in the football *League*.

Lennox hadn't checked in. Typically, we'd speak every day, but my pride flared whenever she left since the first kiss we shared about a year and a half ago. It felt unnatural to let her go after tasting her, exchanging that deep level of intimacy. The more of her time she gave to me, and allowed our affection to grow, the more I weakened as a man. She held all the cards, including my control. I couldn't lie: the shit fucked me up. I hadn't eaten much in days, and sleep was a foreign concept. All I'd been able to do since she left was pour my broken emotions into work. I'd written thirteen songs, even some for Raj. And the nigga ain't have a project rollout in sight.

"You know you can pull up to the crib for the holidays. Wynter loves your Zen ass." Raj shook his head.

Chuckling, I placed my palm to my chest. "Respect to Mrs. McKinnon." Then I took a deep breath. "I'll figure something out."

Launz took a deep pull from his cigar. "I'm beastin' to hear this new material. You got some heat, Tobias?"

"Yo," I exhaled, overwhelmed by exhaustion and passion at the same damn time. "My shit's heavy," I muttered. Raj, to the right of me looked up from the device, the motion so damn fast, it had me glancing his way. "What?"

"Your 'shits' as in plural or possessive?" Raj wanted to know, and I understood why.

A couple of years ago, I wrote a song for his album coining the phrase "my shit's heavy" which referenced a man's balls being full. A man's balls being full would essentially mean he needed a release to empty them. "Content" men usually kept empty balls, which meant they were getting sexual releases regularly.

The phrase didn't catch on like "be my whore," a line Raj riffed at the end of a track, causing a viral moment. But it had been adopted by the culture. So, when I said my "shit's heavy," Raj apparently needed clarification.

"Ah, shit!" He reclined in his seat. "You seen her recently—ahh, man!" he groaned, cupping his face. "It all makes sense now!"

"What?" Launz's forehead wrinkled, eyes swinging between Raj and me.

"Lennox, man," Raj explained. "The nigga seen Lennox!"

Coach's eyes blew up. "Oh! Really? Her?"

"Yeah!" Raj answered for me. "It all makes fuckin' sense now. You calling me the minute I stepped off the damn plane to schedule this session! Yo, now that I think about it, you got my ass in a fucked up space with Blue, man. We've been away with the family for a few weeks, but she likes to have 'mommy and daddy' time when we get back. But I had to be here." He stared into space with wide eyes while pulling on his beard. "Yo, how did I miss this?"

"You get like this after seeing a woman?" Launz asked.

"Hell, yeah!" Raj, once again, answered for me. And in that

moment, I believed I liked it better when he was closed off and emotionless. The color the nigga was giving now annoyed me. "For like three years, now—no. That's when y'all started kickin' it again. I would say... *Hmmm*..." He stroked his beard again. "Maybe two years. It's like every time after the nigga sees—*smells*—her, he's fucked up for a few days!" Raj turned to me. "When?"

I wanted to say it had only been a year and a half since then. I knew this because I'd never forget that second-first kiss. It was a spring night in Orlando. Lennox had just ended her last day of a conference for work. Of course, my love-sick ass made my way down there just to steal a few hours with her for three days. The resort was mediocre, but I managed, understanding it was where Lennox's employer arranged for her to stay, all expenses refunded. It was worth it.

In the morning, she'd grab breakfast at the conference hall a couple of miles away. She'd be there all day then join her colleagues for dinner. By eight-fifteen, she was all mine to kick it with in a neutral place. We didn't go to each other's room, respecting her situation. But damn, those nighttime conversations were every fucking thing. We were like two kids again, no guards or boundaries—other than sex with each other—to our dialogue. Lennox shared her budding desire to get into the nail industry. She wanted to manage and train Black practitioners to dominate the industry. I've wanted that for her since the first time she shared it with me.

That last night in Orlando had a similar natural flow of exchange, only the conversation turned risqué when she asked who I was fucking. That was weird. I knew what I wanted with the girl in the long run, so I set up and stuck to the boundaries needed to make her feel safe with me. So, when the topic went from mattress comfortability to how often the furniture was replaced to the frequency of cleaning *my* sheets after sex, I fucking fumbled.

As we sat in the cut, at night, beneath an umbrella, I turned to her, confused. Lennox's expression was determined as she stared me straight in the eye, and asked, "How many women are you sleeping with now?"

I didn't know how to answer, yet quickly decided on the truth. I told her only one woman. Lennox asked what would it take for me to stop. I shared the answer was simple: her being mine. And that was a gray area. We didn't discuss the obvious. Since we'd been back in touch, Lennox and I had grown a friendship. Yes, my feelings for her were understood, but not the focus. Her well-being had been my push, not my need to claim her from head to toe.

Then Lennox reached over slowly and leaned her face toward mine. I couldn't fucking breathe from the proximity. I fucked enough to know the play, but when you mix your fantasy woman with those parameters I'd put into place, the shit was foreign to me in the moment. But when Lennox leaned forward and pushed her pillowy lips to my mouth, the fragrant scent of her sensual needs opened my lungs, and I could breathe again. My hands gripped the sides of the patio chair because if I touched her, I'd kill the very boundaries I set in place in hopes of having her to myself one day.

Lennox's oral expression of desire was so fucking passionate. Without me touching her, she tasted around my mouth, stroked the side of my face, including my beard, shoulders, and chest like a virgin. She didn't stop until she needed air so much, she heaved, chest caving and breathing loud as she stared at me.

That was the first wake up call to my obsession with this woman. I'd never respected one so much. I used restraint to keep her. Lennox's situation was delicate. There was a child involved, and even I had to have compassion for their dilemma. But from that second on, she felt just as much mine as my own daughter, but more so because Elia would grow to have her own life to share with a knucklehead who, hopefully, wasn't JuJu. If I had my chance at Lennox once again, she'd be by my side till death did us part.

"Is this the petite, light-skin fox with the wavy hair?" Coach L asked, brows in a straight line while blowing smoke into the air.

It was at a *Kings* vs *Panthers* North Carolina home game where I ran into her three years ago. She'd just started her current role at the hospital, and one of the executives invited her to the game to welcome her in. I stepped out during halftime to meet up with a friend of mine, Sheila, who just so happened to randomly text me that morning, asking if I would be in the building to see my *Kings*.

When I told her I would, she asked if I could meet her to say hello. I was game and kept my word.

The remix to my plans occurred when I hiked through a crowd of spirited patrons, but felt a magnetic, spiritual pull to my right. I say spiritual because I faintly heard her name as I stopped to see what the urge was about. The experience was transcendental. The crowd all around slowed and the rowdy sound blurred as my sights landed on a head of sandy blonde and brown curls, deep, trancing, cognac eyes rubbing her peach-colored lips together as she gazed to the left and right.

That rare moment in time began the period of pain and the teasing pleasure of hope for me.

I never saw Sheila that day.

"That's her," Raj answered for my subdued ass.

Launz's connection to Lennox was, ironically, the next season, when he became the head coach of the *Kings*. When they played the *Giants* that year, he did me a solid. He arranged for box seats for Lennox and her girls that homecoming on my dime, of course. But he'd also gotten a chance to meet her during halftime when she and I secretly met up in a private section near the locker rooms.

Launz wouldn't let it go. "Yo, she still with Richardson?"

"You know that nigga's brother got murked by his baby's moms?"

"Murked?" Launz asked him.

Raj nodded. "Clipped, snatched, snuffed…"

"Oh." Launz's eyes blew up. "Ohhh!"

"I feel sorry for the young lady. She's good peoples. Sweet girl," Raj mumbled, glancing down at his *iPad*. "She's got me some fire hits, too. You ain't never answer my question. When did you see Lennox?"

Here we were again with someone else believing I had a pattern of sorts to my behavior. Like Grams, Smite, and Elia, it was now Ragee.

"Let's put it this way," I finally spoke, "whatever you're really interested in from what I sent you, let's try those out tonight, because everything you leave behind will be pitched to Dale."

Raj's head popped up. "Dale?"

I nodded. "He's setting up for a drop."

"When?"

"Why you asking?" Raj asked Coach L.

Everyone found that funny except for Raj.

I finally answered with a shrug. "I don't know the specifics. I don't even know if I'm going to run with him. I just know I'm inspired, and I got shit to get off my chest."

With a twisted mouth, Raj nodded. I knew him well enough to know this wasn't the end of the "will you or won't you work with him" conversation. R&B niggas could be as emotional as high-hormonal, pregnant women. There were times they wanted you the fuck out their faces, but when they needed you, their demands shook the earth. Raj and I happened to be personal friends, so my patience for him was enduring. I knew many of the demons he carried. Raj knew I had a general working knowledge of his traumatized brain. We joked about it from time to time.

Launz's attention bounced between Raj and me, waiting.

Within seconds, Raj sat up in his chair, nodded again, and exhaled. "A'ight. Let's hit this shit then."

He was the first to leave the table for the keyboard on stage.

Lennox

Daphne Taylor peered up from the stack of papers in front of her on the conference room table and pulled in a deep breath. She grabbed the papers, and dropped the bottoms of them onto the table as she exhaled visibly, staring me in the face.

The counselor-at-law was a middle-aged, mocha-skinned woman with locs and a bright smile. Her countenance could be read as cold and no-nonsense, but her tone for the past two hours had been gentle, professional, and compassionate.

"His team back then put in place a pretty iron-clad prenuptial agreement. I've seen several types in my day. This one screams 'you leave with exactly what you brought in, and what was earned while in.' He's never intended on you getting anything, not even after a specified duration of the marriage. Funny how that's turned out for him." She shrugged.

"Either way, this can go reasonably smoothly, as you're not asking Mr. Richardson for anything but the dissolution." Precisely. And it wasn't because Kelvin had anything. He'd never built an empire with his *League* money. Besides, I didn't marry him for profit. I had no agenda, unlike him. I only wanted to be loved and to provide it. The last of any significant money Kelvin possessed had been used to try to save the houses he purchased. I *couldn't* request anything because the man had *nothing*. My husband was the cautionary tale of uncultured men getting drafted with no knowledge of how to preserve or grow their salaries. "However—" When Daphne pulled in another heap of air, my stomach twisted with anxiety. I knew it was an indicator of incoming bad news. "—if he's as combative as you've described, this process can turn taxing for both parties."

"You said he doesn't have to sign anything for the divorce to happen," I reminded her.

"This is true. However, there is a process. You and Mr. Richardson still live together." She thumbed through the stack of papers, documentation of my existence on each sheet. "Your property is owned by you, which is great. You don't have to concern yourself with an expedited move. And there is a minor in question." *Scott...* "According to his custody agreement, you're the sole guardian."

I was recorded as the only legal guardian, but that wasn't the plan. We were both supposed to be in court that day, but Kelvin never showed. In fact, he disappeared for over thirty-six hours. I vividly recalled my trepidation that day. I'd known and cared deeply for Scott, but signing up to be his guardian was one of the most frightening experiences I'd ever had. He'd been living with us for some time by then, but actually signing up to be legally responsible for him—alone—was daunting.

"I am." I nodded.

"If Mr. Richardson wants to shake the table, he could challenge that. You may want to rethink your commitment to the minor. The monthly stipend you receive for his care could motivate his uncle's claim for him."

This was why it had taken so long for me to pursue this divorce. I didn't just learn of the concept recently. It wasn't sex with Tobias or another trip to homecoming that motivated the idea for me. It was Scott, and the precarious details surrounding his care. I'd somewhat gotten attached to the kid. I wanted better for him than what Kelvin and Kelly-Ann would be able to supply. Stability, emotional safety, and trust were elements Scott needed in his care. The money the state provided him would be squandered. I'd never taken a dime of it. Each month, the money is routed into a vehicle for his future.

It was something I'd still been fighting Kelvin over. He'd been requesting access to it since I signed for legal guardianship. His favorite line when I denied him was how Scott was his real nephew and not mine. So, yes. Daphne's premonition was correct. Kelvin would contest custody. Perhaps a judge would side with his claim since he was a blood relative.

I murmured, "I understand." My head spun with all the ugly fears I'd been carrying since Scott had come to live with us.

"But first thing's first." Daphne handed the stack of documents to a waiting clerk as my damp palms gripped the sides of my chair. "You need to be physically separated from Mr. Richardson for a minimum of one year and one day. Your complaint will include his drug abuse and combativeness. It's time to create a physical distance. The state of North Carolina requires it."

I realized I'd been rubbing my lips together as I nodded.

Another year before I was free; technically, three hundred sixty-six days. And finally asking Kelvin to leave could get messy. What would happen to Kelly-Ann? While I couldn't give a shit if she stayed or left, lifting the band-aid from trauma could risk the stability of living in it for so long. If I was really doing this, I had to do it. Pieces of the board would be moved and eliminated. I had to muster the courage to allow it to be. The table would shake.

"Lastly, Mrs. Richardson." My head snapped up to Daphne. "You're not requesting anything like assets or alimony from Mr. Richardson; however, you do have your property and a salary out-earning him. If this is the case when it's time to file, he can also make it difficult by requesting alimony. Some men have pride that won't allow this. However, vindictive men will request the shirt off your back. It could be for something as simple as power or as reasonable as infidelity." My jaw dropped. "I'm respectfully saying, until the divorce is absolute, conduct yourself in a manner that will protect you."

Infidelity.

Was that what Tobias represented? Did me, finally choosing us, put me at risk of finally breaking loose from this hellish nightmare I'd been living?

I was finishing up on a *WhatsApp* text conversation with an engineer in Ghana when something instinctual had my head lifting. It was Chino Brim, sauntering into the formally decorated reception area, nearing me. He stopped, face screwed as recognition kicked in.

"Yo," was how he greeted me.

"Chino," I returned, offering him a shake instead of dap, sensing his guard up from my presence.

Lennox acquired her height from her father. She was five feet and three inches, which was only three inches shorter than her old man. Like him, she had an oak skin tone. However, hers wasn't marred by years of hard living: physical combat, gang tattoos, a hot temperament creating a permanent scowl, or chain smoking staining her lips and teeth like Chino. She'd also inherited his hair—thick, long, and silky curls. The man closely resembled a Compton Crip instead of a Jersey Blood, hence the name Brim. That was his local set. It was eerie how much my girl favored a man feared by countless people around the way.

He tossed his chin in the air. "Whatchu' here for?"

"To visit Pastor Williams like you."

"Since when you come see Mom Dukes?" His brows formed a straight line.

In my rash decision to finally return here, I damn sure didn't calculate running into this guy. This was exactly why it is never good to act on emotions. I typically stayed three steps ahead in planning, always expecting every possible outcome. It was similar to my thoughts on what state of mind Pastor Williams would be in today. I had to plan for everything and expect nothing. So, now, with the bully of E.O. conjuring volatile, high-energy fuel to spit fire my way, I had to be prepared. Uncle Smite being Chino's close friend didn't make me immune to his contempt. Just like with any other hot-headed goon, I had to stand ten toes down.

I was not afraid of Chino Curry. I showed him respect because of Smite and Lennox. That should not have been confused for fear, similar to other old ass men or young cats my age. I'd beat the living shit out of Chino's old head ass and wouldn't think much more of it. But that was impossible. No matter how estranged Lennox and Chino's relationship, I couldn't violate her father's G card like that. I also couldn't bring conflict to Smite.

So, thoughtfully, I pushed against the tension by asking, "How is she today?"

"Since when do you come see Mom Dukes?" he repeated.

It had been a few years; five to be exact. When she was first transitioned here, I came almost right away out of respect. Although I'd stopped fucking with Pastor Williams that summer after she kicked my young ass to the curb when Richardson came into the picture—and she found out I was trying to date her granddaughter —hearing she'd lost some of her faculties pinched at my humanity. The first visit was hard because she was heavily medicated. She was new to the place, and they were still adjusting the treatment plan for her. Pastor Williams didn't recognize me, but I doubt she had many "present" days back then from her changes. I told her and myself I'd return. It didn't happen any time soon.

Guilt had finally mounted in my heart, and I returned almost two years later. That visit hit different because Pastor Williams was on a better concoction of meds fit for her condition. She was coherent but had no recollection of me. The woman even prayed for me. I didn't know how to take that, and gave up on visiting her again. Besides, I carried a conflict in my heart. I'd still been angry.

"I've been to see her since she's been here."

"Why?" Chino's glaring only sharpened.

I snorted. "She's Lennox's grandmother." That's as far as I'd go to explain myself.

Chino shifted weight in his legs, his stare game strong.

"Mr. Elliott." It was the short dude with a sharp part on the left side of his head, orange hair slicked down on either side. He motioned toward the flowers. "Linda will take this gorgeous bouquet for you and prepare it for Pastor Williams," He took the big ass arrangement I'd brought with me from a nearby table. "And I'll take you to her suite."

"Thanks," I returned to smiley faces as he handed it over to the woman of Asian descent, who was equal to his height.

"Right this way." He motioned for me to follow him.

I did as my attention went back to the stewing O.G. dragon. "You good with this?"

"Look, man." He swiped his nose with a deep sniffle. "She a lil'…" He hesitated and I lost his eyes. "She may be in a fucked up mood." When his attention rolled up to me again, out of nowhere, Chino snorted, "You still got it for that fuckin' girl, man."

He was clowning me, or trying to. I ain't have time for that shit. "Respect, O.G.C." I patted my chest while looking back down at my buzzing phone.

I followed after the escort, hoping Chino was cool with me leaving the conversation there. Shit was so complicated between all of us; I didn't like giving energy to Chino or his mother, yet here I was.

When I was let into her suite, old school gospel filled the air. Pastor Williams was being assisted into a seat at the table in her small kitchenette area. What was striking was her preserved beauty and youthful body. No, Pastor Williams was not still a size eight, but she wasn't shaped like a woman in her mid-seventies either. She'd put on a little weight over the years, and clearly had become frail, losing muscle tone.

"Her son just left," the aide assisting her explained. "She got a little worked up. So, we just got freshened up while waiting on you to come in. Can I offer you anything?"

My eyes scanned the aide and the little guy who'd escorted me in. "No. I'm good. Thanks."

The razor-sharp part guy gave a clean bow before turning to leave.

"I'm going to check in on a few things for her evening routine, and will be right back," the aide offered before following the trail of her colleague. "If you need anything, the call button is located there and there." She winked and pointed before closing the door.

I nodded while heading to the table. Once seated, I noticed Pastor Williams smiling at me. The structure of her face had descended from gravity brought on by age, but beauty just as present. Her dark pink lipstick was in place.

"I know why you're here. The Lord as my witness, I was waiting on you to come." Her words shocked the shit out of me.

"Oh, yeah?"

She nodded, pulling a bowl of grapes closer to herself. "That young man who just left here. He was talking about the young lady who used to go to my church." Pastor Williams' shaky hand lifted to her forehead just beneath her wig. Her nails were almost the same color as her lips. She was confused.

"Lennox?"

"Yeah." She blinked. "Something like that."

"Lennox."

"Yeah. That's it." She rolled her eyes. "I can't keep track of all the young folks I ministered to down the years. I had lots of sons and daughters in Christ. Heck, I even got some here. You know? That young man kept calling me 'Ma.' If I had a penny for all the..." She plucked a grape into her mouth and shook her head.

Pastor Williams didn't know Chino today. More than that, Chino came here talking about Lennox?

"What did he say?"

"You know what he said!" she snapped, eyes hitting me hard. "Listen, if she's in a marriage she ain't happy with, she should go. Life ain't like it was when I was a young girl. Women needed men for a living. A nice home, babies, a car, and stuff like that. He said I told her to marry him. He always talking about her. I ain't..." She motioned to her head. "I ain't sharp like I used to be. I'm getting old, got old people's problems. When y'all young folks gonna start to take responsibility for ya'selves and make good, godly choices?"

She waited for an answer.

I was fucked up.

After a pause, I asked, "Do you remember me?"

"Stop asking me that, young man! Just stop!" She leaned into her balled fist, eyes closed over the table. "I'm sick of people asking me that. I'm old. Can't I just have a little bit of peace?"

Ain't this some shit?

She wanted peace, some shit she disturbed in my life eight... nine years ago. And here I was, fucked up, unable to move on from this shit. I loved Lennox. She was that fire in me I thought I managed to put out when she left for North Carolina to marry Richardson. And now, I was back here, visiting the mentally-compromised woman who caused the second most fucked up dilemma of my life.

Eleven fucking days.

I hadn't eaten much or slept well in eleven fucking days. My last smell of her...sight and taste of Lennox was eleven days ago. She hadn't called, and neither had I. Something felt different. This shit was different. Since our first kiss when she'd leave, I'd allow my pride to flare, angry about her belonging to another man. This time, my thoughts were to give her a chance to choose me. She did, after all, say she'd return to me 'soon.' Whatever the fuck that meant, I had to give her space to make her decision.

But...

Fuck! It had been hard after having made love to her. After hearing her cries of pleasure and the evidence of it squirting onto my tongue. I'd finally gotten a chance to taste her garden, some shit I was too young and inexperienced to do when I met her years ago. The thing I tried to get up the courage to do, but had the time fucking snatched away because of *this* lady.

Lennox wasn't just the typical girl a guy crushed on. She was *that* fucking one for me. I'd had the distinct privilege of snagging more than my fair share of women. I was a fit guy with money and influence, and not all that bad looking in the face. Women weren't a fixation for me. They were endless wells for companionship and sensual exercise. I fucked a lot. And I fucked well. My pallet for sex was particular, and I had found my tribe of women just as specific.

Women were the salt of the earth, necessary to sustain human existence. I truly respected them. But I was no needy man. I was no sap for companionship or romance. In fact, there were many things I enjoyed and preferred over the years as a single man. But when you added Lennox to the equation, division turned into wild multiplication, sending my ass over the bridge in a damn straight jacket. I was up here, at a nursing care facility like a damn lovesick teenager or worse: one of those guys in sappy ass romance movies. This woman wasn't well. There wasn't shit she could do for me.

"Okay, Pastor Williams." The aide had returned. "How are we

feeling?" She went straight into the kitchen to place a tray of what I assumed to be meds down on the counter.

"Tired." Pastor Williams shook her head, face squeezing to communicate her irritated mood. "I need to lay down."

"Okay." The woman looked my way as she approached the pastor.

Before she could speak, I nodded my understanding the visit was over.

I watched as she assisted the pastor to her feet and, eventually, they took off to the back of her suite. Just as I stood to leave, I heard, "You know, now I remember." I glanced over to her. Pastor Williams craned her neck over her shoulder to see me. "I helped out in good marriages. There was this...beautiful young lady. Had natural curly hair like mine—" She giggled. "—like mine is under these wigs. Now that I think about it..." Her eyes squinted. "She had the most gorgeous eyes; something like mine, too. Short little thing, but so pretty. Anyway... She was being courted by a basketball or football player. That man had a bright future ahead of him, and he wanted this young lady in my church. I encouraged them to become one."

She shrugged. "They're still married till this day. Happy, too, I bet." Then her face tightened again. "I wonder if they had any children. You and that young man need to go find her. She'll tell you, I'm all for healthy marriages. Should be easy to find her. I bet that husband of hers is a big superstar now." Slowly, Pastor Williams turned forward, and they continued their stroll to her bedroom.

The woman was officially living on a different planet. The defective decisions she made in the past no longer existed in her orbit. If she couldn't remember the year and decision she made that had affected my life so drastically, why should my ass still hold on to the resentment for it? I decided to let the shit go.

After a deep breath, I left Pastor Williams to her mental capacity, vowing to never see the woman again. It was pointless. I didn't exist in her world. Didn't now. Never had.

Chapter Nine

Lennox

"Okay," I took a deep breath, attention going over to the clock posted over the door of the conference room. "I told you I'd try to have you out of here before lunch." My eyes gazed over the room of twenty-seven vexed directors and vice presidents of the hospital system.

They hated me in the moment, I understood. It came with my role, so I'd typically allow it to roll off my back. Today, my resolve was compromised after a three and a half hour training. I introduced and mandated a new program in our electronic system to maintain quality control, something not uncommon for my role as the vice president of quality and risk management. A part of my job was to seek out and research tools to help the facility minimize waste and maximize quality care for its constituents.

My job.

Never in a million years, when I was back in undergrad studying nursing, did I believe I'd be in administration. I wanted to take care of the sick and teach proper healthcare. I wanted to be a nurturer. Instead, my educational path afforded me an opportunity to earn well, all to be a regulator in the field. Again, I wasn't qualified for this role when it availed itself. However, for more than two years, I worked my ass off to prove I had not only been capable to fill the shoes, but personified the title. This meant I had few friends here at work. I'd been able to shield myself against the acrimony, but as of late, my defenses had been compromised.

My clothes had been fitting looser, and my body had been fatigued from working out twice a day. I hadn't been sleeping much. My brain would not shut down to allow for daily restarts. But work? Work had been a natural function, a respite from my domestic turbulence. Until lately.

Today, I inched my way through this training, frequently checking the clock. I needed alone time. There was so much to work out, so many possibilities to sift through. My brain was on fire, and my body was tense and stiff at times.

"If there will be no more questions..." My attention circled faceless bodies, waiting for one. After seconds long, I closed. "Okay. Thanks for your time today. Take the weekend to enjoy, and on Monday, the new features will be installed and integrated into the IIS database." I offered a neck bow before turning to my assistant, silently requesting she collect and pack up my work tools.

I threaded through grumbling, white coats and stiff suits, and began down the hall to the bank of elevators on the other end of the building. This was my common practice to give my colleagues the privacy they wanted to curse my ass out for adding to their workloads. Just as I turned the corner, Ross Lane, the chief of operations for the hospital system appeared.

I didn't expect to see him. He was due to be in an even more intense meeting. Today, the chiefs were in their semi-annual check-in with the head of the hospital systems. Our operations team had always taken the bulk of the agenda, meaning the heat was on us to eliminate waste and preserve budgets. Why was Lane moseying around the hall? His thin lips curled into a smile when our eyes met, arms folded over each other.

"I heard you'd been in a meeting," he began as I slowed near him.

Straightening my shoulders, I returned, "You mean returning home from war within an inch of my life?"

Lane snorted. "It was a great call you made, rolling out the new features on the IIS. I didn't think the time was right, but as our golden girl here, you're always two steps above the fray."

The term "golden girl" reminded me of what Kelvin had once been to Raleigh. And thinking of that reminded me of how I landed this gig. Feeling my cell phone vibrate in my hand, my appreciative smile was grim.

Then Lane pivoted, looking away. "Take the rest of the day off, Lennox. Your shoulders are visibly heavy. Your countenance is twisted into a knot. You need detangling. You can unwind from time to time, you know?"

Huhn?

"Shouldn't I stick around in case you need backing?" I tossed my chin toward the executive boardroom.

Lane shook his head, thin lips poking into the air. "Not today. My golden girl's busted her ass, bringing in systems that'll reduce spending potentially by twenty-one percent next quarter. Your constituents may be ready to grate your ass, but mine will be eating out of my hands by the time I'm done today." He winked before turning on his heel for the boardroom.

I continued down toward the elevator when my phone vibrated again. I'd forgotten to check it. Thinking of all the shit I had waiting for me in my office, including personal dilemmas, I chanced a glance at my phone. The elevator dinged, and when it opened, a gang of people exited off. I threaded through while deciphering the notification. I stopped dead in the center of the car.

It was a text.

It was him.

Tobias.

My heart pounded hard on the wall of my chest. The saliva in my mouth completely dried. He shared his location. What did that mean? I stared at the phone as though it was foreign.

"Floor?" someone asked behind me.

Wildly, I turned around and found a transportation aide. "*Ummmm…*" I blinked, trying to control my breathing. "Seventh." I swallowed nothing. "Thank you." Then I moved to the back of the car, giving the man with the empty gurney bed his personal space.

My attention returned to my phone. Tobias had never done this. I wasn't familiar with the *Find My* feature. But there he was, his profile embedded into a map. Adjusting it, I saw he was here in North Carolina. Chapel Hill.

I dropped the phone to my thigh. Chapel Hill was just over forty minutes from the hospital. Tobias couldn't be in North Carolina. *Could he?* It felt like a needle prick happened in my skull, and tensioned air had been released. The relief was needed, but was also causing a ruckus in my heart. Then I felt a gripping on my skull, anxiety manifesting.

"Ma'am," someone called out. Blinking again, I felt the throbbing of my lips, which meant I was rubbing them together. Then the transportation aide came into view. "The seventh floor?" He motioned toward the panel.

Following his vision, I snapped out of my stupor. "*Thank*—sorry about that." The clicking of my heels helped keep me grounded as I made my way out of the elevator. On my way to my office, I thought of how convenient it was that my boss told me to take the rest of the day off. It was not uncommon for someone on my level to use that autonomy, but on a day like today, when the big wigs were meeting, going missing could be a bad idea.

And I'd be doing just that: going missing to investigate this shared location.

The husky Hispanic guard at the community gate tilted his cap. "Can I help you, ma'am?"

When I felt the gloss on my mouth, I realized I was rubbing my lips together. "Yes. Visiting." What else would I say?

He nodded. "Who, ma'am?"

"Ummm…" I peered down at my phone. "Seven, six, six, seven."

"Your name?"

Noooo!

I scoffed, fidgeting with my hair.

"I have it on the list, ma'am." He smirked. "I just need to verify it?"

Did I really come all the way out to Chapel Hill to embarrass myself?

No. I came despite the risk of humiliation of a ghost of Tobias being in town. What were the odds?

"Richardson," I finally answered. "Lennox Richardson."

He smacked his teeth and inhaled. "I have a Lennox, but not Richardson."

"Curry?"

He nodded then frowned. "Actually, I have Curry and Elliott. Lennox Curry and Lennox Elliott."

Butterflies erupted in my belly, and I could no longer feel my feet when I squealed, "That would be me, *too*—them. Those names would do."

"Okay. Have a good day, ma'am." He pressed a button in his little booth and the gate ascended.

The car jutted when I pushed down on the accelerator because I still couldn't feel my feet. The GPS guided me to the large, three-story home. This entire gated community was affluent. Sprawling lands, sizeable estates. Immediately, I was enveloped in an escaped community, not too far from where I worked or lived, however, nestled away from what felt familiar.

And you have no idea if someone stole the phone of the man you've slept with to lure you to a place where it can be proven you're a cheater. You haven't filed yet. If you're caught, you're screwed, Lennox!

My stomach rolled into knots straightaway, and my right knee began to bounce with anxiousness. The possibility of Kelvin being savvy enough to pull together a scheme like this was farfetched. I hadn't told him I'd be initiating a divorce yet. Still, I was crazy. Had to be. I didn't do shared locations! No call to confirm the recipient.

No text. Just an impulsive need to see him, connect with him…to forget every impending ounce of drama from my unsettled world.

When I made it to the property, I drove down a long driveway surrounded by a forest before the house came into clear view along with two moving trucks, *a Range Rover, Mercedes Sprinter,* a *Porsche 911 Carrera GTS,* and an older model *Escalade.* I pulled behind the trucks against the circular driveway. The back to one was open, the cargo empty. Men in moving gear—knee pads, industrial back braces, and boots—carried large boxes into the garage. After closing the door to my car, I followed them inside the three-car garage. Once they caught on to me, the brief head-to-toe gapes reminded me of my own work gear. A skirt suit, hosiery, and high heels. I left my purse in the car, opting for just my phone and keys.

While ambling inside, there were people coming out. Mostly men, but a woman who appeared to be Middle Eastern, with smooth tortilla skin, fingered her hair while sauntering out of the open house and into the garage. I realized just how thick my desperation was as I continued into the house as though I belonged there. It didn't take long for this whole fishing expedition to conclude. Just into what seemed to be the split, lower level was a congregated group.

The moment I was able to identify the centered energy, those naturally hooded eyes were on me. On sight. The recognition of the man instantly eased my tendons, tingled my nipples, and put all the stressors I'd felt in the rearview. Since seeing him three years ago at the *Kings* game, his heavy presence had been transporting, taking me to peaceful realms, so far away from my frenetic reality. When in close proximity with him, time didn't exist. Outside of his calming countenance and air, every other element was a nuisance.

Tobias wore a black track suit with a *Connecticut Kings* fitted baseball cap. Such identifiable Northern swag here in the country. His attention drawn to me caused the group around him to do the same. I watched as his eyes traveled down my body, studying my shoes. Simple black *Ralph Lauren Celia* pumps shouldn't have commanded such an extended inspection, but it dawned on me: he'd never seen me in work gear.

My belly flipped and sex contracted unexpectedly. I swallowed involuntarily and switched the weight on my legs, feeling instantly self-conscious. He was here. Tobias was in North Carolina, less than an hour away from my job. Staring at him in this strange home felt like an out-of-body experience. Suddenly, I craved his touch, those soft full lips, and big hands. I wanted to smooth my fingers over the thick, sheen waves of his hair beneath that cap. Flashes of his hairy, broad chest came to mind. His capable and globular arms—I wanted it all. Then his attention shifted. I quietly shivered in its wake.

"Attach those *JBL 530*s, and make sure the sound is crisp," Tobias issued an order.

A guy with heavily tinted sunglasses scratched the back of his head while twisting his mouth. "D been throwin' them back and blowin' them out. He ain't chill yet."

Tobias snorted, "That's exactly why I need those speakers on point. He needs to hear what he sounds like when he ain't in gear. All that alcohol and cigar shit ends this week. I got some shit that'll inspire the fuck out of his ass. No autotune, no vocoding. Straight vocals." Then he turned back to the gentlemen with back braces. "That everything?" When the men nodded in affirmation, Tobias pulled out a wad of cash and peeled off a few bills. "Respect," he offered when handing it over to one of them.

The guys in industrial gear left the group, and the sunglasses guy explained, "A'ight. I gotta go pick up a few things for D. I'll holla."

He and Tobias shook hands. "All love," Tobias muttered. "Go, be manager to that nigga. Make this process easier on me."

The sunglasses guy let out a hard titter. "Ha! Ain't shit I can do that'll make your work with that man easier."

Several of the men followed "sunglasses" out. Just when I thought we'd be alone, the brown woman with long, glossy hair reemerged. "So, we're going with the crab bisque and lobster stuffed *sal*—no." She shook her head, appearing to be correcting herself. Just the mention of all that food reminded me I was missing lunch for this expedition. I didn't give a fuck. *Tobias is in town!* "It's the lobster bisque and crab stuffed wild king salmon."

Tobias' big arms wrapped around his torso as he nodded. "You got it."

"Okay. Cool." She began backing away. "I'll be back in a couple of hours."

"I'm locking up," Tobias told her. "So, use the key."

"Okay!" she shouted back, headed into the garage.

Tobias' eyes were on me again, but he still didn't speak. When he rounded me for the garage, the scent of his cologne made my lids close in helpless shame. Unable to move from the same location I'd landed in when I arrived, I could hear the closing of the garage doors happening behind me. Within seconds, Tobias was back in sight. A twitching of his neck was his command for me to follow him. Without question, I did. I studied his broad shoulders, unhurried yet steady pace, and natural swag in his gait. He held a device in his hands, tapping into it until I heard a chime resembling an alarm system.

I followed him into the home with two storied-ceilings and chestnut beams in the great room. The kitchen was an open design. Hardwood flooring ran throughout the entire main level. We traveled down a hall and into what looked to be the formal living room. The space was filled with plush furniture, and a thick wool carpet in the center. Tobias took a seat on a beautiful sofa with intricate floral stitching into ivory upholstery and opulent, glossed chestnut wood framing.

I remained in the door frame, taking in the grandeur of the décor. There were no pictures of people to be found, but the home was attractively draped. Then my attention landed on the man who clearly had a stick up his ass. Tobias hadn't uttered a greeting since luring me into what could have been a trap. He ran his gaze against me impassively, one arm stretched over the top of the sofa.

I needed to break the thick wall of tension. "Whose house is this?"

"Mine." He didn't move an inch when producing the single syllable.

"You bought it?"

"Rental."

"Why?"

His heavy inspection climbed my jittery frame. "Because your selfish ass hasn't had the decency to call...be rude and send a cold ass text to, at least, let me know you made it home safely."

I rolled my eyes away. "You haven't called or texted either. Or did you send them to my burner phone."

"Maybe I should have. Would that have gotten me some attention?"

My pulsed raced. "Is that what we're doing now?"

His neck twisted in a shrug, beard glistening. God, why did I have to be so damn attracted to him? His big, strapping frame clad in black was imposing. It weakened me.

His index finger arrowed toward me. "You brought condoms to Jersey. I wouldn't have pushed you." He retracted the index finger, and pointed his thumb towards himself, voice throbbing with an unfamiliar emotion. "I'm the one who, like a sucker, spilled the beans, telling you I love *you*—"

"Fuck, Tobias!" I grabbed my head, feeling a sudden ache. "I'm about to leave my husband. You think shit is black and white?"

"Last I knew, my heart pumped blue and bleeds red. Ain't shit about life black and white, Lennox. And it won't start with us."

"Then take it back. I'm not trying to hurt you. It would kill me to have you hurt in all of this... This miserable web I've managed to interweave myself into?"

"You don't get it."

"Don't get what?"

"I'm not going no fuckin' where. I'm here...in this. I ain't leaving shit until I leave with what's mine. That's where I fucked up as a boy. I'm a man now, Lennox. And I want you to finally choose me. The question is do you want to?"

Totally flustered, I changed my line of view again. This was too much. Of course, I wanted to be with Tobias. He knew that. I'd just learned the lengthy process of my divorce. What I would do with Scott before Terry's release from prison still hadn't been decided on. Where would Kelly-Ann land? Where would I go? Would I stay in my home? Did I want to remain in North Carolina? What would I do without my job? I made good money, a salary that allowed me to care for three dependents. What would be the likelihood of finding the same role in New Jersey. Even if I could luck up into the same job, I'd need more money to afford the cost of living there. The questions and dilemmas were endless, making the last thing I needed was to fight with the one source of joy I'd had in life.

"Take off your jacket, Lennox." There was a grave, yet seductive command in that request, causing my head to whip to face him. Tobias' expression remained deadpan, but he did reposition himself, removing his arm from the top of the sofa. An immediate emotion swelled in my throat…between my legs. I found myself thinking of the possibilities of being embarrassed, and acutely, Tobias must have sensed it. "I wouldn't ask you to do anything that would bring you harm or exposure. The house is empty. Just you and me. You saw me arm the house on our way up here." Believing him without a moment of dither, I shut down my brain by obediently removing my jacket. Tobias motioned with his chin for me to toss it over the sofa chair nearest to me. That forced me farther into the room with him. "Do the same with your skirt," his command was throaty, evidentiary of his mood.

This time, I moved into action quicker. I reached to my lower back, unfastened the hook, and lowered the zip of my skirt. I shimmied, pushing the cloth down my hips until it hit the floor. After stepping out, I tossed it over the chair, too. Tobias leaned forward, bringing his elbows to his knees, taking in the new view. The hem of my blouse reached my pelvis area, but my thighs, covered in hosiery with lace banded in the middle of each, were exposed as I stood in four-inch heels.

"C'mere, Lennox," the tempered command in that throaty request arrowed straight to my groin.

I sauntered across the room and to him. Tobias sat up straight when I stopped just a few feet away. His eyes skirted the perimeter and he reached for one of the decorative pillows. He dropped it between his feet planted in *Timberland* boots.

Then those heavy-lidded eyes tapped his lap. "Come."

Not fully understanding this command, I did what was natural, which was sit on his lap. The action was awkward, knowing my ass was almost bare in cheeky panties. But the cry of need churning in my core was louder than those self-conscious whispers in my head. I arranged my legs and feet outside of his, but kept my spine straight as my eyelids grew lazy against his delicious scent and thickening beneath me. Woodsy musk, like sandalwood, and a pinch of citrus mixed with emanating heat, equaled all male, something I was unaccustomed to.

"Bend over and touch the pillow," he husked. Awkwardly, I submitted to his command, slowly leaning over until my hands reached the square pillow. My heart beat so hard, I could hear blood rushing through my skull. "Loosen up. Relax," his tenor soft. Then his big, hot hand was on my right thigh and leg, arranging it aside him on the sofa. My heel hooked into the upholstery. "Just relax," he coaxed smoothly again. There was authority and comfort in Tobias' tone, something I wasn't familiar with, but for some reason, it didn't surprise me. The man had endless options for company, intimate or otherwise. That was a truth of my friend I had to adjust to over the years. Tobias enjoyed sex. He took the same care with my left leg, bringing it up on the sofa so both were now astride him.

Immediately, I felt exposed to him. My all bared to Tobias for his review. My essence—my scent was spread out for him. I could also feel him thickening even more in his sweatpants.

"Your birthmark is pretty."

Birthmark? I had one of those back there?

I felt his thumb brush against my flesh. The touch on an unseen part of my body revealed nerve-endings I didn't know I had. My spine shivered, eyes closing again. I needed him in a way I couldn't articulate.

"I wanna spank you," Tobias softly growled.

"For what?"

"You have to ask?"

Then I knew. Tobias wanted to punish me for disconnecting from him since leaving Jersey. It was wrong, selfish. But I wanted it. I wanted him. So, I rearranged myself on the pillow, bringing my ass farther up his legs and stretched the length of my elbows.

"Do *it*—"

WHACK!

The first thrash was delivered before I could breathe enough to brace myself. My face pushed into the pillow as the stinging sensation moved beyond my cheek, interspersing throughout my torso.

Jesus...

"Sorry," he mumbled dryly. "I couldn't help myself. You okay?"

It took me a minute to squeal, "Yes..."

Then he struck me again on the opposite cheek. This one wasn't less smarting, but it wasn't as startling, making it bearable. The next lash was lower, just above the back of my thigh. That one was even less betraying, though still powerful. I found myself dragging my breasts against his leg and arching my back.

"You good?" I nodded against the pillow. "Your ass looks so fuckin' good bruised," his voice was filled with a different emotion this time. It was lust. For me. I whimpered, lifting my hips again, and pushing them back. Then I felt his fingers between the folds of me, causing me to wince with pleasure. "Shit," he groaned. "So fuckin' wet."

I squeezed my already closed eyes.

But my mouth flew open when the next strike met my flesh. Before I could recover, there was another, this one milder. Then there was another. They began to come rhythmically, and my body anticipated them, ass pushing back. A need continued to grow, and I wanted more of his ministrations—not that the lashes weren't good enough, but I felt the need to release the volcanic stirring in my belly.

Then the blows stopped, and like a wounded dog, I collapsed onto his lap, angrily. I could feel Tobias lifting us inches from the couch, revealing his strength. The heat from his mouth was at the small of my back where he used it to rip my lace panties. The strap released my throbbing clit and was slid away. Suddenly, I felt flesh against mine. Hard, muscled, agile flesh. It was between my cheeks.

It was only seconds into Tobias readjusting his dick for me to know it was out. Internally, I cried for it, begging for it by way of telepathy. I was sure it had its own brain. I willed it to me…inside of me. But Tobias had other plans. I felt the head of it run the fleshy crease of me, skipping my entry points, then nestle directly beneath my clitoris.

Tobias was right, I was wet. So wet my body began to move on its own accord. It was an instinctive, animalistic move to relieve the mounting tension. Less than two hours ago, I was in a boardroom presenting to some of the brightest minds in medicine. Now, I was a cheating, scandalous wife, desperate for her lover to aid in her release. And Tobias did. He'd given me his most precious organ to help. As I rubbed against it with feverish need and pace, I felt a digit from his big hand slip into me and circle around my swollen, soppy suctioning. Soon after, he added another finger inside of my sex, stretching my walls.

"That's it, girl," he droned thickly, slowly, and with approval. "Control your pleasure."

Expressing his known ministrations, Tobias seemed to enjoy the erotic parameters he set for me. With his dick against my clit, I stroked, riding it against the pleasure of his fingers, winding against a minefield of sensitive nerves. I could hear my excitement, the slurping from my sex and my ass cheeks clapping together, created the most scandalous backdrop.

Feeling empowered, I rocked and moaned unapologetically until the building in my groin burst with pleasure-confetti.

"*Tobeeeeeeeeeeeeee!*" I cried, slamming my trunk onto his lap.

"That's it," he coached with mastered confidence.

I poured out to him, feeling my heart confirm Tobias. Feeling safe to express erotica is an undervalued space. As my body gyrated over his, I knew in this place, I was liberated, I was empress.

My lungs failed me, I couldn't get control of them. I felt his soft lips on one cheek and big hand gently caressing.

"*But in the midst was an oasis in red, my emancipation, my preoccupation, my everything,*" he murmured densely. "*The only one to wear my ring. I want to give you all I have to bring. You might be wearing black and white tonight, but you will always be my lady in red, the one who made my heart take flight." The Book of Nyles.* My spine shivered, fatty cheeks jiggled over him as I tried breathing into the plush pillow. I knew those powerfully seductive words. Then there was a gentle, reverential smack on my flesh. "I missed you."

A shaky push of air left my lungs.

His big, hot hands were at my shoulders, lifting me slowly. Tobias assisted my right then left leg from the padded seats, mindful of my heels. Gingerly, he helped me to my feet, standing right behind me. My body was languid, recovering from my orgasm as he fixed his pants. Then he rounded me, steady hand keeping me in place. The pillow from the floor was tossed back onto the sofa. When his soft lips met my forehead, I felt instant affection.

"Straddle me," he requested softly.

I obliged when he hefted me into the air, my legs banding around his narrowed waist, arms wrapping around him like a needy child. I had no idea of what was to come next and didn't care. I was with Tobias. The man was always thoughtful and caring. My eyes were closed, body exhausted, as he moved. We traveled throughout the house. Without grunting or effort, he carried me up two flights of stairs. I could tell by the cadence. My mind was slipping between consciousness and tempting sedation. My body between recovery and greed. I wanted him. My body needed more. This web of seduction he had me under felt like we'd done it a hundred times as versed lovers.

There was an unlatching of a door. I could hear it push open. After several feet, I was lowered, regretfully, not wanting to detach from his scented heat. Yes, I was uncharacteristically needy. After years of deprivation of intimacy, I took each second he offered greedily.

It was a bed, my stinging ass distinctively picking up an unfamiliar texture beneath me. I forced my eyes open and saw a wooden canopy above me. Turning my head, the red rose petals captured my attention. They were everywhere and vibrant against the dark bedding.

Tobias backed away, reaching for my left leg. His hands brushed down until they reached my feet to remove my shoe. He paid the same pace to my right leg. Then his fixation turned to my thigh-highs. They were slowly peeled off, freeing my thighs from the tight, laced band. The elastic from my torn panties was removed next. My breathing grew heavy again as I watched Tobias inspect my sex. Wet and throbbing, what a sight I imagined it to be for him. He reached over and patiently unbuttoned my black sheer blouse. His mouth was too close to my hungry body when he banded behind my torso to unhook my bra.

I followed his silent command when he pulled me up to push the delicate fabric of my blouse from my shoulders and arms. My bra was next, and then I was totally bare to him. I believed this was the first time Tobias ever took the time to surveil my naked body. I squirmed nervously. A spell of subconsciousness overtaking me momentarily.

"You've lost a few pounds in two weeks," he observed in a mutter.

"I haven't been eating like I should."

My weight had always been an issue. Gaining was an impossible task until I learned about the magic of proper dieting and weight-lifting a few years ago. Although I'd been able to put on weight recently, losing it easily was a constant threat, which was why I remained consistent with my regimen. *Unless* I went overboard with cardio and not eating as had been my behavior over the past two weeks.

His eyes closed as he exhaled audibly. "Join the fuckin' club."

"Your clothes are still on." I swallowed, needing to remind him. Being fully naked as he peered down onto me both aroused and intimidated me.

Aroused. After the erotic orgasm he gave me downstairs, my body was still revved up for him. I was pretty sure my excitement was leaking out of me at this point, onto the rose petals. I could feel it on my lower cheeks.

And then when Tobias straightened, locked his beautiful gaze on me while toeing out of his boots, I knew I was in trouble. I watched his painful pace as he removed his track jacket, pants, tank, and socks. When he bent over to push his boxers down his thick, wiry thighs, my head lifted from the mattress, not wanting to miss a beat of his nudity.

He stood, chin partially hiked, dick arrowed toward his thigh. He was thick and large, veiny and primal. His balls were enlarged, intimidatingly heavy, and a hue darker than the rest of his body. My tongue swept against the roof of my mouth. Tobias was so unlike my husband. Kelvin was your typical lanky, basketball build at six-feet and seven-inches. He was knock-kneed with a graceless gait from a slant in his long spine. He wasn't particularly muscular, but still possessed athletic strength needed when he was working.

Tobias, on the other hand, was a slab of taut muscle beneath meaty flesh. At six-feet even, the man was tall and thick enough to envelope me for protection and sensual exploration. His pecs were pronounced mounds of shields. His abs were carved, a rippled display of dedication to his fitness. His arms and thighs were evidence of stunning virility. Tobias' gaze on me was filled with ravenous need.

"You're beautiful," fell from my lips like a confession.

"I'm yours," he informed melodically. His big hand reaching for his engorged cock, stroking it.

My eyes closed in pure shame from my lustfulness. I didn't know intimacy with a person other than myself. I masturbated when needed, which could be twice a week or once a month. Since being friends with Tobias, I'd treated myself to several adult toys, ones to stimulate me into a leg-jerking orgasm. Oftentimes, when I closed my eyes to begin my flight, he was the visual behind my lids. But today, in the middle of a Friday afternoon, my fantasy was right here, mere feet away, baring it all to me.

He's about to break me in two...

Feeling dizzy from too much stimulation, my head collapsed back onto the mattress, and I sighed, "I'm married, Tobias."

Chapter Ten

Lennox

"On paper, but your soul is tied to me." His chest flexed as he approached the bed. "I'm yours, and you're mine. I'm about to prove it."

He lifted my legs, arranging them over his broad-banded shoulders, and buried his face in my cleft. My back arched over the mattress, feeling the sensitivity level of my clit return to intense as though I didn't have an orgasm five minutes ago. Tobias' velvety tongue moved with adroit fluency between the folds of my sex with ravenous need. My eyes closed and hands flexed when he took a long dive inside of me, the slickness of his firm tongue caused my toes to curl. His head bobbed and bobbed, creating a stir in my groin.

My plaintive moans began curling into the air, busy hands reaching for nothing in particular. He dove and dove. I rocked against him, feeling my orgasm crest. This time, I was ready, greedy for it as though I hadn't had a release today. The second the pads of my feet began to warm, Tobias' tongue retracted, and his lips bit into the flesh of my labia. That clever touch was good, but it wasn't as intense as what he'd created inside of me. I squirmed, attempting to control his oral work. That's when he reached up and flicked my nipple sending chards of pain shooting throughout my body. Eminent air burst through my lips and my shoulders rolled up until my weight shifted almost to the top of my head.

"Stop being greedy, Lennox," he gruffed. "I know what I'm doing down here."

I panted hard, body clenched as I peered down on his angry face sheened with my excitement. "Okay," I whispered.

Gracefully, his mouth returned, this time into my folds. I bit my lip to temper the pleasure, the bites of pain from his flick dissipating. My body loosened in no time, warming again to his cadence. I didn't know the play, had no idea of the protocol. I'd ventured into sex with Tobias months after we met years ago, but they were a handful of times and always passion-filled quickies on either of our grandmothers' sofas, in his bedroom, and even in the back of a car he borrowed to take me out on a date. Seeing him completely naked and this mesmerizing, seductive, sex-god had been a mind trip.

Just when I'd eased into the rhythm Tobias created with his tongue beating at my clit, feeling perspiration layer my hot skin, he pushed a finger inside me. Circling around my swollenness again, his tongue thrashing slowed. When I groaned in frustration, Tobias understood and swiped weightily and rhythmically again. I found myself pushing down into his face and hand. My nipples bounced deliciously into the air as my shoulders rounded against the mattress.

Then his tongue slowed, but fingers seamlessly remained course. I was unbelievably wet now, audibly aroused. His fingers swished inside me, making a suctioning sound. But I wanted his tongue. However, I knew not to push it this time. I focused on the sensation instead. His fingers felt different from a penis. They weren't as fill-ing, but a bit more manipulating. When they'd rubbed upward toward the front, beneath my belly, heat would flash throughout my body, and I'd ride into it.

The pressure of Tobias' tongue was heavy again, and the speed quickened. Immediately, my body responded, sex moving at the pace he set. I moaned, attempting to communicate just how good he felt, how much I needed to release the mounting pleasure. I was so close, my spine and toes arching over the mattress. My belly began to warm, hips pumping faster.

Then it all stopped.

"Tobe!" I cried.

He stood from between my legs, a condom magically in hand. Tobias' scowl didn't fade a bit as he ripped the aluminum packet with his teeth and applied it. Those hooded lids were as heavy as the appendage bouncing against his thigh as he crawled the bed for me. I scooted up to give him room.

"What game are you playing?" I demanded, horny out of my mind.

"I told you when you left Jersey, I wanted to show you something. "I'm 'bout to."

He settled between my spread thighs and leaned over. My eyes closed as his glossed lips neared me, wet beard in tow. I could smell myself on him before he met my agape mouth. It was mixed with his virile heat and scent, diluting me. Instantly, we were caught up in oral lust. I was so wound up, my head lifted from the mattress, reaching for his delicious mouth. His tongue was just as aggressive as the mere sight of his dick. I knew it would be a painful pursuit, but I was ready for the meeting place of intimacy with him. I wanted him connected to the inside of me.

"I'm ready," I whispered between kisses and tongue tangling.

Seconds later, he was pulling me from the mattress and into a straddling position as he sat on the back of his feet. The thick pulsing of his erection between us disappeared beneath me until I felt it at my opening.

Intimidated, I protested, "You tricked me. I didn't..."

A soft smile shrunk his eyes. "Cum? You didn't cum in my mouth, Lennox?" I shook my head, answering him emphatically. "You didn't cum on my hand either. I didn't want you to." His arms banded around me, big hand caressing my back. Tobias made me feel so small and protected under his coveted frame, even before we began kissing and touching. He was my gentle giant. "You're gonna make yourself cum, baby," a swell of lust thickened his cords as I tried pushing down onto him. My walls more compliant, surprisingly. "I stretched you with my fingers," he coaxed erotically. *Downstairs*. He fingered me downstairs and in here, swirling his thick fingers inside my pliant flesh.

"*Mmmm...*" I moaned when he pushed my body down even farther onto his throbbing thickness.

"Give me your mouth, Lennox."

With closed eyes, I obeyed, grabbing him from the back of his head and greedily offering my tongue. The strands of his beard rustled teasingly against my chin and neck. I squeezed my thighs around his, lifting and thrusting to fit as much of his lengthiness inside as I could. When my groin flashed, my head rolled back, but I held him tightly in my arms, using his big body as my anchor while I rode him. Tobias' head dipped and his mouth was on my nipples sucking, tugging at a direct line to my pussy. That inspired a direction I grinded into. A need built, one similar to his tongue against my clit, strangely familiar to where his fingers explored.

Before I knew it, my movements grew impending, desire spreading like a wildfire. I bucked onto Tobias as though his body was my own, as though he was an enslaved lover, owing me pleasure. The smacks of our flesh dizzied me, the sound of our rabid breathing turned me wild.

"Shit!" croaked from the back of his throat. "You are stunning when fuckin' me, Lennox." The cords of his neck thick with pronunciation as he seemed to endure my weight. "Cum with me."

I paid his words no mind, was too busy enjoying myself, feeling all the feels of his swollenness massaging my insides. His hooks on my shoulders intensified and Tobias' head flew back as he howled, the tips of his beard brushed against my face. The man felt bigger, stretching me even more. But that was impossible, I was still unable to take him all the way in.

"Fuck!" his taut body strained beneath me, his fierce grip on me, his touch nonnegotiable.

I didn't stop, not sure if Tobias was climaxing, but deciding to be caught up with him in lechery. And, *oh, God*, he was deeper inside of me. A lot, and in no time, my groin was preparing to explode. It all happened so fast, but when my orgasm ripped through me, I wailed louder than Tobias. My grip on his big ass was with crushing pressure as he anchored me by the back, and my ass, to thrust deep into me.

"*Tobeeeee!*" shot from my lungs.

I was a fountain of lust, gushing around him as I came. This was an orgasm, I knew for sure. It hit different than the ones I'd had from my clit. Even with pain, an orgasm could rocket through, shooting me into realms of bliss I never not wanted to know again. My hips were in a fit, plunging down onto its target, spine curled backward, and eyes squeezed close. His big hand covering my cheek clutched me into the roiling sensation until the storm subsided and I was left with a galloping heart and burning lungs.

That was…a lot.

I couldn't quite piece together what had happened. Less than two hours ago, I was at work, muscling through another tough day. How did I get to this foreign bed, stripped bare physically and emotionally? That orgasm was an opening to a new pathway. I was feeling, inside of a new dimension. As I peered up to gain view of his handsome face, tightened defensively, I could sense the swift change in energy. I was naked beyond clothes, and even more than sharing my body with him in Jersey did, I'd forfeited any immunity I had to being hurt by him. I'd opened myself to a new dimension with this man. It couldn't be smart. If I'd learned anything from Kelvin, it's you never give your all. Leaving a piece of yourself unavailable preserves you when your partner inevitably fucks up.

Yeah…

Indeed, it was a lot for me. It was so much, I felt a tearing inside my chest and I began to weep.

"*Lenn—*"

I pushed against him to disconnect. "I'm not even fresh. I should have showered first, at least."

"No." His one word final.

"But *I—*"

I was lifted into the air, feeling him plop from me, and turned around until I landed on top of his big, fast-beating chest. Skin on skin, my face above his heart, I tried wiping my eyes. It was useless.

"I don't even know what I'm doing here," I whimpered, feeling disoriented.

"You feel that? My heart?" he asked, wiping my face. "That's why you're here. You own it. It's been waiting on you to come see about it."

"What we did had nothing to do with your heart."

"It's got every fuckin' thing to do with it. Lennox, this shit's getting harder and harder to do."

"Then how do you think I feel, Tobias? I met with the attorney. I'm stuck for another year as his wife. And the clock doesn't start until we separate."

"Then separate." The simplicity in his tone felt impossible for me.

"It's not that easy."

"Why?"

"Because of Scott. Because of Kelvin's mother. They live in my home. And them aside: I have to get Kelvin to leave."

"Then do that. It's your house," he argued calmly, warm chest rumbling.

"He has nowhere to go."

"That ain't true, Lennox. He's home. The nigga got family all over."

He was right about that. Kelvin was from Raleigh. His family wasn't huge, but he had a circle. Yet, I was exhausted. All the fighting. All the lying to my face about being high, about getting clean, about missing money. I'd been doing it since my early twenties. I was now approaching thirty, and my stamina and interest had waned. There was no hope for improving our lives together. Kelvin made that clear years ago. It was now time for me to act on it.

Tobias croaked, "Why are you crying, baby?"

Sobbing between the side of his chest and arm, I explained, "It's too much."

I felt his warm lips and prickly beard at the top of my face. Tobias kissed me tenderly. "The spanking." I nodded, shoulders shuddering from a disgorge of emotions. I felt and smelled the erotic miscellany of scents from his nostrils. Me and Tobias, we had an interesting aroma. Go figure.

"You gotta go back to the hospital?" I shook my head. There was no way I could go back to work in this emotional state. He exhaled again over my head. "Good. You need to rest. Let's get you showered."

I steeled. "Showered."

First was the grumbling in his chest, then Tobias lifted me at the head with a fistful of my hair. He snorted, "I ate your pussy. You need to wash me off."

My forehead wrinkled. "Wash you off? I don't have you on me. You used a condom."

He chuckled deeply from his chest. "I did, and I need to take it off. Feels crazy as hell. But... Never mind."

"Never mind what?" I questioned his grin.

"Nothing."

"Tobias!"

He wouldn't shake that knowing grin. "Nothing, baby." He tried lifting us. "Let's get you—"

I pushed down on him. "I'm fucking emotional, Tobias. Don't play with me. I'll go home!" I didn't feel as strong as I sounded, but would do it.

"No the fuck you ain't, either. You left me hanging in *Samsara*, some shit you better not get used to."

"Then tell me! Didn't you say there'd be no more secrets between—"

"It was just the fact that you ain't know you're supposed to wash after getting your pussy tasted, Lennox. Damn." He shifted from beneath me.

I pushed my torso up by an arm. "And what's wrong with that?"

"The fact that you're telling me ol' boy didn't eat it."

My eyes fell as I thought about that. Kelvin had gone down on me. It had been so long ago, and always so infrequently that it wasn't a piece of knowledge in my repertoire. That hurt. I was so tender.

"Well, I'm sorry I haven't spent my twenties fucking for fun with random people for that level of wisdom—"

"Ouch." He pretended to wince.

"I haven't been single, and readily available to join sex clubs to watch, teach, and learn—"

Tobias' neck swung, and he issued me a deathly gape, "Don't let your mouth get you into some shit a simple spanking can't correct, Lennox. Get your ass in this shower so you can get some sleep!"

Were his words threatening? Yes. Tobias' tone was promising, too. Would he hurt me? Physically? Absolutely not. However, in the state I was warped into, it was more than my body that was compromised. My heart was in trouble, too.

love ∞ belivin

Tobias

I closed the door to the suite behind me while looking across the room for movements. Lennox was still knocked the fuck out, buried beneath the comforter of the king-sized bed. Quietly, I placed my phone and the house remote control on the nightstand, then pulled my shirt up and over my head, and pushed down my sweats, tossing them into a chair against the wall. After pulling the bedding back, I crawled onto the mattress, shifting until I was right against her small, soft body.

Lennox lay on her back, her right knee leaning over the left. The towel holding her damp hair from the shower earlier had opened over the pillow, several curly tresses escaping its fold. Her lips were slightly parted as she slept, and I still couldn't believe she was here with me. The girl was beautiful, unaged from the day I met her at the mall.

Excitement raced in my veins, desire bloomed in my balls, and before I knew it, I was leaning over her tiny body, kissing her parted lips. My greedy ass wanted more, not being able to let the tired girl rest. I reached beneath the comforter and sheet and brushed my finger down the soft bed of her hair and into her folds. She wasn't wet, understandably, but that didn't sit well with my greedy ass. I licked my fingers, pushed back down beneath the bedding and found her pussy again, rubbing it. Her clit was flat, but within a few seconds, it swelled like my heart each time I thought of her.

As I caressed her, dipping into her sweet cave, I studied the muscles in her face. It was Lennox's breathing that changed first. Her eyelids shifted next. How quickly had I worked up a rainstorm between her legs. A part of me felt guilty for exploiting her need, her lack of sexual satiation. Another part of me felt privileged to be the first to bring it to her after a fucked up marriage. Thinking about her dating again after her divorce had me fucked up. Feeling her puddling against my cupped hand, reinstated my confidence.

"*Mmmm...*" Lennox stirred, legs straightening down the mattress then opening, forfeiting to her pleasure.

I kissed her again, my lips tarrying over her mouth. My tongue traced the lining of her lips, tickling her senses.

Wake up, baby...

I didn't want to spare a moment with her. Thankfully, in seconds, Lennox's hand pushed up, shifting the covers to reveal her brown nipple. I reached down and pulled it into my mouth, suckling gently. In no time, her hips loosened, rocking into my touch. I didn't rub too hard, understanding how precious and delicate this area was. It could endure pushing out babies and metal, medical instruments, but it should also be caressed and adorned.

"*Mmmm...*" she moaned again then, suddenly, her eyes flashed open wide before closing.

Her head pushed back into the pillow, towel opening even more. I loved the sight of her hair. It was the colors and curl pattern.

Everything about this girl worked for me. Her determined approach to life, her vulnerability, naivety, and her undeniable strength. When she sucked in her bottom lip, that shit worked for me, too. I continued to polish her pearl, wishing I could taste it instead. By the way her pussy began to push into my touch, I knew Lennox was where she wanted to be, and how she wanted to shoot it out.

Her little hand clasped my arm, pushing to weight my touch against her. I sucked on her nipple, tugging her areola into my mouth. She pushed against her shoulders, ass lifted off the bed. Lennox's mouth opened, eyes squeezed.

"Yes," she breathed. "Yes!"

When her hips began to buck with total surrender, I knew she was climaxing. My excitement grew, and I rubbed faster, applying more pressure until her mouth shot open and she cried without shame.

"*Ooooh! Tobeeeeeee!*"

I flicked my tongue on her nipple faster and faster. Her grip on my arm tightened. My dick pushed into her right hip on its own, answering to her demand. But this wasn't about me. Lennox needed this liberation, this spoil, this sensual care. I didn't stop stroking her clit until she shifted, lowering her ass to the mattress. Then, I knew she'd had enough.

Pulling away, I lay on my back, struggling not to lick my fingers. Chino was right: my obsession for the girl was a real thing. What I'd give to have this access to her every day. Lennox was a woman to behold. She was a man's fantasy, had been mine for too damn long without "being mine."

"Did I sound like a married virgin this time?" She was still panting when looking over at me.

I laughed. "The hell is wrong with you?"

Lennox grinned goofily, face tight as she stretched beneath the comforter. "Don't think I forgot that."

"Not my finest truth."

"Truth can get you into trouble."

"Tell me about it." The essence of her truth—*mine, too*—was drying on my hand.

"Today…" she exhaled, wiping her face, "has been a day."

"It was the orgasm, too."

Lennox turned to me again.

Staring at the ceiling, I admitted, "The spanking wasn't the only culprit for your emotional breakdown earlier." I nodded. "Spankings nip at your ego," I turned to her. "But vaginal orgasms, be it first time or rarely, can fuck your head up."

I watched her swallow, then her sparkling irises rolled up toward the ceiling.

"What are you doing down here?" My head shifted over the pillow, glaring at her as though it was the most foolish question that ever existed, because it was. Lennox rolled her eyes then tossed herself onto her side to face me. "No. The equipment in the foyer. The guys unpacking the trucks. Sunglasses—what are you doing in North Carolina?"

"Sunglasses?"

"The guy wearing the superstar sunglasses in the house on a cloudy day?"

"Oh, Nikko?" I rubbed my eye with the non-soiled hand. "That's one of Dale's managers."

"Dale."

I nodded again. "That's my excuse for being down here. I'm starting my warmups with D."

"In Chapel Hill?"

"Yup. He's from North Carolina. Spent his first twelve years in the country before moving to New York for artist development."

"Wait. You're going to do it? You're going to produce his album?"

"Yup."

I'd started spending time with Dale. We'd speak damn near every day. We hung out a few times a week. In between drinks, appreciating tunes by other artists and musicians—old and new—I observed him. I listened to the shit he said and the important details he didn't. Dale told me he'd shot his first gun down here, caught fish, hunted deer, and lost his innocence. He didn't term it virginity, or making love, or fucking for the first time. So, when I inquired about his first love, he mentioned "the wrong woman from the wrong generation." That, and his body language, told me there was more to the story.

"I know what you do when creating a body of work, as opposed to just two or three songs." Lennox covered her mouth to yawn. "And yet, you find the time to have an attitude with me for not calling you."

I shrugged with my head. "It's been fuckin' disrespectful."

Her little hand covered my heart. "I've been working through things."

"I know. But I'm here. I can help."

With a soft expression, she shook her head. "You've helped all you can these past three years. You've proven to be a trusted friend. One who does not judge and one who can be patient. You've respected my vows until I broke them."

In Jersey. Nah. I wasn't expecting to make love to Lennox last month, and now that I had, I couldn't stop wanting more and more of it.

My heart flashed open for a moment when I shared, "You're my love song on repeat. The one that makes me weak. You're the one powering my hunger, the only one who makes my heart thunder."

"That's so beautiful. Is that for Dale's project?"

I nodded. "By way of my heart."

Sharing personal shit like this with her wasn't hard for me. But I did struggle with putting too much stress on Lennox. When it came to who she wanted to be with in a relationship, I could never forget how I'd lost her all those years ago. More than I wanted her—*and I wanted her bad as hell*—I needed Lennox to choose me. So, expressing my true feelings for her had to be measured.

She reached over and kissed me. "I don't know what inspired the words, but your heart is so pure, everything pouring from it is perfection."

Again, no need to clarify she inspired the words. I didn't want to be that guy.

"What was the conversation like with the divorce lawyer?"

"Scary." She exhaled, shifted onto her back, and fingered her curls. "I walked in there like a big girl and walked out like a child. It reminded me of what I walked into my marriage as. I was a child, thinking I was growing up when, in fact, I was being herded by my grandmother and Kelvin. Don't get me wrong; I was in full capacity of my mind, but it wasn't quite developed for me to understand the weight of joining lives with a man."

With my "clean" hand, I fingered through her tiny ones over the comforter. "I can dig it."

"And my conversation before that with my therapist didn't help. I've been so busy planning my getaway that I haven't been looking ahead: what my life will look like as a single woman."

"You'll figure it out. You always do. I don't get what you mean."

She pulled in a deep breath through her nostrils, turning onto her side to face me again. "When I was in Jersey, at *Crystal K*'s, the girls were all talking about their statuses as women almost thirty years old. You know everyone's married except for Nisha, and even she's not settled. None of us were satisfied. None of the married ones deeply in love with who we vowed to share our lives with."

I couldn't help a soft chuckle. "Not even Mya's 'everything's rosy' ass?"

She shook her head, a grin brightening her face. "Mya wants people to believe she is, but some of us can see through her BS. My point is, this fact didn't hit me right away. It hit me the other day when I told my therapist I was going to finally take the first steps to leave Kelvin." She shook her head, eyes in the distance. "I have no plan beyond that. These past few years, when I knew leaving him was best, it was my only focus. Now that I'm here, prepared to execute, the shit looks scarier than ever."

"Why?"

"Because my whole world is centered around him. Like I said earlier; I have to think about everyone I live with. I own the home."

"That shit'll work itself out. I promise."

She nodded, eyes squinting as though Lennox was in deep thought. "It will, but what about after? What will I do? Will I stay in that house, live with the memories ghosting in there? Will I continue to work and come home to an empty home? As much as I've fantasized about that over the years, the visual now seems so…blue. Will I stay down here without family? What does family mean? I don't even have a support system now."

"I wouldn't want you to *stay*—I mean..." I caught myself. "I know your life is yours to do whatever you want to do with it. But I wanna be in your *life*—stay in your life." Forever.

Her eyes were on me, but in a way I didn't understand. Then Lennox's gaze rolled down the bed. "When the girls were talking that night at the spa, Nisha mentioned still being single at almost thirty years old. She said it's scary out there for people who want something real and monogamous."

"I can be monogamous. Shit, I've been monogamous for yo ass for a while now, and for all intents and purposes, I'm single." She fell out laughing, body falling to her side of the bed. That shit made me crack the fuck up, too. "Word. My ass committed to you without the pussy or a damn divorce certificate."

Lennox couldn't stop laughing.

Her stomach growled. "Damn! What the hell is that, Curry?"

Her humor was silent as she covered her mouth with squeezed eyes. "I'm sorry!" she damn near shouted. "I haven't eaten since my banana and rice crispy cake this morning!"

"A puff rice cake? Yeah." I scooted toward the side of the bed. "It's time for you to eat."

"Eat?"

"I came up here to wake you up because the food was almost done." I grabbed my pants from the chair. "Everything should be done by now." I needed to wash my hands.

"Done? You came up here to tell me about food, but end up fingering me instead?"

A smile teased my face. "I couldn't help it. You're like my little virgin. Before you leave my presence, I have to shower you with as many orgasms as possible."

Lennox held the blanket to her bare chest and smoothed back her damp curls with the other hand. She looked dazed when she asked, "Are we really doing this?"

"Yup." I chuckled. "We are."

A ringing noise woke me from a confounding dream. A good dream. I was somewhere far away—*for the both of us*—with her in a small cottage. We were naked in bed together, and everything felt right. There was no weight hanging over us neither a dark cloud. Nestled inside of a cottage we slept in the dream until the sounds of birds woke me up. It was high noon because I could see the sunlight where were we—*not that it mattered*. The vibe felt unbelievably perfect; she was mine, and I was hers. It was as if we'd been intimate companions for years. Instead of being excited about being with her, I felt contentment and joy. I felt at home.

But…

I wanted to know what type of birds were outside. Were they blue jays, seagulls, or woodpeckers? Just as I thought to leave her in the bed to see what type of setting was outside of the cottage, a phone rang.

Again.

Being sucked out of the dream, my eyes swung around, and slowly, consciousness swelled. I reached over and grabbed my cell phone.

"Yeah."

"Mr. Elliott, I have two vehicles here. One is Mr. Green, who visited earlier."

Nikko…

Shit.

I rubbed my stuffy nose. "Let 'em in. Thanks."

"Will do, sir."

Next to me, Lennox stirred. It dawned on me how the sun was now down. Just as I lifted my phone again, she murmured, "What was that?"

"My phone?"

Lennox yawned. "Duh. Who was it—*wait.*" Sitting up she asked, "What time is it? Where's my phone?"

My mind was fogged. That call reminded me I had a session with Dale tonight. It would run into the morning if I didn't get what I needed from him. Based on the text I received earlier from Nikko about Dale's drinking today, I knew I'd be up all fucking night.

"Tobias!" her tone was low, but urgent. I loved the cry in it.

I turned to her. "Yeah."

"My phone. I think I left it in the living room when we—when I first got here."

Shit...

"I'll get it."

I needed to take a leak, but thought to take Lennox's need of her phone as the priority. If the girl had forgotten about it, being so wrapped up with me, I'd get her whatever she needed without complaint. Plopping down the stairs to the main level, I could smell the food from earlier. Lennox and I ate good. She even cleaned her plate. The fish had her eyes rolling to the back of her head. I'd be sure to tip the chef. In all the talking she did as we ate, and the fucking we did when done, Lennox hadn't mentioned her phone. Today had been unbelievable.

I went down to the lower level to let up the garage door so Dale and the guys could gain entrance to the studio portion of the house I'd had set up. Then I returned to the main level. And, *shit*, her phone and keys damn sure were inside the pocket of her jacket along with the skirt in the living room. I gathered it all in my arm and hand before shuffling back up the stairs, still feeling out of it. By the time I made it up to the bedroom, Lennox, gloriously naked, carried her shoes in her arm as she walked over to the sofa and picked up her bra. Her blouse was next. She held it in the air, questioning me.

Being an ass, I raised her ripped panties in the same fashion. Rolling her eyes, she fought a giggle. "I'll be submitting an invoice for those."

Without a word, I handed her the cell. As I lay her clothes on the couch, Lennox let out a hard shriek.

"I know it's dark outside, but it's almost nine o'clock!" Her face was wide as hell.

Damn. It is?

With her face into her phone as she tapped into it, Lennox moved to the middle of the room then stopped. "I don't know what to say to Scott! He's been texting and calling for two hours."

I thought for a minute. "Tell 'im you've been with some friends, having dinner after work."

"How would that explain me missing all of his calls and texts?"

After a few seconds of seeing worry color her beautiful face, I recalled, "You workout some evenings after work. Tell him you left the phone in the locker."

Quickly nodding, Lennox began typing away. "Wait!" I called out. Then I shook my head. "Scratch that. You don't have gym clothes."

Her eyes rolled up to the chandelier. "I have some in the car. I can throw those on."

I snapped my fingers. "Good call." I jiggled her keys. "I'll go grab your clothes and follow you home."

"Tobias!"

"What?"

"I don't need a chaperone to drive home."

"It's late."

"I live here. I'll be fine."

Taking a deep breath, I shook my head. "Nah. That don't feel right to me." I turned toward the ruffled bed top. "Especially after..." I shook my head. "Regardless of any of that: It's late."

"Tobias."

My eyes shot up to her. "Yeah."

"I'm driving home alone. You have to work tonight."

Shit.

Dale. I couldn't bail on him. We all knew he'd need time to get focused for this session.

I lifted my phone to make a call. "I can get Charlie to follow you."

"Tobias! No!" there was a panic ringing in that cry.

I took a step closer to her. "Why are you acting like I'm a stranger? Like I'm a random ass nigga?" When she didn't answer, just glared at me with those cognac eyes, I knew. "I'm not going to confront your husband. I told you I'd never interfere unless he puts his hands on you or threatens to—"

"I know!" she snapped.

"And you don't have to be ashamed of what I may possibly see if I were to run across him." Richardson had never been a franchise player, or a memorable figure in the *League* for that matter. Lucky for Lennox and his family, the media nor the bloggers had been interested in him enough to feature the nigga in a "where are they now" segment. So, his condition had managed to have been kept low, compared to a Delonte West. Even still, I'd heard through some channels he hadn't been looking good. The nigga has been a full-on, rouge crackhead. "You don't ever have to be ashamed of any part of your life with me. I'll never judge you."

When tears pooled in her eyes, pain cracked in my chest. I stepped back and took a deep breath. Lennox was not going to back down on this, I knew it. She may have had exotic beauty features, small and petite with a body any man would want to protect as much as fuck, but Lennox was no princess in the wild. She was purposeful, resilient, and from East Orange. The woman was Chino Brim from Amhurst Street's daughter. She wouldn't lay down as a victim for shit. And I had to respect her.

Lennox swallowed before requesting, "I'm going to jump into the shower to wash this scent off me. I'll wait in the bathroom for those clothes."

She turned and took off.

Shit…

I refused to get used to this creeping shit. It was fucking unnatural.

Chapter Eleven

Lennox

I paced off of my exit with a white-knuckled grip on the steering wheel. One ambiguous text from Tobias had me forgetting my real world. Scott. Tobias had brought his down here with him. A man of his status could. He'd told me while we ate how this trip was being expensed by Dale's record label. It was all in Dale's budget. Tobias was able to pack up a few instruments, electronics, two people on his staff, and commandeer Dale's team down to a random North Carolina town to work.

How could I be so stupid?

I berated myself all the way to my neighborhood. I knew what was really going on, though. Tobias was that one thing with the power to let down my guard and force me to live in the moment, something difficult to do as a survivor. The more I allowed joy to wash over me, the less control I had. And as I turned down my block and felt my stomach twist, I realized I had to manage joy, too.

It was just after ten when I pulled into the driveway. The lights on the first floor all appeared to be on. When I texted Scott back, he said his grandmother must have taken her meds, and had fallen asleep early. That to me meant Kelly-Ann had taken her SSRIs prescribed for her anxiety years ago. She'd take them at night sometimes to ensure a good sleep. I didn't always agree with when and why she took them, but never judged. Sometimes, I'd go out on the small balcony off my master bedroom and smoke a blunt after a long day, just to cope with the adult male-energy in my own home. That was typically when Scott was either knocked out in bed or spending the night out.

As I entered the living room, my mother-in-law was in her favorite spot, passed out in front of the television. Scott came down the stairs, eyes wide.

"You okay?"

"How long does it take you to workout? I was scared shitless!"

My nostrils flared, but heart shredded. "Scott. Your mouth. Please. You have me scared, too."

His head snapped to the left, attention jumping to Kelly-Ann. She stirred in her sleep, licking the roof of her mouth before going back out. Scott placed his index finger over his thin lips, hushing me. Quietly, I closed and locked the door behind me. Something was off.

"What's going on?"

He motioned for me to follow him. We traveled out of the living room, by way of a short hallway, and into the kitchen. It was there that we stopped. At the door, which led to the backyard, Scott pulled back the curtain of the window.

"Look!" he ordered.

It was dark, with only a night post light from a neighbor, providing a dim view into my yard. After seconds of swiping back and forth over the full vicinity of the property, I saw it. A "new" tree swaying without the wind. A six-foot, seven-inch-tall, thin, tree zombied out. Kelvin's mouth was wide open as he rested on his feet, in and out of consciousness. He was without a doubt high, unspeakably vulnerable, and blissfully, mentally absent of any threats.

"Why is he like that?" Scott sounded unusually like a thirteen-year-old kid. He was terrified. "What is that?"

Fentanyl...

He'd grown into it; mixing the substance with his heroine and other candies. The types of drugs he'd been on had been changing over the years. That part I knew from several attempts at getting

Kelvin clean, and participating in some of his counseling sessions. The inclusion of fentanyl was a natural progression for an addict like Kelvin. I'd made myself familiar with the pulse of the streets between articles I'd find and conversations with the second head of the emergency room unit at work. It was sad.

"I guess we'll never understand. I don't ever want *you* to."

I watched my husband of eight years sway back and forth while standing near the gate of our yard with his eyes closed, spine on a slant, and mouth hung open. This. This was it. This was why I couldn't have Tobias follow me home. It was why I didn't want anything associated with him to see this ugly side of my life. I had been embarrassed. I'd been ashamed. Tobias, for all of the calm, nurturing qualities he demonstrated to me and others in his circle— for all of the patience and endurance he'd exhibited over the years —was still a possessive man from Irvington, New Jersey. All that passion used to produce heartfelt music was akin to the thuggery infused into his upbringing. And as he'd shown today, Tobias was a possessive lover.

So, hell no: I didn't want him near this jarring reality of my life. I'd been transparent about my issues with my husband; however, I didn't want him to see the ugly for himself. Perhaps a part of it was to protect Kelvin. He was thinner, face darker, and posture far from a professional athlete.

No!

No… Tobias couldn't come near this shit show.

And here I was, again, stuck with all the emotions of disappointment. Embarrassment, shame, and fear of being found out didn't accompany it, though. All those times when he lied, saying he wasn't high. The countless occasions when he'd make me feel wrong for questioning what was so obvious. The many events where I ignored his intoxicated cues just to preserve peace. The years I spent with anxiety, waiting for the next shoe to drop because of his drug use.

All of that shit had taken a toll on me. It robbed me of my youth. I knew how to survive being lied to—manipulation, isolation, and loneliness. Possibly the worst of it all was never having been tended to. I'd never been a wife emotionally. Yeah, when Kelvin worked, I was listed as his spouse on some paperwork. Even now, he's listed as a beneficiary of my health coverage plan through my job. But I've never been doted on, dated, revered, or even appreciated for not bolting back home the first year or two of marriage. I stayed even when he'd lost his job with the *League*.

Oddly, this was the very moment I realized the one ingredient missing from my relationship with Kelvin was love. While I'd never been in love with him, he'd never loved me. I could have fallen in love with my husband; I was wired that way. But jumping into marriage when you're hardly an adult without a fully developed brain doesn't yield itself to the vows. At twenty-eight years old, I was now ready to love a man—something of my own. And I'd been working on myself to be able to receive love.

"C'mon," I whispered, taking Scott at his shoulders. It was time to turn away from this circus we'd been living in. "Let's get to bed. We have a long day tomorrow."

We walked away from the window. My days of living with this toxicity were counting down.

I scrolled through opportunities curated on an app provided by a headhunter I'd contracted with. She sent the listing over this morning. I took a break when Scott returned to our table with food.

"Hey, Scott," a young girl with bone straight, dark brown hair called out to him from the other side of the dining room of *B-Way Burger* on Capital Blvd. "Heather and I are sitting over there. You wanna come?"

Scott and I turned to look across the half-filled room at the same time. I knew the table she spoke of because the giddy girls sitting there were giggling shyly when she pointed them out.

"Anna-Bell, don't you see me with family?" Scott hissed, swinging his blond tresses from his face, whipping his neck.

Little Anna-Bell's face blanched. She peered my way then mumbled to him, "Oh. I'm sorry." The girl took off across the restaurant.

I leaned into the table as he took a seat. "That was kind of harsh. Wasn't it?"

Then I began unloading my food from the tray he'd carried from the counter.

"Naw, it ain't." Scott's eyes were low, on task as he spoke. "They're getting annoying."

My forehead wrinkled. "Anna-Bell and Heather?"

Scott bit into his *B-Way* deluxe with bacon then chewed a bit before he answered, "Them and all girls."

"Hey! What's wrong with girls?"

He shrugged, attention going out of the window our booth was against. "Girlfriends don't work for the dudes in my family."

"Dudes? Like who?"

His volume was measured when he advised, "Uncle Kel...my dad." Scott coolly tossed fries into his mouth.

"Why don't you think girlfriends work for them."

He leaned into the table, chin low. "Look at where my father is now." His brows peaked. "Unalive. And why? His girlfriend. Look at what my uncle was doing last night. You ask him why, and he'd say because of his wife."

My head jerked back, but I immediately reigned in my emotions. "Did he tell you that?" Scott nodded while taking a bite of his burger. "Do you believe that?"

For a while, Scott didn't reply. I patiently nibbled on a fry. They were better than *McDonald's*. Scott had boxing and soccer today. I was looking forward to this fast food meal with him in between sports. It was the only occasion I'd get to pry his heart and mind open, understanding the toxic environment he'd been living in that was my home.

A few years ago, when I thought to enroll him into extra-curricular activities, I arranged for his mother's relatives to commit to taking him. Typically, between his grandmother, aunt, and cousin, someone would transport him. However, today, no one was available. One of the two house vehicles was down, so I filled in. While it may have sounded burdensome to make that request of them, to me it guaranteed Scott spent time with family on both sides. As a kid, coming up, I hated that I didn't know many relatives on my mother's side. I would ask my grandmother to reach out to them, but she wasn't passionate about it. It shrunk my social pool and made me feel lonely. I didn't want that for Scott. I didn't want it for any child.

"At first, I did when I was little. And then…"

I tried pouring dressing over my salad to bide my time. *But…* "Then what?"

"He started to say weird stuff. Like calling you ugly and skinny and fat." He shook his head. "That didn't make sense to me. You're really pretty and super nice. So, when I got bigger, I saw he was kinda mean to you sometimes, and…" He shook his head again.

Talking to a teenager—even a new one—could be exhausting.

"Well, yes. Your uncle can be very mean to me. Nonetheless, that has nothing to do with you. If you want to somehow use that energy, recycle it. Make sure when you deal with girls, you show respect." I went about cutting my salad leaves with the plastic utensils. "And as far as your parents go: have you ever talked to your mother about what happened? Like…get her side of the story?" Without the benefit of his gorgeous hazel-green eyes, Scott shook his head again. "Okay. I think that needs to happen before you can begin to establish limitations about the opposite sex."

"I already know what happened. I saw her court paperwork."

"For her trial?" He nodded. "How?"

He gave me the dry shrug again. "Aunt Patty had it out when I came over a while ago—I was small. And me and my cousins…" The shrug. "…we read it."

I was stunned, recalling the nightmare of a time.

"What did you read?"

"That he liked to fight her. A lot." He stuffed four fries into his mouth. "See. Us guys don't need girlfriends." And yet another shrug.

For seconds long, I cut into my salad, and began to eat. It was my distraction to give me time to think.

"You know…" I decided to return to my gloriously, salty fries. "There are guys who are totally fine with girlfriends. They respect them, protect them, and…really like them."

"Yeah. My cousin, Billy's, got one of those," he grunted, eyes rolling toward the window.

"See! It happens…a lot, actually."

"Yeah?"

"Yeah."

"Then why didn't you choose one to be all those things to you?"

My forehead lifted, and I blinked slowly. Exhaling, I admitted, "Great question! *Fair* question." I scratched my scalp, internally debating if it were appropriate for me to really go there with Scott. He was so young, so overly-exposed to shit he should have been protected from. But the proverbial milk had already been spilled. "So, you know my mother's deceased. Right? But did you know my father was in and out of prison most of my childhood?"

That's when Scott's eyes met mine. He nodded, sending oily locs of hair for a swish into the air. "But not that much."

I nodded. "Yup. I didn't really know him—still don't. I mean… growing up, I knew who my father was because he was a gangster in our neighborhood. Everyone knew and feared him. His reputation protected me growing up more than his guiding hand did. He was always…in jail or prison."

"For what?"

"Drugs, assault, weapons…you name it. Some charges smaller than others, but they added up in number, causing me to miss out on having a dad. You know?" I ate more of my salad to pace my emotions. "His last prison stint was for murder." I felt his eyes creep up on me. It was a span of seconds before I could meet them.

"Who did he kill?"

I hesitated again before coming with it. "The man who murdered my mother—"

"What?" Scott's volume was at an alarmed level. I tried to flash a smile to get him to realize his loud reaction. He visibly shrunk before me. "I'm sorry. But…"

"It's okay. I understand. This isn't something I share with many people. If you were there, you knew. If you were not, you're not likely to hear it from me. It's a crazy story. One that possibly led me to meeting you."

"How?"

"Well, possibly my bloodline or my environment...my psychological pathology."

"Patho-what?"

"The things I've seen growing up." I shrugged. "Maybe even consequences of my parents' mistakes."

"What mistakes did your momma make?"

"She was in an abusive relationship with a thug. They dated for years. At some point, she got pregnant with me. That didn't stop him from blackening her eye, though. He was caught by a cop, slapping her while she was nice and pregnant with me. They threw him in prison until I was about four years old."

"Then what happened?"

I took a deep breath. "She'd been dating another guy. Just as toxic apparently. My father wasn't even out for a month when my mother and her new boyfriend took me down to *Disney*. The story goes, after a day at *Magic Kingdom*, back in our cheap motel room, he got drunk and beat her, too. He choked her to death."

Scott's *B-Way* deluxe with bacon dropped to the wrapper on the table. "Shit," he murmured.

"Scott," I weakly warned him.

"I'm so sorry." He blinked fast. "For your momma, I'm sorry, Lennox. Man," he breathed out. "Your life's been..." Scott's eyes fell.

"Pretty shitty?" I snickered then winked when he peered up to me. "It may seem that way, but I've been blessed, too. Your friendship is proof of that."

"Yeah, but I didn't know about your momma, Lennox." My shoulders lifted as I tried to minimize the first recorded trauma of my life. "And your father: he killed the mutherfucker?"

I wanted to laugh at his southern accent, but decided to do the responsible thing instead. Leaning into the table, I threatened, "You know, I'm going to wash that filthy mouth of yours out with liquid soap."

His forehead lifted. "But you just used a bad word, too!"

"Yeah. But I'm grown; you're still getting there. I have more words in my arsenal that can articulate my thoughts without profanity; you should endeavor to get here."

He rolled those hazel-green irises before sipping his drink. "What did your daddy do?"

Oh…

I wiped my mouth while chewing. "The man who murdered my mother was from Clifton—a town not too far from where I'm from. My father knew who she dated—every man she dated—while he was away those years in prison. So, when the guy—Larry, I believe his name was—got back to Jersey, my father knew where to find him."

"How long did it take?"

"For what?"

"For the word to get back to Jersey?"

"Oh. Thankfully for me, just a day. Of course, I don't remember any of this. I was only four. But I, too, read the reports when I got older." I squinted at him. "The Larry guy left Orlando for home right after he did it. Our motel room had double beds. He strangled her in the bathroom while I was asleep. They said, when I woke up, I went looking for my mother and found her slumped over the tub. When she wouldn't wake up, I had the mind to leave the room. A woman from…Georgia, I believe, had met my mother just the day before. They sparked up a conversation about my dress so, the woman remembered me. I must've told her my mommy wouldn't wake up. Well," I exhaled, "needless to say, she followed me back into the motel room and called the police after seeing my mother. The woman had the mind to go through my mother's purse to find contact numbers. She tried a few until she got to my family. That's all it took for ol' Chino—my father—to find out."

As I went back to my food, Scott murmured, "And he found him, and killed him." It was as though he was in awe of a heroic act.

My mouth twisted in a shrug. "I guess he was the only man who could beat her." Knowing his violence extended to women still irritated me about the man. A man who hit women was a true coward in my eyes. Maybe my mother's pathology of domestic abuse had stemmed from him. This was why I found his "descension" upon Kelvin and me in North Carolina hypocritical. He beat my mother when I was in utero. The man could have killed me.

"How?"

"How what?"

Scott asked, "How did your daddy kill Larry?"

"Brutally. Beat him with his hands."

From the funky thirteen-year-old, I heard a grumble to the tune of "Good for the bastard," before he stuffed a gang of fries into his mouth. "How long did he get for it?" he garbled around the food.

"He was lucky. The jury was hung on the first-degree murder charge, and gave mercy by agreeing on manslaughter. He got fifteen. You know: crime of passion, and all." I rolled my eyes. "He was out by the time I turned nineteen."

"That was gangstuh," his drawl pronounced.

"That's my daddy'!" I chirped facetiously.

"You still mad at 'im?"

I glanced up at Scott, choosing my words as I inhaled deeply. "At times, when I'm forced to remember and reflect, I'm still angry with all of the people who governed my childhood. No, I'm not mad at my father for having the passion to kill the man who murdered my mother, but I am angry that he wasn't a better man to begin with. I get angry about his absence sometimes. I, for sure, get salty about decisions my grandmother made when raising me."

"Why?"

"Because her manner of raising me was based upon her time coming up. It was according to a society that was 'once upon a time.' If my father had been a responsible citizen, he could have raised me and that would have allowed me to avoid a few pitfalls."

"Like what?"

A sad and regretful smile stretched my face. "Like marrying your uncle—or marrying so young to begin with."

Scott nodded while peering me dead in the eye. "That's what you meant when you said your story leads up to meeting me?"

"Yeah. My grandmother pushed me to marry your uncle. I don't want to get too deep with the story, but kids belong to their parents. Yes, in some cases like ours, parents aren't the best for the job. But I believe there's still hope for your mother, Terry. At least, give it a try when she comes home in January."

An emotion rolled over his almond face. "You're leaving, ain't ya?"

The first tear dropped unexpectedly. Quickly, I swiped it with salted fingers. I shook my head. "I'm leaving him, Scott. Just him."

"You goin' back to New Jersey?"

I turned to face the window. This shit was hard. There were still a gamut of unanswered questions. I had no job in Jersey. I had no place to live. Taking a deep breath, I braved my boy again. "It's likely. I don't have any support down here."

"You do up there? Your grandmomma's in a care home, ain't she? You don't even talk to your daddy."

"Yes, and correct." My father, though now financially stable, and seemingly on the straight and narrow, still lived in my grandmother's house. I wouldn't go back there even if he didn't. "I'll figure it out, though. When you get my age, and waste so many years on a dead-end road, you develop handicaps. Thankfully, I'm still young. I'll find another job. I'll find a place to stay."

He nodded, expressing his faith in me. "Does MeMaw know?"

I shook my head, sniffling. "You're the second person I've told: the first in the house. I'm waiting to finish developing a plan, you know?"

Scott nodded again, and I hated myself for being another reckless adult in his life. My crime was instability. Kids needed that for emotional development. I was ruining someone else's child when all I'd ever wanted to do for the kid was give him a semblance of a childhood. We found ourselves finishing our food, allowing silence to swell around us. I didn't know about Scott, but I didn't hear the other patrons or the traffic from Capital Blvd on the left side of me.

My mind, instead, traveled to the psycho-pathology I wondered if I struggled with. My mother, by my womanly theory, was broken and troubled. She had to be. If she stayed in a relationship with a man who put his hands on her, there had to be an issue there. And when you add violence to a subsequent relationship, there is, no doubt, pathology there. That would cause me to consider my own shit. Why had I been here in North Carolina so long? I'd been financially independent for most of my marriage, even before Scott came into my life. What was it here, in this pool of toxicity, that I'd chosen to live with?

Psychosis?

Either way, I had to be prepared for my total independence. I didn't want to jump into a relationship with Tobias with baggage on my back like Santa Claus. I'd have to pace myself to wholeness.

"I hope you find a boyfriend who's all those good things to you," Scott's small voice broke my screaming internal fears. When I gaped at him confused, he uttered, "You. I hope you find a guy better than my dad, Uncle Kel, your dad, and me. You're too good not to."

I reached for his hand, wrapped around his soda. "If I ever got wind of you going down the path of those guys, I'll crawl down here on my elbows and knees to set your tush straight. Please believe that."

"Well, you ain't gonna get one with that type of attitude, ma'am." His one brow peaked.

My head flew back and I howled in laughter.

Tobias

Dale, on the phone with his teenaged boys from his first wife, strolled over to the keyboard where I was playing, establishing a chord sequence. He plucked a few notes he thought matched.

"You heard me, Dad?" One of the boys asked.

With the phone on speaker and to his face, he answered, "Yeah, boy! I heard ya ass the first time." Dale was known to sport a permanent smile, exposing shallow dimples. Very few times would you catch him without it to some degree. It was charm mixed with nature. So, when he fussed at his son, I didn't know if he was serious or not. "If I told you not to do it the first time, why would you go behind my back, and sneak into my room?"

That question reminded me of how Dale had full custody of his sons. Their mother, Tika, had a total of four sons, two before the ones with Dale. Oddly, she had custody of none of her children. I could have pried: he'd given me permission to ask anything about his personal life I wanted. It was an exercise to gut him for the project. But I decided not to. Not everything needed to be shared. In the halls of the industry, I was known as the therapist, but outside of making music, I typically didn't give a fuck about people.

"Pops—"

"Pops my ass, bro," Dale interjected. "I'm in the studio. I gotta get back to it. We'll talk about this shit when I get home. As a matter of fact," he scratched his chin, looking toward the ceiling, "everything. Give Milagros everything. The phone, remotes, mice, monitors—everything!"

"Man!" I heard the young man groan.

Dale hung up on him, and that's when I knew he was dead ass serious. "Shit!" He swung back to the keyboard, still trying to add to the sequence. "The shit being in love with the wrong fucking woman will do to you." He scoffed. Then Dale turned to face me. "You got a kid." He snapped his fingers. "A little girl. Right?" I nodded. "Ever married?" I shook my head. "Lucky son of a bitch."

That shit made me laugh. "How?"

"Because too many kids by the wrong woman'll keep you working until you're old as fuck. You know who told me that?"

"Who?"

"Luther."

My face balled. "Luther?"

"Luther, Luther." Dale laughed. "Luther Vandross, nigga!"

Then my forehead stretched. "Word?"

"Word. Luther saw it all, yo." He cracked the fuck up. "But you ain't gotta worry about that. You've been playing it smart, which is why I don't get how you're able to tune in like you do." He tossed his hand toward the keys where I was still playing.

"Why?"

"Because..." He seemed to have been searching for his words. "This type of curation requires a level of experienced passion."

I smiled. "You're right."

With a grin, Dale squinted. "Okay. Answer me this: were you in love with your daughter's mother?"

"Nah. Just a body I caught. Wrong time; wrong body."

"So, how you write the shit you do—compose the fire you do, and you ain't never been in love?" He laughed again.

I gave up on the sequence and turned to him. Rubbing my wet palms over my sweats, I wondered how long we'd been at it. It was Saturday, the day after Lennox ran out of here like a bat out of hell. I hadn't heard from her. A-*fucking*-gain... This time felt different. I wouldn't allow too much time or distance between us. I'd finally got up around one in the afternoon after finishing up with Dale at four in the morning. I texted her while waiting on Dale to return to do more recording this evening and hadn't heard back yet. I'd been checking my phone all session. I wanted to spend some time with her while down here. Even if I couldn't take her out, just kicking it with her had been my favorite pastime since reconnecting with Lennox a few years ago.

"I never said I wasn't in love, D. I've been in love like two...three times."

He smirked. Then Dale swiped his nose contemplatively. "And you never...married any of 'em?"

There was confusion in his tone. Dale was in his mid-forties. Marriage was en vogue for his generation. With mine, it had been fading out. There was no real value to marriage. Too many of my peers didn't see the benefit of combining lives legally and spiritually. We were at war with each other: fuck love. Sex, criticizing, and outsmarting one another was how we engaged. Were those my rules of engagement? No. But it was indeed the race I was in with my female counterparts.

"Nah." I fingered my beard, thinking about the faceless women I'd fucked against the many passionate ones I'd found a genuine connection with, in and outside of the bed. "Marriage for me means forever. I see beautiful women with insightful life-views who know who they are from time-to-time." I smiled at him. "Those are my least favorite."

"Why?"

"Because even after realizing they were above average, I still felt no inspiration to take the relationship further." I shook my head, eyes locked on a random speaker on the wall. "They weren't 'the one.' You know what I mean?" I looked at him.

Dale chuckled. "Shit. Now you've fucked me up. You were in love with them, but they weren't the one?"

"They weren't." I admitted. "There's a difference."

Laughing, he pulled up a rolling stool and sat a few feet away from me. "School me, my nigga."

Shaking my head, I laughed at my damn self. "I ain't about to drop no deep jewels, my G. My shit's been fucked up since I was a kid. I met my "one" before I could fuck her properly. I say that to say, I was so young. And from that experience, no others after it have compared. Love will grow you the hell up. Real love will force-teach you patience. Shit, man, true love will have you craving a woman for years, knowing she's giving her body to another nigga."

"Fuck!" Dale whispered before whistling. "And what do you do with that?"

"You use love to just wait it out." Then I laughed. "You're forced to study love, to extrapolate that shit. Break it up to break it down in lyrics and melodies. *Shit!* Love has leant itself to hooks on rap albums for me—the ugly side of it." I shrugged. "The feel goods and the resentment all come from the same place." I covered my heart with my palm.

Dale looked stunned. Brows high and eyes wild. "Yooooooo." I hated to sound so fucking sappy, but I'd also learned love was pure, so it required honesty. That's what I conveyed to the artists I produced for. You can't address love without being real about who you are and what you're feeling. Did I have my days where I felt like a sappy sucker? Hell fucking yeah! Those were probably the days I didn't call or text. I'd just go into my cocoon. But that place was cold and lonely. My truth was giving my all, including my under-standing, to love. That would draw me out of the cocoon to get back to my truth. *She* was my truth. My love. "What's the craziest shit you've done for love?"

My eyes snapped up, thoughts recalibrated. It took a few seconds for me to consider that. I've tricked a lot on love. It was my joy. I gifted the women I loved with toys that made them happy. Trips, bags, watches, shoes—all of that was in my trick bag. But participating in that type of love language wasn't crazy. Crazy was shit I'd only done with one woman.

"Okay. I got you." I pulled at the ends of my beard. "The craziest shit I've done for love was drive over eight hours to a different state with a gang of Bloods to run up on the O.G.'s daugh-ter's husband."

"What was y'all running up on him for? He hit her?"

"The nigga was a pill head. Heavy. He was talking crazy to the O.G.'s daughter. Doing crackhead shit…fuckin' up the money… stressing her the fuck out. O.G. got word and rounded up his crew. I so happened to be in the room when he called my uncle." Out of nowhere, I busted out laughing. "No shit: I was at my grams' house, telling her how I got invited to play at a party for Erika Erceg. You know her and her family had just gotten poppin' around that time—"

"And she was fuckin…" Dale cut me off snapping his fingers. "Shirez."

"Nah. This was before Shirez. She was fuckin' with D-Struct."

His eyes went wild. "Yoooo! You know who almost fucked D-Struct up?" I gestured with my face. I didn't know. "Divine!" He laughed. "You know who that is. Right? A.D.? Azmir Jacobs, man!"

The lightbulb clicked on in my head. "Oh, shit!" I'd just met him.

Dale nodded while laughing. That's when I understood women were right: men gossip just as much, if not more, than them. That was exactly what this had turned into. It was easy when the Ercegs were the topic. Those Syrian, female-dominated reality show giants would bring it out of you, especially us. Dale and I were two Black men in the industry—he more so than me. Dale was a legend. Had been in the game since about age fourteen. Aside from all of that, the Ercegs—with the exception of one daughter—loved Black men. They were always checking for brothers, which made everything they did gossipy for barbershop chat.

"Yeah. He was with his ex for a long ass time before he married the one he's with now. But the ex fucked around on him with D-Struct."

That's when it clicked. "I ain't heard from or about that nigga in years."

"Because he fucked the wrong bitch!" Dale and I both fell out laughing. "You feel me?" He moved toward me for dap. "Anyway. Back to your ass with the craziest shit you've done for love."

Oh. Right...

"Yeah. I'd just gotten that gig. The original keyboardist dropped at the last minute, and the party was the next night. But when this call came through, I begged my O.G. to let me go. Now, mind you: we're talking like ten to twelve Bloods. So, you know none of them niggas had driver's licenses. When my uncle said no, at first, I reminded him of that. Then he said I could go, but had to stay in the car, and if we got pulled over and caught with guns, I wasn't to claim shit. My dumb ass drove over eight hours to pull up on this nigga. The woman's pops and his crew packed up all her shit, and moved it to a crib she so happened to have stashed away from this nigga."

I was happy as fuck when I learned about it that night. And I felt satisfied when Lennox told me years later how it was Chino who gave her the money and wisdom to do it.

"Oh, word? That's what's up."

I nodded. "But that wasn't the crazy part of the story. What's fuckin' with that is when we were at their old crib, the O.G. took his daughter and her things to the new crib, and I stayed behind with my uncle and a few others. Before we pulled off to follow them, I slipped out of the car, and found the pill head inside the house, packing shit up. Dude is like six inches taller than me. I'd seen him before and could tell his weight had dropped. It was the shit he was on. I ain't give a fuck. I walked into the room he was in and swung on his ass—*BOW!*" I threw a jab in the air.

"Damn!" Dale sat up on the stoop.

"I did. The nigga fell to the floor. He was expecting it—not from me, though. He thought it would come from one of the niggas in there with the way they jumped out on him. So, while he's on the floor, grabbing his bloody nose, I pulled his pretty ass up by the shirt, got close to his mixed-ass eye color, and told him to remember my face, because if he ever threatened or laid a finger on her, my face would be the next and last he'd see. I told him I'd kill his ass. Then I kicked the fucker in the face with my *Timbos*. Knocked him the fuck out. One of the lieutenants was a shortie, Rory. Old head chick that would bust off before you pull out. Lil' thing, too. Ol' girl's like four feet, ten inches, or some shit. Now, she got a legal mind. She was there to tell the O.G.s how far they could or couldn't go depending on the charges at stake. She was standing in the doorway, arms crossed, and I thought she was gonna rip my ass. But she winked, saluted me, then motioned with her hand for me to get the fuck out."

Dale busted out laughing again.

"Word." I nodded. "I wasn't supposed to be there. 'Til this very day, the girl don't even know I was out there, in that shit. But I saw her big crib with her husband, and the one they live in now. I didn't get out of the van for the second one. I kept my ass still, trying not to fuckin' cry like a baby."

"For what?"

I shook my head, defeated. "That I let her marry this weak-ass, dope head for one. Then I felt helpless knowing they had only been married for about two years or so, and he'd been fuckin' up on her. I knew I could love her better than that nigga, and there I was, sitting outside like a fuckin' kid, not doin' shit, but waiting."

"But you fucked her husband up."

"Yeah, but guess who ended up with her that night?" *Again.*

Dale's eyes locked onto me. "That's some shit, Tobe."

"Yeah. For 'the one.'" Feeling fucked up rehashing all that shit, I turned back to the keyboard. Before playing again, I checked my phone, and saw nothing from Lennox.

Once again, I'm this close to the crib you share with him, but won't step foot on the doorstep…

Chapter Twelve

Lennox

"What's going on here?" I asked the first police officer in my path after slamming my car door closed. I had to park in front of a neighbor's house because mine was covered with armed police. "Excuse me!"

The white man with a walrus-styled mustache turned my way. "What business is this of yours, ma'am?" His snarly tone of authority made my blood boil.

"The type that owns the property your compadres are on!" I was snappy because he was being nasty.

Their presence caused anxiety to coat me. It was one of the common emotional and physiological responses I'd learned to cope with since becoming Mrs. Kelvin Richardson.

"Are you Mrs. Richardson?" a female officer asked as she took long lunges toward me.

"Yes."

"She's the wife," the woman told her colleague as she approached me. She stepped into my personal space, I learned quickly it was to control the volume of her message. My neighbors were out looking, or peeking through their windows. Another nightmare I'd lived from time-to-time with no control. "My captain got a call from the judge this morning. Not only did Richardson not comply with the outpatient rehab mandate by the judge, but he approached an undercover last night, trying to cop. When the officer made an attempt at an arrest, he fled. Last night, both under-cover officers were able to identify Richardson—I mean..." She shrugged, and I understood. Kelvin was their prized fighter less than ten years ago. He was also a fucking conspicuous tree in height. "So, the officer got in touch with the prosecutor, his probation officer, and the judge. And the judge..." She gestured toward the house.

Instead of replying—because what the fuck could I say?—I started for my driveway. In my wake, I could hear the two officers informing their flank of colleagues I was "the wife." Inside, Kelvin was pushing his feet into old sneakers. His hair out-grown, clothes wrinkled, face stained with red from a lack of rest and frustration. He was surrounded by officers, radio chirps, and messages from their walkie-talkies filling the thick air.

His hazel-green eyes met me, then the muscles in his face contracted with disgust. "You're never the fuck where you're supposed to be when needed!"

"Excuse me?" I was just with his nephew. After driving him to both his Saturday activities, Scott asked if he could hang out with his soccer teammate this evening. The mother of the friend offered to drop Scott off at home after dinner. Quickly, I was grateful for the last-minute arrangement. Scott wouldn't have to be traumatized, once again, by his uncle's antics. "What's going on here?" I asked Kelvin.

"I need a lawyer. A real one. You can't keep telling me these shitty ass Legal Shield lawyers are helping me!"

"What did you do, Kelvin?" I asked again, my heart racing and armpits misting.

"That's what I've been asking him!" Kelly-Ann wobbled into the room, out of breath, with his wallet in her hand. She must have come up from the basement after getting it. Only Kelly-Ann was allowed down there. God only knew what Kelvin had going on in the basement. I, for sure, didn't want to know. "He don't wanna say nothing. Only yelling for me to call you!"

"Mama!" Kelvin shrieked, eyes closed with passion. "Shut the hell up!"

"Hey!" one of the officers warned him.

Ignoring them, Kelvin stood, now with his sneakers on. His dark glare on me again. "Be a real wife, for once. Use that degree I paid for! Get me a fucking lawyer that works!"

The wind left my chest. It wasn't because I couldn't take his toxic words or energy. I'd been hit with far more viciousness than this from my husband. It wasn't because I was embarrassed about the six officers witnessing my husband's vitriol. Kelvin carried no integrity therefore, I couldn't expect him to demonstrate dignity for me. No. I was astounded by his lack of self-awareness. The absence of accountability.

"Kelvin, what happened to my necklace? The one with my initial in diamonds?"

His head flew back. "I'm 'bout to go to jail, and this bitch asking about jewelry? Oh, my fucking god!"

"What happened to my necklace, Kelvin?" I demanded this time.

"What necklace?" he yelled back.

I liked nice things. Every once in a while, I'd treat myself to more than a manicure, getting my hair done, and being waxed. I liked diamond pieces, a *Louis Vuitton* bag once every few years, and perhaps some *Asè Garb* pieces. I worked hard and should be able to reward myself every now and then. The only problem was I lived with an addict, who, over the years, would steal the breast from a baby's mouth to sell the milk. Kelvin had stolen jewelry I'd received from my grandmother. He'd taken two birthstone pieces my father had purchased for me when I was a child. My husband had taken my entire wallet once, and attempted it for a second time, but I caught him red-handed in my bedroom one night when he thought he would creep inside while I was sleeping.

We slept with locked bedroom doors in my house. It was a sad fact. Once I understood his addiction for what it was, I purchased a safety deposit box at my bank. It was something Kelvin would not have access to under any circumstances just as it was with my bank accounts. I struggled for days wondering why, after returning from Jersey with the *Andretta*'s neckpiece, did I not take it over to the safety deposit box. I'd been beating myself up over it for days since I found out. But in this moment, it hit me.

I wanted to have a piece of Tobias with me in my real life. I wanted something connected to him with me at home. I looked at that necklace night after night when Tobias wouldn't call me all those days. I went looking for it two days ago—tore my room apart —before succumbing to my reality.

That reality was standing in front of me, about to be escorted out by Raleigh's finest.

"I'm done," I told him with spread nostrils and upturned lips. I meant the shit from the pit of my belly.

"Fuck you!" he spit back as they walked him to the door.

I turned in their direction, and spoke even louder, "I'm filing for a divorce. Don't come back here. I don't give a damn what the judge says he wants to do with you. I will have your things sent anywhere in the country you want, but it's all leaving here just like you are!"

"Fuck you, you ugly, hood-rat bitch!" Kelvin channeled the African blood swimming in his veins.

Now, *that* shit turned my stomach.

I tapped the last of my blunt into the ashtray. Before leaving the tiny balcony off of my master bedroom, I tugged on the strap of my trench coat then carried the roach inside. I locked the door behind me, and on my way to the bathroom, there was a knock on the door.

"I'm going to bed." *Shit.* "You okay in there?" It was Scott.

High out of my mind, I didn't want him anywhere near me in this state. "You should have been sleep," I hissed.

"It's almost midnight. So should you!" he nipped right back at me. "Goodnight." I heard him take off.

Now, I was numb to the disappointment I'd normally feel about a thirteen-year-old having to tend to my emotions. Scott wasn't here when his uncle was hauled off by police earlier, but he'd heard about it. His friends from the neighborhood texted him. Kelly-Ann filled Scott in once he was dropped off, too. Once again, I was doused by embarrassment, courtesy of Kelvin Richardson. I hated this life for Scott.

Just as I'd flushed the roach down the toilet, my phone chirped. I didn't jump to check it. I knew who it was. Instead, I moved slowly to the sink to wash my hands, then to the bathtub to turn on the faucet and run a warm bath. *Yup.* A fat blunt, hot soak, and a bag of white cheddar *Cheez-It*s were all I needed tonight. Sauntering back into my bedroom to grab a few things, all I could think about was how I wanted to ensconce myself to lick my wounds.

When I toed into the bathroom again, my phone sounded...*again.* Ignoring it, I caught my image in a long mirror, hanging on an adjacent wall. Bruises. His hand marks were still there, on my cheeks and beneath them. They weren't as red as they were last night when I'd gotten home. They were darkening into a burgundy hue now. The sight of them made my clit throb and nipples tighten into pebbles.

After stepping into the heated water, I took my time picking up my phone. Sighing, I brought it up to my tight eyes, over the water. I noticed more recipients than anticipated. There was a missed call and text from Mya. She said she was checking in. I guessed she was attempting to keep her word of doing a better job at keeping in touch. Right now wasn't a good time for me to respond, so I kept scrolling.

Yup. This one I had anticipated. Tobias, my manstress, was in town, and summonsing me to his den of sin where he did all types of nasty shit to me that I liked too much. And he knew I liked it; and would let him do over and over and over. I'd never known this skilled lover side of Tobias. Ten years ago, it was just...quick, sneaky sex a few times. This. This was sensual sorcery. Pure mind fuck. And I didn't need my brain compromised at this juncture of my life. I meant what I said to Kelvin. I was done.

Being done meant planning my next move. I'd already begun fielding jobs in Jersey. Earlier today, after Kelvin's apprehension, I did a deep dive into an apartment search in New Jersey by way of the popular listing websites. The shit was depressing, reminding me how damn expensive the New York Tri-State area was for no reason. That further dampened my mood, so I gave up. It was Saturday, but I still sent my lawyer an email, explaining what happened today, and asked about any insight she could provide to expedite the separation process. When she surprisingly returned my text within minutes, her news sent me into further despair.

I couldn't kick Kelvin out, although this home was in my name only and had been paid for by me exclusively. Kelvin was my husband and, in fact, a resident here. She advised me to be ready to move if he, predictably, said he wouldn't. That, of course, couldn't happen until January when Terry would be released from prison. And as simple as it may sound, dumping the kid on his mother the minute she's released from prison didn't sit right with me. Ideally, I'd like to provide a gradual re-introduction. The fact of the matter was, Terry would be discharged to her mother's home in Knightdale where other members of her family lived, too. Scott was well acquainted with that family. I'd made sure of it. So, while moving him in there wouldn't be too much of a culture change, Scott living with his mother would be a huge adjustment for him.

And I'd be over four hundred miles away, unable to get to him should shit go awry...

I'll never put myself in this situation again!

I wouldn't. Never would I trust someone with my livelihood, be it with advice for it, or joining theirs with mine. I certainly didn't want to jump from a failed marriage into a passionate affair with a late-adolescent crush. That would be foolish. It would feed into an insecure narrative I'd been carrying. That was how I was weak, never having any guidance from dedicated parents. I'd always felt bastardized as a child and adult. Since I didn't have parents to help establish me as a person, it had been quite difficult to define who I was as a woman.

As a kid, along with the little girls at the church I grew up in, I'd talk about being a mother and wife one day. It was as though that was all we were raised to be, other than to be worshippers. My desires were established before my identity had been. Being a mother right now seemed foreign. My experience as a wife made me never want to sign up for this shit ever again. But I didn't want to be alone. As a wife, I'd been lonely. As the object of my manstress' long-term affection, I'd felt empowered. Why on earth would I marry again?

Sighing, I placed the phone on the floor then lay back in the tub, closing my eyes. I'd be scheduling a session with my therapist first thing in the morning.

Tobias

"Daddy, are you still in North Carolina?" she called out, using her soft tone, created exclusively for me.

"Nah, baby." I rubbed my tight eyes as I lay in my bed, the shades in my bedroom all closed, blocking out the morning sun. "I'm home now." I yawned, "Got back on Monday."

"Oh," Elia chirped into the phone.

"Is it snowing up there yet?"

Elia giggled. "No, Daddy. It's not snowy at home yet either."

"You never know here in Jersey. We get snow sometimes in November, even if it's just once."

"Are you going to Granny's today?"

I pulled in a deep breath, still trying to wake up. It was Thanksgiving Day, and I was back in Jersey, feeling stuck as hell. I went out to a few clubs last night. StentRo had an appearance in SoHo, and afterward, my crew and I headed to *Club Sin* in Harlem. That was lit as hell. I loved the club. No, I wasn't the type to play the dance floor, or plot on women. My reason for being there was recreational. I needed to know what people from that demographic listened to. It was my responsibility to know the vibes happening in there, as well as day-parties, something attended by a slightly older demographic. There was so much energy in a club, so many electric vibes that it could quiet the noise of my personal shit.

"Oh, nah." I yawned again. "Uncle Smite's taking her to her cousin's in Plainfield. You know she likes to get out on the holidays from time to time."

"Then where are you going to eat?"

"Where are *you* going to eat?" I teased her.

"Daddy!" my baby groaned. "You know I'll be here with Mommy's family today!"

"Yeah," I chuckled. "I know. Maybe Daddy'll order something from *DiFillippo's*, and get some work done."

"Working on Thanksgiving?"

"Who do you think's gonna pay for your *Disney* trip next month, lil' girl?"

Elia giggled first. "Daddy!" she groaned again.

My line beeped with an incoming call. I pulled the phone toward my face. "Baby girl, your Uncle Raj is trying to call me right now. Hit me later when you get a chance. If not, I'll stop by tomorrow if you don't get home too late."

"Okay, Daddy! Mommy said we're leaving first thing in the morning. Tell Uncle Raj Happy Thanksgiving!"

"Awwww! I will."

"And Mommy just said don't forget about what y'all talked about. Love you! Bye!"

"Okay. Love you back even more," I replied to her, not quite knowing what Krista could have been referring to. Then I clicked over. "Yo, my baby said why the fuck you calling her daddy on the day of the giving?"

"Oh, shit! Tell my niece—wait. Didn't you say Lia was going to Krista's peeps' spot in Boston?"

Rubbing my nose while stifling a yawn, I answered, "Yeah. I'm just fuckin' with you. She said whaddup, though."

"Give the cutie my love when you speak to her again. Anyway, what's on the agenda for today?"

I placed my hand on my bare chest. "I 'on't know. I honestly haven't had the time to think about it. Elia's ass called, waking me up."

"You went out last night?"

"It was mad real, too," was my way of answering in the affirmative.

"That's what's up. I told Blue you were coming through."

"To Sparta?"

"Where else?"

My face went tight. "You ain't tell that Black woman no shit like that!"

I could hear the laughter in his voice. "How you figure?"

"Because you don't lie to your wife, so why would you start on this fine holiday?"

"Oh, word, Tobe? You ain't pulling up on us today?"

"All the way out to Sparta?"

"Nigga, you only an hour away. You come out here to work; you can't come to be with family?"

I broke character, cracking the fuck up. "Why are you so pressed about me coming out there, choir boy?"

"Because ya ass was in North Carolina with your lil' mistress-boy—"

I fell out laughing hard as hell. When I could speak again, I asked, "Oh, this what we doing, chief? We being petty?"

"Maybe, but fuck that! This is where home is. I get it; you're an artist, too. Your role is to create and produce. I ain't been in this game as long as 'Mr. May/December,' but I treat mine like they should know where they belong. And plus," Raj cleared his throat. "Wynter does have a few things to run past you."

"For who?"

"Who the fuck you think, nigga?"

"I know she's your wife, but Wynter's written some heat for other artists, man."

"Nothing's surpassing my shit on the charts. She writes her best work for me. Last I heard, that was contagious."

That was a small jab. I made no secret of Raj being my favorite contemporary artist to work with, and that said a lot. Brielle and Pixie's talents knew no bounds, but Raj gave me endless vulnerability. It also helped that he, too, was a musician. His throat and mind in music was sick! The nigga hadn't missed since he'd been married, and, coincidentally, reached out to me for heat. Together, we'd been creating chart-topping hits.

"Here we go!" I groaned much like Elia a few minutes ago when I teased her about having to work today.

"I ain't begging. I'm about to head out that way for the holiday giveaway we're doing with T.B., but dinner starts at six sharp, nigga."

I was still undecided. In the back of my mind, I'd still been thinking about hitting up a club in Philly. A budding producer was throwing his birthday party tonight. He'd been trying to get on my line for a while now.

"All the way out to *Spart*—"

"Yeah. Sparta, nigga. All the way!" Raj snapped, partially in jest. "You want me to send the jet to pluck you at Teterboro? That'll get your ass here?"

Raj could be a recluse to some. If you were lucky enough to be a part of his exclusive circle, it went a long way. I knew shit about the nigga I'd never breathe to a best friend. *Tuh!* I also understood this to be a power play. My boy didn't like me spending too much time with Dale. He likely felt like it was him sharing his juice with another artist. So, just as Raj copped to, he wanted me and Dale to know where I belonged, which he felt was with him.

Shit!

I wanted to sleep in for a few more hours, workout, possibly get a hair and face cut, then get ready to party some more tonight.

"Fuck it. I'll be there." I brushed my hands down my face. "Lemme call to see if I can get up with my barber and do some shit. I'll be there. And don't think you laying down ya pimpin' over here, my nigga."

I could hear the smile in his voice. "You know it's all love, brother. You got me, and I got you." Shaking my head, my eyes rolled up to the fan on the ceiling. "One last thing."

"What?"

"Stay the fuck out of North Carolina if that situation ain't feeding your soul."

What?

How did Ragee know—

There was no need to ask. Our circle was small. Someone on my team could have casually mentioned my stay in North Carolina to someone on his, or directly to the man himself. Raj was referring to Lennox, which hurled me into a crazy state of fucking confusion. So, was this push for me to come to his crib for dinner not about his sensitive ass being possessive? Was it about my relationship with the elusive Lennox?

"I don't even know what that means, my G?" I took the rejection route, some shit that wasn't my style at all. I believed in being direct with my confrontations. Everyone in my crew knew this. But if Raj wanted to play big brother, he'd have to be more straight forward. This was an extremely fucking sensitive topic.

Were my friends talking about me behind my back?

"It means when you're without her, you're worried about her. When you leave her, your mood takes a dive, bruh. I'll always respect your decisions, but you can't knock me for making observations on a cat who helped me fix my shit. Are you your best with or without Lennox? 'Cause, I'mma keep it a bean with you: she don't wear well on you at all, Black man. When it comes to her, either you're down or...you're down."

Damn...

When I was quiet for too long, Raj came back with, "Whatever you need. Anything—even if it's to solidify your shit with her. You need to get away? I got the house in *Saint Justin*. You wanna fly out?

The jet is yours. Anything you need to remain whole, I'm here for you, bro. That's on everything."

I hadn't heard from Lennox since she'd left the rental in Chapel Hill six days ago. It wasn't like her to not take my calls and ignore texts for this long. Before her homecoming last month, we'd spoken every day—other than after our second, first kiss when my jealous ass retreated knowing she was back home with her husband. We talked a few times throughout the day. Like my man Pleasure P said on a track, we didn't fuss and argue. I made sure I provided a space of peace for Lennox, understanding what she lacked at home. At most, she'd get on me about resting more, and I'd set her straight on taking care of her glorious body God had blessed *us* with. We laughed and shared…comforted each other.

Now…this. *What in the fuck did I do?* I'd been insecure like a motherfucker. Had I gone too hard on her about caring too much about her husband and his family who lived in her crib? The sex? Did I overdo it? Yeah. It had to have been. With my friendship, I could provide a woman with a sense of liberty. When I made love to Lennox, I exposed my possessive nature. It had to be the sex. It was too heavy. *But I ain't even pull out my bag of toys!* Why hadn't she been hitting me back? I'd been lowkey sick, worrying about her.

I may not have left the state on Monday if, on the way to the airport, I didn't have Charlie, my cousin and assistant, detour to her job. We picked up a cheap bouquet of flowers from a local drug store before the stop. I had him go inside and ask the front desk to see her. I knew security at the hospital was on ten. On top of that, we were flying commercial, and cutting it close. It could have taken her thirty minutes or more if she was in a meeting or training. Or what if she sent someone else down? Lucky for me, as Charlie's goofy ass was waiting for security to call up to her office, Lennox and her team were coming off the elevator, on their way into a meeting. She spotted him first and accepted the flowers. He'd laid eyes on her, and that was all I needed. We made it to the gate of the plane seconds before they shut the door.

"I hear you, man," I finally responded to my guy. "I hear you and appreciate you."

I needed to fall back from this shit with Lennox. If finally being this close to her cost me the worry and bitchiness I'd been feeling since last month, maybe she didn't belong to me. Maybe I'd been viewing this shit wrong all along.

"To God be the glory. It's only love," Raj reassured.

"Always love. See you later, man."

"Peace."

I hung up with Raj then sent Charlie a text about today's itinerary. Next, I shot a text to my barber, who may or may not have been working on the holiday. She'd come through in a clutch all the time for me. Hitting her up early may increase my chances of getting my shit done.

While waiting to hear back, I covered my face with my arm as I lay on my back, head against my pillows. Today, I was without my baby, Elia. Grams and Smite had their own plans, and already, the tightness in my chest from stressing over Lennox had begun. Ragee's words of concern added more weight.

As a kid, I was a loner. I had love around me, but never anything stable. My mother was good to me. A single woman who worked two, and sometimes, three jobs at a time to pay the bills. My pops was a weirdo, nomad keys player, who enjoyed sniffing coke with a glass of *Sprite* during his gigs. When I was four or five, he taught me to play the keys. Before I could get really good at it, he left Irvington.

I saw him sparingly, but definitely knew who the man was. He'd drop off money to my mother once in a while; nothing ever consistent. But his teaching sparked my interest for instrumentation, and I learned how to play even better over the years from music teachers, and an organ player at a church next door to the three-family home we lived in. We weren't members of the church, but my mother made nice with the pastor, and a few of his parishioners in passing, over the years. I got into drumming, and composing eventually, too, through one of their drummers.

When I was a freshman in high school, my mother was diagnosed with pancreatic cancer. That damn demon came on fast and hard, and the shit changed me forever. My whole focus shifted to becoming her caretaker. I learned how to cook, expanded my cleaning skills, and to articulate my words for doctors and pharmacists, who all seemed to have their own languages. Staff from all shifts at the E.R. were familiar with me. Rounds of chemo and radiation zapped her vitality. Eventually, she couldn't work. Moms didn't have much family, and my paternal grandmother did what she could. I'd play for moms when she'd go despondent, had to wash her body, her hair, and even brushed her teeth.

As a kid, your faith game stays on ten. You're taught that "happily ever after" is mandatory. No matter how many times I saw my mother vomit or shit on herself, or go bald, or become despondent, I always believed in her full recovery. That was until that one traumatic experience comes and knocks you on your ass. Mine came twice, and about a year apart.

My mother died in the middle of my junior year. I came in from deejay'ing a party, something I did for a few dollars to help ends meet, and found my mother dead. She wasn't in a deep sleep or unconscious. My girl was dead. There was a different scent when I entered our apartment. I knew before calling 911 that my mother was gone.

Within a week, I moved in with my father's mother. She and I had always been cool, so living with her was an easy transition. What made it breezy was having my father return home after all those years. For the first time, we lived under the same roof. He took me on local gig runs with him. I'd play during his breaks, and even played a few times when he wouldn't show up. He'd keep the money, but I didn't care. There was something right about having a pops, finally.

My uncle, Smite, was in prison at this time. He had a reputation on the streets, one that extended to his big brother, who had returned home a junkie. I didn't get it then, but over years of reflecting, I realized my father coming back to Essex County had nothing to do with me or being home. It was because his coke habit had grown hungry to the point of him violating the people around him. Essentially, pops ran home for refuge.

He died the day after my high school graduation. Two days

before, he came home in the middle of the night with a nasty stab wound just beneath his chest. It was about three in the morning, and he woke me up, somehow managing to not disturb his mother's sleep. Dude needed help. I'd done first aid shit for my mother, helping her with her port and cleaning a small wound from an unexpected fall, but nothing like this. Wanting to aid in his need, I found shit around the house I thought could help. He kept saying over and over he didn't want to go to the hospital. I honored that. I managed to bandage him up as he dozed off. Then, there was the crazy ass cleaning of all the blood he'd lost. I never went back to sleep. After erasing all signs of his arrival home by morning, I showered and left for school.

Over the next day or so, I got to act my age, and be a kid, engaging in all the senior activities, in and out of school. We drank, partied, I deejayed, and tried to get girls. All the fun shit I should have been doing since freshman year. I had so much fun in those two days, my grieving for my mother had numbed a bit, until waking up the day after my graduation with a hangover to EMS flooding my grandmother's house. She'd finally tried to wake him. My father had been dead in his room for over a day. He never left his bed after my novice bandaging. I had to talk to detectives at the precinct. They kept me there for more than half a day until convinced I didn't contribute to his death.

That was the second trauma. Losing my parents after having so little of them forced me to feel every emotion those two elements brought on. I craved love. I loved loving. I cared about people too fucking much in my early years. After my father died, I had to dial that shit back in. I gave love, but love didn't boomerang to me in the same measure. Being raised by a senior-aged grandmother left a lot on the table. Grams was too old to chase me around to play sports if I were into them. She was past her prime and couldn't support my music beyond buying me cheap keyboards and drum set pieces. The woman was worth her weight in gold, but couldn't replace an actual attending parent.

Love or a lack thereof from our formative years shape our hearts. Mine seemed to be too big. Maybe it was due to me being a caretaker as a kid. *Shit.* Had I still been a caretaker? When I looked at how I approached making music, I had to tend to the weak parts of people and manipulate them. I had to inspire them to address and fix those weak parts as well. I was a fucking cheerleader for love in all forms.

But who the fuck is loving me?

I was twenty-nine, and still alone. Laying in my bed on Thanksgiving, arguably the biggest American family holiday there is. Yup. Raj was right: it was time for me to reset my shit.

Chapter Thirteen

Lennox

I brought a cup of coffee to my mouth for a sip as Rachel, Kelly-Ann's sister, entered the dining room.

"Damn," she gestured to my laptop on the table that I'd been on. "You don't let work go, huhn?"

At first, I couldn't decide on my response. It was Thanksgiving morning, and we were at Kelvin's family's house, where dinner would be. We came over in the morning because Kelly-Ann's car was in the shop, and she wanted to help her family cook. Also, Scott's second cousins were in town for the holiday, and they wanted to hang out. So, I brought my laptop with me, only I wasn't performing work duties the hospital paid me for. I'd been on the hunt for an apartment and tweaking my resignation letter.

I decided on a smile. "What were you working on in there?" They'd been at it since before we arrived an hour ago.

"I cut up my vegetables for the roast." She rolled her eyes, voice lowering to a whisper, "I needed to get the hell out of there before I cussed out one of those bitches..." Her top lip lifted in a snarl, revealing her gold-capped tooth—an eighties thing. Even white girls emulated Black culture, still do. There were pictures around the house with her rocking the *8 Ball* jackets I'd seen my father in, in my grandmother's old photo albums. It was hilarious. Rachel had two kids, both by Black men, too. "I said, I'mma come out here to stay out of trouble."

Oh, lord…

We typically spent Thanksgiving here at Kelvin's family's home, so I felt comfortable enough to stay with Kelly-Ann and Scott, as opposed to dropping them off, and going back to my house, only to have to drive back for dinner. Kelly-Ann's family were the Nelsons. There were three sisters, all of whom were relatively close. I guessed they displayed the typical emotional seesaw behavior of siblings. They loved like sisters, and fought like them, too. It was hard to tell for me: I had no siblings to speak of.

The Nelson sisters came from a two-parent household, and lived in this very home. Kelly-Ann, being the oldest, inherited the house when their parents died. However, when Kelvin made it into the *League*, he purchased an even larger home for his mother. Rachel felt the house should have gone to her, since she was the next in line chronologically. It had been rumored that Marcia, the youngest sister, was favored by Kelly-Ann. That could have possibly been why Kelly-Ann told both sisters they could move in once she'd left for her luxury home years ago, instead of going in the pecking order. That still didn't sit right with Rachel.

Rachel, the second oldest of the Nelson clan, ambled into the room for a chair closest to me at the dining room table. I knew right away what it meant.

Gossip.

And their southern accents made the fodder even more entertaining.

Rachel leaned toward me. "She in there playing boss like we ain't all grown."

"Who?"

"Who the hell else?" Her head rounded as she spoke. "Your goddamn mother-in-law! We do this shit every year. This year it changes because you got car issues?" she referred to Kelly-Ann. "Tell me why you ain't got your car, Kelly-Ann! Huhn?" Rachel rolled her eyes then flipped her hair. That struck a thought. All the

Nelsons had a gradient of blond hair, including the parents. Rachel, here, was the only brunette. *Talk about the black sheep of the family.* "We *all* know Kelvin did something to the car. The car drove just fine— hell! It just passed inspection the week before. Then Kelvin started driving it after leaving that mandated, drug rehab program. And all of a sudden, something's wrong? She don't like to talk about that there, though."

I pulled my cup of coffee between my palms, elbows resting on the table. Kelly-Ann never told me what was wrong with the car. She rarely drove it even before Kelvin crashed his *BMW*. It was in pretty good condition. She drove it to Kelvin's court date on Monday morning as I was leaving out for work, but I noticed Marcia had dropped her off that evening, well after I'd gotten home. I didn't ask, so wrapped up in my own conundrum of a future.

"Does she know what's wrong with it?"

She rolled her eyes again. "Tuh! Something with the engine. I heard Marcia telling Cousin Sam about it the other day. But Kelly-Ann don't wanna focus on the truth. She likes to criticize everybody else, and don't like to share her own dirty laundry. She in there bitchin' 'bout how the fridge is on its way out, and that she told me to have somebody come take a look at it or replace it." She clamped her palms to her wide waist. "Do I look like I got money shooting from my pussy?" Rachel counted on her hands. "I got Lil' Jeremy's sports, Layla's gymnastics, still gotta pay my part here, and I done been cut down to part-time at the *Dixie Pig*! I ain't got no rich daughter-in-law. My kids don't make good money!"

This was the same list of grievances I'd heard over the years from Rachel, who I liked a lot. None of the sisters were well off or particularly successful by any measure, but Rachel was the most down to earth. She kept it real, even when it was ugly. And, typically with the Nelson sisters, it was ugly.

"I'm sorry to hear that. What's wrong with the fridge?"

"The light keep flickerin', and Marcia swears it don't stay cold consistently. But who is Kelly-Ann to tell us what to do with our fridge? She don't even live here. She need to be worried about what's going on with her son!" Rachel glanced over her shoulder before leaning toward me again. "You know she mad at you for not going to Kelvin's court date on Monday. Right?" My neck whipped back. "Yup. The nerve of her!"

The nerve of her was right. Kelly-Ann didn't have to support my decision to leave her son, but she could in no way criticize me either. She hadn't mentioned anything to me about this, something she'd had plenty of opportunity to.

We live in the same house!

"She said it made him look bad to the judge that you weren't there. Said Kelvin looked heartbroken and lonely with those cuffs on, standing before the judge. Marcia said the judge ain't have no pity for Kelvin this time. You see all that time he gave him!"

I shook my head. "Time?" When Kelvin crashed his car on school property, the judge finally mandated a drug rehab program. But because Kelvin had always been treated with kiddie gloves in his hometown, and even state, the judge made it a short-term, ten-day program to begin immediately. Kelvin only stayed four of the ten days. I didn't think of the consequences of him leaving prematurely, so emotionally torn between my need to get off this cycle with him and beginning a sexual relationship with Tobias. Kelvin's shit had finally been placed on the back burner of my immediate worries. "She hasn't mentioned anything. I assumed the judge would only have him stay in the program longer."

"He is! Try nine months!" Rachel's eyes were wide with disbelief herself.

"Whoa!" I blinked hard. "In a drug rehab?"

"The judge said if he fucks this one up, Kelvin's going to prison!"

Wow! Wow! Wow! Kelvin wouldn't be home anytime soon. How would he fair in an institution? He never attempted more than a detoxing program over the years, not even when the *League* begged him. Could Kelvin share space with strangers? Take orders from others?

"And watch your friends." Rachel was all in my face at this point. Friends? What friends did I have that needed to be watched?

I didn't discuss my Kelvin shit with anyone but my therapist. "I'm hearing some weird shit with people being fake...having an agenda with your man, girl—"

"What're you in here talking about with your big ass mouth?" Marcia was at the opening of the dining room, neck a shade of flaming burgundy. "You think we can't hear you?" She threw her index finger into the air.

Kelly-Ann was on Marcia's heels, into the room. The woman moved faster than she ever did at home. "I'm not afraid of anybody! I'll say my shit straight to her face if I need to!"

My brows met. "Then what do you need to say, Kelly-Ann?"

She rounded her sister, coming farther into the room. "Alls I said was you should've been in that courtroom on Monday! You're his wife. The judge looks at things like that! You didn't even get him a lawyer!" Her tone was defensively high, but I could tell Kelly-Ann meant those words from her core.

"Why would I be there?"

"Because you're his wife!" Marcia repeated.

"The wife he's stolen from? The wife he berates? The wife he doesn't respect? The wife who's about to pay out her ass for that last accident on school property?"

"He's sick! Okay?" Kelly-Ann argued. "It's a mental health issue!"

"Okay." I closed my laptop. "A mental health issue he's had all of our marriage. That's eight years, Kelly-Ann! So, why is the first time he's doing a residential program it's because it's court-ordered?"

"It has to be when he's ready!" Marcia answered.

"Yeah," the oldest Nelson agreed. "You know how this goes, Lennox. The poor boy is addicted to drugs! It's not his fault. That first accident messed him up, and those doctors prescribed meds too strong for his system. Where's your compassion?"

"Where was yours when you caught him in her room the other day stealing that diamond necklace?" Rachel demanded to know. "Had the *Andretta's* box and all!"

My jaw fell. She'd seen Kelvin steal my jewelry?

"That's it!" Marcia slapped the table with her hands. "She's coming back home. She's too old for this shit, Lennox! What did you expect her to do? Fight him for it? The woman's disabled!"

"Have I treated her harshly?" My pulse began to race, this whole scenario catching me off guard. "I've never mistreated you. Never disrespected you."

"It's about what you've done to my son!"

"Me?"

"Yeah. You! You emasculated him! At first, you just kept to yourself when you moved down here. I guess you weren't happy when he was off, busy playing basketball. Then, when you called up North to your hoodlum daddy, and him and his homies came and attacked Kelvin like that...whatcha think was gonna happen to him as a man?"

I needed to get this straight. "Are you blaming me for your son's behavior?"

"Yes! Yes, I am, Lennox. You young girls think alls you gotta do is be pretty. Then, when the man falls on hard times, he's the only one to blame. Yeah; you got a job. A good one. But then, you think you're all high and mighty. What kind of man wants that in his woman? What good do you bring to the man? He don't even sleep in the bed with you. Ain't never really! You know how awful of a wife you gotta be for a man not to wanna come to your bed?"

Her words hit like acid. "Excuse me?"

"You're cold, Lennox! Your friends say it, too," Marcia announced.

"To him!" Kelly-Ann qualified.

She had to. I'd always been kind to her. I'd had my issues with her lack of support for her son's accountability, but never treated her badly. All this time she'd been kicking my back in to her sisters.

My pulse wouldn't slow, and now my mouth was dry. I wanted to go. My first thought was Scott. He was off with his cousins, and wouldn't be back for hours, likely. Perhaps that was a good thing. I didn't need him hearing this or seeing me leave. Grabbing my things from the table and chair to the right of me, I struggled to keep calm.

"Are you married?" I asked Kelly-Ann. "Are you?" that next one was for Marcia. "Have you ever been married?"

"What does this have to do with how you treat her son? My nephew?" Marcia asked.

"She's doing the best she can with no support!" Rachel argued on my behalf.

"It has to do with the fact that I've been married to a man—"

Kelly-Ann cut me off, throwing her hand in the air dismissively. "Oh, c'mon! It was for his money. Girl, they were all lined up. You were chosen because you were pretty and was in school. You knew what you were signing up for!"

"Do you hear yourself as a woman?" I asked her, clutching my things to my chest. "You've just confirmed my suspicion all these years. He never married me for noble reasons. He brought me down to his hometown and has ignored, embarrassed, and belittled me for eight years. But I was chosen because I'm pretty? Do you remind him of that every time you hear him call me ugly? Your son has taken from me all these years. And at best, he what? Paid for a few semesters of my school? He's stolen from me—"

"He's stolen from me, too, Lennox!" Kelly-Ann was red now.

"Yeah!" Marcia echoed the nerve of a sentiment.

"But he's your son," I made clear, trembling in my heels at this point. "Not mine. I've done this longer than I should have. I've wasted my youth with a man who doesn't accept accountability. He gets angry that I exist. Angry that I beg him to do better. Angry that I don't allow him to drain my bank account or my identity as a woman. He gives nothing!" I shouted. "He validates nothing! He produces nothing! He inspires nothing! He only tears down. And you, as a woman, want to judge me for simply surviving his shit?"

"He's surviving you!" Kelly-Ann returned. "And he's my only living son. My other one's dead from choosing the wrong girl. You think I won't fight for my last living child? You're the problem, Lennox, and I've had enough. I'll be moving out ASAP. He goes, then I go!"

Rachel laughed. "You forget your grandson lives there, too?"

"He don't need her!" Kelly-Ann turned to leave. "We don't need your shit no more, Lennox. None of us!"

My feet began to move. Swiftly, I was into the cramped living room and headed to the door. I could hear animated chatter happening behind me, but couldn't feel my lungs to breathe. All I felt was a need to escape. Once again, I found myself in self-protective mode. When I felt attacked by my husband, I'd hang tight emotionally until I was alone and could process the pain. Kelvin wasn't the pitcher of venom today. In his wake, his family doled it out.

I felt betrayed. For eight years, I'd never felt like family, but never felt better than Kelvin's either. I assimilated, spending time with his family, and helping out when I could. I accepted Scott, and even assisted with money for the family when asked. No, I didn't think I was one of them. But I did expect honesty when it came to me dealing with their troubled relative. I expected women to have compassion for women.

After throwing myself into the car, I tossed my purse, phone, and laptop into the passenger's seat. A single thought occurred, and without any preamble or hesitation at all, I reached for my phone. With a shaky hand, I tapped away.

Tobias

I stopped the track and rewound it again. As I rode on the passenger's side this holiday afternoon, I played with a record I'd

been working on for Dale. Something was missing. Hitting play, I closed my eyes behind my *Asè Garb* sunglasses and listened for the lead up to the bridge. I stopped and rewound it again.

Next to me, driving my car, Charlie readjusted himself in his seat. I threw him a hard ass stare. If he even moaned the wrong way, I'd cuss his ass out. He had my *i7* for the past two days. I'd told him a thousand times not to smoke in or around my property. If he loved weed, I didn't need to know it. When he came to pick me up this morning to drive up to Sparta, I smelled traces of it in my shit. And it wasn't on him. The scent was coming from my ride.

I wish your big ass would say something…

Charlie knew not to even look my fucking way. I hit rewind again. Taking a deep breath, I absorbed every harmony, drum—the entire melody. Instinctively, I began to hum notes, adding a melodic layer. I zoned out, opening my brain to all of the elements. Ideas began to flow.

Then the music cut.

My eyes shot open and caught when the *Bluetooth* was alerting me of a call.

"A call from Lennox. Should *I*—"

"*Yes!*" I damn near barked at the dashboard.

"Okay. Answering."

The call couldn't connect fast enough. "Hello?" I asked, too hard and too soon.

"Tobias?" her voice thick, volume low. Lennox had been crying.

"Yeah. What's good? Where are you?"

It took her a second or two before she answered, "I'm in Raleigh." She sniffled. "Outside Kelvin's family's house."

My body coiled tightly in the car seat. "What's *wrong*—did he hit…" I sounded too thirsty and needed to calm the hell down.

"No." The cry in her throat more evident. "He's in a program. His family… I just got into it with Kelly-Ann. She's moving out. She blamed me for…everything. She called me cold. Me!" She cried.

"Where are you going?"

"*I*—" She hesitated. "I don't know. I'm just so angry. I feel so blindsided, Tobias! What woman feels that way about another woman? A young woman? I swear, days like this I wish I had my mother…"

My eyes closed and I pinched the bridge of my nose. "Head to the airport."

"What?" She whimpered.

"Go to the airport, Lennox."

"For what? I don't have any clothes."

"I need you to listen to me. Get to the airport. I'll fly you up here and get you back home. Just get to the airport."

"*I*—" Lennox couldn't speak. Finally, she mentioned, "Scott."

"Where is he?"

"I left him. He's with his cousins, fishing."

"Then he'll be fine. Scott's with his family. And if Kelly-Ann needs help, she can get help from Terry's mother. She ain't helpless, Lennox. She can step up in your absence." When she didn't speak right away, I repeated. "Get to the airport. I need to make a few calls. I'll hit you back and tell you where to park."

I finally took a breath when she sniveled, "Okay."

Lennox

We were cleared to remove our seatbelts. As I obeyed, my attention shot across the aircraft to Danny G, who was unclipping his as well. He must have felt my curious glare and glanced up. Then he chuckled.

"Girl, we good. See. We landed safely."

I was still stuck on how Tobias arranged for me to fly to New Jersey on Ragee's private jet. Private. I had to park in a smaller lot at the airport, too. It took longer to make it to the airport, park, then board than it did to arrive in Jersey.

The rich are rich for a reason.

"Yo," Danny G tossed his chin toward his window. "Go 'head."

I stood and grabbed my things to see what he was referring to. But then the flight attendant appeared, directing me to the front of the plane. Without hesitation, I began toward the door that was being opened. As I took down the stairs, I tried stealing glances at massive acreage. Lush, green, botanical scenery for days. This was clearly private property. A full estate.

Finally, I looked ahead. The captain and co-captain were at the foot of the steps, greeting me just as professionally as they did when we met in Raleigh. One gestured ahead with his hand. Following his sight, my lungs seized. He was standing next to a golf cart off the runway. Even under a *Kings* baseball cap, I could make out that full beard and robust frame from a distance. My heart burst open as I continued down the stairs, my short legs taking long strides toward him.

Tobias' expression was placid, but his aura expectant. A goofy smile warmed my face as I traveled, mere feet from him. I reached for his thick body before I could touch him. He didn't waste a second to greet me. His scent and heat in low, and damp November temps warmed my soul. I inhaled his strong, protective countenance for seconds long. I had just been a crying mess two hours ago, and now, I felt a deluge of emotions I couldn't control.

I peered up to his hooded eyelids. "I didn't call because I don't want to be one of those women, running from one bad relationship to a savior. I mean…" I swallowed. "I know you're more than that —we're more than just a passionate fling—but I have to feel the ground myself. When I'm with you, I'm floating on air. I'm feeling too much. Then Kelvin got arrested, and I fell into the blues. I've been trying to arrange my exit. My therapist warned me about closing out my affairs with my marriage before being swept up in a tide of emotions with another being or thing. She's right. I shut you out and I'm sorry."

Tobias, still impassive, dug his big fingers into my curls, reaching for my scalp. He gripped my skull firm enough to tilt my face toward his, then dipped down and kissed me. His mouth was hungry. His ravishing pace expressed forgiveness and, oddly, patience. My body thundered, collapsing against his. I wasn't accustomed to this level of intimacy with any man, not even my husband. It was wild for me to be kissing another man out in the open considering my sensitive situation. But I couldn't care less. My heart felt at home against his hard body. I tasted him greedily until he pulled away. His smile had finally arrived, eyes now tight with lust.

"I'mma have to pull up on your therapist. Let her know I'm the real deal. I was made to love you," his delivery thick and assured. "It's a slightly obsessive love, and I see how that can be problematic for you and me. But I'm working to prove I can be the man for you. I'll take you as you are. A year from now, when Richardson's name ain't tied to yours, you won't be better wrapped with a bigger, prettier ribbon. You're perfect as you are. Always have been to me." Tobias pressed his lips firmly into mine in a kiss. "It's late. Let's get you something to eat." He pulled me toward the passenger side of the cart.

"Yuuuurp!" It was Danny G greeting him, now deboarding the plane himself.

Tobias tapped his chest with his hand while moving back to the driver's side. He sparked the engine and switched gears to leave.

"Aren't you going to wait for Danny G?"

"Nah." Tobias pulled off. "Leech got 'im." He pointed behind us to another golf cart.

"This is a massive ass property. Where are we?"

"Ragee's backyard."

Oh... I glanced around, even more impressed. "That was his plane?" Tobias nodded his head. My heart fluttered again for him.

"You good?" Tobias asked me, again, for the fiftieth time since he walked me into an opulent mansion in the middle of Sussex County, New Jersey. Huge.

Huge!

The home had a black and white contemporary theme. The ceilings were tall, some vaulted, and the halls endless. I'd only been inside three rooms, but had ambled past several. This home was a dream. Long and wide windows with garnished treatments. The dining room table we were eating at with eighteen other guests had been the longest I'd ever seen.

I was eating at Ragee *freaking* McKinnon's mansion. *Ragee McKinnon!* And he had a celebrity ensemble at his holiday dinner. Tori *friggin'* McNabb and her family were here. I accidentally walked in on her breastfeeding in Ragee's office, having mistook Ragee's instructions for the powder room. Of course, it was awkward as hell. I couldn't stop apologizing. She was so gracious, unhurried when she told me it was okay. Her husband was tall, meeting her lengthy stature. They looked damn good together. She had been retired for some years now, but still looked super fit.

How?

Trent Bailey, from the *Connecticut Kings*, was here with his family, too. His wife, Jade, was beautiful. Tobias once told me we favored. I could see why he would say so considering both our heights and complexions. Jade worked well against her husband's height and weight, being so petite. I noticed her throwing her weight into him a time or two, Trent's body not effected by the intrusion at all. Her eyes were a beautiful hazel, and mine were a light color, too. She was gorgeous, and so was Trent. It was cool, telling people I'd seen him play live, and now, I was sharing a Thanksgiving meal with him and his family.

Wow!

Yes, I'd known he and Tobias were colleagues. Tobias practically revived Ragee's musical career, although he said all the time, the credit shouldn't go to him exclusively. Tobias and I had been platonic friends for well over a year before our first kiss. He'd wanted me sexually, as I had him, but we honored the friendship before going where our flesh seemed to have "needed" to be. Over the past three years, we talked and talked.

There was very little I didn't share with him once I'd grown to trust Tobias. And he'd shared a lot with me. He spoke about how his friendship with Raj had deepened once they worked on their first, full album collaboration. Tobias had mentioned Raj's wife, Wynter. He'd shared how she was a budding writer with growing success, and how they'd adopted three boys a while ago. I'd even seen Ragee backstage at two of his concerts last year, and the year before, had been in his *Checkerboard* club, in the main room with him, at the same time. But being in his home, watching his chemistry with his wife, their children, and friends, was a different phenomenon. So, maybe I was being weird.

I clenched his big hand intertwined with mine over his hard thigh. Since arriving, the only time Tobias was not touching me in some form was when I used the bathroom before dinner. His hands cupped mine, threaded with my fingers, often were in my hair, on my waist, shoulders, or lower back. Shamefully, I reveled in each second of his aggressive touch.

I grinned his way. "I'm eating." Then I crossed my eyes, stuck out my tongue, and lifted a cheek.

Predictably, Tobias laughed then shook his head. "I got something to put in those deep dimples."

I whispered back just as low, "Oh, you've *got* something to make these dimples disappear, but you playin'."

I realized the inappropriateness of that statement just as it left my mouth and froze. Tobias' reaction mirrored mine for seconds long until his eyes softened into slits. "You wanna elaborate on that?"

With food in my mouth, my jaw collapsed. Did I mean that? Yes. I absolutely wanted to taste Tobias, but could never be bold enough to broach the subject. However, it seemed I just had.

"What're y'all whispering about over there?" Raj asked from the top of the table. We were in the middle, to his left side, him to our right.

He'd been holding court with the table, talking politics, sports, and generally catching up with his guests. I'd been a fly on the wall, feeling an outer-body phenomenon that began before the star-studded dinner. I was with Tobias. Just the thought of it dispersed butterflies in my stomach. I was crazy. Out of my damn mind. I'd just awakened in my bed this morning, only looking forward to a successful apartment search. Then I was completely blindsided by Kelly-Ann's beef with me.

I spoke to Scott on the plane. He and his cousin had returned to the house, and I wasn't there. He was able to piece together what happened. I told him I was fine, and that I'd be accessible to him. I needed some alone time, but was honest when telling him I wasn't alone. He needed to know that. Scott empathized with me more than I wanted him to. I hated that for him. My life had been my mess to sort. Once again, I assured him I would be fine, and he would, too. He made me promise to check in with him later.

"Menophilia," Tobias answered, casually reaching for his tumbler.

The handsome, brawny, bearded man at the end of the table, closest to Raj, choked on his food. Simultaneously, Wynter's eyes burst wide. I was confused as Raj peered at me briefly.

"Oh, shit," the effeminate man, sitting across from us, toward the left, murmured and blinked his darkly, lined eyes as he gazed at Tobias. He wore black crushed velvet that fit like it was made for him, with a *Chanel* brooch pinned to the lapel of his jacket.

Ragee's brows furrowed. "What about it?"

Yeah. What about it?

"Just laying parameters for our impending marriage. Lennox asked about the good ol' Rusty Trombone. I told her I'd have to ask you about *tha*—"

The bearded guy next to Raj's chair pushed back from the table. Wynter collapsed dramatically into her chair. Raj hung his head.

The effeminate man enunciated, "Fuck!" His pronounced cheeks high.

Across from us, Trent murmured, "Shit…"

Tori's husband covered his mouth. Tori appeared as confused as me. Unbothered, Tobias forked a piece of baked salmon into his mouth. I caught when he tossed a cheeky wink toward Ragee down the table.

"Oh, we doing that tonight? In front of my pastor?" Raj gestured toward the man trying to clear his throat and recover from Tobias' cryptic words.

He's a pastor?

He *did* pray over the food—and quite impressively…eloquently for a metro-sexually styled man. His wife was tall and well-proportioned with big, wild, wooly hair. The style worked for her. It told of Nubian vibes with her rich, mocha complexion. These were real-life great-looking couples.

I wanna be one…

My attention returned to Tobias, who still played placid to the ruckus he'd caused amongst the adults at the table. "Bishop knows what time it is," he thickly returned before feeding himself again.

Raj turned to his pastor. "You know what this cat's talking about?"

"Baby," Wynter, on his other side, reached for him. "Leave Bishop alone. I'll explain later." Her tone nurturing and authoritative.

"Nah, man,' Ragee protested. "LeRoy, I know your twisted mind know all the lingo. What's he talking about?"

The epicene man slowly brought his wine glass to his mouth. His face spread into a controlled smile. "Raj, please. There are children at this table. Plus, your pastor's here. He doesn't need to know just how badly I need to repent of my sins and be baptized." He rolled his eyes. "I'll pass."

Even the kids at the table laughed at that one.

"How are those greens?" Tobias asked me almost in a hushed tone before kissing the side of my face.

I'd never seen him so touchy feely. So possessive.

"Good. Really." I spoke up. "In fact, I can't remember the last time I had a Thanksgiving meal where everything was so good. Thanks for having me."

"You're welcome," Wynter returned. "We're grateful to finally meet you."

Raj nodded.

"That's because you've been spending your holidays eating white people's cooking." Tobias reminded me.

Unable to look at him, I shook my head while I giggled.

Touché.

"I see the type of energy you're on," Raj somewhat warned Tobias about his mysterious words earlier.

Tobias chuckled, hand still clutched to mine as he ate.

"You've been determined to get him here, successfully got him here, then you rib him every chance you get tonight," Wynter reminded her husband. "You even tell his crush how you're so happy she's finally giving him a chance, so he can now stay out of bathhouses—" Nearly every adult at the table went up in laughter. "You think he's not going to play the game with you?" Wynter asked Raj.

A cute smirk formed around Ragee's beard. It appeared as if he finally understood Tobias' confounding term earlier. I still hadn't caught on. I'd have to ask later.

Ragee began to glare down the table at Tobias, fork in one hand, knife in the other. It was hilariously predatory. "Tobe know what time it is. I don't mind sharing producers, but family is family. Blood in, blood out. They say keep your producers close. I say keep your family, who understands without judgement, even closer—"

"Oh, Ragee, please!" LeRoy cried, eyes rolling in the air. "We all know your panties are in a bunch because you don't want Tobias to get as close to Dale as he is with you. Could you please grow up and understand, even if they do develop a relationship while working together, there is only one Ragee McKinnon? Let's man up here. It's business until Tobe says otherwise. Grow some"—his mouth balled tightly as his cadence changed, trying to control his next word, and the volume of it—"fucking confidence, and drop it!"

Oh, my god…

Trent snickered across from me. Jade shook her head, smirking over her plate. Tori McNabb held her chest as her head tossed back and she howled into the air. Wynter, snickering, reached for Raj's back for another rub. This crew was brutal.

There was a passion in Ragee's eyes for Tobias, who pretended to ignore him. "Call me petty all you want. I'll be that squeaky wheel."

"Awwwwww!" The pastor's wife cooed. "That's why I love me some Ragee. T.B., too. Y'all don't mind being vulnerable."

Raj pointed with his fork. "And that's the guy who helped me understand how to be that way on my records."

LeRoy shook his head as he mumbled to himself. The kids down that way laughed at him. I smiled, peering up to Tobias. His jaw worked beneath his neatly groomed beard. Just about every man at this table had a full beard. It made me realize something else my culture lacked. I hadn't been accustomed to being around Black men, especially ones that respected one another so. At best, I was used to working with a gang of white men, with a few Black and brown sprinkled in between. That revelation made me feel good about my decision to leave Raleigh.

"Bishop, you've been quiet all dinner until Tobias had you choking on your food," Jade noted to the table. "Everything okay?"

The pastor nodded, eyes closed. He finished the little food on his plate a while ago, I noticed. "I'm fine, Mrs. B. Thanks."

"He's just being E," Trent chuckled. "Ain't that right, Lex?"

Lex was the pastor's Nubian goddess of a wife. Bronzed, thick, and gorgeous. She was far from a BBW, but her length, mixed with controlled curves and toned muscles, made her beauty hard to go unnoticed. She rolled her eyes. "He's perfectly content. Probably a little tired after the fundraiser this morning, but he's content." She studied him as she spoke. "Y'all know he loves spending time with y'all. You guys keep him balanced. Hanging out with you keeps him from leaning too much into his nerdy tendencies, and becoming a holy-roller."

The table laughed. "Not a holy-roller." Trent cracked up.

"Lex, you keep him from becoming a holy-roller," Jade scoffed. "Girl, please!"

Tori found that hilarious. It seemed to me they knew each other. Raj nodded hard, trying to stifle his humor.

"All jokes aside," Tori's husband leaned into the table. "When you're quiet like this, and your eyes are closed, what are you doing?"

They definitely had experience with each other. I simply wrote the handsome, raspy-speaking man off as weird, but not offensive. Tori's husband just confirmed the weird part.

"I'm hearing," the pastor rasped. "Feeling." He shrugged. "Like Alexis shared, I'm content."

"What're you hearing, E?" Trent asked, eyes squinting down the table at him.

The pastor's eyes opened. He sat up and chuckled. "Incongruently, I'm sensing a connection at this table."

Wynter snorted as she peered down the long dinner table. "We see the connection."

The pastor took a sip of water, unhurried.

"Y'all leave my strange man to his Maker. Y'all know he rarely stays on planet earth." His wife rubbed his shoulder and back soothingly.

"He's our guy, Lex." Jade's head fell to the side. "You know we stay fishing for a Word from on High."

Tobias laughed next to me. But the others wouldn't take their eyes off the preacher.

He placed his elbows on the table and rubbed his hands together. "A business deal of sorts. A partnership."

Everyone looked around at each other.

"Who?" Wynter asked.

"We had the collaboration today," Jade explained. "Trent and Raj finally brought your vision to fruition. The Thanksgiving dinner for their charities was a success."

The pastor shook his head. "This feels professional. I'm sensing a career transition. Two radical ones."

That had everyone, once again, glancing around the table. I wasn't the only one confused.

"Oh!" Jade tweeted, straightening her spine while catching eyes with her husband. "I guess this is as good a time as any to share." Trent shrugged at her in agreement. Jade turned back toward the table. "I just closed on the fourth location of my salon business."

"The nail salon?" LeRoy asked.

Jade nodded. "Yup. I've got two here in Jersey, one in New York, and the other in Philly. We're now talking to a contractor about putting together a design for each location. They need to be uniform no matter where they are." She glanced down the table. "Think *B-Way Burger*. Every restaurant looks the same whether you're standing inside or outside. I meet with him next week to see his designs."

"And what's next?" Tori's husband asked.

"Me, cutting a check." Trent's brows lifted. The table laughed at that, me included. Jade melted into him with an embarrassed expression. "She's got lots of shit to do, which is why I've been staying on her lil' ass. She's been sitting on it for years now, being so afraid, thinking it would take away from what she does for our family. It's been a dream of hers for way too long. I'm 'bout to wrap this ball life up. It's time for her to spread her wings and see dreams can come true for her, too."

Jade reached up and kissed him. "You are my dream. Every day."

It was such a cute and sincere, candid moment. I almost felt guilty for watching.

"So sweet," LeRoy cried, his chin resting on his knuckles.

It was. My hand tightened around Tobias' under the table.

"So, what's next?" Tori asked, passing her baby to her husband. "I'm ready to support a Black-owned nail salon."

"A lot." Jade exhaled. "I have to hire staff...train staff—"

"Holy shit," Tobias steeled next to me. His hooded eyes fell on me.

It took a few seconds for me to catch on.

No!

My face opened in terror. I shook my head, attempting to signal Tobias.

"What's going on over there?" Trent asked from directly across from us.

"What do you do for a living, Lennox?" Wynter wore a puzzling expression.

Tobias leaned into me, planting a kiss beneath my ear. "Wrong question, Winnie—"

"Easy!" Raj warned.

LeRoy chuckled. "Good one, Tobias." He winked.

That earned Tobias a giggle from Wynter, too. "Well?" she prompted with impatience. "Does our Bishop still have a perfect score?"

The pastor's wife craned her neck to peer down the table.

Tobias inclined again and whispered in my ear, "Ezra's more than a preacher. He's a prophet. I had to learn that the nigga really knows shit. Just like he knows you're the person who's on the other side of Jade's business needs, he probably knows how bad I wanna eat your pussy right now. It don't help that me and the nigga got a lot of freaky shit in common."

My eyes burst wide, and I swallowed hard. Between his warm, soft lips directly on my ear, and these strangers staring me down in anticipation, plus learning a pastor having *anything* in common with Tobias Elliott, I was spooked.

"Lennox's been in training and management for a major hospital system in North Carolina. Her passion—her dream—for years has been to train Black women on how to service their community in the nail industry with the utmost, professional standards."

Damn. He made me sound like a cover letter.

There was a resounding echo of utter shock in the room.

Chapter Fourteen

Lennox

Well after dinner, the guests were congregated in the formal living room of Ragee and Wynter's home. Of course, there was a live band in the corner. Nothing overwhelming, but certainly beyond just a piano and drums. There were two guitar players and a percussionist. There was also a guy who went between the mic and sharing the drums with another. They performed a sexy tune I loved within minutes. As I danced in his arms, I asked Tobias the name. It was *"Choosy Lover"* by The Isley Brothers. I'd never heard of them, he shared, because they were an older group from our grandparents' day.

Lots of people sang on the mic, including Ragee. He was now belting out Mint Condition's *"What Kind of Man Would I Be"* with a tumbler of golden *Mauve* in one hand. Him being a natural tenor, I was pleasantly surprised at how well he sounded in a high range. He shared the microphone with guests, too, as some simply watched him. He even asked Tobias to sing a few times. Of course, Tobias turned him down. He didn't like to be the singer, preferring the role of the composer.

Tori's husband, whose name I finally knew was Ashton, was a little loose. Hell, we all were. The wine, champagne, and other

244

spirits were flowing freely. Like Tobias and me, Ashton danced with his wife. This song, in particular, apparently had him in his feelings. As Tori swayed in his arms, beaming seductively, Ashton sang the song alongside Raj with passion. It was almost as if the record held sentimental value to them.

When they made it to the part of the song where the harmony broke up, and Ragee sang, *"Makes me wanna say, ohhhhh…"* Tobias leapt in place.

"Whoa!" He turned toward the band. "Somebody's fuckin' up that F minor six!"

"Big time," I managed to hear the pastor rasp.

The pastor. *See!* Everyone was musically inclined.

Raj peered over to one of the guys singing and gestured for him to bring it down. Tobias turned back to me, big hands on the small of my back, and we danced until the song concluded.

Raj laughed. "Jim, man. You fucked up the split key on the bridge. Tobe was about to throw your ass out."

"Pastor, too," Trent chuckled. "I 'on't even know music, but when I saw his head whip around, I knew somebody was off!"

As they laughed, the Jim guy held his face in his hand.

"Why were you so cold to Raj?"

Tobias used his nose to graze the side of my face. "You noticed that?"

I stifled a moan, still unused to being so close to a man; caressed by one, too. "I think the whole room did. I can tell he thinks highly of you."

"He called me out on some shit earlier that stung," he breathed into my ear, causing my spine to arch. "Ain't no biggie, though. Just brotherly love."

"Good. I like that you're around people who seem to genuinely love you. That's so underrated nowadays."

"Your hair smells so damn good," Tobias expressed throatily. He inhaled deeply, causing a cool breeze to graze my scalp.

"You and my hair," I chided lightheartedly.

"I love it." His hand roved up my back, causing me to curve into his hard chest and abdomen. "I can do this shit forever." His words were like a feather stroking my spine, making me shiver.

He smelled amazing, masculine energy teasing my feminine wiles, as we moved in sync.

"You haven't asked about Kelvin's arrest."

"I don't wanna say the wrong shit."

I peered up at him. "You never do. I've gutted some of my most personal shit to you, and you've never said anything wrong."

"We haven't talked in so long. Feels like, we haven't been the same since…"

"Homecoming?" Tobias nodded. "I feel the same. It's like we talk less since…"

"The fuckin' started." I nodded. He reached down and kissed my lips. "You were rubbing them together. What are you thinking?"

"How I've had your body, yet still feel absent from the friend in you. But I've been in a metamorphic phase. I'm renewing myself. Being with you feels so good…so natural, but after walking this through with my therapist, I know I have to make sure I'm not leaning into a convenience. I need to be sure I'm moving into what's purposeful and meant for me. And right now, I want to make sure what's meant for me is good for me.

"Growing up with my grandmother, I never felt at home emotionally or that I belonged. I was just a consequence of my parents' bad decision and, therefore, a circumstance for my grand-mother. That's one of the reasons why I went along with marrying Kelvin. Yes, he was handsome, had a promising future, and told me to marry him, but I went with it because someone I felt I owed something to pushed me."

I loved how his attention was stapled onto me, and Tobias still moved rhythmically, guiding our steps.

"For over three years, you've done a lot for me emotionally. You've been my biggest cheerleader…biggest confidante, my biggest confidence-builder. But I have to make sure this next chapter in life is for me. So, when I do fade to black…when I don't reply—I haven't been replying—it's because I want to make sure I'm balanced with this thing. I have to know I'm making the right decision that's best for me. This season has to be about Lennox." My eyes closed in a rush of passion. "Yes, I feel you belong in it. Yes, I want you in it. But when I'm away from you, now that our passion is high, thanks to us…"

"Fuckin'."

"Yes." I smiled. "I guess. That. The breaks in between just give me that much more confidence that *I'm* in control. I'm sorry it has to be about me. Do I see a future between us? Yes. And it terrifies me. I do see myself being with you, but at the end of the day, it would, invariably, be as your wife. I still have to maintain self-identity. I have to make sure all the baggage incurred from my faulty decision as a young adult has been cleared out before I find myself being your wife. It has to be all about me."

"It's always been all about you, Lennox," his volume so tender.

"I do believe that, coming from you. I love you for that. I do! Still, I have to serve me first. So, while I'll return to New Jersey, I have to be on my own. I have to live on my own. This is something I've never done. I've provided for people over the past six years or so, but I've never done it just for me. Do I want distance from you? No. But I'm old enough to know everything that feels good ain't good for you.

"I'm trying to move into this with just me on my mind. Do I want you there on the other side of it? Absolutely. But if I fall into you before I put myself back together independently, I'm going to end up in a situation where, maybe we will work out, yet I'll always wonder the motivation behind it. Like, what was the motivation of my grandmother taking me in? What was the motivation of my grandmother pushing me into a marriage I had no business in? What was the motivation of me accepting her influence?

"I *have* to figure out what's best for me. Do I think you're good for me? Yeah. The fact that I know who you'll be in my future frightens me. But I need to stand on my own emotionally to have self-confidence. So, during this transition, I'm going to need help, but I'm also going to need space. All I'm asking is that you continue to be patient with me. I have to try me out. I have to temper me. I have to see what it's like with just Lennox as a motive and no one else. I don't want to be another circumstance to anyone. I want to be chosen. I want to be loved, but I have to be those things to me first."

His heavy-lidded eyes were lower than usual as he peered down on me. Tobias nodded, expression placid. And the moment I began to worry about his reaction to my emotional diatribe, his teeth revealed themselves, illuminating the candle-lit room.

"You're going to be my wife?"

Huhn?

Was that all his big ass heard? Out of all the gazillion words I shared to *express*—

Big arms landed on my shoulders, and a face joined our personal space. "Y'all getting married? Can I sing there? In fact..." He backed away, neck swinging in search of someone. "Bishop, can we get you to officiate? Who the best man?" he posed to Tobias.

"If your drunk ass don't stop," Raj's friend, LeRoy, groaned, sauntering past us carrying a champagne flute high in the air by its stem.

So embarrassed, I dropped my face into Tobias' hard pecs.

"Shit," Tobias husked. "I gotta get her back home." He took my hand, and guided me out of the room, leaving Raj hanging.

"Why would you do that to him?" I asked, giggling, on the way down a hall.

"Raj'll be alright. He's been in his feelings over this Dale collab."

"Why?"

"It's what R&B dudes do. Raj knows he's my number one guy. Our connection goes beyond music. The same with Wynter. We clicked almost instantly. She's cool as hell. The perfect fit for his moody ass."

We turned back into the dining room where Jade was at the buffet table with her son, Kyree. At thirteen, he towered over his mother. She sauntered our way to leave the room.

"I'm so grateful for today." She rolled her eyes to the back of her head, lashes meeting. "I've been stressed for months about rolling this thing out. My husband is my biggest supporter, but he's in the

League. He can't help me with this. Then, I have my girlfriends, but this isn't their dream. My husband loves to say, 'your gift will make room for you,' quoting the bible. I haven't been telling anyone how much anxiety I've been carrying in quiet because I had no idea about this part. I only know I want top-notch work and customer service for Black women. Period. I really hope you'll consider doing this with me."

"Of course!" I didn't want to give away how desperate I was for the opportunity. "I'll be ready for our call next Wednesday. I have a few models I want to type up for you, even a few programs available to help with inventory and Q.C.—I mean…" I rolled my eyes this time. "Quality control. My bad."

"No worries. I can't wait!" She turned to leave, laughing. "Such a blessing, girl!"

I waved her off then turned for Tobias. He was standing over one of the chairs at the table that had now been cleaned off by the staff as he typed into his phone. "You said you wanted some of the ambrosia."

"Oh!" My eyes brightened as I pivoted. The buffet was loaded with all types of goodies. "Yes. Ambrosia." Then I gazed his way again. "Business?" *Or your daughter?*

I didn't want to think about the latter. It didn't take long to locate the fruit salad. I scooped up just enough to sample and found a spoon. Then I walked over to Tobias, who was still entranced in something in his phone.

"Are you ignoring me?"

I smiled when he peered my way. "Oh, nah. I'm looking at these flights. There's one in first class—*Delta*—that can have you in Raleigh at four in the morning. That's awkward. I can't have you driving by yourself nowhere at that hour."

My pulse began to beat hard in my neck. "You're sending me home tonight?"

He turned to me, at first his gaze appeared confused. "I know I strong-armed you into coming up here. I told you I'd have you right back home. I'll be a man of my word." His brows narrowed. "You don't want to…"

I knew Tobias well enough to know he was struggling to mask his excitement.

"I texted Scott right after dinner. I told him I'd be home tomorrow. I didn't say when."

"So, what do you want to do?" His attention swung above my head, telling of his thoughts of us extending our time here.

"Well…" My forehead stretched. "You're home—in Jersey. I'm in town…" I wrapped my free arm around his back and placed my chin into his chest. "I haven't seen your wine selection. I'm the only woman who's seen you naked but hasn't been to your home."

Those heavy eyes wrinkled at the side, and Tobias tapped his index finger at the tip of my nose. "I know what you're alluding to. And while I'll never lie about my sensual preferences, I won't allow you to call me a whore. Do you wanna see my private cellar?"

I bit my lip, feeling sexy in a way I wasn't used to. "I want to see your collection. Why don't you treat me like you wanted to when you saw me at the *Bank of America Stadium*, *if* I told you I was single."

A fire ignited in Tobias' eyes, and his amusement disappeared. "You wanna role-play, Lennox?"

"I woke up in my bed in North Carolina, prepared to get through another dry Thanksgiving holiday with my in-laws. Then I end up in Jersey, unscheduled and with a job prospect before I end the night. I don't even recognize the girl who left that bed this morning. Until I arrive back in Raleigh, I want to be anyone else, as long as I'm with you." I swallowed back a tear as I peered up to his beautiful face.

Tobias

She took in every inch of the space she could as we left my wine cellar and traveled into the great room of my spot in Englewood Cliffs. Lennox carried a glass of *Château Blevin* while she perused. In one hand, I held a glass of *Mauve*. In the other, I tapped the universal remote to power on the stereo. *"Dirty Secrets"* by Burna Boy was in motion, and I decided to leave it there.

"And how many square feet is this?"

"*Ummm…*" The feel of my cell vibrating inside my pocket delayed my answer. "Five thousand, six hundred, sixty-seven."

"Just missing that six, six, six curse." She smiled.

I scoffed, "Hell yeah. That's exactly how I remember what it is."

"What year was it built?"

"I'm the second owner. I believe they built it in ninety-six."

"And how long have you been here?" I peeped how she eyed Elia's canvas pictures on the walls in the hall leading toward the great room.

"About four years."

"You were living in Paramus before then?"

"Yeah. Rented out a house, and when I hit a lick with the *Children of Fate* joint, I got some opportunities off the rip from that alone. I reached out to a few people I knew in the industry for a realtor. Let's kick it in here." I motioned into the great room then led us to the bar. Once inside, I pulled out a stool for her. "Yeah. She found this spot for me in no time, and at a fair price. She negotiated her ass off. I see shortie from time-to-time at events. She's been helping me out with some investment business lately." I pulled my glass up to my mouth. "Jaquana. She was a realtor then. Now, she's a whole ass broker."

Lennox's eyes lit up at that. "You think she can refer someone who does…modest rentals? I've been looking for something in my budget all week. Everything's overpriced. I have to protect my savings."

"You selling your house?"

She nodded just after taking a big ass gulp of her wine. "I meet with a prospective agent next week. I had an appointment with one two days ago, but he flaked on me." Her mouth twisted.

"That's fucked up."

"It is. I don't even know how fast the market is moving now. I do think I'll turn a profit, but don't want to throw all of that into paying rent to someone else."

"I feel you. You ever thought about buying something here? Chino killin' the real estate game."

I really wanted her to reach out to her pops. Lennox and I were fucking now, and there would be no man after me. She was mine. I'd make sure not to fumble the bag this time. Due to street politics, her pops had to be informed properly, and not find out randomly. I wasn't afraid of the O.G., but street code was street code. Smite still lived by them. It could affect his relationship with his friend.

"In Jersey? Let me find work first." She laughed. "This state is ridiculously expensive!"

"I'll hit up Jaquana tomorrow. She'll do me a solid and help you find something in your price range. Something non-luxury." I rolled my eyes playfully, wanting instead to offer to help with any expenses she may need. But I knew better than that with Lennox. After her expression of where she was emotionally earlier at Ragee's, my ass knew to keep my mouth the fuck shut.

"Thanks!" She blew out a breath. "First a job prospect, and now a housing prospect. All of this after the hellish morning I had." Lennox glanced around the room. "So, this is where you warm them up?"

"Them?"

Her shoulders lifted. "Your den of lovers."

"Den *of*—" My head rolled back slowly, and I cracked the hell up. "You calling me a whore again, girl?"

"No!" She smiled and pouted at the same time while reaching

for me. "I don't think you're a whore at all. I swear. But we know you like your sex stuff and..." She murmured, "are clearly good at it."

Heat caressed my balls. This was the third response my dick had to her words. Lennox said she loved me earlier at Raj's. She also told me she'd end up *my* wife someday. I wanted to fuck her right there on the spot, but played it cool.

I placed my hand over my heart. "Thanks for the compliments. Feel free to not whisper them next time. But I need to make this clear: I don't bring random women to my home. Remember, I have a daughter. The more people in and out of here, the less sacred this place is for her."

Lennox's eyes fell, and she nodded as though rebuked. "Then where do you go to...play."

I took a sip of my *Mauve*, highly aroused by her mere presence in my home. Not to mention the conversation.

"You know where I *go*—went until I... You know."

Her little hand was on my thigh as she leaned into me. "You didn't have to stop for me." Then Lennox grabbed her face as a hard ass laugh slipped. "But I appreciate it. I'd be nuts if I had what you've given me, and knew someone else was having it, too!"

She was pretty. So fucking pretty even when she was masking her vulnerability.

"Another compliment." I brought the glass to my mouth. "I can get used to this."

Grinning, Lennox squinted her eyes. "What's the name of that place again?"

"What place?"

"The sex club."

I chuckled. "Sex club," I whispered, trying it out for size as I scratched inside my beard. "*The Jux Supper Club*."

"Is it nice?"

"You wanna see?"

Lennox reclined in her seat. Her face flashed in horror. "Are you serious?"

I swallowed back brandy. "I am."

"What would I do?"

"Me." When I could register her shock, I offered, "Or let me… you. It would be fun." I winked before taking another sip.

She dropped her chin then her cognac eyes. Lennox wanted to fuck. Now. I had enough experience with women to be able to read body language. I loved the effect I had on her sexually. Maybe kick-starting that leg of our relationship wasn't a bad idea after all. I finally had more of her. She finally wanted more of me.

My attention shifted to her high heeled boots. They added inches to her petite frame. She wore fitted jeans, and what looked to be a bodysuit under a cropped blazer.

"So, am I getting you a hotel room for the night?"

Lennox's lashes lifted as she looked up from her glass planted on her crossed legs. "I am at my hotel." She glanced around. "Here's my bar. There's the lobby's piano. But for some reason, the piano player isn't there doing his job." Her mouth twisted. "Are you the piano player?"

She serious about this role playing…

"I'm your host, actually. Anything you need, I'm here to provide."

"Right now, I'd like to see my room." Lennox took a sip of her wine.

I placed my glass on the bar. "I'll do you one better. I'll show you to your room and start your shower to begin relaxing you. While you're doing that, I can put something together to really prepare you for a good night's rest."

Lennox's lips twisted, but her cheeks spread. "I'd like that."

"Before we go, give me a number."

One brow lifted. "A number?"

I shrugged with my lips. "Any number. Single digit."

Lennox rubbed her lips together as she thought about it. "Three." Insecure about the random act, she rolled her eyes.

My head bobbed as visions loaded in my mind. "Three. Easy." I gave her a neck bow, impressed by her boldness. "This way."

Although she tried to hide it, she was tense. Her joints were tighter each minute I massaged her glorious, naked body. Now on her back, the chain connecting the clamps I fastened to her nipples moved. Lennox let me put them on without a single protest, confirming my suspicion of her needs. She squirmed on the portable massage table. I wanted to remind her to relax; however, I knew her tension wasn't coming from pain, but from need.

I lifted her right leg over my shoulder as I leaned into the table and kneaded into her thigh. Running the bottom of my palms across her muscles, the glow from the lit fireplace made her glossed skin appear delectably bronzed. After her shower, I had Lennox on a massage table in the middle of my master bedroom, fully oiled. I rubbed her body thoroughly from her neck to her toes, front and back. The venture was quite delicious, allowing me to learn about hidden moles and scars. I even got to see her birthmark again.

When I worked my fingers into the juncture of her hip, she tilted her pelvis, pushing her pussy in the air. Again, telling me where she needed me. I smirked, understanding her desire. Still, I stuck to my plan of learning her body. It would be mine from here on out.

After finishing up with that thigh, I put her leg down, then turned to grab waiting hot stones. Starting from her feet, I massaged them into her oiled skin, moving against her muscles. I made sure to circle them into her belly even through Lennox's contractions; she was so damn reactive. I took my time rubbing them onto each of her arms, finally looping them around her breasts.

I watched her face, and the line between her brows, as it thickened. Her lips twitched, rubbed, and pressed into each other intermittently. When I was done with the stones, I placed them onto a table. Then I studied her body, watching her cues of impatience, enjoying the bold display of her femininity. Reaching over, I yanked at the nipple chain.

"Mmmmm…" Her body tightened from the core.

The tips of my fingers danced down her slippery body onto her bed of pubic hairs. I noticed the wax job had grown in. That told me Lennox had planned to share her body with me last month in *Samsara*; it wasn't from pressure or a request. She willingly gave herself to me.

The second I pushed two fingers down her slit, a gush of air broke through her lips, and Lennox's thighs parted. I went straight down and into her core, my fingers moving exploratively as I watched her every reaction. It took me years to learn how to finger a woman. I heard them complain about men ramming their fingers and, sometimes, whole fists inside a narrow, protected orifice. Not only should those hidden nerves inside be the goal, but politely entering to find them was a priority, too.

From my experience, not every woman's major orgasmic nerve endings were located in the same place. That means not everyone can orgasm in the same positions, neither did they come from the same places inside. So, as I massaged her internally with intention, I watched Lennox's responses. She was so roused, it shouldn't have taken—

"Ooooh!" she moaned out loud, giving me GPS-level instruction.

I stopped navigating and backed up, then waited. Next, I moved a quarter of an inch and stroked there. Her hips bucked toward my hand. That's when I knew I was there, and my fingers stroked and stroked. Lennox's face contorted, muscles tightening everywhere now. With my free hand, I reached up and unclamped one nipple. It was dark, expanding like a blossoming flower. I freed the other as I stirred and stirred against her thrusts. Watching her throw her pussy had my dick throbbing.

Leaning over, I whispered in her ear, "You're the most precious thing to me. My first obsession. My first ray of sunlight after losing my moms. Thank you."

My face shifted over to her right breast, and I flicked my tongue heavily over the beaded tip once, twice, three—

"Oh, *my*—! *Uhhnnnnnnnn…*"

Lennox exploded, rocking the table beautifully. I licked and stroked as her body spasmed wildly. Her arms flew into the air, and she captured my bicep, hugging her torso to me as I flickered and rubbed to her delight. I didn't stop until her thrusting slowed and body returned to the table.

"*Huh! Huh… Huuuh… Huuh… Huh!*"

Lennox was out of breath and completely undone. That's when I knew she was finished. I pulled off her nipple with a long suck.

"*Ooooooh!*"

My hands lazily slid from her soaked pussy, swiping her sensitive clit on the way. That caused her body to clench.

"*Shihhh…*"

Satisfaction opened my face and shrunk my eyes. I loved this shit. Getting a woman off should be taught in schools. But having Lennox boneless and spread wide for me wasn't something any other man should ever know.

I pushed her legs, lifting her spread knees into the air. Then, from the bottom of the table, I reached over and hooked her shoulders to lift her little ass in the air. Her legs were over my shoulders. The material of my shirt prevented her slippery body from falling from my grip. Her neck was lazy, head tossed back, curls swinging in the air.

As I walked us into the bathroom to shower off the oil, I asked, "You okay there?"

"*Mmmhmmm,*" she moaned something lazily.

But I understood the sentiment. I chuckled, lifted her higher until her pussy reached my face, and pulled her swollen clit between my lips before letting it go.

Lennox mewled a deep cry.

"One," I whispered as we walked into the bathroom.

Lennox

"*Tobeeee!*" I cried, gripping the marble, hexagon tiles of the floor while my knees were planted above my head on the stony bench against the wall of his mammoth-sized shower.

On all fours while spicy water sprouted all around, I pushed back into his busy mouth. The whiskers of his beard teasing the back of my thighs, the powerful thrashing of his tongue swiping against my swollen clit—it all told of his sexual ministrations. As my nipples tingled and feet warmed, all I could think about was how many women felt this mastery. How many of them had been bent over in his three-glass-wall shower with him eating them from the back? My spine curved, tits bounced in the air as I rocked backward, my groin churning.

This was the head trip I'd been feeling from sex with Tobias. He was a pleaser, while my husband had seemed to be a taker during sex. Tobias took his time with me, put his mouth everywhere. My husband stopped going down on me within the first year of marriage—after I began reacting to his abrupt, nasty behavior. Tobias made my body feel celebrated, never sparing a glance or touch to any part of it. My husband enjoyed calling me ugly and skinny—and even fat when it suited him.

Kelvin made my stomach churn.

Tobias worked to make my groin churn.

PLOP!

An unexpected smack to my ass had my eyes burst wide. The sting blurred my vision, but when it was over, I was unable to feel my knees or hands. The only sensations were from my breasts bouncing, cheeks slapping against his face, and Tobias' lips and tongue sucking my engorged clit.

My eyes closed, core exploded, sending me adrift and in a fit of shakes.

"*Tobeeeeeeeee!*"

My head rocked up and down like a racehorse as I held the floor for balance. I couldn't control the yanking of my shoulders, and my knees struggled to hold my jerky sex he showed no mercy to. I struggled, for what felt like an eternity, to come down.

When I finally did, and my heaving breaths didn't compete with the shooting water from multiple showerheads, Tobias removed his face from the seat of my ass.

"Two," he murmured.

I was too spent to understand what he meant.

𝒯𝑜𝑏𝒾𝒶𝓈

Her legs were wrapped around my waist as I walked us out of the bathroom and into my bedroom. This felt so fucking good. I could feel the firmness in her thighs, the need in the grip of her arms. Like she'd mentioned earlier, I would have never imagined returning to my bed with her after the way I woke up this morning.

Ragee's words nipped at me. He wasn't malicious, perhaps just wrong. *Damn.* I hoped he was wrong about this. I didn't mean to shit on him tonight. Discerning my moods was one thing, but it was reductive without context. At the very least, I hoped he saw Lennox's light for himself to know she was the real thing. Yeah, our situation was fucked up, but we had the power to right a long ago wrong. Either way, I had nothing to prove. Lennox knew she could call me during a difficult time. And I'd come during her duress.

I was willing to keep my word and get her back home tonight. But the girl clearly had her own desires. I wasn't mad at the agenda. There wasn't much I wouldn't do to ensure her happiness. Fatherhood taught me so much about sacrifice. This woman represented more than ass to me. I couldn't explain my draw to her. It was something I couldn't control.

Just months ago, her body trembled from nervousness when we kissed, our feet inches apart. Now, I couldn't get enough of her cries of pleasure. And Lennox was so damn responsive to my touch. I looked forward to her being my sensual muse.

"Do you have a music system in each room of this place?" she lazily whispered into my neck.

I snorted. "She's alive." I hadn't heard a coherent sentence from Lennox since we'd come up from the bar, and I got her started in the shower before the massage. Then, after she collapsed on the bench in the shower, I washed. After, I left her to wash so I could brush my teeth. By the time I was done at the sink, she'd walked out of the shower. I dried her off and carried her out here. "I thought you tapped out on me."

With her in my arms, I managed to move the pillows on my bed to pull back the comforter. When I placed a knee on the mattress and leaned over, Lennox almost lost her grip.

"Tobias!"

I laughed, helping her to land safely onto my sheets. "A few minutes ago, I was *Tobeeeee*. Back to formalities, I see."

"Shut up!" she groaned, crawling deeper into the bedding.

I followed her, pulling the blanket over our naked bodies. Quickly, Lennox shuffled closer to me, draping her little arm over my chest and thigh over my own. This wasn't good for me. My dick swelled to a standing position. When she giggled, the blood flow to my balls constricted.

"Why do I feel like a teen again—like an older teen. A young, teenaged Lennox would not be in a grown man's bed. Ewwww!"

I scoffed, rubbing my eye. "I hope not."

"This feels amazing. Are we really doing this? Will this be our norm?"

"That depends on what you've envisioned for your norm."

"Would that be before my marriage or after? Those are two different Lennoxes. The one now is less jaded than the one before."

"Tell me what the one before envisioned for her."

Lennox sighed, a giggle followed as her damp hair dripped down my chest onto the mattress, and I was absolutely un-fucking-bothered by it. "Of course, getting a degree was a must. Marriage would have been next for the old me. Then kids." She nodded, softly pulling at the hairs of my chest.

"Kids? You?"

She scoffed, eyes drawing up to my face. "Why not me?"

"I don't know." I took her hand and brought it to my mouth for a kiss, not meaning to offend her. "You've been this…sexy, cool, perfect body, never-aging type of chick to me."

"What does that say about mothers? They're not sexy? They're boring and old-looking?"

Chuckling, I shook my head, intermingling our fingers. "How many kids do you want, girl?"

"*Hmmmm…*" She straightened two of her fingers in the air. "Maybe this many?"

"I've waited eight long fuckin' years for my babies from your belly. Try this many." One by one, I lifted two more of her burgundy-painted fingernails.

"Tobe!" she spat.

"Yell out my name like that one more time, and we'll get started right now." My dick twitched beneath her thigh.

Lennox's eyes lit bright as hell.

Chapter Fifteen

Tobias

I needed to move us away from what my dick was clearly screaming it needed. So, I brushed wet ringlets of her hair behind her ear.

"I'm really excited about this next chapter for you." That was how she put it at Raj's earlier. "You're going to be amazing—you've always been amazing. I'm thinking, in this chapter, you'll be able to see you alone, without the drama. Nothing will compete with you making your dreams come true. I'm almost jealous."

"Why?"

"Because it's gonna be a dope time for you. What human being doesn't want to be liberated and independently making life happen for themselves without the dark shit haunting them? You're going to blow Jade's mind by making her business tight. When the time's right, you should think about partnering with her."

"Partnering?"

"Yeah. Unless she's gonna stop with four salons. This Black nail industry will be revolutionary. She can't stop at four. With you on her side, Jade'll conquer the world." I lifted my head and kissed her. "And I can't wait."

"Why does it sound like you won't be around?"

I shrugged. "I'll be right here."

"Like away from me?"

That made me chuckle. "Where you want me to be, baby?"

Lennox's lips twisted. "I think we know I want you." She shook her head. "I don't want the distance anymore. I want access."

"Well, you'll be back in Jersey. Come to Bergen County."

"I'll go where I can afford to be. But you have to promise me one thing."

"Anything."

"Exclusivity."

I felt my forehead crease. "And, exactly what does that entail?"

"No female friends. No sex."

My chest vibrated from a silent chuckle. "No women. No sex. You're asking for a lot."

With a smirk of confidence, she shook her head. "You've waited for me all this time—"

"And you want me to go back to that?"

"No." Lennox's face sobered. "I want it to be just me." She wouldn't look at me. "Like..." She shook her head. "I don't want to share, Tobias. I want this thing for just..." Those cognac eyes swept up to my face. "...me."

"You're making demands. But what about my needs? I bleed, too, Lennox. I have a heart."

"About that." She traced my chest with her middle finger. "I want dibs on that, too."

"Damn, girl!" I laughed hard. "You're asking for a lot. Just take my fuckin' balls, too—"

She reached over and kissed me. Before I could respond, Lennox was straddling me, the hairs of her pussy brushing down my stomach. I panicked like a motherfucker.

Her tongue felt good. She was aggressive, blowing air onto my face from her nose. Her hands on my chest then moving out to my straining arms. Lennox's ass touched the head of my cock, and she readjusted to stroke the shaft. Shit. She was wet. I felt the warm gel brush down almost to my balls.

I reached up for the base of her head through her hair and lifted her mouth from mine. "I can't."

Lennox didn't stop her gliding. Her face was strained, eyes tight, gloriously fucking beautiful. "Why can't you? Feels like you want to," she whispered, more breaths than bass.

"I can get you off like this if you want, but I can't participate."

Her hips stopped. "Why?"

"Because I'll ejaculate."

Her whisper was filled with disappointment. "Isn't that the point? I want to get you off, too."

And I want you to, too, baby…

I licked my lips, already feeling like a sucker for the shit I was going to say. "I don't have any condoms." I let go of a deep breath. "And you're not on birth control."

She didn't need it. Her husband, so bugged out on that shit, hadn't laid a finger on Lennox since the year I ran into her at the *Kings/Panthers* game. It was something she told me once I began earning her trust.

Lennox grinned, eyes still lusty…tight. "You're shitting me."

"I'm not."

"Tobias, you've got a massage table and nipple clamps here, but no condoms?"

"Remember?" I widened my eyes for emphasis. "I've been celibate for about a year now. There was no reason to have any here. The last time I used a condom—before you—was at *Jux*. There're plenty of rubbers there…for obvious reasons."

The muscles in her face dropped. "You've shown me more fidelity than I've given Kelvin."

I pulled up to kiss her again, slow and deep. "I ain't tripping. Celibacy led me to the act of manifestation. Manifestation's got you here in my bed right now, mad as hell that I don't have a condom to make love to you properly."

"Why didn't we make a stop before we got here?"

"Because I wasn't presumptuous. I had no idea this was how we'd end the night. But I'm grateful." I let go of her and pulled my arms over my head to grip the ledge of the mattress. "Now, I wanna see you get off. Go 'head but be quick. I can't be tortured for too long."

When Lennox didn't move right away, I pulled down one arm and gripped her meaty hip, guiding her into the act. So much blood rushing directly to my cock had me in discomfort and feeling light-headed. This was Lennox Curry, and it was no drill.

She leaned over and kissed me. Lennox eventually began her pacing strokes, thickening me to fullness again.

"Yeah," I whispered, looking her straight in the eye. "Like that." I traced her opened lips with my tongue. "You feel so good, baby."

As she kissed me again, swirling her tongue against mine, I pushed my arm back above my head, and let Lennox achieve her pleasure at will. We kissed, and I strained my body when I felt the pressure was too much. I didn't want to cum this way. Yeah, I could have, but this was about her. She flew all the way up here this morning as an act of obedience. I'd reward her for it. I'd lay there and endure her feminine scent of need, the evidence of her arousal, and the whimpering telling of her enjoyment.

My mouth left her lips and trailed down to her neck. Lennox leaned in, giving me access. When I went farther down to her chest, she curled her spine. I lifted, reaching her right tit. As I nibbled, her thrusting hurried. Her moans grew, tantalizing me. The agility and rhythmic rounding of her hips had my fucking head spinning and I dropped back onto the mattress. I tried controlling my senses, focusing on slowing my breathing and stiffening my limbs, not needing to relax.

"Tobe," she whispered, causing my eyes to blast open.

Lennox reached between us, lifting my dick, cupping it to her. She watched herself polish me with her essence. Her pussy was beautiful, clit a pretty, fleshly hue. *Fuck...* The girl was seducing me...hurting me bad. The head of my cock rolled outward when reaching the top of her cleft. Funny how it could be hard, but flex to her needs, too.

When Lennox's rubbing increased in speed, my heart did the same. The head of me would disappear between her lips for longer and longer periods, sliding too close to her opening. After a while, I felt the first inch of her before she brought me out again.

"Lenny—" I cleared my throat. "You gotta chill." She should

have cum by now. "I'm slipping inside," I tried to warn, the natural bass in my tone fucking gone.

Panting hard with an open mouth and tight eyes, she glanced up at me, still thrusting. There was a sexual aggression in her eyes.

"Your 'shit's heavy' like Raj's song says." She licked her lips, eyes low on mine.

Lennox was present and expressing her desires. The shit turned me the fuck on in the worst way. So much that I closed my eyes. In the span of two seconds, her hand was on the side of my beard—the soiled hand. And a burst of sensation gripped the entire shaft of my shit. Her mouth was on me again when I opened my eyes.

Lennox was humming into my face, her hips delivering choppy thrusts, belly lifting from mine. It all meant one thing. Her torso flew into the air, lips spread, and eyes closed to a squeeze as she howled into the air. She was exploding over me, clenching my dick with a unique clasp. She was beautiful, jolting uncontrollably over me, breasts bouncing, stomach visibly contracting.

"Three," pushed through my gritted teeth.

Clenching the top of my mattress, an unexpected orgasm ripped through my tense body. A heavy groan left my chest as I bucked into her. Through low eyes, I could see her watching me blast off inside of her hot, tight pussy. I struggled to hang on as my soul left my body. A panic was riding just beneath the tide of bliss. But I could do nothing but ride out the spasms of my body and the abandon of my fucking lungs.

Her soft body covered my own as she sprinkled kisses on my neck. Lennox hadn't detached from me. My receding length was still lodged inside her quivering pussy. How could I have gone this long without knowing what she felt like raw? What man could have this and give it away? As her hand ran the sides of my chest and stomach, the shit felt wild. I didn't even have a chance to warn her that I was going to cum. I couldn't even predict the shit.

Lennox brought her mouth up to my ear. "Your teetotaling days are over, Mr. Elliott."

Huhn?

Oh! Herk!

Fuck...

Lennox

I toed from the bathroom into the masculinely-decorated bedroom of Tobias Elliott. This was a new layer of him. Yes, I'd seen parts of his home from *FaceTime* calls, but never in the flesh. The walls were a navy blue with off-white crown molding. The overall decor was highlighted by brass and gold accents. One was a gold sculpture of a naked woman. Her head was tossed back, and one knee was hiked, as she groped a breast. I couldn't deny its sexy placement or the owner's desire to have it.

Speaking of the owner: he was in the center of his bed, body splayed beneath a comforter. He'd awakened me some time ago, reminding me of my need to get home today. Tobias carried me into the en suite bathroom where he planted my drowsy body directly on the toilet. As I relieved myself, he washed up for the day. I took my time, watching him brush his teeth for the second time since my arrival. He was exceedingly sexy; finite and large muscle groups performing the mundane act. He left me in the bathroom to wash and fully awaken. That had done the trick. Now, I could take in the full personality of his private room.

I crawled over the mattress to him as he talked on the phone. Tobias was so abundant; thick and comforting. I just wanted to touch and caress him all over. Was I that type of lover? The touchy-feely kind? I thought of how Tobias might be. He wouldn't take his hands off me yesterday, since I stepped off of Raj's plane.

"Nah, Charlie," Tobias' thick, morning tenor grunted. "No. I said only non-stops!"

I ran my hand up his hairy legs, settling between them. He was wearing boxer briefs while I found a t-shirt of his to throw on.

His eyes were on me when he tried to calmly relay, "I know it's last minute, bruh. If you would've done the search before getting high, I'm sure this shit could've been done by now."

My hands slowly trailed up his thighs to the apex. I slipped my hands under the leg openings of the cotton, passing his bushy, pubic bed until I met the root of his manhood. He thickened right away. Feeling emboldened, I released him through the narrow opening. The veins running along his throbbing shaft were lewdly beautiful. I stared at him, eventually reaching for it. A hard, ridged staff covered in a thin layer of silky skin. Using my index, I ran my finger down the slit of the head and softly scraped the lip of his wide crest with my nail.

A penis.

His penis...

Oh, the action this thing has seen. The miracle it worked with giving me a vaginal *orgas*—

"It's not a toy." His delivery was thick, saturated with virile authority. "Don't play with it. It's for your joy, not a detached body part from the lab at school when you were studying anatomy and physiology."

He remembered when I struggled in that class during my under-grad studies. Reproached, I pushed away, up on my knees, then crawled toward the pillows.

"Get back to me if you find something first," Tobias told his cousin, Charlie. "Bye." Then he placed his phone down and turned toward me. His fingers were in my head, heated scent engulfing me. "Good morning." That was followed by a kiss, one with tongue. It ignited a hunger in me I thought would be impossible, considering his generosity last night.

When he let go, I began to feel self-conscious. Reaching up to my nest of a scalp, I was reminded of my predicament. "I have no brush, no deodorant. Thank God you keep extra toothbrushes."

"My housekeeper keeps the place stocked with things like that." He took a deep breath. "I'm gonna head out to *Walgreens*. What kind of brush? Never mind. Just text me everything you need."

"Like you're going to know the right brush to get."

He pressed his lips together. "You're right." Then Tobias snapped his fingers. "Pictures? Yeah. Send me pix. I can work with that." He leaned in for a final kiss.

"Wait," I called out to him as he turned to leave the bed. "What were you counting last night?"

"Last night?"

"Yeah. When you carried me off the massage bed and into the bathroom, you started with 'one.' Then, inside the shower when we were…done, you mentioned 'two.' And the last time, after I came here in the bed, you grunted 'three.'" I thought about it while brushing my teeth. What was that about?"

"I asked you to give me a number downstairs at the bar."

My eyes blossomed wild. "I said three," I whispered in amazement. Tobias nodded, expressionless. The sentiment made me feel giddy. I didn't want to reveal it to him, so I controlled my giggle as I shook my head at him.

He shrugged then stood. "For the second time, you told me you love me. Three was easy."

"When did I say that?"

"First time was in *Samsara*, the morning you left when I was blasting out my goddamn mind. The second was last night at Raj's when telling me at the same damn time, you'll need your space."

Slipping further down the bed, I covered my face.

I did say that, didn't I?

I planned and practiced those words from my heart the entire flight up. The *L* word wasn't included.

"My cook's here, Lennox! Get ready to eat!" he shouted from inside of his closet.

"This sounds great. Thanks, Jade." I spoke into the speaker phone from Tobias' great room.

"Good. I couldn't sleep last night, so stoked about this."

"I'm excited, too. I'm still here at Tobias', but will be working on my proposals for you as soon as I get settled in at home."

"Awesome!" The cheer in her tone couldn't be missed. "I have someone looking into marketing for employees. I need nail technicians to know we're coming."

"Yeah. Even those young women, who aren't into their careers yet. Letting them know there's an opportunity like this available could possibly motivate an entirely new demographic. Beyond that, they'll take the resources learned from your training and possibly adapt it for their own if they go independent."

"Girl, don't speak about my competitors just yet!" Jade's obvious demand had me cracking up. "Speaking of which, Trent mentioned we're gonna have to define our relationship. Like…will you be a contractor, employee, or a potential partner?"

"Yeah. That crossed my mind, too. It's early yet, but I can tell you one thing for certain: I've been an employee—am an employee—and it ain't all it's supposed to be. I mean, I like collecting a check every two weeks, but I don't like being disposable." I didn't have the money to be a partner to Jade either. At least, not before selling my home, and settling in Jersey. I needed to see if her business would launch successfully before I counted my coins. "We'll definitely talk more about it in the upcoming weeks and months. In the meantime, I'd like to share my vision with you. I'm hoping to blow your mind."

"Girl, yes!"

"Thanks for the links to the state's requirements and list of schools. I'm on it!"

"Great! We'll check back in soon!"

The doorbell rang.

"Yes. We will!"

"Bye."

"Bye."

I stalled a few seconds to see if Tobias' chef would answer the door. When I didn't hear any sounds coming from the hall, I stood. I went to the archway of the room, and still, no movement from the back of the house. When the bell sounded again, I hopped into action.

Approaching the double doors of the home's entryway, from one of the sidelights, I could make out a small body. As I opened one of the doors, I saw an adult joining the child. Our eyes all shot around each other multiple times. Then, I realized who those little eyes belonged to.

Tobias...

"Hi..." I finally found my voice, peering between Elia and...her mother.

Elia looked to her mother for guidance. Krista couldn't take her eyes off me.

It took a while for her to ask, "Is Tobias home?"

I blinked, mind clearing of the fog. "*Ummm...*" My hand went to my head, suddenly self-conscious about my appearance. I wore my bra, his robe, and nothing else. I looked a sight! "*Nuh*—no." I cleared my throat. "No." My eyes shot down to Elia. "He just ran to the store. He's been out a while. I'm sure he'll be back at any moment."

What was next? I didn't know the protocol. Tobias never mentioned his daughter coming by. Krista was here. I couldn't believe it. I hadn't had contact with her in... My eyes roved down to Elia. She was beautiful. Mocha skin cased her little body and she had a full head of hair, parted perfectly down the center, with thick braids hanging from ponytails on either side. Nine years. It had been nine years since I'd been in contact with Krista.

"Well, this is her father's house, soooo..." Krista's head was tilted, eyes narrowed.

Yes. It was awkward. I was being awkward, but again, what was the protocol?

Quickly, I scurried out of the way so they could come inside.

271

"Go get your guards and come right back, Lia!" Krista's maternal tone instinctively bit at my nerves.

Elia paid me another gander, then bolted up the stairs. "Okay!"

"He hasn't mentioned you," the sound of Krista's voice had my attention returning to her.

I'd never forget.

Ever...

"I don't know why he would."

She smirked. "Tobias and I are cool. Why wouldn't he mention you? I mean, we're not besties, but we're adult enough to have small talk about women from his past."

That shit nipped at me. They were keywords used to trigger me. Krista, at five-feet, eight-inches, was taller than my five-feet, three-inch frame. She was thicker than me, too, and had thrown that in my face back then.

I smiled, trying to measure my tone and irritation. "I'm not small. Never have been—in any fashion to Tobias. Neither am I simply a woman from his past. That was you, until you decided you didn't want to play fairly."

Krista scoffed. "Are we still on this bullshit? Our daughter is eight-years-old. I've had a few relationships since then, and so has Tobias. Aren't you happily married, too? Or are you?" Her eyes examined the robe I wore.

"What I am and what I do is not your business. You only need to be concerned about that as it concerns Tobias."

Her brows met. "Why?"

"Because there won't be anymore 'oops' pregnancies happening for you with him ever again in life—this one *or* the next."

She laughed. "You're still stuck on that old ass shit! Like I said, don't you have a whole ass *League*-playing husband? Oh, my bad. He was cut mad years ago. I guess he broke now, and you want back on Tobias' train. He'd be a sucker if he let you do it. You should've stayed when you had a chance back in the day. But you chose money."

"Fuck you!" I was jittery with emotion, ready to explode. "You don't know shit about me other than how you conveniently chose to keep the baby when you discovered there was a me. Your lost, misguided ass got pregnant from a random fuck. When he asked you to get an abortion because there was a "me," your trifling ass stalked me and decided you wanted to keep the baby."

"Lennox, lady!" Her head swung, eyes wild as she smirked. "You think you mattered to me that much? Like…who the fuck were you back then—who the fuck are you now, besides one of Tobias' many whores?"

Pedro, Tobias' cook, finally appeared, going to Krista's side. "Please. Wait until Mr. Elliott returns to continue this conversation," he pleaded with her.

I was past the point of reasoning with now. "I was that girl *you* saw something in. You hated the fact that he really wanted me. He told you we had something special, and you should abort the baby. You refused after learning about me! You don't remember? You told me the whole story via inbox back then."

I'd never forget being torn, hurt, and feeling pressured on both sides. Kelvin and his team were pursuing me at the same time Tobias showed up to my grandmother's house with red eyes, saying he had a baby on the way. Apparently, it happened just weeks before we met. We'd been seeing each other for months! Krista purposely waited to tell him. It was a casual mishap because they were never in a relationship. They'd known each other for some time, but decided to sleep together after a party, then resumed their normal lives.

At some point, Krista found Tobias and told him the news. It was at such a daunting time. Tobias and I had been falling for each other, but my grandmother had just forbidden me from seeing him. Kelvin had been coming around, impressing her. I often thought back to that short span of time. If Tobias had not been expecting a baby, I likely would have disobeyed my grandmother and saw him anyway. I was an adult—granted, but still financially dependent. What was the worst she could have done to me? Put me on punishment? I felt betrayed by Tobias in a way because I'd slept with him three times at this point, something I'd never done so quickly and easily with any other guy. Not even Kelvin slept with me so soon after we'd met.

A young Tobias told Krista she couldn't have the baby because he was trying to pursue something with another girl—a girl he'd seen a bright future with. He even told her my name. I guess that alone sparked her creative research.

"What inbox?" Tobias appeared in the foyer, his hat and coat still on.

My eyes went straight to Krista. "Tell him!"

"Tell him what?"

"Tell him how you searched and found me on *Facebook* back then."

"How?" Tobias demanded.

Krista seemed to be annoyed by it all. "You mean to find you?" She shrugged. "You told me her name was Lennox. I went to your list of friends and there was only one with that name."

"And you reached out to her?" his voice calm, steady.

"I was—what? Seventeen…eighteen-years-old at the time?"

"Yeah. And very antagonistic over a guy you barely knew."

"I knew Tobias long before you came into the picture, sweetie."

"Yeah, but not as a girlfriend or even a prospective one. You were a random. Never me. Not then or *now*—"

"Lennox," Tobias warned, taking to my side with a gentle hand at my waist. "Elia's here."

"I'm not going to shut up." Krista wouldn't win now. Not with all Tobias and I stood to lose. We were in too delicate of a promising space. Her mere presence represented a bad omen. I damn near hated her. Had gone to her public profiles on *Facebook* and *Instagram* when she moved over there. I guess one could say I'd turned into the stalker. Krista was your average, aimless, hood chick. There was nothing special about her. Nothing notable at all.

You could see her lifestyle being upgraded once Tobias finally got his break in music. I could even tell they tried their hand at romance for a brief time after Elia was born. But it didn't stick, because Krista was never the one for Tobias. "I've never spoken ill against you or your daughter. You can ask Tobias. *We've* been best friends for years now, and not one time have I disregarded you or her. But what you won't do is see me and think you got a leg up because of an unwanted and unplanned baby—"

"Bitch, my child is wanted by—"

"Only you two! You won? Big fucking deal!"

Did I just say that?

I didn't mean to—not like that, at least.

Truthfully, although Tobias had returned to my life, and very intimately, he'd returned alone. We didn't see each other much, so I'd only heard about Elia and her mother. I listened without much feedback. Being in his home almost naked, and having them "pop up," peeled back my real, raw feelings of the trio.

"Yo!" Krista snorted Tobias' way. "You think this one's classy? Look at what she's saying about our child—about me! But this is class to you, Tobe?"

That shit grated at me. "It's fucking 'Tobias' to you! And I am the epitome of class and grace, even for mediocre women like you—"

"Ain't shit mediocre about me. I work hard and own my own home."

"Yeah, about that…" I turned to face Tobias, although I was in his tight hold. "Did you ever wonder where her nursing inspiration came from?" I peered over to Krista. "Where are your scrubs? You love showing them off like you're a real nurse."

"Bitch, I am a real nurse!"

"Not the one you want to be!" I yelled. "Not the one I am!"

"Yo," Tobias barked, causing a burst to happen in my mind, and out of nowhere, I caught the wails of a child. "What are you saying, Lennox?"

Elia…

As pretty as she was—as many features as she shared with the love of my life—seeing her was a sore sight for me. She represented what Tobias and I should have had right now. My life could have gone in a different direction had I made simple changes in how I was influenced. I wanted a stable career, loving marriage, and beautiful babies by one man. This man was now soiled with having to care for his daughter, a physical reminder of why I would never be his first.

"What the hell you think she's saying?" Krista's hands went to her hips. "She don't accept your child. Your flesh and blood!"

His head swung to face her with violent speed. "I'm not talking to you," subterranean voice deep, crisp.

Just when things were perfect. I'd awakened in his bed. Last night, I'd gone to bed with a job prospect and a possible solution to my housing need. I'd made love to this man, had given my soul to him without words. I loved Tobias and wanted to get to a place emotionally where we could finally pursue what was ours.

Elia...

Seeing her this morning dredged up another barrier to what I felt we were owed. And I felt like shit for feeling that way.

One foot in front of the other...

Hang on till the next moment...

Soon, this will be a faded memory...

You won't break...

You're built to survive even this...

Before the tears spilled, I twisted out of Tobias' hold. Then it was my turn to bolt up the stairs, rounding Elia's little, sobbing body on the way.

Chapter Sixteen

Tobias

Her office was nice. Relaxing, I guessed. Warm, gray walls and a smooth, lavender carpet. Long, ten-feet-tall windows faced a coffee shop on the corner across the street. Against the wall adjacent to the French doorway was a long, white, suede, tuft sofa. Her walls were framed and decorated. Apparently, Lennox's therapist was a New York Times bestselling author, and a *Mauve* aficionado. There were bottles of it in the brand's different strengths, placed like trophies in one corner.

Strange...

"Mr. Elliott," she smiled, looking down at her tablet before returning to meet my eyes. "I'm so thrilled to finally meet you. I know you have a flight to catch in a few hours. Thanks for making time."

"Of course," I returned stiffly.

"On paper—what Lennox has shared about you all these years sounds...unbelievably promising."

"For her, I am, Doc."

"Tell me something about you I don't know. Give me something real."

"She's your client, Doc. She's probably told you all of it. But from my heart to your ears, she's mine. However you can fix her 'scary, must do things by the therapist's book' ass to ease her into this reality—*her reality*—make that happen. Do it. I'll take it from there."

Every facial muscle of hers seemed to have suspended. "Okay," she sang, expelling air. "Then, let's start with Elia. If you don't mind, share with me your feelings on what happened last week between Lennox and…" She looked down at her tablet. "Krista."

I took a deep breath, chest tightening at the memory. I'd heard from Lennox only three times since dropping her off at the airport to get back home that Friday. I already didn't want to send her home, hating to resume the distance. And I damn sure didn't want to after the blow up with Krista. It was too dangerous. And not because Lennox was upset, but because I was fucking pissed.

My baby girl stood at the top of the steps, scared, and crying at her mother engaging in a vicious, verbal war with a stranger. This all happened in her daddy's home. At the core of the nasty fight? Her daddy. And while my baby cried, I remained on post with the stranger. My life was so fucking complicated when it came to Lennox. Apparently, she had been my priority over my own fucking daughter that day. The shit had been fucking with me ever since. No one stood with Elia, yet I stood right by Lennox's side. I'd since apologized to my daughter for the whole ordeal, specifically about that. Of course, my baby girl told me she forgave me and was fine. However, as a man, I'd been sitting in this shit. Stewing in my weakness.

Lennox Curry…

Lennox texted me when she'd gotten home safely. Then she randomly sent a text at three the following morning, reminding me of how much she appreciates me and wanted to continue to build on what we had. She apologized for her behavior that day and her feelings. She took full accountability, and told me she'd do the work to be better for Elia and me. Of course, she said much more. Her text was a fucking novel, but I abstracted what I needed from it.

"You mean the undying dilemma with the love of my life…" I scoffed. Feeling defensive and angry, I wiped the sides of my mouth.

"My requited love has returned to my world, only to reveal she can't accept the baby that broke us up in the first place."

The therapist's smile was knowing as she shook her head. "You know Elia wasn't the reason you and Lennox didn't pursue your relationship back then. At least, that's not what she's shared with me."

"Yeah, but if you're telling me Lennox didn't mention me having a baby on the way back then being a dealbreaker for her, then she hasn't been as open as you're requesting of me right now."

"Yes. I'm aware of Krista being pregnant at a precarious time. I do understand how it played into the 'break up.' It was an ingredient, not the whole soup. Lennox can deduce the timing of Elia's conception."

"It didn't sound like it at all that day."

She leaned over her crossed legs. "Perhaps that's because this was her first time seeing Elia. From what I've gathered from Lennox, she was on emotional overload with having you support her at the last minute on Thanksgiving. Then, finding possible pieces to the next step in her life with the job and realtor on the same day. She felt you two made emotional and sensual strides toward unity, something she's not had in a very long time." She nodded softly, with gentle understanding. "And she saw your pride and joy. Lennox described Elia as your twin. She couldn't stop raving about how gorgeous she is."

Then her hands abruptly shot into the air. "I should have began this conversation by informing you that Lennox provided full consent for me to share her words about this topic. I was happy, hoping if you heard her perspective from a neutral party, perhaps it would resonate differently."

Chewing on the inside of my mouth, I nodded, trying to process everything. Much of what the therapist said, Lennox had put into that long ass text last week.

"What do you have to say about that?"

"What, in particular?"

"About her willingness to have me share her perspective with you."

I nodded, now understanding the question. "It makes sense."

"What does?"

"Why she would push for me to see her therapist. Why she would ask you to convey her feelings after she showed her little ass in front of my daughter last week."

"Why is that?"

"Because she still wants me, and needs your approval for that single fact."

Her eyes opened wider. "You think Lennox seeks the approval of others? I don't believe that's a fair judgement. I was hoping she'd get a friend to vent to for emotional exchange and positive influence. I was thrilled she found that in you a few years ago."

I shook my head. "No. Lennox don't need nobody's approval for shit." I chuckled. "The woman's an independent thinker to the point of a fuckin' rebellion now." When the therapist's face cracked into a smile, I knew she agreed.

She nodded. "This is going to be a journey—for you all. But I do believe our girl can navigate the muddy waters to get where she wants to be."

"And where's that?"

She shrugged, sitting back. "Like you said, she's likely told you everything. Lennox is rebuilding. Recalibrating within, reframing her mind, and reshaping her heart. She's transitioning into a new woman; one she's choosing, and not surviving. I'm thrilled to be a part of it."

I nodded. "So am I."

"Good. So, don't interfere with the process by thinking you're at an impasse."

I whistled, shaking my head. "It's kind of hard not to. Elia is a part of me. I don't know what kind of man I'd be right now, without her."

"And?"

"And then, I have the love of my life...the masseuse of my soul, telling me Elia reminds her of being robbed of my 'first.' That she could never be the first to give me a baby. There's nothing I wouldn't do for this crazy woman. Do you know how much that fucks with my head? How helpless and unfixable that one thing is? I can't change what happened nine years ago. If I could, it would have happened already."

"Okay. You're going to have to process this. If Lennox is upset about not being a first for you, I think she needs to think about that in the reverse."

"What do you mean?"

"You won't be a first for her either. She's married. Just as some women want to be the first and only to give their man children, men want to be the first to soil their women."

My head fell back, and I cracked the hell up, too loud for a professional setting. When I could catch my breath, I nodded. "Word. That's true. And I ain't even trippin' off that. I'll take her as she is."

The therapist winked. "And trust me, she'll take you the same. I've been at this work for more years than I care to share. More often than not, there are couples who are helpless with no tools powerful enough to fix their union. But then, in between, along come souls like you and Lennox. A couple with real issues, but ones that can be fixed with patience and kindness toward one another. Just hang in there. You'll see."

Seeing her soft, expressive, vestal smile filled with the confidence of a seasoned woman of an African tribe, my chest began to ease. It was as though she'd injected me with hope. My ass needed it before flying out to *Karsyn Cove* to record with Dale.

Lennox

"Damn!" Rachel grunted. "He's had all this *shiieet*. You'da thought five kids lived down here instead of one grown man!"

I walked up the final step from the basement into my kitchen, holding one end of a rolled-up rug while she had the other. My aunt-in-law had been over since this morning, helping me clean out the basement, aka Kelvin's room. The ungodly and sad shit we found down there. Burned spoons, needles, empty lighters, porcelain bowls, countless empty prescription bottles, charred aluminum foil pieces, and half-filled bottles of liquor. We even discovered what Rachel had to explain to me were burnt light bulbs, something meth abusers used to smoke the drug through a straw. It was an emotional task, disbanding his personal space. Either way, it had to be done.

Kelly-Ann had moved out the week after Thanksgiving. She didn't have much. Most of her things had been sitting in storage for years, since she'd lost the home Kelvin bought her. Kelly-Ann employed the assistance of Marcia, Marcia's boyfriend, and his nephew to move her things out. The following day, I received a call from Kelvin. He was still in the residential program, demanding that all of his things go with his mother. He labeled me a few decorative, demeaning titles, all the while needing me to do yet another thing for him. Kelly-Ann was in no position to lift furniture or run up and down the stairs. Marcia had a sprained wrist from Kelly-Ann's move.

So, as a middle ground, Rachel and I agreed we'd take care of the task. The problem was, I wasn't available to do this until the following week, which was two weeks after Thanksgiving. They had to wait. I'd been working for both the hospital and Jade's impending salon business. I'd also been packing my things around here, too. Life had been moving on the fast track for me.

"Okay!" Rachel panted after we dropped the carpet at the curb in front of my house. "That's it for now. I'll get this shit over to the shed in the back of the house till Kelly-Ann decide what she's going to do with it."

My phone pinged with a notification as we trekked up the driveway for the door. It was an email notification. "You want a bottle of water?" I offered Rachel.

"Yeah. I'll take one. Gonna grab my purse from the living room while I'm at it." We walked inside and I headed for the fridge to grab the water. "You know that Scott's been a trooper through all of this," Rachel noted when I handed her the bottle.

My mouth twisted with sadness. "He has. A little too much." Scott's room was still intact. I'd been having him spend nights at Terry's mother's place for days at a time, strategically. I didn't want him to think he was being kicked out. In fact, I hadn't had to kick anyone out. When Kelly-Ann decided to go, her son wanted to follow suit. This thing had been working out for me, putting the anxiety I had after meeting with my divorce attorney last month to rest. But Scott was a delicate matter. "I just hope he isn't saving face for me. The kid has been my protector for too long. It's not fair to him."

Rachel finished gulping back water. "Naw. I spoke to Mitchie. She said he done picked out a room over there. Fighting his cousin that just moved in for it." She laughed.

Mitchie was Terry's mother, and Scott's maternal grandmother. We'd been in touch a lot over the years. She was more hands-on with Scott than Kelly-Ann. Terry was blessed to have her. Mitchie and I had been in talks about me transferring custody of Scott back to her soon.

"Yeah." I snorted, rolling my eyes. "He told me. I think it's cool how he's getting his mother back and a cousin his age, all under the same roof."

"So, what're you going to do? You know, I was just telling my cousin, Sandy, this family must be cursed."

"Why?"

"Because of all the shit we done been through, starting with Kyle getting killed like that...Kelvin losing the *League* and getting on drugs bad. And now we're losing you."

I scoffed, "I don't think your family considers me divorcing Kelvin a loss."

"And that's the problem. Them dumb fucks ain't know how good they had it with you." She offered her hand. "Well, I still wanna be your friend. Maybe if I'm in the area of the hospital during the day, I'll stop by for lunch."

I took her hand with a smile. "Thanks, Rachel. Thanks for everything. Most importantly for being you." That was all I could say. I wouldn't tell her that though I'd still been working, I'd submitted my letter of resignation the week after Thanksgiving. My last day at the hospital would be December thirtieth. I was generous with giving them time to find my replacement. However, I had loads of vacation time accumulated I was still considering what I'd do with.

"Alright, girl!" She grabbed her bag and sauntered to the door.

"Take care, Rachel," I murmured behind her.

After locking the door, I pulled out my scrunchie and fingered my hair. The simple act brought bigger hands to mind. He enjoyed playing in my hair. An ache lanced my chest. I missed Tobias so much. We hadn't spoken much since I left Jersey, but this felt different from our breaks in communication after homecoming. Yes, Tobias was upset with me, and I'd been embarrassed. However, we were…together. I knew this from my urge to send him lines from a Nyles Adams poem while in a directors' meeting at ten in the morning a couple of days ago.

"My love for you is
All of me and none of me
It is all of you"

Within seconds, Tobias texted back, *"Seventeen syllables, three lines of five, seven, and five. A Haiku for You. Sending it right back to you."*

Another example would be when Tobias landed in *Karsyn Cove* to record more records with Dale. He sent me a picture of the water. He also sent a picture of the sun setting over the palm trees. I understood the sentimental value in his sharing. But we were right. I'd messed up bad with Elia. I honestly didn't know I'd been holding on to that anger and regret. It was disgusting and, in between work and research for my move, I'd been trying to think of ways to amend for that nasty behavior.

In the dining room, I sat in front of my laptop. Sure enough, there was an email from Jaquana. She had agreed to help me find a place in Jersey. That was another daunting issue. I'd have to fly up there to actually see these places. When would I find the time? The realtor I'd finally began working with to sell my house had already begun her work. I didn't want anyone in and out of here while I was away.

I spent the next few minutes clicking on images of three town-house rentals. None thrilled me, but two could work. They were all three-story high structures. I didn't want to be hiking up and down the stairs. Then, there was one in Edgewater that was well beyond my price range. I took a deep breath, reclining into the seat. I didn't want to do this. I didn't want the task. Then, I listened hard around my home and heard...nothing. There was no energy here. The place was dead. When good energy doesn't exist in a home, it's time to go.

Sighing, I sat up and clicked on the link for the next prospect. It was a standalone house. My brows furrowed. In *Samsara*. I yanked up my phone from the table so fast it fumbled in the air. Thankfully, I caught it. Then I dialed up Jaquana. She answered almost right away.

"Hi," her feminine voice cultured with charm.

"Hey—" mine was not. I was beyond confused. "I'm looking at the *Samsara* property."

"I thought you'd like that one."

"I *did*—do. A lot!" I blinked successively. "But how is this place only one thousand dollars a month? It has five bedrooms, two of which are masters with en suites. Plus, it sits on an acre and a half with a pool in the back!"

"Yes," she crooned. "All new appliances, a miniature wine cellar, and the furniture is included."

Again, I blinked. "For one thousand dollars?"

Her laughter was breathy. "Yes. One thousand eight dollars a month, to be exact."

"How does this happen? The other prices are north of three thousand without these amenities, the size, the included furniture, or the privacy!"

More laughter. I wondered if I sounded as feminine to Tobias when he made me laugh as this woman had to me. "It's called a pocket listing. The owner's given me exclusivity with this listing, which means I get first dibs. And I'm offering it to you. When do you think you'd be able to come up and take a look at it?"

"A look?" My eyes went wild. I didn't want to tell her I'd stayed in this plush home two months ago. "I don't think that's necessary."

"No?"

"No. I'll take it on sight." Then I went back to the computer screen. "125 Nirvana Lane in Samsara, New Jersey will be my new home." Until I could afford to buy again.

"Oh, my! That's what I like to hear." Just when I thought she'd caution me about taking the place without having seen it, Jaquana shared instead, "I'll have my assistant draw up the paperwork."

"Easy peasy!" I squealed.

"Byeee!" she sang.

"Ba-byeeeee!"

Then I shot to my feet and did a praise dance. I didn't think; I only allowed my body to move celebratorily, the way it wanted to. The last time I'd danced like this was to mock my grandmother!

But I did vocalize, "Thank you, God!" at the top of my lungs. He *had* to be moving on my behalf. These "ways" weren't being "made" on their own.

My phone rang, and when I saw the name on the face, I began to repent right away.

"Hey!" I answered, resuming my seat at the table.

"You answered!" Mya noted, surprised.

"Why wouldn't I?"

"Well, the last time you texted me back you said you had a lot going on."

"I do," I admitted while going back to the tab of the nail tech school I'd decided on. The need to type in my new address was imminent.

"Well, girl! What's going on?"

"I'm moving."

Mya gasped. "Where? Have you told the girls? Nisha and Lisa told me they've spoken to you recently, and I'm feeling left out!"

"No, I haven't told them. So please keep this between us."

"You know I will! Spill!"

"I filed for divorce from Kelvin." Mya didn't react to that. "He moved out. His mother did, too."

"Okay," she spoke in a way to tell me to keep going.

"Yeah," I inhaled. "Well, now I can be free to do what I want. I don't see the need to stay here in Raleigh."

"So, where will you go?"

I delayed for a few seconds to finish the application I'd started two days ago. "Can you keep a secret, secret?"

"You can tell me anything. You know that!"

"Okay. So, I've been seeing this woman. Tricia. We started out as friends earlier this year. But we've...you know..." Mya's hard, audible, scandalous gasp caused me to feel awful. "We're spiritually connected now. Let's put it that way. She's got a place in *Macen Beach*—"

"So, that bitch got money!"

"*Ehhhh*... It's more like her parents invested at the right time. It's been her family's vacation home for a while. No one really visits there, so she asked her parents for it. They've accepted her coming out and okayed it."

"Bitch!"

"Yup, girl. I'm moving to South Carolina."

When I opened the door, I didn't expect to see him alone. He'd aged over the years, but his warm, honey skin was still wrinkled and heavily blemished from brutal fights and scuffs with law enforcement. The blood drop tattoos were still bright and proudly posted. But those deep, caramel-hued eyes and wavy hair pulled into a sleek ponytail still reminded me of my lineage.

"Hey," I tried for soft, but cheery. "Come in."

He strolled inside slowly with confidence, clad in a leather jacket. His naturally slanted eyes gave off an intimidating glare. His powerful silence had men shaking in their boots, and I could see why. Chino Brim from Amhurst Street was a known killer. His reputation stretched from the streets of Essex County, out to the penile system.

Finally, he asked in his infamous, taut tenor, "How long you been here?" His inspection of the living room wouldn't stop.

I licked my lips. "Just this week."

Literally two days ago, I moved into the *Samsara* property. I still had mine and Scott's things at my house in Raleigh. The school I applied to wanted me to come in person to sign paperwork and to sit for an hour orientation. Also, Jade had me meet with a few of her investors to present my prospective curriculum for the training program and policy manual she'd, hopefully, be using soon to launch the business. That was yesterday. They loved my ideas so much, Jade and I were able to throw around some numbers for me to come aboard to help her with the launch. She was generous and rather aggressive. We agreed to put a pin in me possibly partnering with her at some point in the future.

"How'd you find it?"

"*Ummmm…* A realtor—broker," I corrected myself. "I guess it's the same thing, huhn?" I laughed nervously.

He swung around to face me. "Nah. It's not. Two different titles. Which one helped you out?"

I nodded, pulse racing. "She's a broker."

"Who?"

"Ummm…" I swallowed. "Jaquana."

His forehead stretched, then brows furrowed. "Her? How?"

"A mutual friend."

"What kind of friend? She's in the big leagues. Million-dollar homes…celebrity clients." So, I'd heard. "This shit's gotta cost a pretty penny."

I shrugged. "It's a rental."

He nodded, staring at me for a while. Finally, my father looked at me. "Damn. You look just like her," he murmured, close to a whisper.

That spooked me a bit. "Who?"

"Darlene."

Mommy...

My eyes fell. I didn't know how to respond to that.

My father cleared his throat then reached back to scratch the back of his head. It was an uncharacteristic sign of unease for him. "I...*ummm*... I know you may not think so, but she would be real proud of the woman you are. Real proud."

"You're right." I snorted. "I don't believe you."

"I respect that," he murmured while nodding.

When the word-flow slowed, I decided to move things along, remembering my impending travel. "I know on the phone I told you I'd moved up here. I wanted you to see the place."

"It's nice." His eyes brushed the room again.

"And let you know it would be cool if you came over once in a while for dinner, maybe? There's even a pool in the back. So maybe this summer, I can throw something on the grill and we can hang out back there?"

He scoffed. "You cook?" I shook my head. "I 'on't cook either."

"Tobias does."

"Who—" Revelation hit. Then his face tightened. "What you mean?"

Upturning my lips, I nodded. "It's official. We're a...thing." I blinked, showing my slip, actually. In my heart of hearts, I wanted to finally explore love with Tobias. I hoped it worked this time. "A real, for real thing."

"Ain't you still..."

"Married? Yup. I've filed and have to be separated for a full year."

"Ol' boy good with all this?" He gestured the house, which meant my choices—all of them.

I sighed, sitting on the edge of the sofa. *The* sofa. The one Tobias and I made love in front of homecoming weekend. "I don't think he has a choice. The judge ordered him to complete a nine-month drug treatment program. After that, we have three months to remain separated. I think it'll be easy-peasy from there." I giggled.

My father expressed no humor, which could have made the moment less awkward. It didn't, though. I didn't know this man, but the few interactions I'd had with him coming up, mirrored his dry personality on display now. It wasn't offensive because I had an inkling that the man had an ounce of like for me.

He tossed his chin my way, face still deadpan. "He ever lay a hand on you?"

I shook my head with vehemence. "He's all types of fucked up, but violent, Kelvin Richardson isn't. *Or* your trip down there that year may have done the trick." I shrugged.

"Yeah. Now, listen here." He pivoted, swiping his nose with his thumb. "About this Tobias thing: the kid need to come holler at me."

"For what?"

"As a man. He shoulda been the first to tell me 'bout all this."

"But I'm telling you. You're my father."

"How long?"

"Excuse me?"

"How long y'all had this shit going on?"

That was hard to answer. "Officially? For the past year and a half, maybe."

"And he ain't..." He turned away, fist going to his mouth. Then my father rolled his neck toward me. "I just saw the nigga last month, visiting mommy."

"Who visited Grandmother? You or Tobias?"

"We both did! I thought it was weird but let it slide. He a good kid. I just thought he was being a little bit of a weirdo for still hanging on to old shit."

Whoa!

Tobias went to visit my grandmother. I dropped my face in my hand. "That's the problem. None of this is old. It's still an issue for us."

"What is?"

"When Kelvin mentioned wanting to marry me back in the day, even you weren't with it."

"You damn right, I wasn't."

"Why?"

"Because the nigga was a square. A fuckin' goof troop. He couldn't take care of no good girl like you. We eat them pretty-boy, arrogant, weak-ass niggas up in the penitentiary. Real eyes realize. I spotted that pussy-ass in him coming from a mile away."

"Grandmother hadn't."

"*Psssst!*" he spit into the air, brushing me off with a hand-wave. "Say, now, my mother's a old, respectable, church lady. You damn right she gon' think marriage is the way."

My forehead wrinkled. "Why? Had she ever married?" Then I thought about it. "My last name is Curry. Yours is, too."

"Yeah!" he returned defensively.

I stood. "Grandmother's last name is Williams."

"And?"

"Who is your father? Did she marry and divorce him?"

"Nah. Mommy ain't never been married."

"Then whose last name do you have?"

"My pops! What you mean?"

"Who was your father, Dad?"

He pivoted again, turning away from me. "Ah, man. That's that lady's business. I ain't never get into it. I saw him a couple of times as a pup. Ain't no biggie."

"That's my point. Grandmother pushed me to make a weighty decision. When she found out Tobias liked me, she flipped on him. She told me he wasn't allowed at her house anymore. Then, when Kelvin came sniffing around, she practically pushed me down the aisle to the altar."

He sucked his teeth. "Man, that old shit, baby girl."

I laughed wryly. Everyone referred to that period as old. And maybe it was to them, because life kept going. For Tobias and me, it had hiccupped. We'd never aired it out.

"It may have been a long time ago, but it's not old. I swear, I don't harbor ill-will for Grandmother, but I do get frustrated that she's still here, yet I can't confront her about this. I feel like she owes me an apology. Something!"

My father shook his head. "Nah, baby girl. That lady don't owe you or me shit. She looked out when it was time. She raised you from four-years-old to college. She looked out for me. She ain't the one that owes you. It's me. I owe you. If I'da been around after ya Earth passed, raising you right, you'da seen that weak-ass nigga coming a mile away, too." His nostrils spread and I lost his eyes as he wiped the sides of his mouth. His small frame rocked a bit as he stared at the floor. "It ain't easy for me to say all the shit I need to, but…" He exhaled, switching the weight on his hips. "Just put it like this: you inviting me to come chill over here's gonna give me the opportunities I'mma need to keep apologizing. I'm your daddy. I failed you. I failed ya Earth—*may Darlene rest in peace.*" He whispered. "Then I fucked up with you. Let my moms stay where she at. She can't defend herself. I'mma do my best to help you let that shit go. A'ight?"

Fighting back burgeoning tears, with pouted lips, I nodded. He'd never expressed that juxtaposition to me—any at all, in fact. The only time I'd ever felt a connection to him was when he descended on Kelvin years back in North Carolina. That was the one time I felt like a daughter to anyone.

"So, what's up with the house in Raleigh?"

I shrugged, feeling momentarily, emotionally defeated. "I've been considering renting the place out again."

"Word? Why?"

A wry smile pushed onto my face. "Because if there's been anything I've learned from you, it's been to create options for myself. Selling the house may give me a nice payout, but renting it can provide security down the line." I winked.

Expressionless, my father nodded.

"Sara?" I asked into the screen where I was on a *FaceTime* call with Raj. "Sara Peterson?"

"Yeah, man. Sara fuckin' Peterson. She was a sweetheart. Her parents are cool people's, too."

"They live…what? Twenty minutes down the road from your estate?"

"Ten," he corrected me.

"Damn," I whispered.

When the phone rang with a *FaceTime* from Raj, I almost didn't answer. He knew I'd been in *Karsyn Cove*, cutting tracks with Dale. But my gut told me to see what he had to say. The last thing I was expecting to hear about was death. Raj had an older brother with special needs named Arnie. Arnie was high-functioning, but needed supervision, to a degree. So, Raj built him a ranch on the back of his palatial estate. Arnie had a friend, Sara, who was developmentally delayed, too. She was a nice and high-energy Caucasian woman who crushed on my guy, Arnie, so bad over the years. Raj allowed her to come by and utilize Arnie's farm, too. I liked Sara a lot. One year, when working on one of Raj's albums, we found ourselves back at the ranch. Sara asked me to "make her a singer." Within a few hours, we had a song. Sara's parents met us on the ranch, and we watched Sara perform her new track, *"Farm Girl."* It was fun and funny as hell. Sara was a star, truly.

Raj said her parents found her non-responsive in her bed this morning.

"And they don't know what happened?"

With a twisted mouth, Raj shook his head. "It's fucked up."

"It is. How's Arnie taking it?"

"Wynter wants to wait to hear back about the cause before we tell him. You know Arnie's gonna wanna know every detail."

"Yeah." That's how my guy's brain worked.

"You know what this reminds me to do?"

I scratched my beard, sitting back from the sound board. "What's that?"

"To love as hard as you possibly can. If love makes you happy, then love, my nigga. Sara was full of love."

I nodded. "She damn sure was."

"You are, too, Tobe." That gave me pause. "Word. Remember what I said to you Thanksgiving morning about Lennox?" I nodded, running my palm down the top of my head, not wanting to go there. "Although, it was out of love, I'm thinking this Sara shit just broadened my view of you. You're love, too. You speak it, you teach it, you give it. Shit, man, you probably 'fuck it,' too!" I chuckled at that as Raj laughed, clowning me.

"If taking care of people is how God created you, as your brother, I can't criticize you for that," he continued. "After seeing you two together that night, I realized I didn't trust you to be you. You're fuckin' Tobias Elliott, the love doctor, musically. Of course, you live that shit. So, I guess what I'm saying, my guy, is continue to be love. Love your fuckin' heart out. I need it. The world needs it."

I scoffed, not feeling love at all. Thanksgiving Day was a dream. The morning after, the fairytale ended, and a fucking hocus-pocus spell hit my world. Did I believe Lennox was regretful? Yeah, I did. But regret wouldn't erase what her actions uncovered. She couldn't love my baby. I would never ask Lennox to parent Elia. She already had two. Nonetheless, Lennox's acceptance couldn't be negotiated. Yeah, I'd fucked up when getting a girl pregnant back then. Elia was my consequence, but she wasn't a punishment.

My head rolled back, and eyes closed as I groaned. Raj's message was appreciated, but the timing was fucked. "A'ight, man. Much appreciated."

"Love."

"Love."

As soon as Raj disconnected the call, I heard, "Daddy?"

Those soft cords could mangle or heal my heart. I knew them. My head jerked toward the door of the dark studio, and in the bright ass doorway was my baby girl. Aside her were her mother and...Lennox? The softness in her eyes belied her guilt and timidity.

Ripping my eyes away from her, I glanced down at my baby girl. My heart swelled in my damn chest as I stood to greet her.

"What're you doing here, Pear Bear?"

Chapter Seventeen

Tobias

The moment Elia met me midway for an embrace, a little body joined the two women in the doorway. As I lifted my baby from the floor, I noticed the tight ass biker shorts and Jamaican flag-styled tank JuJu wore as he rested with his weight on one hip.

"Hi, Mr. Elliott!" he greeted as Elia hugged me tightly at the neck.

"Whaddup, Ju! It's good to see you down here, kid."

He smiled back somewhat shyly, reminding me of his young age.

"Daddy, where's Dale?" Elia asked.

"Yeah!" JuJu seconded her inquiry.

"Why?" My eyes swung between the two adults in the doorway. "This surprise wasn't for me?"

Elia hugged me tighter again. "Yeah, Daddy," she groaned.

"I mentioned Dale," Krista explained. "and JuJu said he was in. Sorry, Dad, you're not the rockstar for everyone."

As I placed Elia on her feet, I shared, "Dale's out back, freestyling with a few of his choreographers."

"Aren't you down here creating the music?" Krista asked.

I shrugged, eyes brushing down Lennox's body. Her curly waves framed her pretty face. She wore casual, blue shorts with a matching cropped, short-sleeved jacket. Beneath was a simple, white tube bra. How long had they been on the island? She looked vacation fresh with orange lipstick. Lennox couldn't stop looking at me either.

"It's his creative style," I tried to explain. "The music, the dancing—all of it."

"Let's go see if we can watch!" JuJu suggested to Elia.

"Yeah! Yeah!" she trilled, little body tight with excitement.

They were almost out the door when I yelled, "Stay back! Don't let him know you're there!"

Dale wouldn't have tripped at all, but this was business. If he was in the zone he'd been in since we landed, he likely would have pretty much ignored the kids, crushing their fandom. That wouldn't be fair to them or Dale. He was down to earth otherwise.

The kids charged out of the studio. And like a moth to a flame, I glided over toward Lennox. The moment I touched her, one hand going to her ass and the other to her scalp, she melted into me.

"What're y'all doing here?" I asked again, recognizing the tenderness in my voice.

I lifted Lennox's face up by pulling the hair in the back of her head. It was one of my favorite things to do to her, was the same way I wanted to kiss her for the first time, again, a year-and-a-half ago. Each time we kissed was a fantasy come true.

"I'll let her explain her reason," Krista began. "My reason is, after talking—and sometimes verbally fighting—with her on the phone for three hours on Sunday, the next day she called to invite Elia and me to fly down here to surprise you."

My attention went down to Lennox, still suspended in my hold. "Why?"

"Because I've been missing you." Her voice was so small.

"I know. But this is a lot. Expensive, too," I probed for more answers, releasing her hair.

She stepped closer to me, cutting Krista out. "I get it now." She exhaled in frustration.

"Explain."

"I get your...slight obsession with me all these years. The need to possess me. The urge to drown in me, to become one, and own me: mind, body, and soul."

I cocked my head to the side and my forehead wrinkled. "Slight obsession?"

For a spell, Lennox smiled cheaply then mouthed, "Full obsession."

"Well, that ain't my business," Krista made clear. "I was invited —all expenses paid for. The resort is nice, too."

I asked Lennox, "What resort?"

"It's about fifteen minutes from here. A *Hilton* property. The kids love the pools and beach."

My face went tight. "Is that where y'all're staying?" That didn't feel right to me.

"That's where JuJu and I are definitely staying. And if I know Elia, she'll choose JuJu over Daddy here in *Karsyn Cove* any day. I don't know about anyone else."

Again, I glanced down at Lennox, who was now rubbing her lips together. Her little ass wasn't staying at no fucking resort while on an island with me. She'd be right where she fucking belonged: my bed. Her silence and nervous energy told me she knew that. I wanted to taste her lips, throw all of my weight on her, but didn't think she was with it because of Krista. I didn't give a fuck, but decided on modesty.

After grazing her jawline with the tip of my nose, I, regretfully, let her stand straight, but didn't let her go. My hand stayed in her hair, and Lennox's arm roved up the back of my t-shirt. Her touch coated me like a pain-reliever.

"I'm going to apologize, again, to the both of you, at the same time. My behavior that morning in Englewood Cliffs was unacceptable. I explained to Krista how I haven't worked through my issues stemming from nine years ago. Yes," Lennox admitted. "Krista's pregnancy hurt me. It was a big deal to me back then, but if you two have been able to work through it like mature adults, I'll have to suck it up, and do the same." Her other hand landed on my belly, sparking a nerve in my groin. "If I'm going to be a part of Tobias' world—which I am and will—I'll have to share it with Elia, and I don't mind."

Krista nodded her approval.

"And I know you were wrapping things up out here to leave in two days," Lennox explained. "So, I thought a good way of making amends was to surprise you with your baby girl. I knew Elia would be at *Disney* for Christmas. They leave on Christmas Eve, not giving you much time with her after being out here working. I figured the more time, a merrier Tobias."

That shit made me smile.

"Thank you," was all I could return.

"Do you need to finish up in here?" Lennox asked.

I turned around to the sound board. "Nah. I was done a while ago. Was in here, kicking it with Raj on the phone."

"Awwww! About what?" Lennox asked. "Something important, but nothing he needed to *FaceTime* for."

Lennox's giggle made me laugh, too. These R&B niggas were territorial as hell. Raj wasn't fooling nobody.

"Well, I'm going to get settled in while you spend time with Elia."

"And where are you going?"

Lennox blinked hard, a show of sass. "Well, first, you're going to show me to your room. Then you can go."

That's what I thought.

Krista held a tight smile, her brows shooting up in the air. I had a feeling she was picking up on Lennox's territorial ways in front of her. It was all good. Krista and I didn't get down like that. Hadn't in years.

"We good?" That was a common question I asked Krista.

"As long as Elia's good, I'm good. Elia said she forgives her and wants to get to know her since I told her I forgave Lennox. You know me: I'm looking forward, not backward. And I told Lennox, I'm not that insecure, mean, manipulative little girl I was when I got pregnant. Some people grow." Her head tilted toward her shoulder. "I'm one of those few people."

Lennox took a cleansing breath, apparently making a good attempt at biting her tongue.

The island was perfect, especially beautiful at night. Even tucked away on an off road in an eight-bedroom, private, beachfront home, the magic of the tropics still happened. I strolled into the house after seeing Elia and her crew to their taxi. They were off to their resort and would return in the morning for private beach fun. I told them they'd get to meet Dale, too. We'd just finished up dinner here at the house. The chef managed to whip up a satisfying meal of chicken fingers and onion rings for a pair of eight-year-old finicky eaters.

It had been over two hours since I left Lennox in my quarter of the house to "settle in." I made sure food was sent over to her when putting in the order for our dinner. Krista hadn't brought up the money for the house with her man, and I was grateful. Since they'd arrived, my mind had been on cloud nine. I wasn't prepared for that conversation.

The house was shaped similar to a four-leaf clover. Dale had his wing, management had theirs, I had mine, and the auxiliary staff and crew had theirs. Charlie, of course, was traveling with me, but I arranged for him to stay in the quarter with Dale's staff, who likely shared his favorite pastime. Having a wraparound deck, each wing could be accessed in and outside. I wanted a bottle of brandy, so I made a detour to the cellar on my way to my quarters.

Once the *Mauve* was secured, I passed a few people before arriving at a private hallway. The moment I closed the door behind me, I heard cackling. It was an argumentative tone, stopping me in my tracks. I listened for a few seconds longer before realizing it was coming from the deck. The closer I walked, the clearer it became.

"You're a dirty, dirty bitch, Len. You know that! A nasty, gutter bitch!" I knew the only man crazy enough to use those words and tone with Lennox had to be Richardson. And the only reason he did was because he knew Lennox wouldn't whisper a word of it to her father or me. "Pussy? You eat pussy, but you're married to me? You see why I never wanted to fuck your ugly, whore ass. You don't even like dick! How am I supposed to be a better man and take care of myself when my wife's sucking on a woman's pussy?" He chuckled, but still revealed the emotion from his accusations. "You basically take away my home, ma's home, and Scott's home, just so you can go down to *Macen Beach* and suck on pussy while eating other seafoods?" His hard guffaw was filled with derisory.

"That's not true, Kelv—"

"Yes, the fuck it is! I'm still the fucking man, Lennox. I've got eyes and ears on you right now! I hear the beach in the background!"

"I'm not in *Macen Beach*, Kelvin," her cadence even.

"Fuck you! When I'm done with this program, I'm gonna get a lawyer and sue you for cheating! I've got witnesses. You destroyed our marriage by cheating on me all these years with a dyke? You stupid *bitc*—" The call was cut.

"I guess that was the end of your twice-a-week, seventy-five cent call allowance," she murmured into the air.

I leaned into the doorway, eyes cast out to the roiling water. "You munching on carpets and ain't put me on?" It was a joke delivered dryly.

Facing the water, Lennox didn't stir. She sat back against the railing, propping one bare foot on the same step as her ass. "You heard that, huhn?"

"I did."

"They say when you need to catch a snake, field the sources."

"How?"

"Two weeks ago, I was sure to speak with Lisa, Nisha, and Mya over the phone. I told all three I was finally divorcing Kelvin. But I gave three different happily-ever-afters to each woman. They had to be unique to find the leak."

"Did you find it?"

"Yup."

"Mind if I ask who?"

"You already know."

Mya...

"What made you do that?"

That morning of Thanksgiving. When I was at Kelvin's family's house, his aunt, Rachel, told me to watch my friends. When Kelly-Ann came in, vomiting her grievances, she and Marcia mentioned my friends. They don't know my friends—not even work acquaintances. That didn't sit well with me." She shrugged.

"So, *Macen Beach*? I can afford a spot out there. She a stud or a femme?"

Lennox snorted at my corny joke. That's when I knew she was bruised. "You know the worst thing about this?" she asked the water. "It's dredging up this gnawing feeling I get every time a woman never shows compassion or empathy. My grandmother pushed me off onto a man. Kelly-Ann blames me for not being in love with her son through his addiction. Apparently, her sister, too. And now, Mya. She's somehow been communicating with my husband, for god only knows how long, and I never knew. If women don't stand for women, who will?"

I chewed on that for a beat as I watched the dark waves off the coastal line until they broke off into white hues. This was the shit she'd been going through down there by herself. She braved all the shit Richardson's weak ass hurled her way. No one was there to defend her or kick his ass. Never again. No more.

"What do you need?"

Still gazing at the nighttime water, she asked lazily. "What do you mean?"

"When you get this way at home? How do you cope?"

She scoffed then finally looked my way. "A fat ass spliff."

I pivoted to head inside the house. Less than ten minutes later, I was back, tapping her shoulder. Lennox turned around with big eyes, clearly not having heard me walk up on her. She glanced down and saw the blunt and lighter I was handing her. At first, she stalled. She exhaled deeply, shoulders caving. Eventually, she emptied my palm.

And I left my girl to her escape.

Charlie's ass is good for something, I see…

I was stretched out on a lounge chair on the warm sand. My earbuds played old school Boyz II Men from my phone. Their *"Christmas Interpretations"* album was a classic. 'Twas that time of the year, but listening to Christmas music on a tropical island was a crazy contradiction to my senses. Still, this shit was tight; a favorite of mine. I was in a zone, having my senses beautifully assaulted, studying the crashing high tides, and being serenaded by timeless talent.

Then my sight was enhanced when Lennox slowly promenaded my way, one leg swinging in front of the other, kicking up sand. Her curls blew in the nighttime wind, looking just as freed and unrestrained as I imagined she was after her smoke. I'd left her some time ago, on the deck of the other side of the quarter for privacy. It was nice to be sought out.

The closer she came, the more I could make out the tight slits of her eyes. Her taupe romper wore well on her toned thighs and curved hips. Her breasts were free beneath the thin fabric. The woman was a natural beauty. She crawled up the lounger to lay her body on top of mine, and as soon as she settled over me, Lennox's tongue was in my mouth. It moved against mine slowly, lazily grazing my own. I could smell the slight musk from her smoked trees, but what dominated was the vanilla scent of her hair, blowing all around my face. She pulled back, sucking my bottom lip as she descended, nipping at my beard.

Lennox inched down my body until her little hands were at the elastic waist of my basketball shorts. She yanked at it and my boxers beneath. I lifted, allowing her to drag them down, seeing my dick spring out. She pulled them from my feet, then peeled out of the top portion of the romper, exposing her pretty tits. Lennox swung her head to futilely move curly strands from her face. *So fucking sexy…* In this wind, they'd blow all over, uncontrollably. I was ready, excited about her obvious plan to make love to me from on top. Damn, I was ready.

But Lennox didn't remove the bottom of her romper when she reached over to push my legs on either side of the lounger. She squatted over the bottom of the chair, hips spread, and planted her elbows inside of my thighs. I lost my fucking lungs when she gathered my dick in her hands and pulled it to her lips. *Shit.* She kissed me devoutly, sprinkling them down my shaft. I couldn't keep my eyes off of her. It felt like Lennox was in her own world with the companion of her choice.

A soft grunt escaped when she put me inside her warm mouth. Her lips felt good against me, too. She stroked me slowly, grip a little loose for my preference, but I wouldn't complain. My girl wanted to neck me, another first for us. I enjoyed watching her. Lennox pulled me out with an opened mouth then extended her tongue toward her chin and licked the underside of my cock. She was pulling from her NormaJean deep throat bag. The attempt pleased me. Her eyes were tight as hell, her persona was vixen.

I took in her intended vision. She was straddling the lounger with her breasts out as she stroked me with determined care just beneath. It went on and on. I was in no rush to end this rare, erotic leading of my requited love. In due time, I'd teach her how to neck me properly. I'd even show her how to take one nut in two parts, one being in her hot mouth.

Until that time came, I decided to take in the beauty of the present. Relentless wind mussing her curly tresses, R&B legends crooning in my ears about falling in love on Christmas day, and a wanton beauty, under the influence, taking care of me just felt right. All on a sandy beach.

Ahhhh…

I lay back and watched Lennox's passion at work.

Lennox

Gazing at myself in the mirror, I noted, "This is twenty-nine."

Not quite thirty-years-old yet, but the clock was still on. I fingered through my freshly colored hair, questioning why I was up so early. Yes, it was Christmas Day, but it was also my birthday. There were no kids around. Why couldn't I sleep in?

That was a more appealing prospect, especially with how I felt last night, after Tobias had finally crawled into my bed, wrapping his strapping arm around me. I intertwined my legs with his hairy ones as much as possible. Within seconds of his heated covering, I began catching a thousand winks. Then I was abruptly awakened by his Pear Bear calling from *Disney*. By this time, Tobias had left my bed, and I was out again.

"*LENNOX…*" he called from down the hall.

My face lifting in a fake cry. "I'm coming, baby!"

I could smell and hear crackling bacon, so I knew he'd been cooking. But something had been biting at me since I began washing up a few minutes ago. I'd done twenty-nine birthdays and Christmases in my life, all in varying places with different people depending on the years. But this one felt different. It evoked burgeoning emotions I couldn't give a name or reason to.

Applying coral lip gloss, the color reminded me of my grandmother. That thought led into my need to see her. I'd only been back in Jersey for a couple of weeks now, but still. The responsibility to check on her was more reasonable considering the lack of distance now. I'd still been chewing on my father's insistence that I get over my disappointment in her handling of my womanhood. He was right, but I'd give myself time.

Walking out of the master suite, I pulled my phone from my robe. Scott would call at some point today, especially when he opens the new monitors and speakers I got him for his gaming pursuits. The food smelled amazing, awakening my belly as I drew closer to the kitchen. I could hear masculine voices en route.

In no time, his thickness came into view. Tobias stood against the island, eyes narrowed and chin toward his chest. I gaited straight into his personal space.

"What?" I smiled, knowing what. He'd been waiting on me. "I didn't take that long."

"I wanted you to get out here to eat before his greedy ass takes all the food." He gestured across the kitchen.

"Hey, Charlie!" I greeted as he piled pancakes into a plastic container. "Merry Christmas!"

"I'm Islamic, queen," he explained. "But the big deal of the day is you. Happy born day!"

I smiled. "Thank you!" Then I pivoted to stand on my toes and get closer to the face of my bronzed giant. "Looks like there's plenty enough food to me." I managed to kiss his waiting lips. He was always prepared.

Then Tobias took me by the shoulders and turned me around. With a gentle push, he urged me toward the living room.

"Bye, Lennox!" Charlie shouted behind me. "Oh! I hope you like that bong I got you! We gone blow some together soon!"

"The fuck she is!" Tobias bit back nastily.

It disturbed me no more than I was sure it did his cousin, Charlie. I didn't smoke weed regularly, but not even I would want paraphernalia to use it. It would bring back memories of a struggling, soon-to-be ex-husband. Thankfully, I hadn't heard from him or his mother since last week in *Karsyn Cove*. I wouldn't be hearing from Mya again either. The next day, while giving Tobias and Elia alone time at the beach before I joined, I called my "old" friend. I told her what I knew and that she wouldn't ever hear from me again in life. My words were colorful and with finality. After ending the call, I blocked her on all social media and my phone as well.

"Your shoulders are tensing up," Tobias noted over me. "You okay?"

Shoot...

The thought of Kelvin and Mya coiled me in no time. I nodded as we turned for the living room. Not only was there a beautiful Christmas tree set up in there, but it overflowed with gifts. Some were wrapped in traditional holiday paper, and others were in the original designer bags or boxes. And there were plenty. I even saw where he placed the ones I'd had in here already for him—minus the tree. This was why it had taken Tobias so long to come to bed last night. And apparently, he had help from Charlie at some point.

"Merry Christmas, Lennox," he droned.

Cupping my mouth with both hands, I turned to him. "This is a lot." I didn't mean to sound ungrateful and hoped he didn't receive it that way. "Thank you!"

Tobias planted a kiss on my forehead. "You're welcome, but this ain't it." When I eyed him wildly, he took me by the shoulders and spun me around again. "We have to acknowledge another special occasion."

Our travel was short; he stopped at the opening of the dining room. The table seating eight was filled from top to bottom with gifts. Birthday wrapping paper covered some, and high-end designer logos on bags and boxes contained others. There was a cake—a huge cake—in the center of the table. It was an image of me from last week in *Karsyn Cove*. Elia, JuJu, and Krista had gone back to their resort, leaving Tobias and me on the beach as the sun set. Gloriously tipsy, Tobias and I role-played being a model and photographer meeting on a shoot. I gave my best Tyra Banks poses as I sipped on *Mauve* with melting rocks.

The image on the cake was me doing the exact same pose as the brass image in Tobias' bedroom. My head was tossed back, and one knee was hiked, as I groped a breast in a string bikini hiding very little. I wore a covering while the kids were around, of course.

"Damn, was it freeing to take that cover up off ," I breathed out, gazing at the cake.

"I could tell. I couldn't decide which picture I liked best. But I think this one captures you damn near bare and...loving yourself. Loving on yourself." His hairy face moved closer to my ear, and he whispered. "Look at where your hands are. It's like you're enjoying you." His chest covered my back, and I could feel him thickening behind me.

My eyes closed at the instant arousal I felt from his heat, words, and encouragement. "That's like the sculpture in your bedroom," I whispered, loving the heady space I was in.

Tobias didn't reply right away. "I guess it could be." He lowered his mouth and kissed my neck. Immediately, I swelled between my thighs. "But I like your interpretation of femininity better."

He moved from behind me and toward the table where he scooped frosting with his index finger. "*Niña's Sweet Cakes* at your service." He brought the dollop of frosting to my mouth. I watched his burning gaze on my lips until I opened. I swirled my tongue and the delicious cream cheese frosting around his finger, pulling it further into my mouth. When I let it go, Tobias' gaze returned to my eyes, now filled with hunger.

"Some days, I feel weak for loving you the way I do," I murmured.

"Why?"

"Because I wonder if your love for me feels so monumental because no one has ever committed to me, my heart, my well-being, or my happiness like you."

And that's when I was able to name the now-exploding emotion. As an adult, waking up to Christmas Day was just like any other. And as a woman low on love, waking up to my birthday was just as mundane. I didn't get the urgency in Tobias' demands this morning. It was just another day to me.

But not to him.

"And lucky for me, no one else ever will." He crushed me into his chest, lifting me from the floor by grabbing me at the ass. Tobias took my mouth hungrily.

"I'll be like..." Jade Bailey, in the middle of Ragee's plush, contemporary kitchen, threw air punches. Like...she spread her feet apart, had her fists in the air, throwing mock jabs.

Every one of us around the palatial island was in a laughing fit. I had tears in my eyes.

"For real!" Jade declared. "I'll be like 'bop,' 'bop,' *BOOM!*'" Her air jabs synced rhythmically with her demonstrations. When she returned to the crowded island, she wore a smirk. "Boy, that bitch know she don't want none of this. Not even Terrell! He hates women so bad, with his gay ass. No disrespect, darling," she amended to LeRoy, the only male in this conversation—stately dressed, too.

"None taken, sweet peach. Terrell is a ponk, and I told him straight to his face at *Art Basel* one year." He snapped his fingers, thinking. "It was that year he was on *IG Live*, talking about 'Ragee's nice and all, but Luther Vandross wouldn't sit with him if he was alive.' I said, 'you fucking right Luther wouldn't sit with Raj, because his ass was so goddamn catty, especially when it came to competition!' But that aside, Raj could never be Luther, neither does he want to be. He's in his own lane."

"Exactly!" Wynter agreed.

"And if I was there, I would've hooked his fat ass!" Jade demonstrated a calmer air punch, cracking us all up again. She was nice and tipsy, and I loved it.

This was nice. The night of Christmas, which was my birthday. After spending the morning opening gifts and making love, Tobias and I got dressed to visit his grandmother and uncle with gifts in tow. Then, we drove up to a party at Ragee and Wynter's in Sparta. It was mostly the same crew that was here on Thanksgiving. Tobias took me on a tour of the estate before the sun set. I even got the chance to meet Raj's older brother and visit his ranch.

Oddly, on the ride back to the main house, Nisha texted wishing me a Happy Birthday and Merry Christmas in a thread we have with Lisa. Lisa sent her well-wishes, too. I replied to them both asking for a time next month when we could get together. I had more settling in to do, but coming clean to them about the fib regarding what I'd been doing during and after my divorce proceedings needed to be cleared up. I'd tell them about Mya, too.

Tonight, I was able to talk more to the ladies. Wynter was really sweet and just as down to earth as Tobias described her. Tori wasn't as talkative as the other ladies, but made sure we had a one-on-one conversation, making me feel welcomed. Jade was funny as hell, but the biggest nurturer. Bishop Carmichael's wife was a riot. She was blunt, smart, and so Harlem. She even cussed a little, which was funny. She referred to her husband a lot, especially when she was "going off." It was cute and telling of how much of an influence he was to her.

LeRoy was the classiest man I've ever met. He was dressed to the nines and had one of the broadest vocabularies around. Apparently, he was a world traveler. All night, people mentioned being surprised to see him so soon after Thanksgiving. LeRoy mentioned being a companion to several wealthy men around the globe. Why did I believe him? He seemed to fit the bill with his faux accent and poised posture. I learned a lot about this celebrity circle in just a few hours of drinking, eating, and cutting up.

Laughing, I asked Tori, "And she's talking about your best friend?"

The world knew Tori McNabb and Brielle were best friends. Tori cameoed in Brielle's videos, danced at her concerts, and had even been seen vacationing with her. And Brielle was at many of Tori's fights before she retired a few years ago. Ragee and Tori were best friends, too, which was cute. I remembered reading online how both Brielle and Ragee sang at Tori's wedding because she couldn't decide between the two.

I also learned Tori had two step-daughters. It was good to see another woman express a similar guilt of her husband not always having his girls on the major holidays. I'd have to figure out my role in Elia's world, even if it's simply to love her daddy and be kind to her. Whatever it was, I'd do it.

Tori shook her head while rolling her eyes. "I go through this every time we get together and Jade gets that damn *Mauve* in her. If

I try to defend Brielle, then Jade'll be whooping my ass! Okay?" she fell into laughter.

"Tuh!" Jade was back in her fight stance. "You don't know about that '*Tori The Banger*' shoulder roll! It be ready, bro!" She demonstrated over and over. My stomach hurt because I laughed so hard. "See, they think because we're short we can't fight. Can you fight, Lennox?"

"I never had to." Between being O.G. Chino Brim's daughter and the pastor's granddaughter in East Orange, no one really bothered me. *Until I got married.* "But let somebody roll up on my man"—I winked—"and they'll see these E.O. hands." I faked a jab, mocking her.

As everyone laughed, Jade ate it up.

"I'm telling you! That bitch don't want it with me!"

Trent quietly walked up behind her. "What bitch?" he asked, pulling the glass from her hand then taking a sip. He frowned in disgust.

"Who else?" Tori rolled her eyes.

"When the news reports on Brielle waking up with only one leg, we're pointing the police to your Alpine mansion to look for the voodoo doll." LeRoy smoothly informed.

Adorably, Trent rolled his eyes into the air. "Fuck, Jade! You ain't learn nothing from Bishop's '*Eight Principles of Letting it Go*' classes a few months ago?"

Jade rolled her hazel irises this time, as she pushed her weight into his chest and hissed, "I'm just playing, Trent. Dang!"

"No, your little ass ain't."

"And my husband put his foot in that course," Lex looked to be stirring the pot.

Or perhaps that's what some of us who laughed thought because we'd all been drinking a lot at this point. Seeing Trent lean down to whisper in Jade's ear as she faced the crowd had me craving my own big bear. I gazed past them foolishly. This place was too big to see from one room to the next.

When I brought my attention back to the room, I caught Trent tossing his neck at the people gathered at the island. Immediately, he swung Jade around in a swift and gentle manner I could guess she was used to.

"So, you said you're in *Samsara*?" Tori was at my side, really close. "When I was trying to find a house *years ago*, my realtor showed me a few out there. Do you know what the word *Samsara* means?"

"No," I answered, noticing everyone was grabbing their glasses and plates, and following the Baileys out of the kitchen.

Weird...

"Let's go in the living room. I'll try and act out my bourgeois ass realtor, and how she ran down the definition and told me that each road in the town has significant meaning, too."

"*Uh*—" I grabbed my drink. "Okay."

Chapter Eighteen

Lennox

Raj's living room was outfitted with two keyboards, a drum set, and microphones tonight. Just as on Thanksgiving, there was live music and serenading by talented guests. The place was decorated festively, providing a warm holiday, convivial energy. People buzzed all around us, even random strokes of the keyboards sounded occasionally. The drummer hit a few sequences, too, every now and then. It was just random. The vibe was chill, but could be weird for those not understanding the hosts' musical inclination. I was still adjusting myself.

Tori and I found seats on a sofa where she had me spooked.

"A cycle of karma?" I gasped, eyes wide.

She nodded. "Yeah, but you said Nirvana Lane, so that ends the cycle. Nirvana's like the final state of karma, and covers pain." She screwed her mouth, gazing toward the twelve-foot ceiling. "Right?"

"I hope so," I noted animatedly. "Or else, I'm calling that Jaquana lady up to find me another place!"

"Jaquana? You've worked with her? She's our broker, too! My husband and I were working with her at the same time and didn't know it." Then she clarified, "We weren't married then. Just still trying to figure our shit out."

Just as I was about to respond, there was an urgent *shhhhhh*'ing around the room. They were telling us to be quiet. At first, I thought it was rude, and was a little embarrassed to be that detached from the room. But of course, I yielded, glancing around for the point of it all.

Music...

Okay. They were ready to begin Christmas carols?

From my vantage point, I could see Raj behind a keyboard and two men with microphones. One was the pastor.

"Okay, guests. Can I make a request of no recording of the next few minutes? We have a videographer here for this very reason. Please." There was a practiced authority in his tone, yet it was supplemented with humility. "Please. No pictures or videos. Just be present in the moment. Thanks."

Then the pastor looked over to the other guy—a short fellow, whose wife was a riot earlier when they'd arrived. Heavy in stature, she rocked the dopest bleach-blonde mohawk. He motioned toward the instruments.

Seconds later, I heard a soft, timid tenor. It was a man, singing about falling in love on a special day. There were a few encouraging responses from the guests. I tried scanning the room for the mild, yet passioned-filled voice. Raj was my first guess, but he was playing with a closed mouth. The pastor and short guy with mics had unmoving mouths, too. Who was that singing?

Then, out of nowhere, the short guy with the mic animatedly demanded, "Up, Tobe!" while yanking his arm in the air as though directing a choir.

Tobe?

I leaned over my lap to crane my neck to see the keyboard hidden from my view. Indeed, it was Tobias singing, big body curled over the board tensely as he sang.

Shit...

My heart swelled protectively. Tobias didn't like singing publicly, only for work. It was a talent he was known to hide. Why would he put himself out there like this?

Then there was a shift in the keys and the pastor, Raj, and the short guy began harmonizing. *Damn!* Even the pastor could sing! *Again!* This crew was different. A free concert was happening here.

The pastor took a seat next to Tobias on the bench. He placed the microphone on the keyboard while Tobias sang about being all he needed and never thought he'd fall in love on Christmas Day. He seemed to fixate on Tobias' hands and eventually played alongside him. Strange until there was another chord shift, and Tobias abandoned the keyboard, leaving the pastor to play and sing.

The short guy continued to direct even when singing background. When the crowd opened for me to have a direct view of Tobias, my pulse began to bang in my neck. He sang about how Christ came down on Christmas and it was the same day he'd fallen in love. When his hand lifted my way, I couldn't breathe.

In this moment, it was clear. Tobias was serenading me in front of his friends. I knew this was not easy for him, but he sounded pitch-perfect, and was so damn handsome. I stood, wanting to run to him protectively, however couldn't. It would embarrass him. But I needed to touch him for comfort.

Then Tobias fingered me to come to him. My feet moved before my brain. I was at his big body, trembling with glassy eyes. He was doing this for me, and I felt his passion. I got the message. Tobias was telling the world he was in love with messy me. Yes, I was still married, but his love for me had been heightened on Christmas Day, my birthday. The tears fell, and suddenly, so did Tobias as he riffed fluid notes. He took to one knee.

My knees buckled, heart pounded.

The short guy came over to take Tobias' microphone while using his own for background vocals. I trembled in my heels at the sight of Tobias pulling a box from his pocket. With shaky hands, he opened it to a diamond so radiant, I couldn't make out the size or shape with the tears welling in my eyes. Completely sobbing, I fell to my knees to join him. I didn't give a damn about the ring; I just wanted him. To hold, protect, and secure his heart for the rest of my life. I'd never get bored inside of his arms. There was so much space there, I could stretch out, and even share with Elia.

"You're such a fool," I cried in his chest.

"I know. I am," his thick croak picked up in the mic. "Only and always for you. I know you didn't expect this, but I wanted to make your first birthday with me one you'll never forget. How lucky am I to have friends who could help me do it in such spectacular fashion?" The room laughed, moved by his humor. "I also know right now may not be the best time to make this type of commitment, but I can't wait anymore. I need to know…when the time's right." He pulled my face up to meet his intentional gaze by the hair on the back of my head. "Will you marry me, Lennox Alexis Curry?"

The short guy had taken over Tobias' riffs, creating the most romantic backdrop as everyone waited with anticipation.

I tried getting my sobbing under control. "I hate I waited this long to love you," I admitted. Tobias kissed my wet lips encouragingly. "I'd marry you tonight if I could."

"*Ut!*" the short guy broke his notes to trill. He glanced around animatedly. "We've got one, Bishop!"

A gravelly voice spoke into a microphone and rasped, "It would be my pleasure."

My attention was fastened to the love of my life. I nodded. I cried. And continued to nod. Of course, I'd marry him once I got my affairs in order. Deep inside, I felt spiritually joined to him for years. We'd just have to work on the legal part of it.

"Here they come," Charlie murmured from behind the wheel of the sprinter rental.

I glanced up from the back, and through the tinted windows, I could see her small frame take down the stairs in one hundred-twenty-millimeter heels. It was a beautiful November day in North Carolina, where the weather was still mild. She stressed about her outfits down here for months before the divorce proceedings were scheduled. I understood why, but hated having her worry. Seeing her in cropped dress pants with an *Asè Garb* monogram print, sleeve-less cape helped me note the compromise. It covered her well as she strutted with the sun beaming in her face.

Behind her was her father, O.G. Chino. He'd been with her these past three days as Lennox's divorce was being finalized. Richardson didn't make it easy on my girl. He didn't want to just sign the fucking papers and go about his life. Nah. He wanted to fuck with her, demanding spousal support.

Bitch...

Seeing Chino's short, but stocky ass following behind Lennox to the sprinter, I was happy I made the call of having him down here with her all these days. Another compromise. Lennox's father and I had words about me not having told him about our affair. It wasn't as explosive as it could have been. Maybe because Smite was there to host it. I was able to get him off my back by assuring I'd aide in him and Lennox establishing a relationship finally. Having him involved this week was a demonstration of that effort. Unfortunately, I had work, leaving her to the proceedings without me.

I'd flown in from Detroit, filling in my dates for Dale's promotional tour. The album dropped less than a month ago, and he'd been spreading the word, touching major, and some local, radio stations as well as podcast shows. I'd been asked to do a few as the executive producer on the project. It was worth the effort. The album streams were unbelievably high, and it had been number one on *Billboard* for weeks now.

I flew into North Carolina this morning, missing Lennox and Chino by minutes as they attended the last day of court. She tried to tell me it was unnecessary since she'd be returning home to Jersey today. Not hearing any of it, when Charlie booked my flights for this run of the tour, I was sure to have him do Lennox's and Chino's as well. Yes, I'd just gotten off a flight, and would have to endure another in a few short hours, just to make sure I was here supporting her in some capacity.

Charlie left the driver's seat just in time to meet Lennox and Chino at the rear passenger door and opened it. They assisted Lennox's hike inside. She was two steps into the sprinter when she noticed my legs. Her eyes roved up to my face and in a span of two seconds, I identified recognition, relief, joy, and...pain. My body tensed as I stood to grab her. She hugged me tight as Chino hopped in.

I pulled her face to me by the back of her curly waves. Her brown roots had dominated since she dyed it for her birthday almost a year ago, and I loved the look on her. She clung onto the wings of my back as I kissed her, fucking up her gloss. "You good?" I asked, examining her eyes.

"I will be," she whispered.

"What the hell that mean?" Chino hissed. "I been asking her since the judge ruled in her favor, what's wrong."

Lennox ignored him, taking a seat. I leaned over to offer him dap. "Good to see you, O.G."

"Appreciated," he returned, but quickly went back to his daughter as I sat next to her. "If that tweakin' ass muthafucka ever fuck with you again—"

"I'm fine!" Lennox shut down his rant. "Really." She tried to soften it with a smile. "Thank you. But I'm good." Then she opened her cape, revealing her round, seven-month belly hidden beneath high-end garb, and exhaled deeply while falling into my side.

We entered the rented home through the garage. I trailed behind Lennox while holding her cape over my arm. From the back, she didn't even appear pregnant. However, that ass had swelled similar to her belly. Pensive, I knew to wait until Lennox was ready to speak to learn what had gone down.

We spoke every day again, several times a day. Our communication was even more frequent than it was before we started fucking a year ago, during her homecoming trip. Lennox had been keeping me abreast of everything happening in court. Richardson had done exactly what he told Lennox he'd do while we were in *Karsyn Cove*. He'd gotten a lawyer. According to his aunt, Rachel, who'd check in on Lennox from time-to-time, the attorney took him on pro bono, still admiring Richardson's short-lived career.

Richardson thought he'd had a case and even revealed how much he'd been in touch with Mya for some time. He tried to accuse her of infidelity. Of course, when Lennox and I learned about it, we were scared out of our asses. Not only did Lennox's attorney prove to be competent, but my girl seemed to have some "creeping" savvy to her as well.

Richardson claimed Lennox visited Jersey last October and had stayed with her "lover." Kelly-Ann wrote a statement agreeing with her son's allegations. He tried to use Mya's story of Lennox staying at a cheap hotel, which was suspicious. She said she had reason to believe Lennox hadn't stayed there at all. Richardson's attorney tried to argue how Lennox could have easily said she was staying there, while actually not staying there at all. This theory was shot down when Lennox's attorney got a sworn statement from Lisa that she'd actually been inside of Lennox's hotel room, and had seen the room had been used by her. They also used a picture Mya had taken of her and Lennox in the room before they parted ways.

It was a fucked up attempt and wasted Lennox's money on attorney fees. Either way, it was worth it. Richardson couldn't prove the cheating, and therefore wasn't granted alimony. Besides, Lennox didn't have a job. She completed the nail tech program so she could write the curriculum and policies for Jade's salons. Her initial payments had been to an LLC she established earlier this year. However, when she performed hours for her license, her low income was paid directly to her as an employee at a random nail salon.

Another move to protect her against his greedy ass. So, on paper, Lennox had no means of paying him shit. Lennox's lawyer had been able to effectively prove how she was a neglected wife for most of the marriage. Yes, we should be in celebratory mode, but Lennox was not.

Maybe because she knew it appeared we'd dodged a bullet on the infidelity claim. All those sneaky links over the past four years. The homecoming two years ago when I had her bring her girls to Raj's club, *Checkerboard*, just to steal a couple of hours in the same room as her. We snuck off to his office for a kiss and rub down fest. Raj knew, but her girls didn't.

Videos or pictures of me proposing to her on her birthday could have been leaked. We could have been caught the time I met Lennox in Florida during her work trip when we had our second-first kiss. It could have been the time I had Coach Launz get them the box suite at the *Giants* vs. *Kings* game. Or last fall, when I rented this very house so close to their home, using Dale's recording as an excuse. *Shit*. Lennox had, *in fact*, been with me last homecoming when Richardson alleged the cheating took place. He simply had no proof.

"Okay, man," Chino started as we made it to the opening of the living room. "What's going on?"

Lennox had moved past the room when she tried, "Dad—"

I swung around to face him, "O.G., I know all you wanna do is support her, and you did. You've held her down these three days in court."

"The fuck, I *know*—"

"And now, I'm here." I tried reigning my temper. He was annoying the fuck out of me now. "Her man is here. I'll take over. You filled in when I couldn't. She's my responsibility." I looked him dead in the eye.

Chino took a step back, almost squaring me as he shot daggers, too. Again, I wasn't afraid of Lennox's father. He may have still been feared in the streets, but this was my world. Lennox was my lane he wouldn't cross. And if he tried me, I'd lay his little ass the fuck out.

Behind me, I could hear Lennox trekking for the bedroom. Ahead of me, behind Chino, Charlie was there, anxiously tense and closely watching.

"Aye, yo, Tobe, man." He sniffled, swiping his nose. "I'mma let you have that, but watch the way you talk to me, man," his volume fair. "I'm her old man. I'm only here to help. You feel me?"

Biting my tongue, I gave him a nod and turned off down the hall.

The moment I closed the door, Lennox was on me. Her little body curving around my chest and abs. As she hugged me, one hand went around her shoulders, and the other to her belly. For a while, we didn't speak. I knew to wait.

"He was good these past few days," she spoke into my chest. "I've actually seen a sweeter side to him."

"Good."

"It's just...I needed..." She peered up at me. "It's been a rough few days, and I didn't know how the judge would rule with alimony. I feel like...I just needed to see you, be right here."

I stroked her belly, hoping to soothe her, and possibly wake the baby to feel a few kicks. "I'm here."

"I'm embarrassed."

"For what?"

"All of this. This big deal made for nothing. His mother sitting in the courtroom day after day, supporting him and avoiding eye contact with me. I took her ass in when the sheriff put her things on the street. Mya wouldn't give the statement of having been in the *Red Carpet Inn* with me that morning. She watched me pack. That heffa is evil personified, and for what?" We would never know. Lennox still had her blocked. "Having to put Lisa and Nisha through this. Hiding my belly from the world. It's all embarrassing." She peered up to me. "We should be celebrating the album's success, not visiting North Carolina to finalize my divorce." Lennox rolled her eyes.

I exhaled, still rubbing on her. "Just think of the good days that are coming. *Shit*. You can think of old, great days."

"Like your birthday?" She grinned devilishly.

I scoffed, nodding. "My birthday. The event that likely got us this." I quickened my caress of her belly.

"Yup. That day. One of the best." Then her smile faltered. "I just…" She rubbed those soft lips together. "I'm ready to get out of here."

I glanced down to check my *Richard Mille* for the time. "We've got a few hours before our flight out. Come on. We can grab a bite at a restaurant near or at the airport." That was one thing I had to learn about Lennox's pregnancy: I had to keep her fed. It improved her mood.

"Wait," She exhaled. "I've got to see Scott. I told Terry I'd be there by two."

I reached for her hand. "Let's go."

Without a second of hesitation, she took my hand, and allowed me to lead her on.

Lennox

Epilogue

Tobias' birthday, seven months before...

***

I turned away from the bathroom mirror and faced the door.

Whew!

Okay...

I smoothed down my thighs, being sure I didn't apply too much *Grayson's Skincare* seduction oil. My nipples were exposed in the nude, sheer bra as my breasts nearly spilled out. And my belly. I was full, having eaten a delicious steak and lobster dish downstairs at *The Jux Supper Club*. The ambiance loosened my anxiousness about the facility's reputation. It was a...regular—high-end albeit—restaurant in New York City. The ambiance made you forget about the sensual dungeons above on the higher floors. And the spirits were definitely top tier. The vintage *Mauve* I had tickled the beds of my feet, revving me up for what was to come after dinner.

Dessert.

Dessert as in me.

It was the night of Tobias' thirtieth birthday. Figuring out what to gift the man who seemingly had it all and could afford more was a difficult feat. That was until one day, while performing my required hours for my nail license, it dawned on me. Three of Tobias' favorite things in this world were Elia, sex, and me. I allowed him time to spend the morning with Elia. She "treated" Tobias and his grandmother to breakfast. I'd given him his gifts before we left his home for the night. Now was his adult time with me.

I incorporated his second and third favorite things. Sex with me at *The Jux Supper Club*. Tobias still had a membership, though inactive for the past year or so as he patiently waited for me to finally take the reins of my life. Secretly, I'd held on to guilt for that. Did I like the idea of him sleeping with other women? Hell no! But it wasn't like he'd brag about it to me. Tobias didn't kiss and tell. What he did was share his proclivities with me to the extent of belonging to this organization. I understood on the other side of that were women who shared in the lifestyle as well. Women, who I was sure were attracted to my teddy bear. He was disturbingly handsome, worldly articulate, innately caring, extensively traveled, considerably wealthy, and indisputably well-endowed.

Of course, I'd open my mind to his kink. I guessed another trait Jade and I had in common was our jealousy when it came to other women. Having Elia around and now, being out openly with Tobias, dating, I'd grown possessive. Fully aware of this, I purposely did not touch Tobias when Elia was with us. He tended to show signs of physical affection in front of his daughter, which was fine by me. But I was cognizant about my conduct when with the two of them, and refused to taint my reputation in Elia's eyes. I wanted to be liked and accepted by her, too.

I let out another long, nervous breath. On the other side of that door were props, toys, and apparatuses that could intimidate a vanilla woman like me. Also out there was a gentle giant, who would likely transform into a frightening sex-god. My eyes squeezed, crushing my lashes. I wanted to please him so bad, and prayed I didn't screw this up.

One last breath expelled before I opened the door. I toed out onto the heated wooden floor, a contrast to the marble in the bathroom. Soft notes of jazz tunes flowed in the air, easing the tension in my shoulders a bit. I located him across the massive "lab" of a suite, peering up from his phone. The tight grooves of his back outlined his virility. But when he turned around to face me, the sight of his leather pants loosely hanging on his structured hips caused my breasts to feel heavier and nipples to tingle. That piece of his lower abdomen beneath his exposed belly button, where his pubic bed lay, entranced me. I involuntarily swallowed my primal reaction to him. He'd shaved. Of course, Tobias did. He knew we'd be at the club tonight. Was that something he did when playing here?

He sauntered over, a hunger in those thick-lidded eyes burning me. My lungs jumped, and simple breathing got ahead of me. His eyes roved around my breasts down to my belly button, and finally landed on the matching, nude, sheer panties. I'd gotten waxed for this occasion, just as I'd done last October for homecoming.

"You look amazing," he droned, impressed.

Stretching the tension in my neck, I blurted, "You do, too."

Tobias chuckled quietly, low eyes on my body before circling me for a full view.

"Are we really doing this?" There was a muted confidence in his delivery, a know-how he carried. I nodded with little conviction. "Good. I'm not going to scare or scar you tonight. I'll save that for another visit. I do, though, look forward to bruising you a little." Then a blow cracked my one cheek for emphasis. Tobias was in front of me again, gazing hungrily down on me like prey. "I'll allow you to look freely tonight, but moving forward, no eye contact until I give you permission. Understood?"

Sheesh!

I dropped my chin. "Yes," I whispered.

Then his big hand was at the back of my skull, gripping a fistful of my hair, forcing my face to him. "I said next time. Tonight, I need to see those cognac irises to be sure you stay with me all the way." His brandy-scented breath hit my face, deluding me.

This was everything. No stress. No surprises. Yes, Tobias could freak me out in this "laboratory," attempting to blow my mind.

However, this wasn't a fear that could disrupt my mental health. There was an exchange happening here. We were giving to one another. Here was peace.

There were no surprise traumas. No gut-churning discoveries. Four months after escaping my life in North Carolina, I'd begun to adjust to peace. Balance really did exist. Love did exist. And my fidelity followed behind it.

Tobias tsked. "Your eyes are closed again," he droned thickly. "What are you thinking?"

I kept my eyes closed, but grinned contently. "How I may finally be experiencing what perfection in life is."

"Oh, yeah?" His hand still gripping my hair, making a nod impossible.

"Yeah."

I'd heard from Kelly-Ann two months ago. She tried stopping by the house in Raleigh to get a few tools from the shed just to learn it had been rented to a young, Haitian couple. Kelly-Ann felt she should have been notified and reminded me we were still family. Keeping the conversation brief, I assured her I'd send money for whatever tools she had in the shed. Everything in there had been put at the curb for the following trash day. It was gone.

Scott and I checked in with each other, at least, weekly. Terry and I spoke often, too. I made sure of it. So far, Scott had settled in well with his maternal family. Having a cousin his age, who'd recently moved in, may have been the trick to the quick adjustment. Mya had tried contacting me for weeks, back in January, through Nisha and Lisa. I guess it had taken her that long to truly understand she'd been blocked as I told her. Both Nisha and Lisa had agreed to not get involved with this one. I was grateful for their compassion.

School had been great for me. At first, I approached the need to appease the government in order to obtain a license simply to teach and provide a business plan for the industry with lackluster. Blame the snooty master's-degreed girl in me. But learning something new had been intriguing. It had also been paramount to building a formative business plan and training model. I truly believed Jade was about to shock the industry with this business. I was thankful to have a hand in it.

"Yeah," I breathed as my beam widened.

"How?"

"Everything. You." My eyes opened. "The peace of my home. School's been great—" A record scratched, and I took a step back.

Worry creased that space between my eyes. "What's wrong?"

"Shit. Shit. Shit!" I covered my mouth. "My rent is due today. I forgot to pay it."

"That's no biggie." Tobias dismissed, still in authoritative mien. But this was my real life.

I shook my head. "My mortgage gets paid automatically. But this rental is weird. The company uses *Zelle*, so there's no invoicing or automatic opt-ins." I went looking for my phone. "Pretty weird."

"Why?" he asked, still standing where I left him.

"Because, apparently, the entity I rent from is an LLC."

"And?"

"And big corporations typically have their own electronic system set up for payments. This one does...*Zelle*." I scratched my head, peering around the room. "Do you know where my phone is?"

Tobias' head shook softly. "Don't worry about it."

I snorted, "Don't worry about it, get evicted, and come live with you in Englewood Cliffs. Simple." I started for the bathroom.

"Lennox, don't sweat it. It ain't important now!"

That shit grated at me. I'd been a provider for six years, solely responsible for securing boarding and utilities. My life may be freed of that overwhelming responsibility; however, I was still an independent woman about my business. I would never tell Tobias to blow off one of his many obligations just because it didn't suit an agenda.

I swung around. "Who are you to say that?"

His eyes fell and mouth twisted as he switched the weight on his hips, exposing a corded vein going down to his nether region. Tobias shook his head. "Just let it go. Come on."

I scoffed. "I have to pay my rent, Tobias. It'll just take a minute. We have all night. Why are you bugging?"

"Because it ain't important."

I turned fully to face him, breasts bouncing in the air. We never argued, but I couldn't roll over on this. "It's your birthday; April third. As you requested that morning I left you on the floor in *Samsara*, I'm yours. So, again, I'll ask: Who are you to say?"

"The owner of the fuckin' property!"

My eyes ballooned. "My place in *Samsara*?"

"Yes. Pay tomorrow. Pay next week. Don't pay this month. It don't matter. The money is routed into an account that I'll use to pay toward the wedding!"

What?

I shook my head. "You own that house? How is it possible? You told me you rented it for the week in October for us. For me."

"Yeah." He brushed his hands roughly down his face. "I also told you I needed to up my investment game. Real estate is the most common route. You told me you liked the house, so I had Jaquana help me get it."

"Wait…" I was stuck. "Is that what you meant when you said she'd been working on some things for you?" Tobias nodded. "Tobias!"

"What?"

I didn't know what to say. When I learned of the house's availability, I jumped on it. It was too good to be true. "I was easy bait for her."

"Don't start that. She was only doing me a favor."

"Only a thousand dollars a month for that big ass house!" I thought out loud.

"Hey!" he hissed with a silent warning. "I get it's fucked up that I went through those measures to help you land up here, but watch your damn mouth. We're in a scene here where your attitude will get you punished in ways you don't wanna know."

My lungs seized at the bite in his tone. "Tobias—"

"Here, it's Big Daddy."

Big Daddy?

Okay…

I pivoted, then toed in his direction. Incongruently, a stir began in my groin. "Is that what 'they' called you here?"

Tobias shook his head. "It's what *you* will call me here."

That gave me pause. "I already have a *fath*—"

"Who is small. And I'm not. He's also not a daddy. I'm your Big Daddy. Got it?"

Why the hell was this off-the-wall shit turning me on. It was the authority in his message, the firmness in the delivery. *This* was really Tobias' arena. It was his play. And in that moment, I knew; he could claim me; heart, soul, and mind.

His eyes roved down my body lazily. "I don't like that cheeky smirk you're wearing. I think it's time I temper your arrogance." He swung his chin across the suite. "Get on the spanking bench, Lennox."

I knew the leather, padded, wooden apparatus he referred to. Tobias went over every toy and piece of machinery here when we arrived.

I obeyed, stretching over the triangular contraption, cupping the sides. I attempted a deep breath to prepare myself, but moved too *slow*—

WAP!

The first lash landed harshly on my left cheek. My body curled over the black, leather pad, hands gripping the sides even harder.

"That was for your arrogant smirk. Now, I'll introduce you to the flogger." Lust coated the man's throat, telling of how satisfied he was with catching me off guard like that. "Remember the rules I gave. If anything is too much—*pain or pleasure*—use the safe word."

I wanted to roll my eyes, still reeling from the smarting blow, and having him remind me of the rules. He'd been going over them since I told him about this birthday gift. I knew the goddamn safe word!

SWOOSH!

Another blow. This time, the bite had tentacle measures, spanning over more than one of my cheeks. I even felt a bit of it on the back of my thigh.

Shit!

I was gasping now, the ache swelling before subsiding. I endured five more of those before Tobias had mercy and assisted me from the bench—rather, he snatched me off, swinging my throbbing body in the air, almost when I caught the sight of a flogger on the floor. The offender.

He kissed my belly then groaned, "You're so fuckin' perfect. So tough. So strong. Nothing can break you." Next, I was being lowered onto the high-posted bed. "You taking those lashes like a G got me horny as fuck. I wanted to play, delay my pleasure and yours, but fuck it. It's my birthday." Graciously, Tobias arranged me onto my side, facing off the bed. I watched him peel out of his leather pants with athletic grace. He grabbed his engorged dick in one hand and stroked himself, one of my favorite sights. "Open up, Lennox," he growled, approaching me with his hand in motion.

I felt the cry between my thighs, even with the throbbing of my ass. It was all happening so fast. Tobias gripped my head with the other hand and fed himself to me. Right away, I went to work, enduring the invasion of his fat, mushroom head, tasting the lip of him as he pushed into my mouth. He went deep, reaching my throat then pulled back. Tobias repeated the act several times more before beginning shallow thrusts. I loved it. Loved getting him off this way. Since my first time in *Karsyn Cove*, when Tobias didn't "respond" right away, he's instructed me on the pressure from my hands and motion of my tongue needed to get him off. It had become an intimidating act, but one I now craved.

In this position, Tobias maintained control of the pace. I tightened my lips beneath and swirled my tongue over and under his head as I bobbed. Managing to peer up, I saw my bear was beginning to lose it. This wouldn't be a long session. I wanted him undone. The thought of it made me throb below, and I reached down between my legs to relieve myself. Without breaking his stride, Tobias pulled my hand up, placing it around his big balls. It had been days since we'd last made love, so he was definitely "full."

Tobias' moves grew precise, hips taut. The vein coursing his forehead protracted and his face was strained. *Shit.* My groin cried from torture. I knew it was time. Within seconds, hot, creamy liquid squirted into the back of my throat. I tried relaxing my sphincter to allow him inside; his cum became too much, eventually spilling from the sides of my mouth.

There was no time to complain. Tobias lifted my body again, this time landing me on all fours. Greedily, I spread my knees, widening my hips with desperation. Swallowing his cum, I moaned, begging him for expediency. Sometimes, Tobias could move too slow with the purpose of delayed gratification. But right now, my hips squirmed, expressing my need of him.

"*Ahhhhhh!*" pushed from my abdomen at his aggressive thrust inside of me.

I was unbelievably wet, flesh hardly protesting his entrance. This was what I loved, too, about his lovemaking. Tobias had his aggressive moods where he'd move quick with savage carelessness. His big hands wrapped around my waist as he pounded me from the back. The arching of my spine invited more of his imposing girth inside. The sounds of our flesh slapping together was primal, further arousing. My neck couldn't hold my heavy head. I felt when he reached up and unclasped my bra, freeing my titties. My nipples were being licked by the air from the urgent movements of his hips.

His grunts over my head, each time he pounded me, echoed in my clit, giving it stimulation of sorts. Tobias moved so fast, tirelessly. His handling of me so rough, tenured. Possessive. It all spurred my orgasm, and my head shot up as I howled, "Oh! Oh! *Tobeeeeeeee!*"

Spikes pricked my feet, heat blanketed my core, and a delicious ripple tightened my brain. He pounded and pounded, grunts growing louder with each thrust until Tobias pulled out. He urged me to face him and fed me his engorged, wet flesh again as he held the base. Eyes strained, neck tossed back, lost to bliss, the love of my life squirted in my mouth, releasing again. I sopped up each drop he gave like cattle being fed grains.

Grunting when emptied, Tobias pulled out of my mouth and heaved up on the bed. He stretched out, panting wildly. Still swallowing back his essence, I crawled over to him. His arm banded around me.

"I'm out of practice," he couldn't catch his breath.

My eyes went wild. "Out of practice? You just came twice, in the span of three minutes."

Licking his lips, Tobias shook his head. "Same nut, two different drop offs." He slapped my ass. "I've got lots to teach you. Just don't use it to manipulate me or with someone else."

Bringing my thigh up and near his dwindling erection, I promised. "So long as you love me, you'll have my fidelity."

I swear...

"Shit!" he groaned, this time frustration looming.

It was one of those unexpected, bad news type of regretful groans I'd lived with for eight years.

My entire frame tensed, post-coital vibes be damn.

"I didn't use a condom," he graveled.

The wind left my lungs. "Tobias, if you coil like that again over some shit that ain't breaking news!" I was so disturbed and relieved at the same time, I couldn't finish my thought. "I'll make an appointment tomorrow for birth control." I patted his taut abdomen. "Happy birthday, baby. Life's great."

My body eased, limbs loosened when he reached down and kissed my forehead. "We ain't done," he murmured.

"I know better." I giggled with closed eyes, contently, and blissfully.

Where I belonged.

The ***END***

For more visual, click here for my website.

~Love Acknowledges

Visuals: **Indelible Images** – Mae, you're amazing. Such a professional optimist. I pray my peers get to experience your magic. Thanks so much for "getting it!" Brian – We FINALLY got you! Whew! I guess patience is truly a virtue. LOL!! You've been AH-mazing! Thanks so much! Elena – This is like the second time I saw a model and envisioned my client at the same time. Thanks for this! My absolute best to you in all your endeavors!

Beta Reader: — Yorubia, aka Uncle GWORL, yes I FIRED you! However, I used you for a passage in this book I felt was tricky. *Then* you know what happened? I fired your arse again! Ha!

Research: Special thanks to Adrienne G. for assisting again with legal matters. You're a gem! I have to thank Dr. Tang Barnes for always being a medical reference for my crazy stories. Love you, chica! xoxo KJB, you've been the N.C. plug with this one. Love you!

Christina C. Jones aka CCJ — Thanks for your genius and generosity. You're pure magic, woman!

Interior Artist: Cedeara Ardell McCollum — Thanks, baby girl, for the imagery you've designed for my books! Love you always! *Pssst...* You can read them now! LOL!

Proof Reader: Tina V. Young — You're simply amazing! There's no way I could appear this put together without your brilliant mind and generous heart! I love you dearly!

Editors: Zakiya Walden of ***Zakiya's Voice*** — Thanks a million times for everything! May it all come back to you in good portion!

Sitara Thomas — Hats off to you! I mean...the juggling act you had to perform and with limited time was certainly impressive. Thanks for everything!

MDT: *Tsk. Tsk.* You doubted me again. "Make another Love." LOL!! Thanks for everything!

Master, my ***Jireh***, my ***Rohi***, Psalm 63:3 (NIV) "Because Your love is better than life, my lips will glorify You." *Father, I bless You for Your enduring love.*

~Other Books by Love Belvin

Love's Improbable Possibility series:
Love Lost, Love UnExpected, Love UnCharted & Love Redeemed

Waiting to Breathe series:
Love Delayed & Love Delivered

Love's Inconvenient Truth (Standalone)

Love Unaccounted series:
In Covenant with Ezra, In Love with Ezra & Bonded with Ezra

The Connecticut Kings series:
Love in the Red Zone, *Love on the Highlight Reel, *Determining Possession, End Zone Love, Love's Ineligible

Receiver, *Pass Interference, Love's Encroachment, &
*Offensive Formations (*by Christina C. Jones)

Wayward Love series:
The Left of Love, The Low of Love *& The Right of Love*

Love in Rhythm & Blues series
The Rhythm of Blues **&** *The Rhyme of Love*

The Sadik series:
He Who Is a Friend, He Who Is a Lover & He Who Is a Protector

The Muted Hopelessness series:
My Muted Love, Our Muted Recklessness, & Our Reckless Hope

The Prism series:
<u>Mercy</u>, Grace, & The Promise

~Extra

_____

You can find Love Belvin at www.LoveBelvin.com
Facebook @ Author - Love Belvin
Twitter @LoveBelvin
Goodreads: Love Belvin
and on Instagram @LoveBelvin

Join the #TeamLove mailing list on my website to keep up with the happenings!
Click here (with WiFi) to join!

www.ingramcontent.com/pod-product-compliance
Lightning Source LLC
Chambersburg PA
CBHW021216260626
47172CB00002B/455